The New Vigilantes

BOOKS BY JAMES D. HORAN

FICTION

King's Rebel
Seek Out and Destroy
The Shadow Catcher
The Seat of Power
The Right Image
The Blue Messiah
The New Vigilantes

NONFICTION

Action Tonight
Desperate Men
The Pinkerton Story (with Howard Swiggett)
Desperate Women
Confederate Agent
Pictorial History of the Wild West (with Paul Sann)
Mathew Brady: Historian with a Camera
Across the Cimarron
The Wild Bunch
The D.A.'s Man
The Great American West
C.S.S. Shenandoah: *The Memoirs of
Lieutenant Commanding James I. Waddell*
*The Desperate Years: From the Stock Market Crash
to World War II*
Timothy O'Sullivan: America's Forgotten Photographer
The Pinkertons: The Detective Dynasty that Made History
*The Life and Art of Charles Schreyvogel: Painter-Historian
of the Indian Fighting Army of the American West*
*The McKenney-Hall Portrait Gallery
of American Indians*

The New Vigilantes

by James D. Horan

Crown Publishers, Inc., New York

FOR GERTRUDE
WHO SO FAITHFULLY STAYED WITH THE HOUNDS

© *1975 by James D. Horan*
All rights reserved. No part of this book may be reproduced or
utilized in any form or by any means, electronic or mechanical,
including photocopying, recording, or by any information storage
and retrieval system, without permission in writing from the
Publisher. Inquiries should be addressed to Crown Publishers,
Inc., 419 Park Avenue South, New York, N.Y. 10016.
Printed in the United States of America
Published simultaneously in Canada by General Publishing
Company Limited
Design by Nedda Balter

Library of Congress Cataloging in Publication Data

Horan, James David, 1914-
    The new vigilantes.

    I. Title
PZ3.H7838Ne   [PS3558.065]   813'.5'4   75-1416
ISBN 0-517-51871-6

Contents

BOOK ONE:

THE ALIEN WORLD

Chapter 1

Trevor David—Reunion of the Hounds

How can I forget? It was April 10, a few minutes after four, the day Nixon delivered that speech on the Far East. There was this kid, probably a Madison Avenue agency messenger, a bundle of mats under one arm, the other holding a radio blaring hard rock next to his ear while a guy in a two-hundred-dollar suit shouted that he should listen to his president instead of that crap. But the kid only grinned and said who the hell was Nixon compared to the Stones? Mr. Two Hundred Dollar Suit gave me a disgusted look, shook his head as if dismissing everyone under seventeen as doomed, then walked away while the kid played out the tune, humming and doing a few shuffling steps until the light changed and off he trotted.

It was a stunning afternoon, bright and clear with the spring sunshine making panes of ice on the upper floors of the Pan Am Building. It might have been a great day for the history books but, like that kid, it had a different meaning for me; one year ago the eight of us had said good-bye at Clark Field; now Stu Harlow was making good his promise to bring us together for our first reunion. His brief note had said April 10, 4 P.M., so it was not only to the day but the hour.

Stuart Fitzroy Harlow III, Major U.S.M.C. (ret.), a very precise man.

As I stood on the sidewalk of Park in the upper Forties, gawking up at the gleaming obelisk of black stone, the scene at Clark came back to me; an emaciated Harlow, a crisp new uniform hanging on his frame like a shroud, coming down the plane's ramp followed by seven POW wraiths hung over from trying to make up for all the beer and booze they had missed in four, five, six, seven, or eight years.

Stu was very brief at the microphone, nothing cornball about flag or country, he simply told the crowd how thrilled he was to be home and proud to have spent the last eight years in the company of what he called the bravest men he had ever known. Then with a grin he said he had only one comment for Charlie and held up an index finger. The crowd had been begging for something to cheer about and gave him a big hand, providing television and the print press with the first dramatic break in a rather solemn afternoon, while the straight-arrow brass, most of them leaders from behind, looked on proud as parents at an Eagle Scout ceremony.

Behind us I heard a newsman ask an army PRO, "Isn't this the group the Vietcong called 'The Hounds'?" I was tempted to turn around and tell him the full title according to Hanoi's propaganda broadcasts was "The American Hounds of War Dedicated to Killing Vietnam Men, Women, and Children." It was that crazy commandant of Tong Le Mai, the jungle prison camp in the south where we were held, who gave us the name in one of his daily outbursts. But it was only funny to Charlie's guards when they kicked us out for inspection "to make sure the American Hounds didn't have any fleas." They made us stand at attention in the village square until the sun pressed down on our brains like a branding iron. One morning we fell over like bowling pins leaving only Stu standing, swaying but standing. Twice the guards knocked him down with their rifle butts, but each time he staggered back to his feet. From where I lay on the ground, sweat rolling into my eyes and the world swaying and dipping, I could see him fight to get to his knees, pause, then with a great effort stand upright. Finally the guards got weary—I guess they even felt the heat—and drove us back to the stable. We were like a bunch of staggering drunks and I remember asking Stu why the hell he didn't stay down. His swollen lips had trouble forming the words:

"The only way you can beat these bastards is by doing what they think is impossible. . . ."

It is obvious to me since I came back that for the next couple of generations at any cocktail party, family dinner, neighborhood bar, union gathering, or even a couple of guys meeting in the supermarket, there will always be two vociferous camps—one supporting the war in Vietnam, the other condemning it. Shorn of all politics, one fact still stuns me like a stone flung in my face—I spent almost seven years in a prison camp in a war that had only losers. And back in Tong Le Mai that's the way we felt—eight forgotten losers led by this indomitable guy who insisted we had to be winners.

As the war slowly ground down and the guards became younger and more vulnerable, Stu went out of his way to cultivate them—not in the hope of getting better treatment but to lull them into a false sense of security. When we decided to execute Stu's escape plan, they would be dead within minutes. We accepted the fact we might join them, but that's how desperate it was in those last days of Tong Le Mai. Thank God, peace came.

At the Clark Base Hospital there were several days of medical examinations, briefings, and interrogations before we all said good-bye. As Stu was walking toward his plane, he suddenly spun around and came back.

"By the way," he said casually, "I'll see you in New York a year from now."

"What do you have in mind, Stu?" I asked.

"A reunion. I've been thinking about it since we came in. Keep in touch with them, Trev."

He was again our leader. I snapped a command and seven badly hung-over guys gave him the best salute this side of Pearl.

I suddenly resented this glorious, serene afternoon and the busy smug people who hurried by on their private errands. I felt like reaching out to grab one and inform him this spring day, 1974, was an important date, a very important date, the first anniversary of the day their countrymen had returned from Charlie's prisons. But I knew what would happen, either some guy with leaden eyes would casually brush me aside or another would politely murmur that plastic New York farewell . . .

"Have a good day."

Oh, well.

In the months which followed our return I became a clearing house, forwarding to Stu the few addresses I could find. He wrote me every week or called, most of the time demanding that I join him in New York. But Manhattan offered no hidden charms for me. After graduating from Missouri's School of Journalism I had worked for AP local filling-in for days off, vacations, and swing shifts, mostly in Foley Square, Criminal and Supreme courts, and the Federal Building along with some shifts at police headquarters before I went inside. I spent my last tour in Rockefeller Center on lobster rewrite before I transferred to the Atlanta Bureau, a few hours from Riverview, our family farm not far from Jonesboro, Georgia, where the Davids have been since before the Revolution. This is Margaret Mitchell country and some folks insist that our rambling farmhouse on the Flint River is really Tara, but my great-aunt who runs the place will tell you her friend Miss Mitchell informed her privately she didn't use any of the fine old places in the county as the model for Scarlett's home.

While I was tramping every one of Riverview's prime acres trying to find peace in the rhythm of nature, the Pentagon put out a story they called "The Hounds of Tong Le Mai," a dime novel title which made me want to throw up. The Atlanta Bureau advised New York I had been second senior officer in the camp, so they asked me to do a six-part series on the Snakepit, which is what we called that goddam place for excellent reasons. I had to turn them down. I also refused an offer from an old newspaper buddy in publishing "to do a book," as he put it. I wasn't ready to return to that tragic senseless war.

All I had to do was let the name Tong Le Mai clang in my memory and almost instantly the smell of ancient manure filled my nostrils. A thousand years ago. An age ago. A million light years ago. As I stood there in that wonderful spring sunshine, I shook off the memories and instead concentrated on what was behind the banks of glass of this beautiful black stone building—the sparkling fountain, the forest of ferns, and the beautiful women crossing a sea of red carpet. In golden script across the doors was the legend: The Eldorado Hotel of New York, with a mounted figure like a proud Cortez, complete with breastplate and charger. Under it was: Owned and operated by Harlow Hotels, Inc. Stuart Fitzroy Harlow III, President.

After spending seven years together in a fifty by fifty wooden building, there aren't many details of his life and family a man can hide. But almost from the day we returned I was being constantly surprised on how much Stu had managed to keep to himself.

I knew his family had been in the hotel business for many years and, while I suspected he had it made after the unexpected death of his father during the winter, I never realized his wealth until the day I asked a reporter in financial to check out Harlow Realty, Inc. Even he was impressed.

The company operated several of the nation's largest hotels, and Stu's father had pioneered in building retirement developments, starting on the east coast and moving to the Southwest. I wondered how Stu had taken it, from Charlie's stinking stable to golden boy in a penthouse on top of the world. I was sure he hadn't changed, but on the other hand there's one hell of a difference between Tong Le Mai and Manhattan.

I was also anxious to find out how deep an imprint a year had made on the others. I had received a few brief notes but some of my letters had been returned with the disturbing purple stamp "Moved, not forwardable." Yet, only a few nights before I left Atlanta, Stu had promised everyone would be at the reunion.

I let an invisible hand swing open the doors and sweep me onto the lush carpet, soft as a pine needle floor in sweet Georgia.

4

"Can I help you?" an admiral in full dress asked. Instead of fruit salad he had "Eldorado" neatly stitched above his pocket, with a tiny Cortez riding toward his shoulder seam.

"Penthouse," I said with the air of a lord to the manner born.

"Your name, sir?"

"Trevor David."

He consulted a clipboard. "Ah, yes, Lieutenant Trevor David, United States Marine Corps, retired."

He rolled it off like a Queen's man reading the Honors List, and I wondered if I should kneel.

He admonished me gently. "Mr. Harlow has called down several times."

"The plane was late."

He sighed. "We just can't depend on anything these days. This way, please."

Well, that took care of the nation's problems . . .

"Mr. Trevor is here," he said softly to the starter of the private elevator.

The starter, dressed like a lesser admiral, whispered into a phone, then touched a button. Doors hissed open.

They both beamed. "Arrangements have been made for your stay, sir," the one with the clipboard said. The doors closed and the elevator, a cherry-paneled box with mirrors and hand-tooled leather seats, ascended with the noise of velvet rubbing velvet. It came to a stop, the door opened, and there was Stu. I have always wondered what there was about him that changed a room. His rugged, handsome face dominated by the intent green eyes that I knew could become as cold and menacing as a frozen sea, or was it his conscious magnetism and air of enormous confidence and fearlessness that made you want to follow him anywhere, to do anything?

Believe me, I wasn't put off center by his flashing smile; you can't live with a man for seven years in a place next door to hell and not know his capabilities; Stu was no ordinary guy. In his company grave misfortunes became tolerable.

We didn't shake hands, we almost broke each other's rib cage.

"God, it's great to see you, Trev! How've you been?" He stepped back to give me a fast, measured look. "Any more trouble with eating?"

He was referring to the problem we all had when we were released; the starvation diet at Tong Le Mai had shrunken our stomachs so badly none of us could retain solid food in the hospital at Clark. Booze went down but not steak. The doctors suggested that we eat small quantities of bland food until our digestive tracts returned to normal. It was weird, even the orderlies came in to watch eight guys washing down jars of baby food with Scotch. . . .

"I'm back on steak, how about you, Stu?"

"I've gained fifteen pounds and feel great."

I studied him while he was talking. I couldn't believe this was the same man I had said good-bye to at Clark Field. It was only April but he was deeply tanned—a few weeks at the Golden Gate, the Harlow hotel in the Caribbean, he later explained—and there was little doubt he was in the best of condition.

"How about nightmares, Trev?" he asked.

"They were bad when I first came back. One almost scared my aunt half to death. I was in solo with that damn block of wood across my legs. I woke up under the desk. How about you, Stu?"

"I get them now and then. Remember what the headshrinker told us at Clark? They would gradually wear off." He gripped my arm. "God, it's good to see you again, Trev! You know, of course, you're not going back this time . . . you just have to stay here."

"We'll talk about it, Stu."

"The hell with talking! That's what we've been doing all winter! You should see my phone bills!"

"As I told you, I like AP and I like Atlanta . . ."

"You'll like New York better," he said with a casual wave. "Come on in, the guys have been waiting for you."

"Is everyone here?"

"Everyone except Max. He had an emergency at the hospital."

"Why the hell did he establish a practice up there? That's a dangerous area."

"I begged him to open an office on the East Side, but no, he insisted on going to the upper West Side. By the way, did you know his wife is pregnant?"

"That's great!"

"Let him tell you himself. He's as proud as a peacock."

"I think you told me his wife was a nurse. Heidi, isn't it?"

"Right. They met at the hospital. She's only been over from Holland a few years."

"How's his arm?"

"Not good. They did a bone graft at Walter Reed but it didn't help much." He added roughly, "The bastards! The great humanitarian Viet Cong!"

"Where did you find Star?"

"Sam finally located him in Canada."

"Canada? The last address I had was in Brooklyn!"

"High steel gave out in the World Trade Center. There wasn't any work so he began hitting the sauce. Rather than go on welfare, he went back to the reservation to live with his grandmother. How long was he in the Pit? Five?"

"A little over six years. He came in right after Bruckner. By the way, how's Tom? All I ever got was a postcard."

"Not good."

"Is he okay?"

"He's had a tough break. You talk to him, Trev."

For a brief moment in that lush foyer we were back in the Snakepit and I was making my daily report.

6

"You're going to find some of them bitter," Stu said quietly. "It hasn't been a good year."

There was a moment of silence, then Stu held out his hand and I took it. There was no need to say anything. He swung open the door and there they were, holding up whiskey or champagne glasses or cans of beer to welcome me.

This is by no means a war memoir, in fact when I finally sat down at the typewriter I had difficulty in recalling dates, names of villages, battles, and objectives. I want nothing more to do with Nam; I had assigned it to the deepest niche in my memory. Yet in that instant when Stu opened the door and I saw them again, I was overwhelmed by a flood of memories—not of war but of the seven men with whom I had shared the bitterest years of my life.

Stu was first man in the camp, I was second. He was captured in IaDang Valley, southeast of Pleiku, in November 1965, the first major engagement in which American troops had been used. A year later Charlie overran our positions near Kontum in the Central Highlands. I have always tried to reconcile this irony—a big chunk of my life had been traded for a jungle hill that never had a name, only a number on some divisional map.

As a first lieutenant and senior officer I was separated from the rest in the first village we were taken to, stripped and interrogated by a V captain. Standing in my shorts I gave him only my name and serial number. The captain laughed and informed me in perfect English he would do his best to change my mind. After six months in solo, shackled like a wild animal, I found out what he meant. When they came to get me, I couldn't walk, so they dragged me to the captain's office. He silently handed me my "war criminal's confession" and I signed it. At that point I would have gladly signed a petition to the Vatican to have Ho Chi Minh canonized.

You're either a liar or a fool if, reading this, you insist it could not happen to you; just give us your body and we'll show you how simple it is. In no time we will make you say what we want you to say.

Although I had signed their document I was kept in irons for another few weeks to cure what the captain called my "bad attitude," a phrase all POWs in Nam heard many many times.

As the tides of war changed I was moved from village to village, finally arriving in Tong Le Mai, Christmas week of '66. It was a shabby jungle village built on the outskirts of an abandoned rubber plantation. In the center was an old French cavalry stable which the V had turned into a prison. Doors had been added to the stalls along with a wooden bunk, a chair, and a horse blanket. There were no windows, only a peekhole in the door for the guard. When it closed you were buried alive in a foul-smelling darkness so thick you could almost feel it. There I was shackled, in other words flat on my wooden bunk with a notched two-by-four and a locked iron bar across my legs. At this point I didn't know if I could hack it any longer, I was ready to give up. I was skin and bones, with long shaggy hair that I was certain made me look like a faded replica of Robinson Crusoe.

The second night I heard a faint muffled voice from the adjacent stall. I couldn't move but I banged my head against the wall. It gave me hope: at least another human was living in that endless darkness filled with the stench of ancient manure.

After a week they gave me a document which I signed. To this day I have no idea what it was but they told me my "bad attitude" had been temporarily cured so they removed the leg irons. That night I began tapping on the wall to answer that faint voice. I searched desperately for a cup to duplicate the old college trick of putting some kind of receptacle against the wall to find out how your roommate was doing with that great-looking blonde. All I had was the horse blanket, another one of Charlie's incongruities. The heat was unbearable but they gave us blankets "for our welfare."

I finally rolled the blanket into a horse collar, put my head into it and talked to the wall. I almost wept with joy when I heard a muffled but audible voice say:

"Merry Christmas. I'm Stu Harlow. Who are you?"

God, did I feel like the Count of Monte Cristo!

Stu and I communicated like this until they gave us a few minutes outside for exercise. The war was going badly for them, and the first time I tried to speak to Stu a guard's rifle butt sent me sprawling.

However, we had our "com"—communication—which was as important as living. Gradually they loosened up and our exercise period was stretched to an hour. That was the winter of '67 when Tom Bruckner was brought in. He was a lieutenant and navy pilot whose Crusader had been shot down on a strike. Charlie hated pilots, and Tom was treated brutally. He later told us how he had been beaten, stoned, and kicked in a series of villages before he reached Tong Le Mai. During an exercise period Stu managed to mouth an explanation of how to use the horse blanket. The three of us soon had com.

Kenny Iron Star came next. He was a Special Services sergeant, a full-blooded Mohawk from, of all places, Brooklyn, which I learned to my amazement had a community of Mohawks, some of them skilled steelworkers.

He had tried to escape three times on the trail and showed the results. Both eyes were swollen shut, he had a smashed cheekbone and a split lip. He was tied like a mule, a V corporal told us with a grin, because he had acted like a mule. To cure his "bad attitude" Star received a long dose of solo. When he finally joined our slow-moving circle in the exercise area, his swollen face had subsided and his split lip was healing but those dark flat eyes held a ferocious hate. It didn't take him long to get on the horse blanket telephone.

Prisoner four was Sam Hoffman, a Spec 5 communications expert, I say wizard, who had been ambushed on a patrol. In those early days

Sam was a plump little guy who looked like a solemn owl. I always thought that he could have been easily picked out of his high school graduation photograph as the student most likely to win the Westinghouse Science Award. Sam took his place in our circle. The Pit would trim him down to a gaunt scarecrow with enormous dark eyes.

The war continued to mount in intensity and every week groups of prisoners moved north through our camp.

After Sam, Rudy Webb joined us. We watched him come in, a rumbling cursing giant bound with ropes so tightly he could barely shuffle. He reminded me of a Gulliver with a rust-colored stubble, harassed by a group of jabbering brown-skinned Lilliputians who poked him with rifle butts and bamboo rods. Rudy was a PFC captured in one of the countless, forgotten jungle fire-fights in the Central Highlands. Curiously he wasn't killed by the V, who apparently kept him as a sort of American trophy to put on display in the villages. He was bruised and scratched by barrages of stones and sticks, but this big guy was undefeatable. When he saw us he broke out into some gin mill tune, sending the guards into a frenzy. Before the batch of prisoners left there was a loud argument over Rudy, the guys who had captured him were reluctant to give him up. Finally the camp's commandant settled it; Rudy stayed behind.

The one prisoner who received the most brutal treatment was Arnie Harper. Arnie had been a CIA agent in Indochina since the early sixties. He had worked with Special Services on intelligence and rescue missions in Laos and Cambodia and before his capture in '68 had maintained a relay post, directing air raids. He was returning from Saigon when he was betrayed to the V by a frightened headman of a village where he had stayed for a few days. Before he arrived in Tong Le Mai he had been "questioned" for months. This was Charlie's favorite trick: a guard tied your wrists and elbows behind your back with a nylon cord about fifteen feet long and a half inch in diameter and bound your legs in such a way as to cut off circulation—the result was excruciating pain.

Arnie told us later he had made a vow with himself that if he knew he was on the verge of betraying the location of the relay post, which is what Charlie wanted so desperately, he would attack his guards and force them to kill him. But apparently they believed his story that he was a civilian worker and sent him to Tong Le Mai. He was in bad shape when, prodded by a guard, he hobbled painfully into the stable.

The last prisoner to enter the camp was Max Findeloon, an army captain and doctor who was captured after the V overran his forward aid station in the fall of 1970. Max's arm and shoulder had been shattered by a grenade burst but his first concern was for a young corporal who had been shot through the lungs. Max had done all he could on the trail but the kid died a few hours after they reached the village. In the heat, dead men were put underground as fast as possible so we buried the kid a few minutes after Max said he was gone. Stu ignored the yelling, threatening guards to lead us in a brief prayer before we tossed in the dirt.

In Tong Le Mai there were no niceties about either life or death.

Max, who had gone into the army immediately after his residency, was the son of a Michigan tulip grower. He became the camp doctor, treating not only us but Charlie's guards and the villagers for everything from leprosy to the clap. He was serene, vulnerable, unshakable, incapable of hate. For him the terrible realities of Tong Le Mai existed only to be forgiven. To all of us, perhaps even secretly to some of the guards, there was something almost spiritual about Max. When I hear the word *bravery* I think of Max, sweat dripping off his face as he whispered instructions to us how to set his broken bones..

Gradually his arm and shoulder atrophied, and while Max knew he would never operate again he cheerfully insisted he could still be a consultant and anyway they're the ones who make the money . . .

During the years we were in the camp we saw many commandants come and go. Some were formally correct, others indifferent, a few sadistic. The unforgettable paranoiac one we called "Colonel Shakespeare!"; we gave him the nickname after he made us listen to a long and hideous poem he had written and dedicated to the V army.

In one of his unpredictable rages he gave us our nickname, "American Hounds Who Make War on Vietnam Men, Women, and Children." The guards took it up as they gleefully kicked us out to "inspect us for fleas," as they called it, and other prisoners passing through made up stories of our bravado until we became known as far north as the Hanoi Hilton.

Twice Stu stood up to our wild-eyed commandant and each time spent weeks in solo. Then one day Rudy, who had been helping the villagers haul some logs, told Stu he had seen a patrol coming in with Red Cross packages. We were desperate to get them; they contained not only food but badly needed medical supplies.

A short time later a V combat photographer on his way north stopped in the camp. When he was passing the stable, Stu called out to him in French. Happily he answered. We watched as they talked; after a few minutes the photographer gave Stu a cigarette and left.

That night in the stable while we smoked the precious butt to a glowing end, Stu told us the photographer had refused his suggestion he take our picture because there was no propaganda angle. Stu then presented his plan to tip the photographer to the Red Cross packages and get him to take Shakespeare handing them out to us. There would be benefits to this outrageous lie, if the photograph got out it would notify our families we were alive.

I pointed out Hanoi would undoubtedly distribute the print, the East German news agency would pick it up and service AP and UPI who would wirephoto it to the States where I predicted wide coverage. As always we took a vote; Stu's plan was unanimously approved. He had an additional suggestion; we would give Ho Chi Minh the classic salute by

10

each man closing his right hand but leaving the middle finger sticking out. This was gleefully accepted, along with Max's urging that we all look as doleful as possible, an easy bit of playacting.

We couldn't wait for the next day when Stu again called out to the photographer. This time we could see he was excited. Stu told us he had jumped at the idea and said he would ask the commandant about the packages that evening over dinner, but promised Stu protection as the source of his information.

Now that he had him in a bind, Stu demanded we get several packages as a reward. The photographer was angry but agreed to do what he could.

At first Colonel Shakespeare was furious. He clearly intended to use the packages for his own men or as barter. However, he recognized the photograph's propaganda value and agreed to pose with us. In the morning we were marched to the village square and ordered to line up before the grinning colonel who looked like an evil Santa Claus guarding his packages of life. First came a rambling lecture. The photographer was probably mesmerized because he never caught our extended fingers. Later we learned the *Pueblo* prisoners did the same thing, but ours was the first to come out of the southern prison camps and caused a stir back home.

We did get our packages and the picture received wide coverage in the media, print and TV. Large city dailies encircled our fingers and captions praised our courage in defying the Communists. More important, it told our families we were alive. Looking at a copy I find it hard to believe I was that gaunt, sad-eyed stranger. As my aunt observed, we looked worse than the Yankees who came out of Andersonville. . . .

The picture enraged the POW wives who by now had their own organization and knew how to pressure Washington. A Georgia paper discovered I was the great-grandson of a Confederate cavalry officer and for weeks the Stars and Bars flew over editorial pages in the south.

But we paid for it. A furious Hanoi sent Stu into solo for a month, we were confined to the stable, and a bewildered Shakespeare returned to combat along with the photographer. Stu came back to us, a defiant bag of bones in foul-smelling rags; we had lost the battle but won the war of Tong Le Mai. From then on you could sense the uneasiness of the guards in dealing with Stu; I guess they never knew what to expect.

The new commandant was cold and formal. As he told us in our first meeting, "Your people are bombing and killing my people and that I don't approve." He pointed to us, "And this I don't approve either."

The next day we each got a banana and an extra plate of what we called sewer greens soup. Max solemnly urged us not to throw out the cockroaches and bugs, at least they were protein.

For all the years we were together, Stu was accepted as our leader, not only because of his rank—as a Marine Corps major he was senior officer in the camp—but more because of his personality and courage.

11

Obstacles, hardships, even torture only seemed to stimulate him. He infected us with a fierce spirit and a determination to survive because we knew he would do more than he asked of us. He stood up against Charlie, demanding medical supplies or better food. All of us signed the so-called war criminals documents, but not Stu. He couldn't be broken, and as a result had more solo time than all of us put together.

From almost the first day he arrived in Tong Le Mai, he had planned the camp's policy of resistance. As he explained, if we surrendered totally to Charlie's demands we would become dead inside, human zombies to be manipulated at their whim. As Arnie once recalled, Stu put his head on the tracks and we followed him. Actually by our resistance we forced Charlie to become brutal but at the same time this strategy, adopted by the other prisoners in the north, eventually exposed their inhumanity and caused international pressure to bear down so heavily on Hanoi that treatment slowly improved after 1969.

After 1969, we were no longer locked up at night and the restriction against talking was lifted.

Our basic method of passing the time was talk—the three prime subjects were food, sex, and escape. In the last year the latter was most important. Stu had devised a plan that had a million to one chance of succeeding, and we unanimously voted to try it. Each day our position was becoming more desperate; from 175 pounds I was reduced to 115, Stu had broken out in a series of painful boils that Max had to lance daily with our sliver of a knife; Arnie had a serious mouth infection after he had extracted two teeth with a rusty nail; Star was developing beriberi; we all had malaria, and despite Stu's threats, pleas, and promises we were finding it more and more difficult not to let ourselves die inside.

In the years we had been in the camp we had seen other Americans only once. This was Christmas in about '72 when we were taken by truck to a church in a small town. The guards led us in and lined us along one wall. Across the aisles were several other American prisoners. Prisoners from both sides of the church were taken two by two to the crib. The guy I knelt down with looked as bad as I felt.

"Can you read me?" I whispered.

"Yeah," he whispered back. "You guys the Hounds?"

I was stunned. That was the first time I realized anyone knew we were alive. I started to rattle off our names but when a guard started toward us I began pointing to the manger.

Then Charlie distributed hymnbooks—it was all for their propaganda camera crews—and we began singing. Stu nudged me, and I noted that in between phrases of "Silent Night, Holy Night" he was interjecting his name and camp:

"Silent Night, Holy Night,
"My name is Major Stuart Harlow,
"We are in Tong Le Mai . . ."

I did the same thing and nudged Tom who followed me and so on down the line until POWs along both sides of the aisle were bellowing out Christmas hymns with some strange variations. Before we left a great deal of information had been fed into the prison grapevine.

That night we put together what we had heard and came to the conclusion something big was brewing on the outside. That was the only reason Stu didn't put the escape plan into action. The visit to the church really saved our lives. A few months later we were herded into the village square and told by the camp's commandant that negotiations were going on in Paris and we could expect to be released soon. Then one day we were taken in a truck to the Hanoi Hilton, and from there on a plane to Clark where we had said good-bye to Stu.

One year ago.

Instead of a giant scarecrow, Rudy now looked like a huge, well-fed professional fullback out of condition from drinking too much beer. While the others cheered, he lifted me onto his shoulder and marched across the room to the bar.

"Give the lieutenant a drink, bartender," he roared. "He's got a lot of catchin' up to do . . ."

Tom Bruckner was tending bar. He was still the quiet, introspective man who, I recalled, loved flying more than life itself. To take Tom out of the air was like grounding a swallow. Now there were strands of gray in his curly dark hair and, except for a brief smile when we shook hands, his thin, distinctive face was solemn.

"It's great to see you, Trev," he said as he made me a drink. "What's happening?"

"Nothing much, Tom. How's it with you?"

He bent over to fumble with the ice bucket. "There are times when I wish that damn ejector had never worked."

"Come off it, Tom," I protested in surprise. "It can't be all that bad."

He said almost wearily, "A week after I came back my wife's lawyers served me with a copy of the decree she won three years before. She's got a goddam family! Two kids and a jerk of a husband who kept saying how sorry he was so often I felt like strangling him."

He gave a short laugh. "Five and a half years in a stinking horse stall and for what?" He shrugged. "Hell, I'm sorry, Trev. We're here to have a good time and I'm busting your stones with my troubles."

"Look, Tom, if there's anything I can do . . ."

"Sure you can. Forget it and have a drink. Stu didn't want a regular bartender so he elected me. What'll you have?"

I took my scotch and water to the wraparound windows and the stunning view. It was an eye-catching room, almost theatrically so. The deep red in the thick carpet was matched by the heavy drapes ready to be drawn across the night. There was a wall of books, a beautiful eighteenth-century writing table, a grand piano, and a huge semicircular couch by the open fireplace. Dominating the mantel were three wild-eyed cowboys in bronze thundering into town: Remington's famous "Coming through the Rye." How many times had I heard Stu tell the story of how his father had won the sculpture in a Montana crap game when he was starting in the hotel business, only to have his mother condemn it as a monstrosity fit only for a dark hallway?

There was a beautiful stereo but no color TV; this clearly was a room for work, meditation, and the talk of friends. I thought it reflected a lot of Stu, virile, with an eye for comfort and a sense of dramatic beauty.

"Isn't this place a knockout, Trev?" Sam Hoffman said as he joined me. He pointed to Brooklyn. "That's where I came from. Bensonhurst. What a difference!"

Like all of us Sam had filled out. Once again he was a chubby Mr. Science who would always look uncomfortable in the most expensive clothes.

"How's the world treating you, Sam?"

"Great. You know I have my own business now?" He gave me a dignified card which read: The Hoffman Agency. Investigations, private and industrial.

"I remember you wrote me last winter you were with a big private detective agency."

"Only for a few months until I got my back pay. Then I opened my own business. Actually it was Stu who talked me into it. He gave me a big boost."

"Oh? What did he do, Sam?"

"He handed me Harlow Realty on a gold platter, you know, checking out personnel and stuff like that. Then he introduced me to two guys who were opening a big discount store in the city and out on the Island. They gave me all their business." He said proudly, "You wouldn't believe the electronic stuff I have, Trev, real sophisticated. TV cameras, some with telescopic lenses and owl's eye . . ."

"What the hell is an owl's eye?"

"You can shoot at night. Then I have the best transmitters, the kind the Bureau—the FBI—uses." He lowered his voice. "Hell, I even have a laser beam outfit that can pick up a conversation at half a mile when the door's closed!"

"I think you could have taught those Watergate burglars a few things about their business."

"Watergate? Forget it. They were amateurs."

"Are you married, Sam?"

"Who needs it, Trev? Besides, what woman would stand my hours? Not that I'm lonely, baby. I met this woman, Leah. She kept telling me how liberated she was and how we could have this wonderful relationship. Without marriage, that is. I said fine. She's good looking, believe me, like a model, and she can make lentil soup pretty good, but of course not like my old man . . ."

"I got your letter telling me how your father died. After all those stories I felt as if I knew him."

"Menz told me they found him on the floor. That was two years before we hit Clark. How do you like that kick in the head?"

There was no need to ask who Menz was. Sam's stories of his father, chief maintenance man for Menz's Pickle Works in South Brooklyn and the eternal seeker of fine farms, had always been funny, no matter how many times Sam told them.

"How's it going at AP, Trev?" He snapped his fingers. "Hey, how about your Georgia peach? What's her name?"

"Leslie."

"Yeah. Leslie. No wedding?"

"I'm in Tom's class. She had a family by the time I got to Atlanta."

"See what I mean? Who needs it? But what the hell, you can't blame 'em. Who wants to wait for a ghost? My family even sat shiva for me." He lowered his voice. "You got off easy compared to Arnie . . ."

"What happened, Sam? I wrote to him but I never received an answer."

"Remember how he was always talking about his wife and kid?"

"A little girl. She was born while he was in Nam."

"Right. He never saw the kid. They were both killed in an automobile accident three years before he got home. A goddam drunk rammed their station wagon. He stayed in his town only long enough to visit their grave and put his house up for sale. I found him in Chicago for Stu. Let's go over and say hello . . ."

I was wrong when I said that all of us had filled out and changed slightly. Arnie Harper was still the same lean, hungry-looking guy from Tong Le Mai. Somehow he always reminded me of a Hemingway prizefighter. College football had left him with a slightly battered nose that went well with his light blue eyes, tight curly blond hair, and crooked smile. Maybe that's why the CIA picked him; he looked like anything but an expert on guerrilla tactics who could speak fluent Chinese and several dialects from Burma, Laos, and Thailand, where he had been stationed for years investigating the drug traffic.

Arnie had been recruited in college, Princeton, of all places, where he majored in Far Eastern history. He had an affinity for languages and his initial assignment was the Indo-Chinese drug traffic. Before the first Green Beret "advisers" were sent to Nam, he was organizing an intelligence system with the Montagnards.

Arnie was not garrulous; he was more of a loner than a mixer. When he talked in the Snakepit it was usually about Far Eastern politics and China. He said that before Nam opened up he had badgered the home office to give him a China assignment, at least station him in

Hong Kong, but the agency kept putting him off; Arnie thought it was because they had lost a few good men who had been sentenced by the People's Court to long prison terms.

If Arnie had had a favorite subject it was his infant daughter born while he was in Indochina. It was clear his big romance was his wife, a high school sweetheart. His tour with the relay station was to be his last; he had planned to return to the States and do graduate study in Georgetown with the hope of joining the State Department's Far East desk.

As I walked across the room to join Arnie, who was talking to Star and Rudy, I felt sick as I recalled how desperate he had been to see that little girl and her mother, a blonde, blue-eyed beauty who, Arnie insisted, could play tennis as well as Billie Jean King.

"Hey, Trev!" Arnie said jumping up to grab my hand. "How's it going, man?"

"Fine. How about you, Arnie?"

He gave me that familiar twisted grin.

"Oh, I had a few tough ones but nothing I couldn't handle."

"I wrote to you but the letters always came back."

"I've been moving around." Then quietly, "Do you know I'm with Stu now?"

"Doing what?"

"Development scout, whatever the hell that means."

Sam broke in, "So are Rudy and Star. They're out in the Southwest. Harlow Realty has a big thing going out there."

Rudy, a slightly drunken grinning giant, asked, "When ya gonna join us, Lieutenant?"

"I'm thinking about it. How've you been, Rudy?"

"Great. Me and Sittin' Bull are teachin' 'em construction out there. You want a drink, Injun?"

Star held out his glass. "The same."

"How about you, Star?" I asked. He looked lean, dark, and dangerous. I always told myself that when Star grew old he could replace the Indian on the nickel.

A shrug. "No complaints, Lieutenant."

"How was the reservation?"

"Fine for blanket Indians. You still on that newspaper?"

"Wire service. Associated Press. I'm a rewriteman."

He shook his head. "I'd go nuts sittin' at a desk all day. Right, Arnie?"

Arnie put his arm around Star's shoulder. "I'm with you, buddy. Do you know this is the driest Indian in the West, Trev?"

Star made a face and groaned so loudly we all laughed.

"Ginger ale. How much of this shit can you drink?"

"I found him in Canada," Sam said proudly.

"One day up drives this Cadillac," Star explained. "My grandmother almost died. On the reservation anything but a pickup truck

16

means trouble. He's a young guy in a blue suit. He says he's from a hotel in New York City and the major wants to see me . . ."

"I said, 'I only know one major,' " Star continued. " 'Yes sir,' he said, 'his name is Harlow.' "

" 'But the war is over,' " I said.

" 'So they say,' he said. There was no foolin' around with this guy so I just got in and he drove me to the airport, gave me a ticket, and here I am. Big Chief Ginger Ale."

"Arnie said you hired him, Star, and Rudy," I said to Stu as he joined us. "Sam says he's checking out your help."

Stu nodded. "That's the only way to stay in business these days—either hire relatives or friends you trust. I don't have any relatives so I depend on friends." He added, "Star and Rudy have done a great job."

"We caught 'em usin' reject doors last month," Star said. "I had all I could do to stop this big goon from leanin' on the boss carpenter."

"They're both out in New Mexico," Stu explained. "We're building a big retirement village on the edge of the desert. I think it will be one of the most beautiful places in the Southwest. At least I hope so. That's one of the things I want to talk to you about, Trev."

"Hey, Injun, how about some pool?" Rudy shouted from the bar. Beyond him was a billiard room with a pool table and deep leather chairs.

"Drop over if you want to see a massacre," Star said.

"Go ahead, we'll join you in a minute," Stu said.

Star, Rudy, Arnie, and Sam drifted into the billiard room and I followed Stu to the windows.

"How do you like the view, Trev? On a clear day you can see clear across Jersey to the Poconos."

"It's really beautiful. Is this your office?"

"Office and apartment. Come on, I'll give you the five dollar tour."

There was a smaller room with a desk, sofa, lounge chairs, and a revolving bar. A bedroom held a startling surprise; a click of a button and the ceiling moved back to reveal a plexidome that looked right into the heavens.

"It's fantastic when it rains," Stu said lovingly. "I have a couple of dames who beg me to call them when it rains. They say there's nothing like screwing to thunder and lightning."

"No one special?"

"You know what I always said, Trev. Marriage, kids—the whole bit is not for me. I think I told you I was sorry as hell your plans didn't work out."

"I'm like Tom. She had a family by the time I came back. I couldn't blame her."

"No, I guess not. You heard about Arnie?"

"That was rough. I don't know if I could have taken it."

"Arnie said he went home, closed the house for a couple of days and just sat there, making love to Jack Daniels. He said for the first time in his life he really cried when he found a scrapbook his wife had prepared of pictures of his little girl from the nursery to almost the day they were killed. What really hurt was what happened to that drunken bastard who rammed their car. His license was revoked for a year and he got a two-hundred-dollar fine! A revocation and a lousy fine! They should have thrown him in the can and forgot the key. A week after he got home, Arnie turned his house over to a real estate man and took off."

"How did you find him?"

"Sam found him in Chicago. It took some talking but I finally got him to join us. He's moving around the country, spotting sites for possible developments."

"You know damn well Arnie doesn't know his ass from a hole in the ground about real estate development. Star, Rudy, Arnie, Max, Sam, Tom. Now me. When did you join the Salvation Army, Stu?"

He leaned on the windowsill and studied the streets congested with the evening traffic. The cars looked like toys, their impatient honking faint and far off.

"That's the way I want it," he said firmly. He went on, musingly, "Do you know this Christmas, Trev, it will be almost ten years since we first talked in the stable! Ten years! Remember what I said at Clark? The bravest in the world I called you guys. I meant it then and I mean it now. Hell, you seven guys are all the family I have left! I think that hit home at Dad's funeral last winter. The only kin in the chapel was me, the other people were business associates. There's a couple of cousins somewhere out West but we haven't heard from them in years." He was silent for a moment. "I know this is going to sound weird, Trev, but in a way I'm beginning to miss the Pit."

"Stu, for Christ's sakes! You're talking about eight years in hell!"

"Then maybe hell has its good points," he replied with a wry smile. "I know it's crazy and I have never mentioned this to anyone." He held up a hand to shut off my protests. "Of course I don't mean the degradation, starvation, or brutality. It's more abstract. For one thing, the uncertainty and challenge of every day. We didn't know from morning to night what was going to happen. We had to outguess them every day." His voice became taut and his eyes narrowed as he looked out in the gathering dusk. "We were alive then, Trev! Christ, how we were alive! We were hungry and dangerous, ready to do anything to survive." He turned to me. "Just like Shakespeare and the Red Cross packages. Remember how we screwed that crazy bastard?"

"Who could forget?"

"The guy who came down from Washington to tell Dad we were alive gave him a copy of the picture. He had it framed." He pointed across the room. "Every time I look at it I find it hard to believe . . ."

Behind us there was a wild whoop. We turned to see Tom rushing

18

from behind the bar toward a slender man formally dressed in a blue suit, white shirt, and dark tie who was entering the room with the hesitancy of a new boy arriving for his first party.

He grinned and waved to us with his left hand; not even the padding of his suit could hide the deformed shoulder and arm that hung like a broken wing. He was immediately surrounded by the others who boiled out of the billiard room at Tom's cry. I noticed that while they ruffled his thick blond hair and wrung his good hand, even the exuberant and slightly drunken Rudy didn't swing him up like a doll as he had done me; to all of us Doctor Max had been precious and fragile.

"Here's Max," Stu said. "I knew he'd make it."

When we joined the others, Max, standing in that grinning circle, didn't say anything for a moment. Then someone gave him a drink and he raised the glass.

"Thank God, we're all here," he said, clearing his throat.

He went from man to man, pointing in mock horror at Rudy's growing beer gut and smiling in approval when Star silently held up his glass of ginger ale.

"And you, Trevor?" he asked, formal as always. "All is well?"

"Fine, Max. How about you?"

"In seventh heaven. Did Stu tell you? I'm going to be a papa."

"I heard the good news. Congratulations."

"God knows how many I've delivered." We touched glasses. "They were all important but this is the big one."

"Now that everyone's here let's go down to dinner," Stu called out. "We have a private room and a menu as long as your arm. Rudy, if I catch you goosing the waitresses I'll throw you out the window. Star, you sit next to him."

Rudy cupped one of his big hands. "Just a little one, Major?"

"You heard what the major said, Fatso," Star said.

"You know somethin', Injun?" the big man replied. "I think I may have to lean on you."

The elevator door opened and Stu waved us in. "Okay. One floor down. And the bar's open."

It was another beautiful room with many windows and that great view, a bar in the corner and a large oval table with flowers and gleaming silver.

"They first had it set up with a dais," Stu said, "but I said the hell with that, everyone's an honored guest tonight."

As he had said, the menu was long and varied. The serving seemed to go on endlessly. Perhaps it was psychological but every plate was cleaned.

"What about you, Max? How is it *really* going?"

"I have a good practice, a lovely home, a beautiful wife who will soon give me a beautiful child," he replied. "What more can a man ask for?"

Stu said, "They did a bone graft at Walter Reed."

"Legs, not arms, are important on the West Side," he said with a grin. "Every patient lives in a top-floor walk-up."

He was the same old Max.

Stu leaned over. "I keep warning him he's going to get ripped off by junkies one of these days. Maybe you can talk some sense into him, Trev."

"Stu's right, Max. Why practice up there?"

"A physician goes where he's needed," Max replied.

"Yeah. A goddam hallway at two o'clock in the morning!" Stu said, exasperated. "All those bums have to do is call him!"

"Stu, they're not all bums," Max protested mildly. "There are good families up there. Hardworking people. They need a doctor, even a one-armed one."

"I've been reading about that Wounded Knee business," Stu said abruptly. "What do you think of it, Star?"

Star gave us a faint smile. "At least it made you white bastards listen for a change."

"I thought it was very effective," Stu said.

"In what way?" Sam asked.

"For one thing it proved television can be a political weapon. It made a direct appeal to the public. I think it also showed how to circumvent the natural process of government."

"In other words you stage an event to get across your philosophy?" I asked. "Exorcising the real demons in prime time?"

"Ah, that's the magic phrase—prime time," Stu said. "I think you'll see more of this. If your event is imaginative enough you get instant global communication. Wounded Knee, taking hostages, the plane hijackings—all demonstrate that it is possible for a small group"— his wave took in all of us —"to intimidate the strongest of governments. All you need are blood and pagentry." He turned to me. "And you people are the conduits, Trev. Print and television."

"But that's blackmail," Max protested.

"Of course it is," Stu admitted. "But there's another side. Take Wounded Knee. Ask Star about conditions on some of the reservations. They're unbelievable. Somebody had to kick Washington in the ass."

"I still think it's wrong," Max said stubbornly. "You go by the law and you get the same results."

"But who can wait that long, Doc?" Star asked. "Let's say the state wants reservation land to build a dam. The Indians say, 'Hey, State, that's where our ancestors are buried!' Does the state care? Hell no. Five years later the court tells the state it was wrong. What does the state do—tear down a twelve-million-dollar dam? No, they give the Indians a couple of bucks and that's it."

"Nam is the best example of what Stu is saying," Arnie put in. "Kids grew up eating dinner while we took Cannonball Hill. When they received their greetings they said, 'Screw you, Uncle,' and either took off or joined a demonstration. Do you think that would have happened if there hadn't been television?"

I could not help but notice how easily we had fallen into the old routine; after what was laughingly called chow in the Snakepit, we would discuss and argue on any subject from the sexual ability of Vietnam men to the efficacy of bananas in treating malaria. In the last few years when they didn't lock us up any longer, the young guards would stand in the doorway of the stable and listen to our sometimes violent discussions. If the subject had a sexual theme, Arnie would translate into Vietnamese, which never failed to make them giggle.

We exhausted television and the Indians' cause and continued by denouncing the society we had come back to, an instantly bitter and favorite topic. Sam touched it off with his story of how he was plagued with troubles two days after buying a new car.

"... The dealer was a big fat guy sitting behind a desk and chewing on a cigar. 'Hey, I bought a car here yesterday for eighty-five hundred and this morning you had to tow it in. What gives?' I asked him.

" 'We're fixin' it, ain't we?' he said.

" 'Yeah, but I want to know what's wrong.'

" 'It happens all the time,' he says. 'It's the factory. They send us crap. What am I supposed to do?'

"When I ask him why he sells crap he tells me he has to feed his kids.

"A few days later it's towed back again. This time a guy in a gas station informs me I have no motor mounts. The same guy gives me the same story, it's not his fault, it's the factory. I called the factory and after ten dollars in phone calls I get something called customer relations. They made a million promises but nothing happened." He ticked off on his fingers, "Five trips to the dealer, about three hours on the phone, including a call to my congressman who sent a letter saying absolutely nothing and I still have my hand up my ..."

"What happened to the car?" someone asked.

Sam gave us a gloomy look. "I loaned it to this woman to go out to the Island to attend her nephew's bar mitzvah. Then I get the keys in the mail. When I called her she really gave it to me. It seems the car went dead on the expressway and it cost her thirty bucks for a tow job. This time the transmission froze. I had it brought back to the guy with the cigar. It's still there ..."

"No one gives a damn anymore," Tom said.

"Star and Rudy can tell you about builders," Stu said.

"One guy was named James," Star said. "I told him if his first name wasn't Jesse he was named wrong."

"I still think I should have leaned on him," Rudy grumbled.

"No matter how you look at it, it's a lousy stinking world we came back to," Arnie observed. "Everybody's out to screw you."

"There's only one way to beat 'em—do it to them before they do it to you," Sam pointed out.

Max exploded, "My God, what a bunch of cynics I have for friends!"

"Remember, Doc, what the Frenchman said, cynicism is only experience," Arnie observed.

"What the hell did you guys think you were coming back to?" Max asked. "You were nuts if you thought it was a perfect society. It never was and it never will be!"

"I admit New York City was far from perfect when I left," Stu said, "but Christ, it can't be compared to what it is now! And that's not only New York. I made a tour of our hotels when I came back. Take Chicago. Detroit, Pittsburgh. People can't even go to church anymore after sundown! Hell, four kids stabbed a guy to death outside Penn Station yesterday because he wouldn't let them snatch his suitcase. The oldest is sixteen!" He sipped his wine. "What troubles me is the attitude of the people, they're becoming conditioned to it all. Now a cop killing is a two-day newspaper story; the day he's killed and the day he's buried with our chuckleheaded mayor getting indignant over his casket."

"And look at those kid gangs," Sam said. "I saw one on television the other night. The bastards were movie stars! How many people they mugged doesn't seem to matter." He held up his hand. "Listen to this: one day two of my guys tailed this thief to the South Bronx. He was stealing a store blind, and in order to make a case we had to know where he was stashing the loot. They tailed him to a tenement and looked for a phone to check in. Every booth was ripped off. They finally got one in a bar. When they came back to the car a gang of punks told them they had prevented some kids from stealing their battery so it would cost them fifteen bucks."

"Did they pay it?" Tom asked.

"Of course they did," Sam said. "It was easier than the emergency ward or the morgue."

"How about the police?" Max asked.

"The police?" Sam said. "In Dodge City?"

"What's this Dodge City?"

"Dodge City, Fort Apache. Tombstone. That's what the cops call parts of the city where it's open season on them. They only go in with shotguns and in groups. Like one guy told me, 'Up there the pension doesn't look so big.' "

"What happened when we were gone?" Max asked sadly.

"They let the goddam world fall apart," Stu said grimly, "brick by brick. . . . They just didn't care."

Our discussion broke off when the lights slowly dimmed and a line of our very attractive waitresses appeared with the flaming baked Alaska while some guy with a great tenor voice sang "Auld Lang Syne." Sure it could be classed as pure American Legion cornball but, goddam it, I sat there with the others, a frog as big as a fist stuck in my throat. Even Rudy didn't make a pass at the well-stacked blonde who served him.

22

When the lights went up a guitarist appeared who made sure the sombre moment didn't last. He went around the table playing the songs we remembered, "Bits and Pieces" from the Dave Clark Five, The Beatles' "She Loves Me," Simon and Garfunkel's "The Sounds of Silence," until Tom said we sounded as ancient as a bunch of Civil War vets. There was one more ceremony; each waitress read off a name and presented its owner with a small package. In it was a beautiful leather folder containing the photograph taken of us as we landed at Clark. Under it was a list of our names in gold lettering and the title:

"The American Hounds of Tong Le Mai."

"Now we have a whole weekend before us," Stu announced. "It's a little late now but I have a movie I think you'll like. Tomorrow I have a box at the Garden. If you don't like that, just tell me what you want and I'll see that you get it. In the evening there will be a cocktail party. I'm sure you'll like the company. Tickets for a musical will be left in your rooms. If you're not occupied come along. Sunday we have a few things planned, so I'll be in touch . . . now if you want to hit the sack instead of the movie by all means do so. Remember, everything in the Eldorado is yours." He pointed a finger at Rudy, "Except that big blonde, Rudy. She's got three kids in Brooklyn."

We got up, languorous, well fed, content. On another floor was a small movie theatre with deep, engulfing seats. It was a fine whodunit, but long before the suspect was revealed I was fighting to keep my eyes open, while Rudy's snores competed with the make-believe gunfire. After it was over we broke up, some going to the bar or off to bed.

I awoke with the sun streaming in and the phone ringing; it was an impatient Stu demanding I join him for breakfast.

The weekend passed all too quickly. The cocktail party was a huge success, at least as far as I was concerned. She was dark and petite, a copywriter in a Madison Avenue advertising outfit who desperately wanted to get into the newspaper business. We ended in bed in the early hours of Sunday and said a cheerful good morning on Monday. No strings, just a promise to keep in touch. All in all it had been a fabulous three days.

I had promised Stu I would spend my week off with him. Frankly I wasn't in any hurry to get back to Atlanta. Over breakfast Stu renewed his old argument that I was only wasting my time on a wire service rewrite desk and should join him.

"The company is now too big not to have a full-time publicity director," he said. "We've been getting along with a PR outfit in Philadelphia but they're too far away and frankly I don't think they have newspaper experience. I need someone to put together a staff and issue a weekly magazine, newsletter, or whatever the hell you want to call it, for our senior citizen villages in New Mexico, Arizona, and California, and take over the publicity for Eldorado and the other hotels. Name your figure, Trev, and add a generous expense allowance along with a suite set aside for you in every hotel or town house complex we operate. And no one's going to be on your back if you decide to check out your staff in our Golden Gate in the Bahamas. Believe me, the job needs more expertise than sweat. What do you say?"

"Let me think it over for a couple of hours, Stu. I'll get back to you this afternoon."

"You'll be doing me more of a favor than I'll be doing for you, Trev. Businesswise it's been a great year, but lonely as hell after Dad died."

"Arnie, Star, Rudy. Sam. Tom—even Max. And now me."

"That's the way I want it," he said firmly. "As I told you I need people I can trust. To have guys you can rely on guarding your back is better than a million dollars in the bank. At least that's the way I feel."

"What will you do with Tom?"

"I want Tom to open an office for the Harlow interests in Washington."

"You plan on taking over something in Washington?"

"No, but I still want friends down there. A big wheel in the oil lobby owes me a favor. He's promised to introduce my people to the right contacts."

"You mean someone who'll do a favor?"

"Let's say someone who will see that our proposals get a fair hearing." He took a slick-looking brochure from his pocket. "This is a copy made up by one of our competitors for the Interior Department. It's no secret in the hotel business that two of the big parks in the West will eventually be opened for public skiing. I want to make sure our bid gets a fair shake. If you decide to come on, I want you and Sam to go to Washington with Tom."

"Sam's a private eye, Stu, how does he fit in?"

"Sam is practically an employee of Harlow Hotels. I even have a piece of his company."

"Sam said he couldn't have made it without you."

He dismissed the praise with an impatient wave.

"I only gave him a lift. He's damn valuable to us. Last winter I had him spend months entertaining cops from desk sergeants to inspectors who work in the areas where we have properties. You would be surprised at what a free room and a night club tab can do. Three weeks ago we had a fag murder in our East Side hotel. There's nothing you can do about them, they happen in any house. One of Sam's friends was in charge of the homicide. On television we came out smelling like a rose. It all adds up."

"But if you don't have any hotels in Washington—"

"New York isn't America, Trev. We have millions invested around the country. Sam's made his police contacts in New York; now I want him to do the same with the federal agencies."

"How about me? What can I do down there?"

"I think it's vital for a hotel chain to have friends in the newspaper business, especially in New York and Washington. If a legitimate newspaper guy wants a free room, dinner, or a show, all they have to do is call you. No strings attached, no favors wanted in return. It's as simple as that." He finished his coffee. "Now I'm going back to work. Why don't you spend the rest of the day thinking it over? When you have made your decision, give me a call."

I had lunch with the old Federal Building man who had broken me in and was shocked at how he had aged. But as I strolled along lower Broadway to Trinity churchyard, a favorite spot, I reminded myself that seven years had been torn out of my life. During that period my widowed mother had died, along with some uncles and cousins, old friends were bald, bearded, moustached, married, divorced, dead, or gone from town so long no one knew their addresses. More important were the changes in the country for which I had fought and given those seven years. Even the old reporter pointed that out when we were moving around the courthouse. I had inquired about a favorite court attendant who never failed to tip the pressroom when a star witness was ready to appear before the grand jury or a judge was about to hand down an important decision. I was startled when the reporter told me he had been killed, stabbed to death on a Worth Street subway station at the height of the rush hour by a thief who then calmly took his wallet, watch, and ring while a crowd watched; no one interfered. What was doubly shocking was the casualness with which he recited the details. He shrugged when I pointed this out.

"You've been away a long time, Trev," he told me, "and in that time a lot of things have happened to our society. You've come back to a cold-blooded world where it's every man for himself and don't you forget it!"

When I returned from Tong Le Mai I had almost fled back home. I was desperate for old faces, for love, beauty, security. Maybe that's why the South always snares its people, the blood kin and the choking tendrils of the heart. I received the usual publicity, my old high school had a banner, "Welcome Lieutenant Trevor David, U.S.M.C.," and there were endless parties, dinners, and civic luncheons. I guess it was to be expected, my family had been in Fayette County since 1723 and Riverview or the "David place" on the Flint River, which still showed bullet holes of Sherman's bummers, was a tourist showplace. My great-grandfather had been a colonel in the savage house-to-house fighting in the Battle of Jonesboro, when the Confederate cavalry tried to halt Sherman's March to the Sea. But Riverview still didn't give me the peace I wanted; even when I returned to AP in Atlanta I was restless and uneasy; things didn't seem to fit anymore. I had come back to a whole new society in which a "credibility gap" had become a national institution, skepticism was a pervasive attitude, and people followed the dictates of their own morality, not their government's. I was dumbfounded the first time I saw a massive demonstration in New York, but the newspaperman I was with casually dismissed it as "nothing—wait until you see what they do to some of the consulates . . ."

I felt we had survived Tong Le Mai because of our unity and for years we had practically lived on loyalty. Now paradoxically the very war in which we had fought and given years of our lives had caused a good segment of the country to have lost faith in the wisdom and intentions of our leaders.

Then one day, a month after I returned home, a letter signed by several students, two of them Nam veterans, denouncing me and all the POWs as the "real war criminals" was published in the local newspaper. It was no hysterical, irrational antiwar outburst but a calm, lucid, and sincere document. The letter produced an unprecedented controversy; members of the David clan from all over the county stormed into town to berate the editor, the American Legion let go a few indignant blasts, but there were some who agreed with the authors of the letter. It left me shaken. As my wise old aunt observed, Southerners always seemed obsessed with heroes and villains but they usually turn out to be the same men.

It was not the first cry of disapproval I had heard, other POWs had told me of their bitter experiences. I was finding out you really can't go home again—even as a so-called war hero. . . .

However, it was only a local cause célèbre and quickly faded from public interest. I returned to AP and gradually slipped back into the routine of a wire service rewriteman. Old friends were kind and thoughtful, all of them going out of their way to make sure I was at ease. Before Nam the newspaper business had been my whole life but now I felt something was missing; what the hell was a row over the state budget compared to planning how to quickly strangle your young guard so he wouldn't give an alarm?

I found myself becoming vaguely uneasy, uninterested, and discontented. And the nightmares, while not as frequent as when I first came back, were still frightening. I was always in the stall, chained to my bunk with the stinking darkness so thick it seemed to weigh like a blanket, threatening to smother me. Once I awoke, crouched in a corner, to look up into the frightened face of my aunt.

I spent a weekend with a psychiatrist at the local VA hospital. He listened sympathetically and gave me some tranquilizers. I threw them away and came to the conclusion I had to move on, even at the cost of leaving the newspaper business.

The week I had taken off to join the reunion was really a time for decision, where to go, what to do.

In the serenity of the old churchyard I wondered if Stu might be right, perhaps it was better to be with your own kind, with companions who had been tested in the same pure white flame. What the hell was there to decide? After I left the graveyard—there must be some hidden symbolism there—I found a telephone and called Stu.

"Welcome home, Trev," he said simply.

I spent my first months with the Harlow chain setting up PR staffs in each hotel or retirement village across the country. We had many dry runs before I was satisfied with the expensive weekly magazine that would serve the chain. While the format remained the same, each hotel or project added its own local cover in color, inside matter, and community ads. By midsummer I had assembled a bright young staff that put the pieces together almost automatically. I also accompanied Sam and Tom to Washington and met the lobbyist, a hard-eyed veteran of the capital's wars. He wore a plastic smile, talked endlessly without saying anything, and had an impressive storehouse of the drinking and sexual sins of our nation's lawmakers. He also admired Stu; a comer, he called him.

Tom and I set up an office and accompanied the lobbyist visiting congressional offices, attending cocktail parties, private dinners, formal affairs, and even a White House reception. I also did some missionary work on my own. The former Atlanta AP city editor, my old boss, was now chief correspondent of a powerful newspaper chain.

Impeachment was the top story and over dinner he told me the fascinating inside facts of the political maneuvering and infighting, all a part of that tragic, historic summer. Of course, we cursed the Yankee fat-cat reporters who lived by the official handout and ignored the old-fashioned legwork. He also introduced me to other bureau chiefs and reporters, Washington's real working press. I made sure they knew that whenever they came to New York they were welcome to stay at the Eldorado and have dinner or an evening at the glittering Conquistadores Room with their wives, mistresses, or matinee shack-ups. As Stu said, no strings. I spread goodwill like a new commuter sowing grass seed in April.

Sam, meanwhile, cultivated his own circle of friends in Treasury, the FBI, and Dangerous Drugs. Instead of free rooms and nightclub tabs, his goods for barter were information, gossip, rumors about the underworld, free-lance thieves, and the activities of the various police departments around the country.

After the uneasy days of Watergate, it was every agency for itself in Washington, and Sam's tales about interagency rivalry and the clashes between bureaucratic giants were shocking. As usual it was the public who lost out.

ristmas at Riverview with an assortment of kin and was
k to join Stu and the others for a rousing New Year's
g back I can see how we had fallen into place. Instead
Tong Le Mai, we had a gold-plated hotel in the heart of

New York City where we shared our mutual loneliness, restlessness, and uncertainty . . . together we were aliens in another hostile country. . . .

The first few weeks of the New Year saw us scattered around the country; Star and Rudy were in the Southwest, Tom in Washington, Arnie in Arizona, Sam busy in New York checking out a series of annoying room thefts in the Eldorado, while I shuttled about making sure our newsletters and hotel magazines were competently edited. Our salaries were excellent and fringe benefits superb. It was a placid life with some periods of boredom, but for me the movement and variety of scenery and people were excellent therapy. It was evident we were all relaxing, with Nam growing dimmer every day. Once a month we gathered at the Eldorado to attend a meeting presided over by Stu. It was always a wonderful weekend. I never realized until much later how the business meetings always seemed like a council of war. Even the buying of a choice piece of property for development became a military campaign with Stu as our chief of staff. But we all looked forward to these meetings, it was like a widespread family gathering for a clan reunion. . . .

One week in March I spent in Arizona tearing apart and putting together the magazine which served our big retirement village. It had never been right from the very beginning, the beautiful color shots and the text didn't ring true to my ear. I worked with my staff to plane time, then discovered I had missed it. The day had been miserable, everything had gone wrong; printers had become incredibly stupid and the bright young reporter I had chosen as editor had suddenly become a dullard.

The flights to New York were filled and I had to wait for hours until I finally got a seat on a line that stopped at every eastern city except Hoboken. It was midnight when I finally reached the Eldorado; a hot shower and drink finally restored my good humor.

I checked the desk for messages and found Sam had been trying to get me or Stu. I had him paged, called his apartment and exchange, but couldn't raise him. The night manager told me Sam had seemed upset and had them page Stu at some hotel banquet but had missed him; he didn't know what Sam wanted. I left messages all around and went back to the AMs. Like a good lobster rewriteman I read them from page one to Personals before I put out the light. My last thoughts were about Sam—what could be so urgent . . . ?

The ringing of the phone yanked me out of a deep sleep.

For a confused moment I was back in Atlanta and the AP operator was summoning me to work, but instead of that syrupy voice it was Stu's, harsh and demanding:

"I'm down in the lobby, Trev. Join me as quick as you can."

"What's up?"

"Max's wife was raped and murdered . . ."

I threw on my clothes and rushed down to the lobby. A cab w

the curb and within minutes we were on our way uptown. The rain had stopped. Under the lights asphalt gleamed like a dark, glistening river.

"I just got in from that damn hotel owners' banquet when the desk clerk waved me down for a phone call. It was Sam, he had been trying to reach us all night—"

"I know. I got a message when I came in."

"They paged me at the dinner but I had left early with a group from Miami. The clerk was about to turn him over to you when I came through the door. Sam gave me only a few details. Max was out on an emergency. He found her when he came in."

"Good God!"

Heidi, pretty as a blue-eyed Dutch doll, all dreamy-eyed and proud of the life which stirred within her, now a broken, violated thing? It can't be true, I told myself, such a thing couldn't happen to Max! Not Max, dear God, not Max!

"Sam also said something about the cops shooting the guy that did it. I think he said he was a junkie."

"Jesus!"

"How do you like that?" he said grimly. "A guy spends years in a prison camp, suffers all kinds of hell, and comes back to have his wife murdered by a junkie." He punched his knee with his fist. "Goddam this city!"

There were squad cars, cops, and a motley crowd outside the old brownstone. In the lower window I saw the sign: Max Findeloon, M.D. Hours 1-2. Wednesday by appointment.

If I knew Max, Wednesday was like any other day.

A short distance away cops and plainclothesmen stood about the rainwashed outline of a human figure drawn in chalk on the sidewalk.

"The junkie's dead," I said.

"Why do you say that?" Stu asked as we got out of the cab.

I pointed to the chalked figure. "DOA."

A young cop at the top of the stoop barred our way.

"Relatives," Stu snapped. He opened the door and we walked into a long narrow hallway filled with dark mahogany, carpeted stairs and a bronze figure holding a lamp at the foot of the banister. In the rear of the hall a patrolman's stilted monotone briefed the lobster trick reporters from police headquarters how he had killed the junkie.

"... then my fellow officers went into the alley. As I came up he ran out of the cellar—you know the space under the stoop—and started down the street. When I ordered him to halt he turned with a shiny object in his hand—"

"Was it a gun?" a reporter asked.

The cop stopped his mechanized account and slowly put a finger through a hole in his hat.

"It wasn't any goddam water pistol, buddy."

Just then Sam appeared at the top of the stairs with a slender white-haired man. He rushed down when he saw us.

"Stu! Trev! God, am I glad to see you. What a night!"

He whispered something to the white-haired man who nodded and joined the cop being interviewed.

"Thank God, Inspector Finnegan—he's a friend of mine—got someone from the medical examiner's office up here in a hurry," Sam said, rubbing his haggard face. "The bastard used a necktie to strangle her . . . Max kept injecting her with stuff trying to bring her around . . . he was like a wild man . . . it was horrible . . . I'll take Nam any day. Finally I got Finnegan to send a radio car to the hospital to bring back a doctor friend of Max's. He's with him now. . . ."

Max was stretched out on a worn chaise longue. He was dazed, fragile, his eyes red from weeping. Sitting alongside him was a short fat man with thick glasses.

"They killed her, Stuart," Max whispered brokenly. "They killed her and our baby . . ."

"This is Dr. Auchincloss," Sam said, nodding to the fat man.

"I've given him a sedative,"Auchincloss explained. "He's going under."

"Heidi," Max sobbed. "Heidi . . ."

Stu asked the doctor, "Is there anything we can do?"

The doctor gave him a puzzled look. "Do? What can anyone do? A woman has been murdered. A pregnant woman. A horrible crime. And this poor man." He closed his bag. "He is a fine, fine man." He said softly, "You are his friends? The ones who were with him in Vietnam?"

"We were all POWs together, Doctor," I said.

"I knew a little of his story from the administrator. He never talked about it but he did mention his friends. One day I asked him about Vietnam but he only smiled and repeated what that ballplayer said. The black man."

"Satchel Paige," I said. " 'Don't look behind you, somebody may be catching up.' "

The old man lumbered to his feet. "Maybe Max looked behind him." He held out his hand. "I'm sorry, very, very sorry. If I can be of any help please call me."

He closed the door softly and we were alone with Max. The sedative had taken effect and the sound of his heavy breathing filled the room.

"He can't stay here," Sam said.

"We'll take care of him," Stu replied. "Sam, you go down to the hotel and tell the night manager I want the suite next to the penthouse. I don't care who's in it, have it ready in an hour." He looked at me. "Somebody will have to make arrangements for the funeral."

"I'll do it."

"Also see if you can find out where her family lives. Max once told me it was a little town outside of Amsterdam—"

"I'll get the hospital administrator out of bed and check the Dutch consulate."

"Send a cable in Max's name. Just that she died. Then go over to Campbell's. Tell them to send me the bill. You will have to pick out a plot, too." He added bitterly, "Here we are making her funeral arrangements and only a few hours ago she was alive and carrying a child! All because of a goddam junkie!"

"I'll go down to the hotel," Sam said. "My car is outside. Trev, I'll drop you off at the hospital."

We were at the door when Stu said, "Tell the others what happened."

"Are you staying here?"

"I wouldn't want to be any other place" was his quiet answer.

Three horrible days, the saddest of my life. We were an uncomfortable band, each trying in his own way to share Max's grief.

There was a steady stream of mourning nurses in white, solemn doctors, and people from the neighborhood; blacks, whites, Orientals, young, old, vigorous, feeble, junkies. They either jerked Max's hand in a self-conscious way, their eyes darting about the room as if they expected a bust, or they wept on his shoulder. Max carefully listened to each one—even the guy who whispered his latest symptoms—so after a time it appeared he was doing all the consoling.

We felt out of it, standing about with the uneasiness of strangers in that room heavy with the scent of hothouse flowers; not so much as strangers in Max's hospital world but to this special world of death dignified, so natural to the others but to us still baffling and unreal, a formality we scarcely knew anymore.

The most shattering moment was at the cemetery when Max held out his hands, pleading and crying softly, "Heidi . . . Heidi . . ." as Stu and I supported him. On the trip back to the city he leaned back and closed his eyes. All he said was:

"I don't know how I can go on without her."

But Max did—at least to us it seemed that way—and picked up the pieces of his shattered life. He returned to St. Dominick's, opened his office, and insisted on living in the same apartment.

We had dinner with him at least once a week and practically kidnapped him for a night of the theatre and a gathering in Stu's penthouse suite. We even went as patients, Rudy for a nasty infected bite from some desert fly, Tom for a strep throat, and Arnie for the flu; we made up infections to see him.

But life went on and the impact of that sudden brutal crime gradually faded as we slipped back into our daily routines. On the surface Max appeared to have recovered, and until the morning Sam called Stu to rush over to the shabby brownstone for the second time, we never suspected how totally defeated he had been.

Max had committed suicide.

It was a bizarre replay. Once again Inspector Finnegan cajoled the reporters to remain outside, while we sat in the scrupulously clean room and listened to Sam tell us how carefully Max had planned to kill himself.

He knew that an upstairs tenant, a night worker, passed his apartment about six o'clock so he pinned a note on his door asking him to call the police. The cops found him on a couch, a note to the medical examiner written on his prescription pad advising the ME he had injected himself with two grains of morphine. A letter tucked inside his jacket—he had refused to meet death without a tie—was addressed to Stu. It contained a bank cashier's check covering the loan Stu had given him to open his practice, along with another to cover his funeral expenses, and a third assigning what was left of his humble estate to St. Dominick's children's ward. Only recently I discovered Stu had turned over the check made out to him to the children's ward also.

Wearily, sorrowfully, we went through the funeral process again. After the funeral we returned to Stu's penthouse where he read us Max's letter to him. Later he gave it to me and I quote in part:

I feel like a man who has stepped out of the 19th century, nothing is familiar. I am even a stranger to medicine. When I left, life was sacred. Now the law tells us we can destroy it. At the hospital it happens, five, ten—even more times a day. The other men just shrug it off but I can't. It bothers me, I know it may be old-fashioned but I can't change at this point.

My patients are frightened, uncertain, hostile. They regard their neighborhood as a sort of private barony with the drawbridge drawn up over the moats of the city at the first sign of dusk. My God, there are more guns in this block than in four cowboy pictures! I had a kid about sixteen come into my office the other night. When he took off his coat a gun fell out of his pocket. When I asked him what he was doing with a gun he seemed surprised I asked the question. "For protection, Doc, whatsa matter with ya?" he said.

When I came home from Nam I was tired, I guess battered is a better word. The week I told you I was going home to Michigan for a visit with my parents I really spent in a VA hospital consulting a psychiatrist. My depression was worsening every day. Then God sent me Heidi. I felt as if I had been reborn, that a new future beckoned, even in that grubby little flat she loved so much. We had lots of plans for when the baby came. You know what I thought about her pregnancy. This would have been the brightest, the most wonderful day in my life. A child. My child!

Her senseless death has made it impossible for me to go on. I tried, God knows how I tried, but it was too much. The old depression came back and now I have nightmares. I am back in Tong Le Mai. I wake up bathed in sweat, expecting any minute to hear the guards open the stable door to take one of us out for questioning.

32

*And about that wonderful reunion you gave us, Stu. I
wanted to say so many things to all of you, to tell you how
much you mean to me ... you are my brothers ... always
... I cannot hate that poor unfortunate who killed
Heidi. ... I can only wonder at the forces that drove him to
it—God have mercy on his soul. The drug is taking hold ... I
must close ... it's an easy death ... go to sleep and ...*

The words ended in a scrawl. It appeared he stuffed the letter and
checks into the envelope as he felt the last feeble beatings of his dying
heart. . . .

After Stu carefully folded the letter the silence was almost
unendurable. Someone turned on the stereo and the soothing music of
Mancini flowed over us.

"Do you ever get the feeling it's us against the world and the
world is winning?" Stu asked suddenly.

Arnie answered him with a short laugh. "All the time."

"If I go out after nine o'clock I feel like Gary Cooper in *High
Noon* listening for that train whistle," Tom said.

Stu pointed to the darkening city. "Just like Max said, every
neighborhood is a barony with guns. It's not only New York, it's all
over. But we didn't make this goddam world, we were in limbo."

"It's drugs, Major," Rudy insisted. "That's what it is—drugs! Ask
any cop. We're goddam prisoners of the junkies!"

"I happen to think you're partially right, Rudy," Stu said. "There
is no doubt junkies are a hell of a problem in this city." He added
shortly, "Without junkies, Max and Heidi and their child would be
alive."

"The drug problem is national," Tom put in. "When I came home
the local paper had stories about state police raids. The pictures showed
the junkies were kids. Boys and girls. Hell, for some kids it's a way of
life!"

"Oh, I agree drugs are a big reason for what's going on," Stu said,
"but I also think it's only a part of the whole damn picture in this
country." He added impatiently, "It seems as if no one cares anymore.
Take Max. And Heidi. She was murdered, he killed himself because she
was murdered. And what happened? One headline in the *Daily News*.
Five paragraphs somewhere in the *New York Times*. Thirteen seconds
on the television news broadcasts. Goddammit! Don't they know what
killed them? And I'm not talking about the junkie that cop knocked
off—I'm talking about society. What did it do about Max's death?" He
slammed his fist down on the table. "Nothing! Not a goddam thing!
Remember that hotelman's dinner I went to the night Heidi was killed?
Two guys from San Francisco got indignant over their cocktails about
crime in their city. By the time they ordered their second drink they
were telling me how tough it was during the energy crisis. One guy said
he had to walk a mile to work! I don't know—everyone seems asleep,

walking around in fantasy land. Somebody has to do something. I mean it!"

"Like what?" I asked him.

"Wake up the country, Trev! Tell the people they're in a state of siege and they don't know it."

Arnie said, "The house is burning down . . ."

Stu said seriously, "I'm not kidding, Arnie."

Arnie shook his head. "Who is?"

Stu continued in a harsh, bitter voice, "I never thought the people in this country would come to this—afraid to walk down their own streets, to go to church, let a few punks with guns pull off kidnappings and call them political. And they're tolerated! Why? Because we're all too busy with our own concerns. To hell with our neighbor. In my opinion this idiotic society we came back to stinks."

He got up, poured himself another drink and went to the window.

"At least we're together," he said. "They want to buck us? Let them try it."

"Cut one and we all bleed, Major," Rudy said. "Right, Injun?"

Star nodded, he was never one to waste words.

I can recall that scene as if it happened only a few months ago; the lights were winking on in the city's towers and Stu's face was lost in the shadows. He appeared as a silhouette against the glass.

Cut one and we'll all bleed. It wouldn't be long before Sam and Tom proved Rudy was right.

Chapter **2**

Sam Hoffman-
The Raid

As Leah said, I deserved what I got. In the first place, what was a nice Jewish boy from Bensonhurst doing in Connecticut looking to buy a farm with those crazy chickens, cows, and a lake, no less?

My explanation is not simple. It involves Leah, South Brooklyn, Strout farm catalogs, Menz's Pickle Works, and a lot of my old man before I can come to the point of why Tom Bruckner and I were in Connecticut where it all happened. Frankly, I now wish I had never left Brooklyn.

I guess we should start with Leah, who is my favorite woman. Besides being great in bed she is the only one who can make lentil soup like my old man; thick, with plenty of frankfurters, potatoes, and not too much onion. She also agrees with me that it's better the second day.

When I first met Leah I put it on the line: I'm not looking to get married. She said that was okay with her, so we began what I thought was a wonderful relationship. We both agreed that if we met someone we liked better, we would split with no hard feelings.

Leah is strictly a city girl who is lost above Ninetieth Street and below Washington Square; even the Sheep Meadow makes her nervous. A little caterpillar? Forget it. She gets hysterical.

So how could I tell her about the wonderful dream me and my old man shared for years? Solly the electrician, he was known in Bensonhurst and Borough Park, the guy who could fix anything from doorbells to dynamos. Dummy jobs, he called them, but the extra bucks he made came in handy. His regular job was maintenance man for Menz's Pickle Works in South Brooklyn; a million times old man Menz told me, "A regular Edison, that Solly." I will now state flatly he was a genius, not only an expert with the wires—you should have seen the burglar alarm system he put in for Menz when the junkies started robbing back in the fifties—but he was also a private detective, a piano player with a great tenor voice, and standup comedian who on special occasions provided the entertainment for McCormick's Bar & Grill in Astoria. He was also a superb cook. Like I said, a genius.

While he was happy to play the piano and entertain, his true loves were electricity and being a private eye. Once, twice, maybe three times a month a lawyer in Queens would give him what my father proudly called "a case." It was always the same, tailing some joker in a matrimonial jam. I went along because who would be suspicious of a guy with a little fat kid? We jumped in and out of subways, grabbed cabs, and walked countless miles. I don't think there's a section of the five boroughs I can't name, street by street. I can also tell you where certain stores are located. Know why? Windows are excellent for watching your "subject" in the reflection on the pane. As my old man pointed out it was best to use three-cornered jobs; you can move from one end of the window to the other and see north and south.

I loved those crazy days and nights. I never got much homework done, but what I learned about life you don't pick up in classrooms. By the time I was fifteen I could split a pair and install a tap as good as my old man. He said I had a natural touch.

We were partners in everything, from private-eyeing to repairing Menz's ancient electrical system in that old warehouse filled with the most delicious smell in the world, Menz's Kosher pickles. Wonderful.

My father raised me after my mother died when I was seven. He worked for Menz so long he could name his own hours. He was always home, cooking up a storm when I came in from school. You can't buy food like he made. I swear it.

He was slender with olive skin, thick dark hair, and long pointed sideburns; a Spanish pimp, my aunt Marilyn called him, but what the hell, we didn't like her either. Every time we paid her a visit which was not too often I can assure you, she always wound up the evening opening a little canvas bag and showing us her diamond rings and pins, caressing and cooing to them as if they were flesh and blood. Sick, my father always said when we left, crazy sick.

We had fantastic times; once a week to Loew's Oriental, into the city to the Paramount, with dairy on Sunday at Famous on 86th Street and Bay Parkway. When we took those "excursions" he dressed to the nines, wraparound polo coat, A. S. Beck's blue suede shoes, a dazzling tie, and always the white shirt. He was a very puritanical guy when I was with him but I knew he wasn't exactly lonely. Ostensibly we dropped off at B & G next door to Hanson's after a show to see his "theatrical buddies" but I noticed we always wound up with a babe at our table, usually a good looking hoofer with a phony name like Gigi from the Latin Quarter.

But the most precious thing we had, above and beyond the *zaftig* chorus girls, the movies, and an occasional turn at McCormick's—even the electricity and private-eyeing—was what we called The Secret. Every extra dime he or I made went into a large pickle jar. When we had enough for bills I made a trip to the bank.

The object was to buy a farm, land we could own. Not a stamp-sized piece of ragged grass littered with rocks and beer cans but a picture-book house painted white with black trim, a barn with a weathervane, chickens, ducks, pigs, a dog or two, and a back porch where you could see the mists gathering in the valley at twilight.

My father first got the fever a few years after my mother died. I will always remember the farm catalogs, Strout was our favorite, but there were others stacked in a neat pile in the corner of the kitchen. Thompson's Farms, American Homes and Farms, and numerous others from small town real estate dealers.

Stickball, even ring-a-levio, went by the boards when a new catalog arrived. We would sit at the kitchen table and go over it page by page, with my father reading aloud the descriptions, rolling the words over his tongue with loving care. We would go right through, first page to the last.

Menz had an old car he let my father use for keeping it in shape, and one or two Saturdays a month we went "farming," as he called it. I got to know Connecticut, Jersey, Pennsylvania, and upstate as I knew the city; back roads, lanes, towns, villages, crossroads, you name it, we hit it. I even got to know the agents and some farm families. They couldn't resist my old man when he sat down to *tummel* in the kitchen. If it was near dinnertime and his epicure's nose told him something was in the oven, he really put on a show. The cow-kickers loved him, and before you knew it two extra plates were on the table. Sometimes we stayed overnight, a few times a whole weekend.

I can still see my old man in his loafers, slacks, and Borough Park sports shirt solemnly discussing crop rotation, dairy mechanization, the widening of county roads, and state's rights over flowing brooks with some farmer as if my father had been born on a farm instead of in Brooklyn.

Even after I had graduated from high school and gone on to the

National Institute of Electronics—I modestly point out on scholarship —I gladly accompanied my old man on his "farming" trips.

By the time I went in the army, Menz was in kosher foods, the tottering old warehouse had been replaced by a stone building on the Island; everything was mechanized and my father headed a round-the-clock staff of electricians, porters, and handymen. The "farming fund" was up to six thousand, a good-sized deposit. The night we reached the six grand mark was celebrated in Famous with my father giving his *spritz*, which left them rolling between tables.

But we never made the deposit. I was drafted and before we knew it we were saying good-bye and cursing LBJ and those clucks in Congress who sent me off to fight a war in which everybody was a victim.

In Nam, in Tong Le Mai, I was desperate to let my father know I was still alive. When we reached Clark I learned it was too late—he had been dead for almost two years.

There were no cheering crowds or bands to greet me at Kennedy, only old man Menz in his Cadillac. He told me what happened. After the M.I.A. telegram came, my father gradually slipped downhill; Menz said he seemed dead inside. One day when he didn't show up for work they found him on the floor. A stroke, they said, but I know it was a broken heart. Believe me, that was a bummer; it didn't seem possible I wouldn't see him running out to the ramp to hug me and promise to fill me with yesterday's lentil soup until it poured out of my ears. I floundered around for a while trying to find myself in the old neighborhood, but it wasn't any use. The apartment was gone, but fortunately old man Menz had had his lawyer take care of our effects and the bank account, which now contained an impressive fifteen thousand—the last deposit had been made four days before he died.

The major really saved my life. I had been working with this big private eye firm installing security systems and wondering what the hell I was doing with my life, when one day he called. Trevor David, he said, had sent him my address. Trev, another great guy, had been keeping in touch with all of us after we left Clark because the major wanted some kind of a reunion.

I never knew what a big man Stu was until I went to see him in the Eldorado. What a setup! He's a forceful guy, and before I knew it I had agreed to go into business for myself. Sam Hoffman, Private Eye! At first I hesitated but after he put the figures down in black and white I went *shlepping* back to Bensonhurst, my head in the clouds. Well, to make a long story short, Hoffman's Agency was an instant success. I not only got all the Harlow hotel business, but Stu introduced me to two guys who own the Dangler Discount Stores in the metropolitan area and they signed up. It's hard to believe what has taken place within the year. I came home a nothing, now I'm on top of the heap.

My first job was rounding up everybody for the reunion; the next was cultivating the cops whose precincts covered Harlow properties.

This made sense to me. Hotels are big business, and it's impossible to keep out the Murphy men, sneak thieves, high price whores, violent drunks, and the rest of the creeps who can bring grief to innocent New York businessmen. I told Stu we should go beyond the local cops and spread a little grease downtown, like Identification, Missing Persons—not to get secrets but, more important, service. He agreed, so every few months my contacts get an envelope. It pays off. For example, I give them a list of prospective employees; most of the time they're clean but twice I caught ex-cons, one had done time for rape. Can you imagine this guy delivering room service to some woman who might be carrying a bit of a load because she's mad at her husband or her boyfriend? He sees skin and explodes, and Harlow hotels end up paying a fortune in damages.

Cultivating the New York cops I could see, but I was puzzled when Stu sent me, Tom, and Trev down to Washington: my assignment was to make contacts in the federal law enforcement agencies, Trev was to spread goodwill among the newspapermen, while Tom opened a Washington office. Only much later and after a great deal had happened did we finally realize what Stu had in mind.

Well, I got to know a few guys in the Bureau—FBI—and one or two in Dangerous Drugs, Customs, and the Department of Justice. It's the old story, one guy introduces you to another, then he in turn invites you to a cocktail party—cops, federal or local, seem to move in the same social circles.

You must also observe the niceties of petty corruption; you don't come right out and flatly ask your contact for information, it's done obliquely, "dancing around" we call it, but you finally get what you're after if you observe the rules. In a way some of my Washington contacts walk both sides of the street. I also have information they want; gossip of activities of other law enforcement agencies, current investigations, who retired or who was busted, raises, divorces, marriages, mishaps—cops, federal agents, marshals, sheriffs are as gossipy as women at a tea-and-cake luncheon.

What free time I had was divided between Leah and looking for a farm. When the money started coming in, I was determined to make my father's dream a reality. I felt I owed it to him; after all those years of planning, scrimping, traveling, dreaming, it would have been an insult to his memory not to have one; Solly the Electrician's farm, it just had to be.

I went through the catalog bit again, gradually discovering the old enthusiasm. As I read the glowing, familiar phrases, fine drainage . . . deep well . . . buildings in perfect condition . . . trout stream . . . off county road . . . barn and other outbuildings. . . .

It might sound far out but I began to feel close to my old man, once again we were in the kitchen sharing pastrami on club with celery tonic as he circled the good ones with his Blaisdell black electrician's pencil and made with the jokes.

A few months after we buried Max I found what I considered a good buy in Connecticut; one hundred and twenty acres including a working farm and a lake, along with a dozen rented cabins. It was something that could both capture the dream and provide an income; I could sense my old man's smiling approval.

I called the agent and we made a date to look over the place on a Saturday afternoon. I knew Trev was a Georgia farmboy and I wanted him to come along and give me his opinion but he wasn't due in from the coast until late Saturday. Tom was my next choice. I could repeat word by word the stories he had told about the bungalow colony his family had owned on a Vermont lake when he was in high school and college.

Tom said he was glad to get out of the Washington zoo for a weekend and besides he had to talk to Stu, so he came into town and we made the trip to Connecticut. It looked like a good deal. I was impressed with the farm and the buildings but the lake and cabins left me cold. The agent insisted the owner refused to sell separately; it had to be the whole package.

While we were in the owner's house discussing terms Tom rowed around the lake. I thought he was up to something when I saw him pull into a dock and talk to some guy, then use the anchor to haul up a handful of weeds. When he returned he gave me the eye, so I told the agent I would get back to him.

After we left the place Tom filled me in. The tenant he had spoken to had a grudge against the owner and spilled his guts. Not only was there a crack in the small dam which they had patched up, but all the cabins had septic tank trouble because the summer colony had been turned into an all-year-round community. Then Tom took a few damp strands of weed from his pocket. The lake's bottom, he said, was thick with vegetation and the owner's story about great trout fishing was crap; there wasn't enough oxygen in the water to maintain game fish. In order to get the state to stock the lake, I would have to dredge out the water lilies and deep growth. Combined with the drainage problem, the angry tenants, and the poor condition of the dam and lake, the property was not worth half the asking price. No wonder that guy didn't want to sell the farm separately!

Just like Arnie said, they're out to screw you at every turn . . .

It was getting dark and according to the signs we were still a long way from Manhattan so I suggested we turn in at the next spot for a beer and something to eat. Tom thought that was a great idea. We were traveling on a back road, and nothing seemed to be open. I thought we would have to wait until we reached the parkway when I spotted a neon sign:

BIG BEAR TAVERN . . . BAR AND RESTAURANT

The sign was like a beacon. I swung into the parking area about fifty feet off the road. It was a one-story log cabin with pickup trucks and battered cars crowded into a small lot. Hard rock made the walls shake.

40

The years I had spent with my old man pounding the bricks, shadowing some joker with hot nuts for a dame not his wife, had developed my instinct and now this instinct told me the tavern was a bad scene. But Tom waved away my objections and pointed to a smaller neon sign shaped like a beer mug flashing in the window.

"What the hell, Sam, at least we can get a beer."

One small beer and lots of trouble; I should have known better. . . .

I followed him in and we took stools at the bar. The place looked like Abe Lincoln had just left. The walls were of logs with split rail rafters. Guns, a deer's head, two stuffed bear paws on a plaque, a dusty American flag, and bowling trophies were behind the bar. Pasted on the mirror was a picture of a woman with fantastic knockers. From the background it appeared the photograph had been taken in this bar; some hot nights they had.

Off to one side a large group around a pool table was watching a guy make his shot. I had spent every Saturday morning we didn't go farming at the Jewish Community House in Bensonhurst and after several years playing for quarters at the J's pool tables, I was as good with a cue as any hick hambone so I turned to watch him. He was a big guy with an ash-blond crewcut.

I guess he became conscious of me because he slowly looked up and his eyes shifted from me to Tom. There was such a look of undiluted hate it shook me and I turned back to the bar.

Tom was dressed in slacks, an old air force jacket, and boondockers. I was more fancy: I wore a sport jacket so old the Ladies Auxiliary of the local synagogue would have refused it for their rummage sale. But the guys around the pool table were not exactly in tuxedos, they had mud-splattered pants and khaki shirts; I pegged them for construction workers.

The bartender, a dirty apron around his big gut, slowly ambled down the length of the bar. What the hell, I thought, this jerk looks like he doesn't want our business. When I asked for two beers he slid across glasses of foam, took our dough, slammed down the register and started to walk away.

"Can you spare any more foam?" I said. Of course he didn't answer.

Suddenly the blaring music broke off. The quiet after that wailing was like somebody stopped beating your head with a mallet.

"I always wanted to kick the shit out of an officer," someone said.

It was the big guy who had been bending over to make a shot. He stood there at the table, cue in one hand.

"I don't like the smell of this joint, Tom, let's split," I said.

Tom looked down at his glass. "No son of a bitch is ever again going to make me do something I don't want to do," he said quietly.

He pushed his glass across the bar. "Bartender, a beer please."

The slob hesitated, but I guess Tom's easy but determined order still had an officer's ring and he came back, filled our glasses with more foam, and returned to the end of the bar. I was gulping down what little beer there was in the glass when suddenly I heard a swish next to my ear, a clump like someone kicked a melon and Tom flew off his stool. He spun across the floor to slam up against the pool table where someone pushed him toward the big guy with a shout: "Here's your boy, Whitey."

Whitey's fist smashed into Tom's face and he went down. I lunged off my stool but a guy with a cue jabbed me back.

"Take a seat, little man, or I'll fan your ass so hard you won't be able to sit down for a week," he said, waving the cue in front of my face. I almost got away again but this time he tore my shirt down the front as he forced me against the bar.

"Okay, you're next," he said. "Now watch your buddy get fragged."

There was nothing I could do but curse myself for not bringing my gun; for what they were doing to Tom I would have gladly blown out their brains.

Whitey was methodically beating Tom from one end of the bar to the other. When he feebly tried to defend himself Whitey would shout gleefully, "Oh, you want to fight? Okay. Let's go," and then smash him with hands like hams. Finally I couldn't stand it any longer and kneed the guy in the big muscle of his thigh and hurdled the bar. The guy with the cue began hopping around. The bartender started for me but I grabbed a bottle, smashed it on the rail and put the dagger ends to his big gut. An old South Brooklyn trick, it works well in the sticks.

Fatso froze.

"Leave him alone or he gets it," I shouted.

Whitey stopped giving the boot to Tom. "Grab him, Richie!" he yelled to the cue man. When Richie started for me I leaned on mushguts, just enough to let him know the jagged ends were ready to slice his liver.

"The next time it goes all the way in," I told him.

"Let him go, Whitey, he's had enough," the bartender ordered.

"Tom, can you get up?" I shouted.

With agonizing slowness Tom got to his feet. I almost drove the broken bottle in deep when I saw him. His face was a bloody, battered mask. His teeth were gone and his cheek had been ripped by Whitey's boot.

"March, you son of a bitch," I told the bartender. He knew he was close to a hospital because he almost tiptoed around the bar, waving aside the guy with the cue. Tom felt his way to the door and we got out, the broken bottle planted in that flabby gut. After Tom had crawled into my car I pushed fatso so hard he fell between two trucks, flopping about on the ground like a cursing whale. I left the yard on two wheels.

A gas station attendant told me how to reach the hospital. In the emergency room the intern took one look at Tom and ordered him into X Ray. While he stitched him up, I called the cops.

Now comes the incredible side to the story. The chief, who could have stepped out of an Al Capp cartoon, came to the hospital. He made a run to the bar and returned to inform us the bartender was considering filing charges of assault and battery! However, he was willing to forgive and forget if we just continued on our way. He claimed to have ten witnesses who were ready to swear we started the fight with Whitey over an argument about the war. In fact they claimed Tom barely missed Whitey's head with a pool ball. The chief also pointed out that no one in town would doubt the word of Whitey who was, as he put it, "a real patriot" and "war hero"!

The chief then very casually said that if we wanted to go back to headquarters we could file charges. However, he added, if counter-charges were filed against us we would have to be arraigned by his desk sergeant who could not set bail. Whitey, because he was a local taxpayer, would be paroled. The best we could expect was a Monday afternoon appearance in county court. Meanwhile we would have to spend the weekend in a station house cell.

I couldn't believe what I was hearing. It was unreal. Luckily the chief was called to a phone when the intern came out supporting Tom, barely able to walk. He said he had taken fifteen stitches in his scalp, several in his cheek and bound up his ribs, one of which at least was broken. This was in addition to assorted scrapes, bruises, and cuts.

"Get going while you can," the intern whispered. "This Whitey is homicidal. It happens every time he decides to use somebody for a punching bag. The chief is his brother-in-law and Danny, who owns the bar, is their cousin. They're all Swains, the family controls the township from dogcatcher to mayor. When he comes out I'll tell him you headed north. That will give you a chance to reach the Parkway."

I got away from there as fast as possible and didn't call Stu until I found a phone on the West Side. He had the hotel physician waiting and after a cursory examination he ordered Tom taken to Lenox Hill Hospital. There they found another busted rib and a badly sprained thumb. A plastic surgeon was called in and said Tom needed work on his cheek. Next came a dental surgeon who shook his head. The stumps of four broken teeth would have to be extracted and repairs made to several others badly chipped.

Trev had arrived by the time we got back to the hotel and I went over the whole story. When I finished Stu looked at Trev.

"What do you think we should do?"

"We should call the cops."

"Cops?" I said. "They're partners with that goddam bar, Trev!"

"I mean the State Police."

Stu picked up a bottle and walked to the fireplace where he smashed it. He held up a ragged end.

"Did you hold this to the bartender's guts, Sam?"

When I nodded he continued. "They have ten witnesses ready to swear Tom and Sam started the fight and got the worst of it. Sam could easily be indicted for felonious assault with intent to kill."

"How about the county DA, Stu? Christ, there must be somebody . . ."

"State Police. DA. Take your pick. The evidence will be the same, the word of Sam and Tom against ten or more witnesses. They wouldn't have a chance even if the State Police or the DA wanted to make a case."

He tossed the broken bottle into the fireplace. "And maybe they wouldn't be too happy to make a case. You know these small town political setups, Trev; they're almost impossible to buck."

"Hell, this is the metropolitan area, Stu, not some redneck village in Georgia."

"Georgia. Connecticut. New Jersey. New York. Pennsylvania. Wyoming. Every state in the union has small-town dynasties. I say the hell with the cops or the DA. I have another idea."

"What's that?"

"We'll do it our way."

"You mean go up there?"

"Something like that."

"Stu, that's crazy!"

"Somebody has to teach them a lesson."

"We'll let the law do that."

"What law?" he said scornfully. "A hick tavern owns the law!"

"For Christ sake, Stu, do you realize what you would be risking just to kick some hick in the ass?"

"It's more than that, Trev," Stu said quietly. "I'm up to here with the Whiteys who push people around because they have a gun or a knife or a gang at their back! You can't keep taking it forever." He motioned to me. "You say go to the law. Sam told you what happened when he went to the law! What should we do? Forget what they did to Tom?"

"You could be ruined if we were caught, Stu. Is it worth it?"

"I sincerely believe it is."

"Well I sincerely believe you're being quixotic."

"Perhaps. But it would haunt me to know that those bums are in their dirty little tavern playing pool, waiting for some poor guy to come in off the highway to buy a beer only to end up in a hospital because maybe he was an officer. Or maybe because Whitey doesn't like the way he wears his tie. Or maybe because he carries an attaché case."

"If you found the same situation in Pennsylvania or Idaho would you do the same thing?" Trev asked.

"If someone hurt you, Sam, or any one of our guys in Idaho or the state of Washington and the circumstances were the same, I'd sure as hell do something about it." He added almost gently, "Trev, you don't have to come along."

44

They studied each other for a long moment. Then Trev said, "I still think it's juvenile but count me in. Somebody should go along to keep you out of trouble."

"Get all the guys together," Stu said briskly. "Star and Rudy are on the Fire Mountain Village Project. Tell them to get back here at once. Sam, you and Trev go over to the hospital and see if Tom needs anything."

I could see Trev still didn't like the idea but I was ready to click my heels. That's what looking for a farm in Connecticut did—it turned me into a bloodthirsty Zorro. . . .

Later that night when we saw Tom in the hospital his face was dark blue and swollen, a bloody bandage covered his torn cheek, his hand was in a splint and his ribs bound.

"His car must have been totaled," a nurse observed.

That's how bad he looked.

Stu made it a military mission; find and fix, maneuver and penetrate, main attack and reserve. Star and Rudy looked the part of construction workers, so they cased the bar. From their reports Whitey and his gang were the local toughs, mostly itinerant construction workers, well diggers, and scroungers who made a living in the backwoods with a pickup truck. They had a pool tournament going and were at the tavern every evening. I worked out the retrograde operation. About a half mile from the tavern I found a dirt road which took me deep into the woods where a heavy chain with an old-fashioned lock barred the way. There was a sign on the chain: STATE PROPERTY: HUNTING AND FISHING FORBIDDEN

I easily tripped the lock and continued down the road for several miles until I met another lock and chain. A short distance beyond this point the road led into a blacktop which eventually brought me to the Wilbur Cross, then the Merritt and Hutchison parkways, and finally the West Side Highway. It was a long roundabout route but it did avoid the areas covered by the local police alarms.

As our company commander always said, preserve the integrity of your retreating forces.

Meanwhile Trev and Arnie were maneuvering, Trev to the neighboring towns and Arnie to the state courthouse. Trev, like a homing pigeon, went to the local newspaper.

After a few drinks with the editor he had the picture; Danny, the bartender, and the police chief owned the Big Bear Tavern which had a bad reputation. Somebody must have been on the take because its license had never been lifted although there had been numerous fights and once a shooting in the place. Somewhere in the setup a tow car business monopolized all highway accidents; rumors had the chief's fingers in that pie. The editor also told Trev the chief had a speed trap but the fines allegedly went into his pocket and not the town's treasury.

The editor was a former rewriteman on one of New York's defunct dailies, and when Trev asked why the hell he hadn't done anything about these people he just laughed. He explained his publisher owned a string of rural weeklies and depended on municipal advertising and goodwill; he certainly wasn't going to make any waves. As he pointed out to Trev, guys he had worked with in New York were still looking for jobs or had been forced out of the business. I will always remember Trev quoting what this editor said: "To change one thing you'll have to change everything . . . and in my personal opinion the bastards up here aren't worth it."

I guess Max would have called him a cynic. . . .

Trev found a little more on the record when he looked into Whitey's branch of the family. His uncle, the mayor, owned a real estate agency which also had a monopoly. Only recently they had pushed a variance through the city council over the protests of a homeowners' group to build a complex of garden apartments on choice land which had been designated for a park on the drawing board.

Trev talked to some of the people and their stories were typical of what can happen when a local political group takes over. After they had appeared at the Town Hall meeting their tires were slashed and sugar poured into their gas tanks. Of course the chief was very cooperative but pointed out unless they had evidence his hands were tied. Most changed their phone numbers after a series of obscene calls. One man was forced off the road to wind up in a ditch; he not only received three stitches in his lips but his car was smashed. He was a salesman and this meant he was out of a job for weeks. He led several of his neighbors to a lawyer to force the police to press charges against Whitey and his gang, but the lawyer pointed out they could be sued for false arrest if they were not able to produce supporting evidence. The battling salesman finally left town. But Trev found him.

He admitted he had tossed in the towel after almost daily visits from the health inspector (bad drainage, new septic tank needed); building inspector (bad electrical system, must be replaced), and others. It was a typical small-town political dynasty with one family controlling the community's municipal system from mayor to dog-catcher. After I heard those stories I considered that Tom and I were lucky to have gotten away with our shoes.

In the courthouse Arnie located corporation papers which confirmed the stories Trev had dug up; the chief owned a half interest in the bar through his wife, as well as the towing service. Simultaneously with whatever action we took an anonymous report giving the details was to be mailed to the State Liquor Authority and the State Highway Commission.

We planned to hit the tavern at 2100 hours Saturday night. The bartender wouldn't be touched but his stock was to end up as broken glass. Rudy, in charge of delaying action, would work on the cars in the yard and be in reserve. With the exception of Rudy we would all wear ski masks; fictitious plates were to be discarded on the trip back to the parkway. The guy who had threatened to fan me with a cue stick would be given a taste of his own medicine; Star was our unanimous choice to take care of Whitey. Looking at Star I could even feel sorry for that big slob . . .

Star was not only a Black Belt but was an expert in something called Taijojutsu, a combination of karate and several other combat techniques developed for the shock troops in the Japanese police. Then there was Aikido which was a bare-handed form of defense in which the other guy's momentum is used as a weapon. When he was in Special Forces, Star was assigned to the guy who teaches the Tokyo police and became an instructor. He even knew Mojo which is a little-known Japanese art of rope tying. In the Snakepit he showed us a lot of tricks; in seconds he could whip a rope made of shoe laces around your wrist, it was as good as handcuffs. I've seen him work out and he was deadly; in my private opinion his invisible foe was always a white man.

Months away from booze and plenty of hard work in the searing sun of the Southwest had turned Star into a slender, muscular, hard-faced guy with thin lips and cold dark eyes.

Stu's final orders were brief and to the point; we all knew our roles. Once on the highway we slipped into a pattern, cars evenly spaced, everyone dressed neatly, no drinking, no weapons, only this time I carried my licensed .45. To make sure there were no flaws Stu had made reservations at a restaurant north of the bar. If by any weird twist of fate we were stopped by the police the explanation of what we were doing was simple; we were on our way to a quiet birthday dinner.

We scrambled when we hit the parking lot. The moon was up, the sky a dark dome studded with stars. Star silently pointed to Whitey's pickup truck. A black powder cap would be attached to the ignition. When the key turned the head would split; just an extra bonus in addition to the slashed tires and sugar in the gas tank.

I could not help thinking as we slipped on our masks that because we had been screwed by the law, one of the most important and wealthiest guys in the city was leading a bunch of former POWs on a raid against a hick bar to make sure a chowderheaded son of a bitch got what was coming to him—and I, son of Solly the Electrician from Bensonhurst who only wanted to buy a farm, was giving his automatic a last minute check, once again ready to take off on a patrol and praying to God that if there was a fire fight he wouldn't end up in a green body bag with dog tags dangling from his foot. An extraordinary situation ninety minutes from Manhattan. Right?

We crossed the yard as Rudy moved like a shadow from car to car, the air hissing from punctured tires sounding like a nest of disturbed rattlers.

We inched open the door to be hit by the throbbing beat of Alice Cooper. Except for a pyramid of light above the pool table the place was dim and smoky, even the bartender had joined the group circling

47

the table. I yanked off the receiver in the phone booth, Arnie cut the cord of the phone behind the bar, and Trev pulled the plug of the jukebox. In the sudden silence a piece of ice tinkled in a glass. For some weird reason I remembered a bar girl in Saigon named Jackie.

"What the hell is this?" a voice demanded.

Stu held up his hand. "This is no stickup. We're only paying Whitey a return visit."

Whitey wasn't frightened. He hunched over his cue and peered at Stu through the drifting smoke.

"Yeah. I'm Whitey. Whaddaya want with me?"

"We heard you like to kick the shit out of officers."

"Any day. Anytime. Anywhere."

"Fine. That's why we're here."

"Who are you?" someone shouted.

"They're the guys we roughed up the other night," Whitey said with a sneer. "Now they came back with their buddies." He handed his cue to a friend. "I guess we'll have to teach 'em another lesson."

"What are we waitin' for?" one of the pool players yelled as he turned his cue around for a club. "Let's go!"

He started to rush forward. There was a grunt and a thud as Arnie floored him.

I decided it had to look good so I took out my piece. It was a .45 automatic, all chrome that gleamed like a jewel in the dim light. I worked the slide back, clicked home a round in the chamber and released the slide. Then I casually put it on the bar. That's all. No words. No nothing. Just baby on the bar.

When you have seen all the guns in the world one doesn't mean much; hell, even a .22 short can kill you just as well as a mortar. But in a bar even a pea shooter looks ominous. They backed up and I knew they wouldn't give us any more trouble.

Stu pointed to Star who had slipped off his polo shirt. He looked almost black in the dim light.

"You can start with him."

"Want me to skin this little nigger for ya?" Whitey said with a grin as he took off his shirt. "It'll be a pleasure."

That was the wrong thing to say, Whitey, I told myself.

"There's only one rule," Stu said. "No quarter."

"That's fine with me, pal."

Whitey was huge but with a growing tire of beer fat around his middle. He had enormous shoulders and fists like rocks. Compared to him Star was a dark reed of a man.

"C'mon, nigger," Whitey shouted. "Let's see how good you are."

Star was almost nonchalant as he moved in to meet Whitey, who skillfully feinted and lashed out with a cross. Star blocked the powerful blow with his arm but it flung him against the pool table. There was a cheer as Whitey rushed in with a killing roundhouse. Ball game had it landed. But Star easily ducked to face Whitey's open belly. He drove his open hand, stiff as iron into the big guy's kidney area.

Whitey grunted and bent over clutching his gut. Star jumped back and gave him a vicious kick in the face with his heavy boondockers. Whitey desperately clawed at Star, but the Indian now had his own way. Methodically, mercilessly, he went to work. I guess that for Star Whitey wasn't just a big bully with a blond crewcut, he was the whole V army, the guards and commandant of the Snakepit, and every white man from Coronado to Custer. When he had finished Whitey was a battered bloody giant who finally crashed into the phone booth then slowly slid to the floor.

"Okay. He's had enough," Stu said quietly. He turned to me. "Where's the guy with the cue?"

I pointed to Richie, the hero who had threatened me with a red ass. He immediately started to protest.

"Wait a minute. You got the wrong guy. I didn't touch anybody. Right? Did I touch you?"

He was another husky construction worker, deeply tanned and with arms like two-by-fours. But that little demonstration had suddenly drained his courage.

"Ask your friend, mister. Did I do anything? I only warned him not to mess with Whitey . . ."

"That's right, you didn't do a damn thing," Stu said savagely. "When a man was hit from behind and beaten, did you lift a hand? No. When his friend tried to help him, you threatened to make sure he wouldn't sit down for a week. Well, let's see how you make out. Drop your pants, you no good son of a bitch!"

It was a weird tableau; the staring, sweating faces in the smoky light, Whitey, battered and bloody mumbling to himself in the corner, the big guy nervously fumbling with his belt buckle. He must have felt like a real *schmuck* standing there in striped shorts and his pants around his ankles.

"Off with the shorts and bend over the pool table," Stu snapped.

The guy reluctantly followed orders.

Stu pointed to a little guy who kept showing off his bad teeth in a nervous smile.

"You start. Everybody get a cue and line up behind him."

"What do you want me to do?" the little guy asked.

"I want you to fan his ass!" Stu said. "Isn't that what he wanted?"

The big guy started to get up. "Now wait a minute . . ."

Arnie pushed him down and Stu waved to the little guy.

"Get going. If you don't know how to do it, we'll gladly show you."

The little guy hesitantly raised the cue and whacked the ass with a pretty good rap but not hard enough to satisfy Stu.

"Show him how to do it," he told Arnie.

Arnie's cue raised dust from the little guy's pants and he leaped like a rabbit.

"That's what we mean," Stu said. "Everyone gets five shots."

This time he left five red streaks across that hairy moon with its owner yelling and cursing. The line moved slowly, cues whistled through the air, I think they enjoyed what they were doing. Before long the big guy was no longer cursing, he was begging. His buttocks now were bright red and ridged from the fanning by his pals. There were some still in line when Stu broke it off.

"That's enough," he told them, "you can get in your shots after we leave." He pointed to the bartender. "Now it's your turn."

"You touch me and I'll get every cop in the county on your tail," the bartender blustered. But all that bravado was show, he was shaking in his shoes.

"You're not important enough to touch," Stu told him calmly, "but your stock is." He nodded and Trev and I went down to the cellar. We carried cases upstairs until there was barely room to walk behind the bar. We also found a couple of extra hammers and a hatchet which we gave to Star and Arnie. While they ripped open the cases I started on the bottles behind the bar. At the first tinkle of glass the bartender went berserk.

"You crazy bastards," he screamed, lumbering to the bar, "get away from my stock!"

Arnie ignored him and swung at the open box. There was a crunch of glass and the smell of scotch filled the air. The bartender turned to Stu.

"For Christ's sake, tell 'em to stop! That's all my stock. It's my bread and butter . . ."

Stu walked over to the bar and picked up a bottle of bar whiskey. He filled and downed a shot glass. Then he did the same thing with the same brand but from a box. He filled the jigger again and pointed to the little man.

"Have a drink."

Showing every rotted tooth the guy quickly gulped down the whiskey.

Stu filled another one.

"Now try this one."

The shot glass emptied in a flash.

"Notice any difference?"

The little guy looked thoughtful. "One does seem a little weak."

"It's the same brand," Stu said. "Have another." And again he filled the glass with the bar whiskey.

The shot vanished.

"How about it?"

"Not as good as that one," and he pointed to the bottle from the box.

"Know why?" Stu asked.

The little man shook his head.

"It's watered," Stu told the group at the pool table. "Your friend

50

here has been selling you watered booze. I figured you've been cheated so drinks are on us. Give them what they want, gentlemen."

We became bartenders for those motley bums, bottles of Chivas Regal, J & B, Canadian Club, you name it, we dished it out as fast as they could drink. The jerks never noticed we opened the taps as we started for the door. They kept dancing away from the shouting, frenzied bartender who clawed vainly at one bottle, then another. One guy went over to the corner and poured a bottle of Seagram's over Whitey. Even the guy who had been fanned forgot his red ass and went to work on a bottle.

Suddenly Whitey appeared, groping his way along the wall. He was battered, dripping whiskey and defeated.

He said in a hoarse voice, "I'll get you . . . I'll get you. . . ."

Stu studied him in an oddly reflective way.

"If I ever hear that you have hurt an innocent person again," he said quietly, "I'll come back and kill you."

Then we filed out into the yard to find a grinning, impatient Rudy, who happily informed us every tire had been slashed and every gas tank was now a sugar bowl.

The trip along the dirt road was almost leisurely. We bent the plates and flung them into a pond along with the ski masks weighted with rocks. In a short time we merged with the busy traffic of the West Side Highway.

Stu had a surprise for us when we reached his penthouse; there was a buffet and a bar. In war you do queer things. I had been on several bad patrols with some of my buddies wounded and killed, but every time we came back all we wanted to hear was a mess call. I can still see myself sitting against a tree putting away the food, the blood of some guy I had bunked with for months drying on my fatigues. Maybe it was a nervous reaction. Maybe it was callousness. Maybe we were numb. Now I discovered I was hungry as hell. I filled my plate with roast beef, potato salad, cole slaw, and a few slices of bread, selected a cold bottle of beer and joined Arnie on a couch.

Then Stu hit a cup with a spoon and in the sudden silence raised his glass.

"To the Hounds of Tong Le Mai," he said with a grin.

"To the Hounds," we shouted and emptied our glasses. I felt invincible, like there wasn't anything we couldn't do together. I knew from their faces the others shared my emotion.

After we quieted down Stu rapped again for order.

"What we did tonight is an example of what we can do as a unit. I never had any doubt we could accomplish our mission"—he smiled—"without casualties. Perhaps we bent the law a bit but maybe it needed bending to save the next guy who might stop off for a beer from a merciless beating."

He added quietly, "And we squared the account for Tom. Our way."

"Cut one and we all bleed, Major," Rudy shouted. He slapped Star on the back. "We can do anything together. Right, Injun?"

"Maybe we can do something about those goddam junkies," Arnie said. "You know one of them ripped off my attaché case the night I came back to the city? I parked down the street and left it on the front seat when I walked over to the hotel garage to see if there was any space left. When I came out the bastard had busted the side window, opened the door, and stolen the case! I wasn't gone more than five minutes!"

"How do you know it was a junkie?" Trev asked.

"The cops at the precinct agreed it had to be a junkie. When I told them the stuff inside was only some notes I had, they laughed at me when I said I wanted to report it. One detective showed me a bunch of complaints they had taken down in one day: TV sets—one guy's car was left on blocks, they took his wheels—jewelry, a cash register, two hundred pounds of brass fittings cleaned out of a plumber's truck. It was hard to believe. The detective told me that just before I came in they had booked a junkie. He was making off with a guy's car battery and his two suitcases when they nabbed him. And on Park Avenue!"

"It's not the junkies, it's the pushers," Stu said. "The problem is god-awful. Dad told me when I came back, the businessmen of the city have been warning City Hall that narcotics is definitely a part of street crime and the cops agreed with them."

"Then why the hell doesn't the city do something about it?" Trev asked.

"It's a complex situation," Arnie said. "It goes all the way back to Southeast Asia."

"Yeah, I remember those stories you told us in the Pit about when you were out there," Rudy said. "You said they even have armies . . ."

"The big drug syndicates have troops armed with the best stolen weapons from the Nam ammo dumps."

"How long were you out there, Arnie?" I asked.

"Before I went to Nam? About three years. The Agency sent me out there in about 1962 when Treasury discovered big loads coming in from Burma." He made a triangle with his fingers. "Laos. Burma. Thailand. The Golden Triangle. We had a combined operation with the Thai Special Narcotics Organization and the Burmese Frontier Police. But out there money talks and we didn't get very far."

"But how the hell does it get here?" Rudy wanted to know.

"Money, Fatso," Star interjected. "Lots of it."

"Right," Arnie said. "Palms are greased from Asia to New York. They have a smooth operation."

"I would like to do something about drugs in the city," Stu said abruptly.

52

"I'm afraid that's like saying you want to do something about cancer," Arnie told him. "The only way to beat it is to find the cure."

"You have to start somewhere," Stu said stubbornly. "Suppose you offer the junkies a lot of money to turn in their connections to the cops?"

"A junkie would rather turn in his mother to a gang of rapists," Arnie said bluntly. "It's like pissing up a rope, Stu."

"I mean a big citywide campaign," Stu said doggedly. "Get the best people together to put up a great deal of money. Excite the communities. Send out sound trucks around the schools—hell, there must be good kids who will work with the cops—"

"In Bed-Stuy or Brownsville, they'd have the truck cleaned and the driver mugged within twenty minutes," Trev broke in. "Stu, it just won't work. Even before I left for Atlanta the cops were having a hell of a time selling themselves to the kids in this city."

Stu said, "Dammit! Somebody has got to do something. Someday! How the hell are we going to survive? It's not only in New York—it's all over. Like a plague."

We sat there, looking at him. The Hounds of Tong Le Mai, who had followed him to successfully raid a backwoods bar and punish its bullies, did not have an answer.

For a couple of weeks everything was peaceful. The only thing that appeared in the local Connecticut newspapers was a short story about a "gang of out-of-town hoodlums" who had slashed some tires of cars in the tavern's parking lot but had vanished before the police arrived. Evidently the chief had persuaded Whitey and the bartender to keep their mouths shut and to view the beating and the loss of stock as experience.

Stu had correctly predicted that because of politics no one would move against this band of backwoods thieves. Arnie went up to the state house a few times to check the list of liquor revocations but the Big Bear Tavern never appeared. Their tow car business monopoly continued and, as the embittered salesman told Trev, Whitey might have gotten his lumps but it was business as usual with those *putzes* still in the saddle.

Tom finally came out of the hospital, shaky but again in one piece.

The dentist and the plastic surgeon had done a great job; there was only a tiny thread of a scar on one side of his cheek where Whitey's boots had landed and the bridgework was perfect. One thing the hospital couldn't stitch up or make new was his spirit, which had taken a hell of a beating back in the bar. The major spotted this and sent Tom and Arnie out to the Southwest to report on a big piece of land the company planned to develop. Tom was in charge of aerial surveys and

Arnie told us this did a lot for his morale. They kept flying around the goddam desert until Arnie said he was dizzy, but by the time they got back to New York Tom was in good shape.

As for myself I hate the city in the winter with all the slush and crap, so I kissed off Bensonhurst and took Leah to the Golden Gate, that Caribbean job Harlow Realty owns, to live it up for a few weeks. Then one day I got a call from Trev to come back; Stu wanted to see us all in a hurry, something about a plan he had. . . .

Chapter **3**

Trevor David-
The League

In the beginning I was against our actions in Connecticut for two reasons: self-appointed judges and executioners never solved anything, and then from my newspaper experience I was aware of the possible consequences of such a plan. It horrified me. I could see the picture; the local wire service stringer excitedly informing his bureau desk that a millionaire New York real estate man named Harlow had been arrested leading a bunch of former POWs on a retaliatory raid against a backwoods bar to beat up a local resident the police chief called a war hero! On a dull night in any city room a story like this would be welcomed with hosannas. I shuddered when I closed my eyes and visualized the *Daily News* line. Even after I saw Tom in the hospital I tried to get Stu to contact the State Police, the DA, or even the governor's office. He had many influential friends who could make sure his complaint got a hearing but Stu was adamant in his theory that local politics would prevail and the best we could expect was a slap on the wrist for Whitey. He predicted that no matter what we dug up on the bar or the police and sent to the proper authorities, little or nothing would be done. Privately I agreed with him, any southerner who knows the backcountry can tell you about small town political dynasties.

But to combat local politics in a backwoods county miles from Forty-fifth Street and Park Avenue was, as I told him, quixotic. Yet despite my misgivings I went along. To refuse would have been unthinkable.

Curiously, as I got deeper into our plans I found myself caught up, less apprehensive of the consequences if something went wrong, like a cop unexpectedly pulling up to the bar.

I have no lucid explanation of why I abandoned my usual good horse sense. I could say it was because of what had happened to Tom, but that would be too simple and God knows we were anything but simple men. Sure, Tom was as close to me as were all the others and his torn face and battered body were infuriating, but looking back I don't think we were all that altruistic. Maybe we were bitter over a world we never made.

Then again maybe because we had spent seven years in hell we were seeking a scapegoat. Maybe Stu was right after all. The serene life we had reentered was dull compared to the daily, hourly trials and challenges of Tong Le Mai. We had come back restless, uneasy, suspicious of everyone and everything, at ease only when we were together. A good example was myself. After I had spent the Christmas holidays at the farm, my old Aunt Lucy kissed me good-bye and urged me to try to relax more. I was surprised. I thought I had projected the perfect image of the returned hero, properly humble and finally accepting the world. My aunt shook her head.

"Not so, dear," she said holding my hand. "Do you still like Dancy?"

Dancy was our foxhound, only a pup when I left but still a friendly, frisky animal with a deep baying cry, the joy of any hunter.

I was puzzled. "Of course, Aunt Lucy, why do you ask?"

"Because every time Dancy entered the room and you were talking, you'd stop and watch him walk all the way across until he flopped down. You did the same thing when Grandfather David's chime clock sounded the hour . . . and then there's something else—but maybe I'm just a talkative nosy old woman, Trevor—"

"No, please, Aunt Lucy, go on."

"Well, I just don't know how to put it, but you seem so unemotional, Trevor. Sometimes it's hard to know how you feel about anything."

What my aunt was saying was true. I had buried my emotions back in Tong Le Mai—to survive, I had to. When my aunt had told me Leslie was married and had two children, she was stunned that I simply nodded and asked her to give Leslie my best wishes. Sex was a routine, hedonistic act; I wanted no permanency, no ties, no entanglements.

The other shrewd observations my aunt had made were true. Before we did anything in the stable of Tong Le Mai, we first talked about it. We planned it over and over—sometimes simple projects like changing the straw in our stalls. Then we did it—not once but two or three times. For the first few months when I returned I couldn't bear to wear a wristwatch; I felt time was spinning away off my wrist. Before Nam I never noticed the constant noise of the AP city room; when I returned there were times when I physically froze while starting to write a new lead or bulletin. I would sit there like a stone man until my understanding city editor would nonchalantly take it away and slip it to another man. The big moon-faced clocks which told us the time in every country around the world some days seemed to be getting bigger and bigger, and I imagined I could hear each individual tick above the endless clatter of the teletypes.

As Stu once said, we all returned in slow motion. . . .

When I arrived back in New York I watched the others; they were doing the same things Aunt Lucy said I had done at home. For the first time I noticed how we abruptly broke off our conversation if a waiter entered the room; the wail of a siren in the streets below commanded our complete attention; sounds of strangers were still potentially hostile.

Rudy may have said it best, cut one and we all bleed.

Whatever the motivation I went along with Stu's plans. Curiously, the deeper I dug the more contempt, even hate, I felt for Whitey and his gang. Classic Freudian transformation of the enemy? I don't know. But what I do know is that I was as keen and alert when we hit the tavern as I had been in that last fire-fight when Charlie swarmed over our positions and sent me to Tong Le Mai. I left filled with a great deal of self-righteousness and satisfaction at what we had done to the battered Whitey and the weeping bartender whose stock had been reduced to glass splinters. Looking back, I can only regret that what should have ended as a comedy became a giant step to tragedy.

The incident at the bar gradually dimmed as we all settled back in our daily routines; Star and Rudy returned to the Southwest where Harlow Realty was building that huge retirement village, Tom, now recovered from Whitey's brutal beating, was back in Washington. Arnie was moving about the country "scouting" development sites, Sam was in the city recruiting and training a security team for a hotel in the South recently taken over by the company, while I was shuttling around the chain checking and revising our publications and trying to solve any problem dealing with the media.

Each time I returned to New York I gave Stu a formal report of the good and bad publicity our hotels and communities had received, new publications, costs and budgets, changeover in personnel, along with my recommendations. Whenever possible we had dinner, went out with casual dates, played tennis or handball or spent a skiing weekend at a private club in Maine where the women were stunning.

This one night we had a casual dinner in a wonderful fish place off Third Avenue. It was a pleasant evening and we had decided to walk back to the hotel. As I recall, it was about Twenty-Eighth Street when we noticed a small crowd gathered about a cop who stood at the entrance of an empty store.

"What's up?" I asked a man who was shaped and smelled like a beer keg.

He silently pointed to a figure of a boy hunched up in a corner of the doorway. He was slender, dark-skinned, with a mop of curly black hair and wearing a grimy Mets T-shirt. He appeared to be about sixteen and looked to be sleeping.

"What happened?" Stu asked. "Was he hit by a car?"

"Maybe it would have been better if he had been hit by a car," the man said as he walked away.

"I used to work for AP down at headquarters," I told the cop. "What happened?"

"OD," the cop said. He reached over my shoulder. "Thank you, sir," he said to the walking beer keg who handed him a blanket. He knelt down and almost tenderly covered the slender figure.

"The needle is still in his arm," the cop said bitterly as he stood up. "The bastards." He raised his voice slightly. "Anybody know who this kid is?"

"The Spanish guy who works in the bar on the corner thinks he knows who the kid is, officer," the man said. "He went up to the tenement to ask some people."

We stood there for a moment in the tight silence, staring down at the blanketed form.

"My God, he's only a kid," Stu said unbelievingly.

"We had another one last week," the cop said, "a fifteen-year-old girl. She was hustling to satisfy her hundred-dollar-a-day habit. The cop who found her told me she was pregnant. How do you like that?"

There was a commotion near the corner. Several men and women hurried toward us. Without any orders from the cop, the crowd silently parted and they swept through the human aisle with a stout woman in the lead. She gave the cop a bewildered look.

"Her boy Carlos is not come home all night," one man explained.

"This is Louie from the bar," the man who brought the blanket explained, "he thinks maybe it's her kid."

The cop nodded and silently bent down and pulled back the blanket.

The woman's scream tore the silence like a knife. Shouting and wailing, she fell to her knees, clutching the dead boy to her breast. For a brief moment I was looking down at a Vietnamese woman who was holding her dead daughter killed by one of the Cong mortars that had wiped out her village. Then a radio car with flashing dome lights screeched to the curb and two cops jumped out.

"Okay, folks, let's move on," one said, gently but firmly pushing through the crowd, while his companion joined the other cop in trying to lift the hysterical woman to her feet.

"Let's go," Stu said softly and we left.

I don't think we said a dozen words all night; that woman's tormented cry was too loud in our ears.

I was out of town for a few weeks and when I returned my secretary told me Stu wanted to see me as soon as possible. I found him in the penthouse where he had a screen and movie projector set up.

"I want to show you some movies," he said as he closed the blinds.

For the next half hour I saw a fascinating documentary done in 16 mm of the New York drug traffic; junkies meeting their connections on streets, outside bars, even on the steps of a church. It was done casually as though the drug scene was a legitimate part of daily life in Manhattan. The most extraordinary scenes were what Stu called "The Junkies' Flea Market." This showed junkies displaying their stolen wares on newspapers spread out in a deserted parking lot. The buyers, who were their connections, openly traded glassine bags for loot.

"Where the hell did you get this stuff?" I asked as he pulled back the blinds.

"Did you ever hear of the Metropolitan Anti-Crime Committee of some years ago?"

"Vaguely. I remember reading something about it when I was in college."

"The committee was put together by my father and the Langfords—"

"The owners of the big Fifth Avenue department store?"

"The same. Jay's the chairman of the board but Reba runs the store. He's in his eighties and she's in her seventies. They were Dad's closest friends. Together they raised hell with the old Anti-Crime Committee. Dad was almost paranoid about what narcotics were doing to the city. The committee hired a couple of ex-FBI agents and they obtained these films by using an old delivery truck with a hole cut in the side. The police gave them all kinds of static. Once they tipped off the junkies and they almost turned over the truck. When the DA blasted the committee for obstructing official investigations, Dad and the Langfords held a press conference and distributed stills from the films.

"Now it's coming back to me. The pictures were all over the papers."

"It was a one-day sensation," Stu said with a short laugh. "As most things happen in New York, it was forgotten and the committee folded. After Dad died last winter his secretary showed me a file of clippings. He fought against narcotics up to the day he died. He kept warning the city that some day drugs would be in the school system. He wasn't the only one, there were other businessmen who agreed with him but they were only a few voices in this goddam noisy city. I guess no one heard them. Maybe if they had, that kid we saw the other night might be still walking around."

I waited, I knew there was something more besides this old film.

After he mixed us a drink, Stu picked up a blue folder stamped with a gold emblem. He read the formal title:

"Report of the Mayor's Select Committee on Narcotic Addiction and Sources of Supply in the City of New York."

He added: "All week I couldn't get the kid out of my mind; it seemed just a damn horrible waste of life. I guess I was just waiting to take it out on somebody, so when I attended that civic dinner last Saturday night I hit the mayor with it. I thought he would give me his usual Harvard brush-off but he floored me by not only listening but inviting me back to Gracie Mansion for a drink." He patted the report. "I left with this."

"I don't think I've seen anything in the papers on it, Stu."

"You haven't. It's still secret. There are only three copies. The mayor had one, the police commissioner the second, and the commissioner of investigation has the third. This is a Xerox copy."

"What does he want?"

Stu shrugged. "Help, I guess."

"He needs all he can get."

"I know he hasn't been the greatest mayor in the world but I guess we've had worse."

I challenged him, "Name them."

He laughed. "He admits he couldn't win a popularity contest in the city today. What's the consensus of the reporters who cover the Hall, Trev?"

"Most of them claim Mayor Dwight Kerr's the biggest foul ball New York ever had. He's made practically every mistake that could be made. Christ, just look at the city!"

He patted the blue folder. "A good part of the reason why is here."

"Well, come on, you have me all excited. What's it about?"

"First let me ask you this, Trev. Do you remember reading some months ago about how a twelve-year-old kid was found dead of an OD in Harlem? Just like the other night!"

"I was in LA at the time but I read about it. Weren't there a couple of follow-up stories?"

"One of the papers dug up a medical examiner's report listing the deaths of three other kids due to drugs. In fact, the ME's annual report was shocking, the kids dead from OD were younger than ever before."

60

"How young?"

"Thirteen. Twelve. One was ten."

"Didn't the city council start an investigation of the board of education?"

"You know what a city council investigation is, Stu—"

"Bullshit."

"Right. Every politician jumped on the bandwagon. For a week you would have thought they just discovered there were narcotics in the schools. It was ridiculous."

"What about Kerr?"

"He did the usual City Hall fakeout, he appointed a committee and hoped everyone would forget about it. But this time he apparently used good people. Did you ever hear of George Horatio Derby?"

"Of course. The Golden Boy of the legislature. The youngest state senator in the country. One of my first assignments for AP was to help the regular guy down at the Federal Buildings cover his hearings."

"What hearings were they?"

"The Legislative Watchdog Committee. He was chairman. Usually they're a fake but he did a great job. He started with some small-time mobster who got a phony parole and before he was finished he had every big-time hood in the state under subpoena. He was like a bull in a china shop. Party lines didn't mean a thing. I lost track of him after I went down south."

"Well, he was appointed U.S. Attorney, Eastern District. I used to see him on television announcing the indictment of this guy and that guy. It didn't mean much to me but Dad thought he was the greatest."

"When did he leave the U.S. Attorney's office?"

"He didn't leave, he was kicked out after the new administration came in. He ran for Congress but was clobbered. Then he went into private practice and married Betsy Van Lyden."

"She sounds like money."

"Lots of money. One of her ancestors owned as much Manhattan real estate as John Jacob Astor. I've seen her around at a few parties. She's become a bit of a lush. Well, the mayor appointed Derby head of his committee to look into drugs."

"Who are the other members?"

"Were you working for AP in New York when Chuck Brigadier was police commissioner?"

"Cornelius Brigadier, Old Iron Ass?"

Stu laughed. "Is that what they called him?"

"He was deputy commissioner when I covered the lobster shift at police headquarters a few times for vacations. He was a tough old bastard. When the commissioner died of a heart attack he got the job. What ever happened to him?"

"Dad told me Brigadier and Kerr met head on after a shootout between the cops and some black militants who stuck up a Fifth Avenue bank. Old Iron Ass sent them in with guns blazing and plenty of tear gas. A cop was killed but they blew the blacks to pieces. For a time it looked like Bed-Stuy and Harlem would explode and Kerr went through the roof. He told Brigadier to resign or be fired. He resigned but hates Kerr with a passion. He never got over losing out, he had only been commissioner a few months when it happened. He retired last year from Con Ed, where he had charge of security."

"And Kerr appointed him to this panel?"

"Derby insisted on it. He and Brigadier have been close since Derby's days as the federal prosecutor. He told the mayor he wanted a professional, not an amateur. What the hell, it's years since Brigadier got out, it's all water over the dam."

"Actually Kerr made a shrewd choice, Stu. They can't say he rigged his committee."

"That's true. The way the city's going, he can't afford too many more mistakes. And everyone's screaming about junkies and street crime."

"Any others on the mayor's committee?"

"The Langfords—"

"What the hell are those two old toads doing on a narcotics committee?"

"Money and prestige. The mayor got them to underwrite the committee's expenses. But don't sell them short, Trev. Dad always said if you want to know what's going on in the city, ask Reba. She has terrific contacts among businessmen and politicians. She knows where the bodies are buried and has been head of the Fifth Avenue Merchants Association for years."

"It looks like Kerr didn't miss a trick, Stu. When he gives out the report, his press agents can boast he not only appointed his worst enemy in the interest of objectivity, along with some distinguished New Yorkers, and the whole report didn't cost the city a dime."

"Oh, I wouldn't call Dwight Kerr completely altruistic," Stu said dryly.

"When did the committee submit their report to the mayor?"

"Months ago."

"What's he been saving it for?"

"The truth is he never expected them to come up with the stuff they found. He was very frank with me; he said it scared the hell out of him."

"Wasn't the police narcotics bureau reorganized, Stu?"

"Right. Now it's the Metropolitan Police Bureau of Dangerous and Controlled Drugs. They put in a career cop, Inspector Frank Miles, to head it. Did you ever hear of him, Trev?"

"No, but that doesn't mean anything. I've been out of the city for years. And I only covered police headquarters to fill in for vacations and days off. What about Miles?"

"He's a friend of Derby and thinks Brigadier was one of the great commissioners. I met him at the dinner. He's a sharp guy."

"So what happened after the mayor put his report on the shelf?"

"It didn't stay there too long. Both Derby and Brigadier began prodding him. Now he must do something about it."

"Any politician will tell you, Stu, that the danger of a committee is in its report. Usually they turn out to be harmless, but if it's good your public relations man releases it on the day of a big catastrophe so it's buried while you pray no one on the committee is planning to run for office. The Langfords are out in this case but what about Brigadier or Derby?"

"Dad always said Brigadier would do anything to get back as PC to vindicate himself."

"That leaves Derby."

"Frankly I don't know, Trev. I'm sure Betsy would love to be First Lady. She knows politics and is always on some kind of committee, running charity balls, that sort of thing."

"I still don't get your connection to this report, Stu."

"There wasn't any until I read it. Kerr told me privately the reorganized police narcotics bureau has been a disappointment. He believes there are cops still on the take. Now if he gives out this report every mother and school board in the city will be on his neck. He's got to come up with something new."

"Don't tell me you're going to provide that new thing . . ."

He grinned. "Maybe. Anyway, let me read the report. I'll skip the graphs and charts and technical stuff and stick to what I think is the heart of it."

Stu read slowly, picking out the highlights. The report was surprisingly good. It did not deal in rigged statistics, half truths, or badly researched material. It was obvious a lot of time had been spent examining records and files in the medical examiner's office, the police narcotics bureau figures, and talking to people in precincts that covered places like Bed-Stuy, Harlem, and the South Bronx. It was written in a grave, almost solemn manner as if the members of the committee had been stunned by the facts they had encountered. But to me the language had a vague cop accent.

What it said in brief was this: Despite Rockefeller's New York State Drug Law which demanded life imprisonment for pushers, a sharp rise in the distribution of drugs had taken place. Opium derivatives like heroin were not only back on the streets but the contents were pure gold, more powerful than before and probably from Indochina.

After peace in Nam had been signed, Indochina's yearly drug crop rose from seven hundred tons to one thousand, with New York City as its main distribution point for national markets. These were the mechanics of the traffic familiar to most Americans who had seen scores of television documentaries and read numerous newspaper series on the subject. But the latest and most shocking disclosure in the report had to do with the customers of this new drug scene; the terrifying opinion of the panel insisted a new and powerful international drug syndicate with underworld partners in the United States, probably within the metropolitan area, was smuggling in large quantities of powerful drugs with the object of creating an entirely new market among American elementary school children, the war generation that had been raised on violence, that had eaten its dinner with the six o'clock news showing maimed, burned Vietnamese children, razed villages, and GIs dying. These were the kids who had eaten their McDonald hamburgers and French fries as they watched kids, scarcely older than themselves, loot stores, hurl Molotov cocktails, and contemptuously dismiss their adult's world as unkempt, unmoral, and uncomfortable. It was the stuff of the sixties, their television Pablum.

After the war in Vietnam ended, this six o'clock news generation found the Woodstocks gone, Times Square a menace, Haight-Ashbury a ripoff, and the East Village a jungle. There were no more thrilling marches or great causes, only apathy. Drugs were their heritage. Drugs, more powerful than ever, were ready to bring back *Easy Rider* and the wild glorious days.

This was the new market, an eager army of many customers. Sixth grade. Seventh grade. Eighth grade. Younger if they had the money. No ID cards were necessary.

"God, that's hard to believe!"

"It's not exaggerated," he replied. "It's all true. The mayor admits it, so do the cops. They've known about it but can't do a thing and that goes for the federal people."

"Why not?"

"Very simple. Whoever is bringing in the stuff happens to be smarter than they are. The mayor says the rumors are that a couple of federal stool pigeons have been knocked off in the past year. Word has gotten around that if you talk you're dead. It's become worse in the last few months."

"Just what the hell do *you* intend to do about it, Stu?"

"Form the Five Boro Anti-Narcotics League," he said calmly.

I groaned so loudly he laughed.

"Stu, you're only asking for headaches!"

"Hear me out, Trev. I know it's been done before only to go down the drain but I'm sure this time it will be different."

"In what way, for Christ's sake?"

"We're going to become legal bounty hunters."

"You mean like the guys in the westerns who bring in the badman for the reward?"

"In a way—I'm putting up a fund of a hundred thousand dollars—"

I whistled. "For what?"

"To help cops catch pushers, I guess is the simplest way of explaining it."

"I'm dense. Doesn't the state have something like this?"

"They offer a thousand dollars but the program has fallen apart."

"How will the league be different?"

"We'll be offering five thousand for a conviction. But it can vary. Like the lottery. The reward can go higher."

"Subway bounty hunters."

"Stop mocking it, Trev; these are desperate times for this city."

"I'm not mocking it, I'm trying to tell it like it is. Who decides the amounts?"

"The cops. Inspector Miles will appoint a board to make the decisions. It will be out of our hands."

"How about those ancients, the Langfords and Derby and Brigadier—where do they fit in?"

"Kerr called them from Gracie Mansion, they've all agreed to be on our committee. We'll meet the Langfords at the Mansion with the police commissioner and Derby and Brigadier later."

"*Our* committee?"

"Sure," he said casually, "you and I are going to run it, the other guys can pitch in . . ."

"How did you ever come up with this idea?"

"Actually it's not mine, it's Dad's. One of Kerr's first white papers in his campaign for mayor was on narcotics. Dad liked his ideas and he got the Langfords and some other business people to support him. They raised an awful lot of money for him. My father always insisted that street crime and narcotics were linked, so when he saw the city going to hell and the mayor fumbling around he offered him this plan some years ago. But Kerr kept stalling. Finally he got this report and told Dad he was going to reorganize the narcotics bureau. He promised that if this didn't work he would consider Dad's plan for a Five Boro Anti-Narcotics League."

"Do you really think this league idea will help solve the narcotics problem in the city, Stu?"

"To be candid? No," he said blunty. He held up a hand to stop my questions. "This is the same thing I told Dad. To me it will be a waste of time and money. I'm no expert, but common sense tells me the only way to deal with our narcotics problem—not only in New York but all over the country—is to stop the main source, the Mafia or whatever the hell they call it. You know, the big racket guys who finance the buying and the smuggling. You heard what Arnie said that night. The bastards have regular armies over there." He shook his head and said slowly, "Some day, Trev, the people of this city will get so mad at what is happening to them that they will march down to City Hall, kick whoever's there out on his ass, march across the street and do the same thing with the police commissioner, then tell the politicians to get someone in their place who can do the job or else." He shrugged. "The trouble is these days people don't get that mad anymore, they only get inured."

I reminded him, "This time we'll be buddy with the law."

He held out his hands. "We have to."

"And the cops?"

He said in a resigned voice, "We can't do without them. I'm sure there are just as many honest cops as there are crooked ones."

"I'm only pointing these things out to you, Stu—it's better to know your problems in the beginning than later. Buck big-time narcotics and you're up against big-time money and big-time political connections."

"Well, for what it's worth, the mayor promised us complete cooperation."

"Did you want the others in on this?"

"Definitely. We need a tight organization," he said. "That's why the old crime committee was successful. It was a small group of businessmen who knew how to keep their mouths shut. When they had something to say they released it at a regular press conference. I want you to help me run the league and direct all its publicity. There will be plenty for the others to do. Arnie knows a lot of stuff about drugs from when he was working for the CIA. I want him and Sam to run down to Washington."

"What's in Washington?"

"Frankly I don't know. But Sam's made some good contacts down there and Arnie still has some friends in the CIA."

"Didn't you say the feds had two stool pigeons knocked off?"

"That's what Kerr heard from the cops. He claimed the feds are worried."

"It must be quite a mob if the feds and the cops can't make a dent in their operations. I hope you don't expect—"

He held up a hand. "I'm only doing what my father really wanted more than anything, Trev—to try to help the city. I don't plan to play cops and robbers."

It's strange how some phrases stick in your mind:

I don't intend to play cops and robbers. . . .

I sent out word to the others and a week later we gathered in Stu's penthouse and listened to him read the mayor's secret report and describe his plan for the league and the dinner that would launch it. They were all enthusiastic about the plan and when Stu called for a vote it was unanimous.

"How do you intend to work it, Major?" Star asked.

"We'll run ads on TV and in the newspapers listing a box number and a telephone number. Star, Rudy, and Tom will monitor the phones. Trev will go along with a couple of detectives to pick up the mail. We keep the original and give them a Xerox. We'll also have sound trucks outside the schools, and handbills."

"Who determines who gets the money?"

"It will have to be the police, there's no other way."

"What's this about a dinner, Stu?" Arnie wanted to know.

"It will be on the thirteenth in the main ballroom," Stu explained. "It's going to be the biggest this hotel ever had. Trev and I are working on that now."

"This time we're going to be asshole buddies with the law," Sam said. "Let's see how we do."

66

"I like the other way better," Star said. "You go in and do what's to be done and get out."

"What the hell do you want to do, Injun," Rudy rumbled, "kill every junkie you can find?"

"It's one way, Fatso," Star replied. "Who asked 'em to become junkies in the first place?"

Arnie pointed out, "The report doesn't name who runs this syndicate. Are they independents? Mafia? South Americans? Blacks?"

"Apparently even the cops or the feds don't know," I told him. "The mayor told Stu the feds are worried."

"They can't be amateurs with this setup."

"Want to make an educated guess, Arnie?" Stu asked.

Arnie hesitated. "The Agency got involved in that domestic spying episode in the sixties but was never interested in the local crime picture, so I can't toss around the names of mobsters, but for openers I'd say it's either a group in Burma or the Chinese in Thailand. They have to have the money to buy off government agents and cross over the border into South Vietnam where they can get it out by sea. They probably have a deal with the Union Corse."

"What's that?"

"I guess you can call it the Mafia of Corsica. They've been dealing with the drug merchants in Hong Kong for years."

"Why do you believe they might be in it, Arnie?" I asked.

"Because when I left Thai to go to Nam, we had solid evidence the Corsicans were dealing with the connections in Hong Kong and smuggling the junk into Marseilles where they operate the big refining factories. From there it gets into the States."

"This is what I can't understand," Stu said, exasperated. "You people knew all about this years ago. Probably Treasury, Customs, Drugs, the whole bunch of them in Washington—"

"They all had the same story from their own agents," Arnie said promptly. "It's no secret. Spend a few bucks in Rangoon and you can get all the details you want. Don't forget, opium-growing over there is a way of life. I remember talking to a farmer in the hills. 'If you put me in jail, my son will grow the opium. If you put him in jail, his son will grow the opium,' he told me. That's the way it is."

"I can understand that," Stu said, "but Marseilles isn't fifty miles outside of Rangoon. What's the matter with the Sûreté? Or the French police?"

"You need evidence—hard evidence," Arnie pointed out. "Witnesses and informers have a way of disappearing. The Union Corse is very powerful. It not only runs the drug factories in Marseilles and the southern coastal cities but also owns a lot of politicians. The honest ones are told to either take the money or forget about their wives and kids. Those Corsicans are tough, and they have fantastic connections. The Allies had to get their help in the invasion of the south of France, and De Gaulle used them against the OAS in Algeria."

"What do you mean by hard evidence, Arnie?" Tom asked.

"The only way you can crack a real big drug syndicate is by having a contact inside the organization. Someone who can tell you who, what, when, and where. That's how you get the hard evidence to place before a grand jury and which will later stand up in the courts and on appeal. Some of the agencies in Washington work for years on a case before getting a break."

"I wonder what kind of guy runs this setup?" Stu asked, half to himself.

"I'll give you an off-the-cuff profile," Arnie offered. "First of all he must be someone the Corsicans trust. Then he has only professionals who know how to keep their mouths shut. And he's smart, damn smart, and has great organizational ability. The most important thing is, he's not well known to the cops or to the federal narcs. He may turn out to be an American hood who's been living for years in Europe."

"You know something?" Stu said. "I'm getting a terrible yen to know who this guy is . . ."

There is no magical formula needed to put together an organization of the type Stu had in mind; only two ingredients are necessary—money and political benediction. Stu provided the cash and Mayor Dwight Kerr the blessings of City Hall.

Then, the dinner, there must be a dinner to kick off these quasi-official organizations. Certain things are compulsory: celebrities, what are always described as "leading" politicians, and a "keynote" speaker. If it's the mayor, that's a grand slam. He gives the message to the municipal flock that lots of private—not city—money is being used and City Hall likes it; in other words, throw a wrench into the machinery at your own risk.

We had our first meeting with the mayor, Police Commissioner Theodore Fitzgerald—"Teddy Fitz" to the men who knew him when he walked a beat out of the old West Forty-seventh Street precinct years before Stu and I were born—and the Langfords. It was held at Gracie Mansion with Kerr "pouring" as *Variety* would say. We would have a separate meeting with Brigadier and Derby who could not make the Mansion gathering because of business commitments.

Fitzgerald, a sharp-featured man in his sixties, wore a perpetual frown as if to alert all who met him how deeply he felt the weight of human weakness. He had been one of the few cops in the Depression who had gone to college at night to win his BA and later a master's and doctorate. He was the first head of the John Jay College and had worked in almost every bureau of the department. He was called a "progressive commissioner," although I thought he liked machinery more than people. He was familiar to most New Yorkers for his frequent appearances on TV or in the papers demonstrating some new gadget that was guaranteed to help combat crime. After three years most New Yorkers yawned or wrote bitter letters to the editors, wanting to know when Fitzgerald's new systems would allow them to attend night church services or ride the subways without getting mugged.

The New York cop on the beat, the most cynical of men, viewed Fitzgerald with bored indifference. He was an impressive speaker with a marvelous talent for finding statistics to prove his theory that computers were as good as the man on the beat. In a few years he would happily disappear into the clicking world of IBM.

Jay Langford was a sad-eyed wisp of a man who could be shaken by a passer-by's healthy sneeze. But when he spoke it was in a startling high voice edged with command. I decided I would not like to work for him. In contrast his sister, Reba, was a joy. Despite her millions she was an earthy old woman who had never left Hester Street, which she proudly informed you was her birthplace and where she had spent the happiest years of her life managing her father's five pushcarts. She had a sharp voice and flashing black eyes which seldom missed anything. I came to the conclusion she had been a fantastic toss in the hay—half a century ago.

Like her brother she was petite, with dyed jet black hair pulled back in a nineteenth-century bun to accentuate the dead white face. The rings and brooches she wore could be traded for a king, but her earrings were infinitesimal diamond chips given to her by her mother the day she graduated from P.S. 17 on Baxter Street. At least this was the carefully cultivated legend distributed at her annual birthday press conference by an expensive Madison Avenue advertising firm.

In every administration since LaGuardia's the Langfords had financed many civic programs; their favorite had been the Metropolitan Anti-Crime Committee which they started with Stu's father. "Madam" Langford, as she insisted on being called, gleefully blasted the cops and DAs as chuckleheads who couldn't catch a cold in Siberia.

Mayor Kerr welcomed them as visiting royalty. We watched, fascinated, as she dug deep into a voluminous handbag to come out with a gold jigger. Kerr, evidently familiar with the ritual, calmly filled it with Canadian Club and put a glass of water beside the jigger. Her brother vanished into a deep chair.

She downed the jigger and followed it with a sip of water. The mayor quickly gave her a refill.

"Who's this?" she said eyeing me.

"Trevor David," Stu said. "He's in charge of our public relations program. Trev worked for Associated Press in New York and down south. We were together in Vietnam."

She gave me a searching look. "Did you ever cover one of my press conferences, young man?"

"No, Madam. I was assigned to the courts, mostly Federal Building."

She turned to the mayor and said firmly, "I want him to handle our publicity."

"I told the mayor we have a fine deputy commissioner, a former *Times* man in charge of the department's community relations—" Fitzgerald started but Madam Langford cut him short.

"So who needs a *Times* man? Let him stay a deputy commissioner. I want this boy to handle our publicity. He looks smart to me. Right, Jay?"

"He looks like a smart boy."

She turned to me. "So start working, young man."

The mayor cleared his throat.

"I believe you and Jay have read the report I prepared. What it does is to—"

"Don't repeat it," the old woman said, "we read it." She asked Stu, "A hundred thousand dollars you're putting up, Stuart?"

"That's true, Madam." The tiny figure in the chair leaned forward.

"Why?"

"You know it was my father's plan. You also know how he hated drugs and what they are doing to the city."

"Your father was a good man, Stuart," she said.

"The fund will be in his name." He looked over at Fitzgerald. "I hope it will help."

"This is no new story," she said bitterly. "For years and years the businessmen of this city have been warning you people what drugs are doing. Times Square you can forget. Now it's the East Side. What art gallery keeps open after six o'clock? Two weeks ago they killed an old man in his store. For thirty years he had been in one spot. A good man. So what happens? A punk comes in and kills him because he needs money to shoot poison in his arm. Does it make sense?" She shook her finger at an uneasy Fitzgerald. "It's a disgrace, Commissioner. A disgrace."

"The police are doing all they can, Madam," Kerr protested. "We all recognize that it's a monstrous problem. Now this plan for the league is splendid—"

"For a hundred thousand dollars it should be a jewel," she snapped.

"We intend to give you people all the cooperation you need," Fitzgerald said stoutly.

She eyed him in silence for a moment.

"Can you afford not to, Commissioner?"

A wave of angry red started to move up from his neck to his face and he looked to Kerr for help.

"What we would like to do is get started at once," Kerr said quickly. "Reba, will you and Jay serve on the committee with Mr. Brigadier and Mr. Derby? Stu will be chairman."

Stu put in, "We were hoping you and Jay—"

"We put up twenty-five thousand dollars for the report, Stuart," Jay Langford reminded him.

His sister waved that aside.

"Don't talk about peanuts, Jay, when Stuart's putting up a hundred thousand dollars." She turned to Kerr and Fitzgerald. "Do you really think this plan will work? Offering the public money to inform on pushers? Didn't Rockefeller try this?"

"The state's program offers a thousand dollars to anyone turning in a pusher, ma'am," Fitzgerald explained.

"So what do we have that's so different?" she asked.

"More money, ma'am," he said. "We will offer a reward of five thousand."

"So now we have to pay the community to be civic-minded and help their own children?" She leaned over and called out to her brother. "Jay, you heard the mayor. What do you want to do?"

The little man peered from around the side of the chair like a weary gnome.

"She asks me but she has already made up our mind. You tell them, Reba."

She gave her decision in clipped tense syllables. "Three, maybe four times during the last month people have asked us to join this and that and I said no. Jay and I are tired of being do-gooders. What does it get you? Headaches. But this time it's different. We have known Stuart since he was a little boy and we loved his father. Maybe his plan will be a nothing. Maybe it will do some good. We hope so. If you prove to us that it works we'll match Stuart's money."

Kerr and Fitzgerald were obviously startled by her offer.

"We'll make it work," Fitzgerald said hastily. "You can expect a hundred percent cooperation—"

"Just make our city safe, Commissioner. Put the bums in jail and forget the machinery. Now I must go." She waved aside Kerr's eager hand and got to her feet. "Jay, you going to the club?"

"I'm going to play a little cards," he said. "You take the car. The mayor will give me a lift."

"My car is in the driveway, Jay."

She turned to me. "Young man, you can escort me home."

The surprise must have showed on my face.

"You don't have anything to worry about," she said, patting my hand. "Twenty, thirty years ago maybe but not now." She warned her brother who had emerged from the embrace of the deep chair, "Remember, ten o'clock take the pill. Only two drinks . . ."

Langford shook his head. "Seventy-five years old and still a *yachneh.*"

Stu gave me an amused look. "I'll see you back at the hotel, Trev."

I knew he was biting his tongue to keep from laughing.

"One last thing," I said.

They all turned to me.

"Do you intend to release your report?" I asked Kerr.

"Frankly I haven't thought about it," he said. "Suppose I talk to my people here and call—"

"No," Madam Langford said firmly, "let's get it decided now. This is our public relations man, he should know."

Kerr turned to Fitzgerald. "Fitz, do you have any objections to giving it out?"

Fitzgerald couldn't frown much more. "Well, I should talk to Inspector Miles in the narcotics bureau and—"

"You're the commissioner," Madam Langford said impatiently.

"Let's give it out," Kerr said abruptly. Then to me, "Do you need the exact release date this moment?"

"Not right now," I said. "Suppose I write a general release for the AMs about the report and give it out on the afternoon of the dinner. Whoever is the MC or the keynote speaker can discuss it. We may make page one of the *Times*."

"I told you he was a smart boy," Madam Langford said.

"He's a smart boy," Jay echoed.

"Will you liaison with our publicity people?" Kerr asked. "And the police department's?"

"Of course," I told him. "But what about the formal report?"

He said quickly, "Suppose you and my people work it out?"

"So are we all finished now?" Madam Langford said.

"I guess for the time being," Kerr said.

She put her arm, thin as a reed, in mine but refused any help from either me or the chauffeur in getting into the limousine.

"I can call you Trevor?" she asked as the car joined the East River Drive traffic.

"Please do."

She said flatly, "You don't like this business."

"I don't recall saying that, Madam."

"I didn't say you did. In my business you have intuition."

"And this intuition tells you I don't like Stu's plan?"

Those dark searching eyes defied me to lie. "Am I right?"

"I told Stu he was going to have a hundred thousand headaches."

She pressed me, "Why?"

"One hundred thousand, even a million, isn't going to solve the city's narcotics problem."

"So what's the answer?"

"It's complex, Madam, there's no simple solution. Both Stu and I agree that first the source must be choked off. The government—somebody—will have to do that job."

"So if Stuart thinks that way, why does he invest his money?"

I fenced. "I believe you knew his father?"

"He was our closest friend. So you know the story of how he went to the mayor with this plan?"

"Stu told me the whole thing. What did *you* think of Mr. Harlow's idea?"

She took a cigarette from her bag and I lighted it.

"That was five, six years ago when Stuart's father went to City Hall. Then maybe it had a chance. It could have been a crusade with good people, businessmen who had been with us on the old crime committee—"

"Why can't we get them now?"

She shrugged. "Those who haven't left the city are sick of promises. You should hear them at the association's luncheons!"

"You sound as if the league doesn't stand much of a chance."

"Well . . ."

"What do you *really* think, Madam, does it stand a chance?"

"No," she said flatly.

"But you and your brother just endorsed it."

"Stuart's father was our closest friend," she said shortly. "The fund will be in his name, that's enough for us."

"But you said if it works you'll match Stuart's gift—"

"An easy promise to make the politicians work harder. But it won't succeed, young man."

"You haven't told me the reason why," I insisted. "Is it the committee?"

"Time changes everything," she replied with a vague wave of her hand, "even people."

I didn't like what I was hearing and it irritated me that I was unable to pin down this old woman, but before I could ask another question she said brightly, "Ah, here we are," and the car swung into the curb as a doorman ran out to open the door.

"You will come up for a drink," she said. It was more of a command than an invitation, so I meekly followed her and the fawning doorman to the elevator.

There was still time to get the answer to my question.

The Langford apartment on upper Park Avenue was huge, with old-fashioned fourteen-foot ceilings, fading frescoes of landscapes, rolling pastures, and a shepherd boy sleeping under a tree. I'm no antique expert but I sensed the furniture belonged in a museum. There was an étagère displaying fragile vases, and dominating one wall was a large oil of an old couple, stiff with Victorian formality.

"My mother and father," she said proudly. "They had a little dry goods store on Hester Street and, as you know, five pushcarts." She pointed to a small gold-framed photograph. "That's me and Jay. The name then was Leshovitz. My parents were Galitzianer—from Poland."

A grim-faced girl of about ten, wearing a dress to her calves and high buttoned shoes, and a slightly older boy in knickers standing by a pushcart stared out at me.

"Jay says why keep talking about the old days? I say why not? I'm proud of my mother and father and Hester Street. Great people came out of the East Side, young man. And you didn't have to be Jewish. Was Al Smith Orthodox?"

She waved me to a chair and dug down in that voluminous bag to produce the gold jigger. She filled it and remembered I drank scotch and water. She held up the jigger and we toasted the newborn Five Boro Anti-Narcotics League.

"I saw your face when I pulled out my jigger," she said with a chuckle. "A crazy old woman, you said to yourself. Do you know something, Trevor? I pay a lot of money to make people think that way about me. Remember this, never do anything without half an eye on your audience." She downed the whiskey and took a sip of water. "Suppose I was a nice quiet old lady. Do you think the mayor would listen to me? He'd pat me on the head, take my money, and send me home. But he knows better. Once a year the press comes up here. I give them a show. They print my picture and everything I say. Not stupid things, good things about the city and the idiots trying to run it. City Hall and the politicians know it's not just a silly old lady talking, but the voices of the merchants—the ones with money for their campaigns. When we have a meeting of our association what do I hear? 'Tell them like it is, Reba,' they say to me. 'You be our spokesman.' So I wine and dine the reporters and take care of their wives, and they put on television and in the newspapers what we want the public to know. If I say there are too many potholes on the Avenue, the next day a truck comes and they are filled. If I say we need more police, the commissioner promises to put on more men. City Hall knows this old lady represents a lot of important people."

We sat like this, chatting, making small talk, feeling each other out. I was impatient as hell, I wanted to know why she thought the league would never succeed.

Frankly her remark made me uneasy but I wanted the right time to hit her again with the question.

It came after the maid had brought a tray of sandwiches and coffee. They were a happy sight; I was hungry as a winter wolf.

Over coffee she glanced at her wristwatch and sighed.

"Where does the time go, Trevor?"

I managed to look grim.

"Once time was all I had, Madam."

"I almost forgot," she said quickly. "You were with Stuart?"

"Almost six years." A meaningful pause. "They were rough."

It produced the reaction I wanted. Those shrewd black eyes became soft and motherly.

"You poor boy, it must have been terrible," she said.

74

Now she was primed.

"Madam," I said quickly, "why did you say in the car that the league wouldn't work?"

This was such a change of pace that she was obviously taken aback.

"What difference does it make?" she snapped. "We endorsed it—"

"If we're going to be working together on this project, don't you think we should share all the information we have?"

After a moment of silence she said abruptly, "How well do you know Mr. Derby, Trevor?"

I explained that all I knew of him was from my newspaper experience, covering his early days as the Golden Boy of the state legislature and listening to the political prophets tell of the great things that awaited Derby in the future. However, as Stu had explained, he had slipped very badly and was married to a society woman who liked politics, charity balls—the limelight.

"What else did Stuart say about her, Trevor?"

"That she was also a bit of a lush."

She slipped off her ring, examined it against the light, and put it back on.

"There's no more money. She spent it on foolishness. She owes everybody on the Avenue. Twice she gave us bad checks. Jay likes George so we tore them up." She added flatly, "She's a bitch."

"Perhaps I don't see what that has got to do—"

"You asked me and I told you," she snapped. "In the old days you could tell a man by his wife."

"Why don't you like Derby, Madam?"

The shot in the dark found a target. She looked annoyed.

"My young friend the district attorney?"

"I only want your opinion."

"People get older . . . they change . . . you change, young man, I change . . . we all change . . . that's the way life is. . . ."

"If you were the mayor would you have picked Derby?"

"If it was my money? No."

"Can you tell me why, Madam?"

"It's only an old woman's opinion," she replied impatiently. "Is it so important?"

"Let's say I respect your opinion."

She threw her head back and laughed.

"From someone who doesn't work for me? Thank you, my dear Trevor."

"That's why I would like to know what you base your opinion on."

She gesticulated violently as if dismissing some unpleasant creature.

"Must we talk about this man all night? He is not that important to me!"

It was as frustrating as trying to pick up mercury.

"You've known Stuart since he was a boy. You said you and your brother loved his father. If there is anything about Derby that we should know—"

"Do you honestly think Stuart would drop Derby because of an old woman's instincts? Now answer me truthfully, Trevor."

"Frankly, I don't."

She gave me a triumphant look.

"Then that's your answer, young man."

Somewhere in the depths of the apartment a telephone rang. We both listened to the muffled voice of the maid answering it. In a moment she was at the door.

"It's Mr. Langford, ma'am."

She was obviously relieved. "That Jay," she said with mock anger and hurried from the room.

She returned in a few minutes.

"The old man's club broke up early tonight," she said brightly, "now he wants to go to Lüchow's for pancakes . . . perhaps my chauffeur . . ."

It was obvious I was being dismissed.

"Please don't bother, Madam. I can catch a cab."

"When do you meet Derby and Brigadier?" she asked as we walked out to the foyer.

"In a few days. The mayor said Derby is out of town."

"He's in Vegas," she said.

I had all I could do to keep from asking how she knew.

"I never got around to getting your opinion of Brigadier."

"He's an old man who can never forget he was once the police commissioner."

Going back to the Eldorado in a cab I wondered why Madam Langford had never answered my question about Derby.

Chapter **4**

Sam Hoffman-
Washington

The night the major and Trev had their meeting with Mayor Kerr and the rest of the brass up at Gracie Mansion, Arnie and I left for Washington. The major had told us what he wanted—information, as much as we could dig up. Arnie and I agreed that when we reached the capital we would split up, he would look up his old CIA contacts, and I would concentrate on the jokers I had buttered up during our last visit.

I've been hearing a lot of stuff that since Watergate the agencies are buttoned up tight. Crap. If you have the right contacts and they trust you, they'll talk. Of course they're not going to give you all the innermost secrets of their bureau but a smart guy can always put two and two together. You don't have to be a *melamed* to know what's going on—at least in Washington, the leakiest capital of the world.

Arnie is not the best traveling companion, and I was glad we had decided we should go our own ways.

On the way down to Washington, he showed me several pamphlets bound together in a folder.

"What's it about?"

"Technical stuff from the mainland."

"In Chinese!"

"Of course. I told Stu I'm looking around to tie on with some mission going over there. But it won't be for a while, they're still keeping things tight."

"What would you do in China, Arnie?"

"Move around. It's a fascinating country. How the hell much can you take of New York?"

"Leave me in Bensonhurst. I had enough moving around. By the way, who are you going to see in D.C.?"

"A couple of guys. Maybe they're not even with the Agency any more. How about you?"

"I'll shop around. What do you think of that report the major read?"

"Lots of cop gossip."

"It's not going to be easy if they knocked off two narc informers. That gets 'em up tight."

"Don't worry about it, somebody in D.C. has the answer."

We split in Washington; I didn't hear from Arnie but I didn't score for a week. I wined and dined three guys from Dangerous Drugs, Treasury, and Customs and got nothing. They all swore they hadn't heard about any investigation like the one I described. Something told me they were lying, and that made me more determined than ever to latch on to something.

It's a funny thing about investigations: you plot, plan, scheme, and get nothing, then when you're ready to give up something comes zooming in from left field. That's what happened after I had spent a fruitless day wooing a guy from the narcotics section of the FBI. I was trying to hail down a cab on Pennsylvania Avenue when someone grabbed my arm.

"Hey, Sam! What the hell are you doing down here?"

I turned to look into the face of a *putzo* named McCarthy, Chickie, as we called him in high school, a slippery-assed Irisher who had robbed more jukeboxes and pinballs than any five guys in Bensonhurst.

"Hey, I saw you on television the day you hit Clark! I just turned it on and there you were." He stepped back. "Christ, you put some of it back on, man! What's happening?"

"Nothing much. How's it with you, Chickie?"

"Great." He added almost defensively, "I was over in Nam too. With the air force. Christ, was I glad to get out of there!"

His voice lowered a notch. "It must have been tough, Sam. Did they work you over much?"

It was the same old crap; everyone wants to hear about the blood and torture. I was about to brush him when something made me ask where he worked.

He looked around as if there was a spy in the nearest refuse can.

"Bureau of Dangerous and Controlled Drugs," he said softly.

I swear I gulped. Now he couldn't get away from me. We made a date for dinner and I went back to the hotel full of great expectations.

I wined and dined this *schmuck* and his wife, a dizzy dame with a hairdo high as an African anthill, admired their two kids, demons if I ever saw one, and told them a million lies about Tong Le Mai. I took them out a few times, and they even had a cocktail party for me. I let them plan it, I knew Chickie wanted to impress his neighbors in this new development. Fine. Maybe me and my lies could do some good.

A few nights before the party I told him I couldn't make it, it was clear he would have liked it better if I had kicked him in the stomach.

"Christ, Sam, you got to come! Laurie has invited about thirty people! Hell, it's in your honor!"

"Well . . ."

"Come on, Sam, if you don't come I'll look like a jerk."

Then I gave it to him. I had told him I was a private investigator but now I fed him a cock and bull story of how I had been hired by a rich guy who intended to make a run for the mayoralty and wanted me to dig up all I could on New York's current narcotic traffic. He was no dope, and this made him pause for a moment but I spotted a glow in his eyes when I added he would find five hundred dollars in cash in his kids' toybox if I got what I wanted. We shook hands on the deal.

They were nice people at the party and I tried not to feed them too much crap. Some of the stories I made into eyewitness accounts instead of the atrocity gossip we had heard from guys moving through our village or in the Hanoi Hilton just before we flew out.

They ate it up and the party was pronounced a success. I guess it enhanced Chickie's social prestige; I don't know.

What I do know is that he not only came across, but I developed another contact at the party, a mousy little chick named Kate. She not only had a great body, but more important she worked as a secretary to the section chief of a special strike force investigating narcotics in the New York area. Her boss was a sort of liaison between the New York and Washington offices. Beautiful.

I knew this was no rush job. It was obvious Kate was lonely as hell, but she was also from Vermont and a rockbound New England family. Not a prude, let's say she wasn't a pushover. But on the debit side she was thirty-five, no Raquel Welsh, and there wasn't a line outside her door looking for a date.

Kate had been in D.C. for ten years and knew the town; she was a bit of a longhair so I had to listen to a lot of Brahms and Mozart in between sitting through a revival of Bogart's pictures. She lived in a cozy apartment in the Rock Creek section of Georgetown, and while I could have pushed to stay overnight I decided to play it cool. A sweet goodnight kiss, a short wait until she got into her hallway, a wave, and that was it.

After a few refusals I finally accepted a Saturday night dinner because by this time she must have been wondering if this *meshugeneh* from Bensonhurst might be a gay who gets his jollies from lutes, flutes, and old Warner Brothers pictures. She was dressed like a chick in a *New Yorker* ad with just enough expensive perfume to get the juices going. There was candlelight, a great meal, plenty of booze, wine, and soft music. I had to laugh to myself, it looked like Kate was trying to seduce me!

By the time I made my first move she was drooling. The only time we left that nice wide couch was when I went out to move my rented car so those Georgetown cops wouldn't give me a clamp, which means a towaway job and a hundred-dollar fine.

It was a perfect weekend. We had brunch at Crepes, did some drinking at Poor Robert's, and toured those Georgetown antique shops whose prices are obscene. And always we came back to that sweet little apartment.

Instead of hitting Kate with some requests which could have scared her off, I decided to use amateur psychology. I went over my whole story of the Pit to the point of showing her my "scars," actually I do have a five-incher from a gook who massaged my back with a bamboo strip on the trail to Tong Le Mai. This, of course, got her all soft and motherly. Then I gave her the same yarn I had handed to Chickie, how I was a private eye employed by this mayoralty candidate who was dedicated to riding the pushers from the city and hired me to help him out. However, because I wasn't getting anything in Washington from my official friends I would probably have to go back to New York because my employer was willing to keep me in D.C. only as long as I could feed him reports.

Nothing more. I left that to soak in.

My homemade psychology worked; a few days later she called, whispering in the phone she had something important to talk to me about. I went *shlepping* over to Georgetown, and sure enough Katie baby had come through. She had worked overtime and after the office was empty had copied in shorthand as many reports as she could find. Some were meaningless but there were a few gems; for over a year in an investigation called "Grand Slam" the New York feds had been trying to pin down a source that was supplying a combination of pushers selling "multikilogram quantities" of excellent heroin and cocaine and whose customers could include schoolchildren. The government had spent over $100,000 in drug purchases, involved ten thousand man hours which had begun with the purchase of one kilo of heroin to an undercover agent and eventually led to a buy of eight pounds of horse. One report read:

"Informant BR states he can arrange for the purchase of a large shipment but must leave the country. Date or details are still in the

80

negotiating stage. BR suspects Corsica. It is important to contact Colonel B on this. BR informant says he is dealing with pusher who is making sales to Major Walton Elementary School on West 126 Street where the young DOA took place. (See Report 4B, April 4)"

Then came the big one. It was marked URGENT AND CONFIDENTIAL:

"Informant BR murdered this morning. His body was found in the cellar of tenement, Lenox Avenue and 132nd Street. Homicide West contacted his sister through prints. F reported BR uneasy at last contact. He told F he is afraid he will be found out and be killed. Have arranged meeting with F."

Scrawled in pencil was "Goldfield Lighting," probably an out-of-office field cover, I told myself.

We had a start. It was an occasion for a great night with Kate, and in the morning I casually asked her to try to find out who F was and to get anything more on that lighting company. Now she was hooked by both intrigue and romance. Two nights later I not only had the info—F was Gus Fargo, manager of the stock room of an electrical supply house on Ninth Avenue—but also the contents of a second confidential memo advising Washington another informer nicknamed "Fats" had also been murdered.

Chickie didn't come through half as well but that was because of his position. He had laid it on to me in the beginning, but finally confessed he was only a clerk in identification. However he was great on gossip and had one good potential—he was a drinking buddy of a lush agent.

He had found out the government was trailing this New York drug group but had gotten nowhere. He had heard two informants had been killed and the strike force was working with a secret federal grand jury in the Eastern District but everything had ground to a halt.

The agent had told Chickie it was the toughest investigation he had ever been on, he was convinced the pushers they had grabbed honestly didn't know who was running the combination. The top bosses were smart, professional, and very tough. Apparently there wasn't enough money to make anyone talk.

I put five C notes in one of his kid's dolls which made him happy. What he gave me was worth one but now I had him on the hook; the other four were insurance for the future. . . .

Then Arnie showed up, red-eyed and yawning. Three of his old friends had dropped out of sight, another was married with three kids and a mortgage and was working for an insurance company. He couldn't care less about narcotics. But Arnie had scored with the last one.

This guy had been in Thailand since late '72 and, after the war finally spluttered out, was assigned to the American team attached to the Thai Special Narcotics Organization, the same outfit Arnie had worked with in the early 1960s. He had come back with a jungle blood infection that had resisted antibiotics and was undergoing treatment at a Washington hospital specializing in tropical diseases.

As he explained to Arnie, the harvesting and smuggling of drugs had increased since the war started to close down in Nam, Thailand, and Cambodia; official corruption and indifference had not changed. Caravans were back on the trails leading in and out of Burma.

However, recent reports of big buys disturbed American agents in Thailand and Saigon. A query to the Brigade Criminelle in Paris had produced the news that the boys could be connected with the Union Corse and perhaps organized crime in the United States. It was impossible to judge if this had any links to the new syndicate bringing drugs into New York and other large American cities. Arnie's friend had promised to see what more he could get.

"It's funny," Arnie said, "but this guy wasn't very friendly in the beginning—"

"I thought he was a friend of yours."

"You don't have any real friends in the Agency," he said. "I just happen to know the guy. In fact he said he was authorized to make me an offer to come back."

"What did you tell him?"

"I told him to shove it. He's gung ho and didn't like it."

"But he's talking to you?"

"That's what I can't understand," Arnie said thoughtfully. "He was giving me the brush until I started talking about China and how I wanted to get in."

"Why should that loosen him up?"

"You got me. But after that he got on China and how the Agency was working like hell to get someone on the mainland. He even hinted they might put me on the China detail but I told him that if I ever went there it would be as a civilian."

That night I said a tearful good-bye to Kate with fervent promises—which I intended to keep—to return as soon as possible. I also gave her my private number and planted another seed—if she dug up anything good I could persuade my fictitious mayoralty candidate to send me *shlepping* back to D.C.—and her cozy little apartment.

One thing puzzled me and I brought it up with Arnie on the way back to New York; we now had a good start with lots of legwork to be done, but what good was all the stuff we had dug up? As I got it from our meeting, Stu's plan was to put up lots of coin to help rid the city of pushers preying on school kids. I was all for that, but where did Corsican smugglers and a big secret investigation by the feds in New York fit in?

Arnie wasn't much help. He said that knowing the major it wouldn't be a wasted effort. . . .

When we arrived in the city Stu and Trev were meeting with Cornelius Brigadier, the former PC, and George Derby to complete plans for the big dinner which would launch the league, so Arnie and I continued to check out some of the details we had from Washington.

82

I had a hunch Gus Fargo, manager of the stock room in that Ninth Avenue electrical supply house, was an ex-con. That hunch proved to be correct; my contact at police headquarters pulled his yellow sheet, which showed he had done time for bringing in junk from Mexico but had been clean for five years. It was one hand washes the other, the feds got him a job and used him as a field contact for their informants. We decided to keep away from Fargo—he would alert the feds five minutes after we left him. A pipeline in the medical examiner's office gave the names and addresses of all homicides within the past year; the fed's murdered BR turned out to be Bartolo Rodriguez. A sister named Marie who lived in Brooklyn had identified the body. "Fats" was a Cuban bartender named Charles Ortiz, who, like Rodriguez, had dropped out of sight. His tortured body had been found stuffed in the trunk of a stolen car. The ME's records showed he was over three hundred pounds.

Marie had moved, but Arnie and I found her in a dirty, noisy dress factory in Union City, New Jersey, just across the river. She was a tired, dispirited woman in her late forties, beaten down by years of trying to survive in Spanish Harlem. She didn't even ask for our identification when we asked her to step outside.

We sat on a fire escape overlooking a busy street, and in a dull monotone she told us all she knew; it was a typical deadly story played out every day, hundreds of times in Harlem, Bed-Stuy, and the South Bronx.

The family had come from the slums of San Juan to the Golden City only to find the same stench, the same rats, the same bitter grinding poverty. Their father dropped out of sight and their mother got a job in a factory. Bartolo became a junkie in school, his list of arrests was long—ten times according to his yellow sheet—until he was finally sent away for sale and possession. Five to ten didn't help much and a few months after he was paroled he was back on the street pushing horse. This time he made a buy to a federal undercover agent and was grabbed with a fair amount of junk. The feds waited until he was found guilty then offered him the usual deal, his sentencing would be delayed if he played informer. Bartolo agreed and began making buys. That was a year ago. Evidently the feds were in no hurry and let him operate as if he was back in business. His story was that he had paid an agent to dilute his testimony to get him a suspended sentence.

Bartolo told his sister that after a few months when the agents were satisfied he was giving them a fair shake, they actually got him an SS and in fact had the assistant U.S. attorney scream about it in court. This was interesting, the elaborate cover showed the extent of interest the government had in this operation.

The junkie also showed his sister a shoe box filled with hundred-dollar bills which he said had been given him by the agents to make a big buy. Shortly before he was killed, she said, he had become very nervous and drank a lot. Then one day, a few weeks later, a homicide detective escorted her to Bellevue morgue where she identified her brother's body. He had been shot in the back of the head, executioner's style, and the corpse showed signs of ghastly torture.

Two tears rolled down her brown cheeks. She shrugged. That was all.

The father of Ortiz, who had made the morgue identification, was the super of a tenement in the South Bronx. We found him, a small meek man, stretched out on a couch in his basement apartment, listening to a shrill Spanish singer.

I flipped open a shield in a black case. Actually it was only my private investigator's identification, but there wasn't any need for playacting. The old guy was eager to talk; the story he told of his son was pathetic.

Since he was a small boy Carlos had always wanted to be a cop but he was too fat and couldn't pass the physical—city police, transit, housing cops turned him down. He couldn't even get into a private guard company. The reason was obvious from the faded, much folded snapshot the father showed us; his son was over three hundred pounds, it probably would have taken a derrick to get him into a guard's uniform.

But Carlos was well liked in the neighborhood and was a guy who could be counted on to do a favor. He was also a good bartender. His father's voice filled with pride when he told us his son had graduated from "college" and showed us his diploma. Arnie and I solemnly examined the cheap framed document; it was a certificate stating that Carlos Ortiz had graduated from a Third Avenue "Mixologist College."

Carlos finally got a job in a busy tavern that was not only the crossroads for the numbers mobs but also a meeting place for wholesale drug dealers. Somehow this jovial, ponderous man, who wanted to become a cop more than anything else, was recruited as a police informer. The bait? They would help to get him on the department. Carlos was an excellent finger man, and with his help the narcs sent several important pushers to jail. But then, as his father said, he tried to make a deal with someone downtown in the police department—an immediate appointment in exchange for a lead to a new and powerful syndicate moving large cargoes of drugs into the city from Indochina and possibly the source of the drugs being sold to kids.

When there wasn't an immediate reply to his demands, Carlos turned to the federal agents who gladly took him over. In a few weeks he disappeared; one day they found his huge body stuffed into the car trunk.

The old man wept as he told how they had to cut away part of the trunk to remove his son's body. When he tried to talk to the federal narcs or the cops they just shrugged; as far as they were concerned, fat Carlos had never existed. . . .

We now had a partial picture of the feds' investigation. It was clear the government had an extraordinary interest in this new international

84

narcotics syndicate that so far had claimed the lives of two informers, countless man hours, and lots of Uncle's cash.

Of course we had not answered the big questions: who was running this new setup and was this the outfit selling drugs to kids as outlined in the mayor's report?

But we didn't feel too bad; after all it appeared the government with all its resources apparently didn't know a hell of a lot more than we did on that score.

That's what I thought until I received the call from Kate suggesting that I hurry down for another dinner by candlelight and a lesson in shorthand. . . .

Chapter **5**

Trevor David- Dinner at the Eldorado

About ten days after our conference at Gracie Mansion, Stu and I met George Derby and Cornelius Brigadier at Derby's house on East Fifty-sixth Street. The league was progressing smoothly; Arnie and Sam had returned to Washington while Star, Rudy, and Tom were scouting locations for the secret telephone office we intended to establish. I had also contacted the PR men for City Hall and the police department on the releases prepared.

The police department's Deputy Commissioner of Community Relations, the usual municipal euphemism for a press agent, was a former reporter, a professional who knew the answers. But the City Hall character was another story; he was not only stuffy but stupid. It was impossible to pin him down as to when the full report would be issued by the mayor's office. I warned Stu if it was given out by the Hall before the dinner, it could diminish the news value of our release.

I prepared one release for the AMs and wire services, touching on the report and its contents with the expectation that our MC would supply more details. I also wrote a release for the PMs, or what remained of New York's afternoon papers, combining the future plans of the league along with excerpts of the report. With City Hall's press agents uncertain how they intended to handle the release of the formal report, I had to walk a tightrope between the morning and afternoon papers.

However, the big thing was television and I had little difficulty in persuading the newsrooms' M.E.s that the dinner would be worth covering; not only would there be big names but hard news.

I discussed with Stu the difficulty I was having with the City Hall people.

"You have to watch those goddam politicians," Stu said. "As Dad always said, without any effort they can tarnish the most innocent, well-intentioned motives."

I also discussed with Stu Madam Langford's dim view of Derby but, as the old woman had predicted, he dismissed it with a shrug. I was only beginning to realize how devoted he had been to his father. It was a paradoxical situation; he was convinced the league would fail, but at the same time was doing everything to make it a success.

"I don't know what she has against Derby," Stu mused in the cab on his way uptown to Fifty-sixth Street. "But I can believe Betsy's broke. She's been pissing away her money for years."

"The old woman said they owe a fortune on the Avenue and stuck them with a couple of bad checks."

Stu laughed. "Maybe that's the answer."

"I don't think so, Stu. I think she honestly mistrusts Derby for some reason"

"I think the old girl is trying to make something out of nothing."

"She didn't have any kind words for Betsy."

"Oh? What did she say?"

"She called her a bitch."

"Oh God," he groaned, "that's all we need, a couple of women trying to cut each other's throats."

"I wouldn't worry about it, Stu. What the hell, it's only a volunteer organization."

"Yeah," he said gloomily, "but you don't know how these volunteer things can suddenly become political. . . ."

To change the subject I asked, "What do you think about the stuff Arnie and Sam dug up?"

"It's good information."

"What are you going to do with it, Stu?"

"I haven't decided yet. At least we know as much as the feds or the cops."

"When did they go back to D.C.?"

"Last night. Sam got a call. It may be something good."

"Do you intend to tell Kerr or the others?"

"No. Let's keep it among ourselves for now."

Derby's brownstone was in the middle of a well-kept block just off Park. There were saplings protected by circular iron fences, flowers and plants in jugs and vases on the stoops, and gleaming polished brass doorknobs.

It was an older but still handsome Derby who met us at the door. His fashionably long black hair was graying but he was still as trim as I remembered him presiding over the legislative hearings in the Bar Association building years before. He looked like a fading fullback or an enthusiastic Sunday farmer. But something told me booze and not God's outdoors had given him that spurious ruddy look.

"This is Trevor David, George," Stu said, turning to me. "He remembers covering your hearings when he was a reporter for AP."

"Hi, Trev," he said in the classic, jovial politician's fashion. "Hell, that was a million years ago! Come on inside, Chuck's here."

He ushered us into an attractive room with the tips of the trees visible above the old-fashioned window seat. A baby grand was in one corner across from the fireplace and a bar appeared to be anything but ornamental.

Brigadier, who stood up to greet us, was a rock of a man with close-cropped white hair, a nose like a blade, and cold slate-colored eyes that took our measure in one swift glance.

"Stu, I think you know Chuck Brigadier," Derby said.

Brigadier said, "Oh, we've met on the peas-and-creamed-chicken circuit. How are you, Harlow?"

"Fine," Stu said. "This is Trevor David, my associate."

Brigadier's grip was like a vise closing over my hand but I returned it and he gave me a knowing smile.

"Trev worked for AP in the city some years ago," Stu said. "He's going to do our publicity."

"Oh, yeah?" Brigadier said and I could sense him assuming a defensive crouch. "I knew a lot of the boys who covered headquarters. Did you ever work in the old building?"

"I worked out of the shack a few times on vacations," I said.

"The shack was a tenement the reporters used as a pressroom behind old police headquarters," Brigadier explained. "Now they have a nice place on the second floor of the new building across from City Hall." He added with a short laugh, "If I had my way they'd be five blocks away."

"You sound as if they gave you a bad time, Chuck," Derby said.

"They were a pain in the ass," Brigadier said. "If they caught a cop with his hand in the till, you'd think it was Dillinger."

"What did you do when you caught a cop with his hand in the till?" I asked, taking the sting out of the question with a friendly smile.

"Slam the door shut and break his hand," Brigadier promptly replied. "But I wouldn't tell the world about it. Bad for morale. A cop goes home and his kids tell him other kids say all cops are thieves. In any big organization there are bad apples. You have to weed 'em out. Not talk about it."

"Well, now that we have the police department squared away," Derby said, rubbing his hands, "let's have a drink. What'll you boys have?"

He mixed the drinks and waved us to seats on the couch.

"Here's to the league," he said solemnly. We drank to that and he said, "The mayor called and filled me in about your meeting. What's the next step, Stu? The dinner?"

"I guess that's it. Trev and I are working on it now."

"Do you have a chairman picked who'll emcee it?" he asked quickly.

"Why no, not yet—"

"If you don't I'll take it," he said casually. "That is, of course, if you don't have anyone else in mind."

"No, not at all," Stu said, "that will be fine."

"I have an old biog somewhere around," he said to me. "You can use it."

"Sure," I said. "By the way, the mayor gave us permission to incorporate something about the report in our release. I've written two—one for the AMs and one for the PMs. I hope the mayor's people don't release the full report on the afternoon before the dinner."

"Your worries are over," he said grimly. "I talked to him an hour ago."

"Oh? A change in plans?"

"Damn right. I told him to count me out if he was going to release that goddam report right before our dinner. You know what would happen."

I told him I had warned Stu that if City Hall released the report, that story would be on page one and the dinner would be only a sidebar.

"Damn right!" He turned apologetically to Stu, "I'm sorry, Stu, I don't want to make waves but I also don't intend to become a patsy for City Hall."

"Frankly I don't care," Stu said with a trace of impatience. "I just want the league to get going. Now who's going to release the report?"

"We are," Derby said firmly. "I can sketch it out in my opening remarks."

"I'll redo the releases," I said.

"Great," Derby said, "I told the mayor he could give out the full report the following day."

"We weren't born yesterday," Brigadier observed.

"As I said, I don't particularly care," Stu pointed out, "but I want everyone to understand one thing—this is a civic organization. I don't want it to become a political battleground."

"Of course," Derby said smoothly, "but what the hell, let's get as much publicity as possible for the league, Stu. City Hall can work its own side of the street."

The league get publicity? I asked myself. It was beginning to sound more like a platform for Derby . . . he impressed me as a fast worker.

"How's the dinner shaping up, Stu?" he asked.

"Fine. Trev and I have some good names. We could use a whole lot more."

"You got them. The other night Betsy and I made up a list of people you might want to invite. You know, good window dressing. Politicos. People in television and the theatre Betsy knows. Photographers like that kind of stuff. Right, Trev?"

I nodded.

"If you want, Betsy will work with you. She knows a hell of a lot of people here and on the coast. She's been doing charity work for years and has been on a lot of political committees."

"That will be fine."

"Good. Do you have a card? She'll give you a call and you can get together."

Madam Langford's "bitch"? It could be interesting. I gave him my card.

Brigadier cleared his throat. "As I understand it, Stu, you're giving five grand to anyone who turns in a pusher?"

"That's right," Stu said. "You know the league was my father's idea."

"I remember him going down to the Hall with it," Brigadier said. "Later he told me the mayor got him to hold it up. That guy's a great con artist."

"Dad agreed to give the new narcotics bureau a chance," Stu explained to Derby.

"Whose idea was that bureau?" I asked Brigadier.

"Mine," he said proudly, "but they never gave me credit. I spent a year on that thing." He waved a finger at me. "That's what I mean, young fellow, about the press. I told the inspectors if there was a leak I'd bust 'em all to captain." He gave us a wink. "There wasn't a peep out of any of 'em. When the time was ripe I called in that fellow who writes The Cop of the Month Award and gave him the story. He took care of the cops, I took care of him."

"How do you like Fitzgerald, Commissioner?" I asked, knowing the title would make him preen.

"Oh, Teddy Fitz is a good man," he said condescendingly, "but I can't see him as commissioner. He's too damn much for computers. Sure, they're important, but no machine ever caught a mugger. Before I left I told the Queens leader he should get a real cop in there, someone the boys like and would follow . . . but no, Fitz was City Hall's man."

I couldn't resist it, so as innocently as a newborn I asked him, "But I always thought politics never entered into the police department, Commissioner."

He stared at me as if I had spit on the rug.

"Don't believe it, young fellow," he snorted. "Politics! Christ, man, the city runs on it! From the guy who picks up your garbage to the guy who runs the subway! It's all politics." He nodded to Derby. "That's what I'm trying to tell George . . . the guy at the Hall who knows how to pull the right strings can make this city run like a clock."

I still don't know what made me say it, the words just blurted out. "Are you going to run for mayor, Mr. Derby?"

For a moment the silence was solid like ice, then Derby laughed, a little uneasily.

"Oh, don't mind Chuck. He and Betsy have been pushing me for years . . ."

"I bet this time we'll push you over the brink," Brigadier said smugly.

Derby waved him off. "Let's get back to the league. Stu, is that five thousand dollars only for possession?"

"I'm not interested in junkies, George, only pushers."

"They should bring the chair back," Brigadier snapped.

Derby ignored him. "Will the department make the decisions?"

"Inspector Miles of Narcotics will make up a committee," Stu replied. "It will pass on every—well, I guess we can call it reward."

Brigadier put in, "Sonny Miles is a good man. I'll have to talk to him."

"There'll be a mail drop and a phone number?" Derby asked.

"You're not going to get stoolies to walk in off the street," Brigadier pointed out. "Rockefeller found that out."

"The state only offered one grand, we're offering five," Derby said.

"You'll get a lot of small stuff—"

"We're not interested in street people," Stu said. "We want the pushers. The bigger the better. We're hoping this time the community will cooperate. It's their kids. . . ."

"By the way, how did you fellows like the report?" Derby asked.

"It was a good job," Stu said. "The goddam thing gave me nightmares."

"We found a lot more than we expected," Derby said. "Some of the fellows I know at the bureau gave me a hand and Sonny Miles helped Chuck."

"Oh, so the local cops know about this new setup?" I said.

"Of course they do," Brigadier said indignantly. "Sonny Miles dug it up months ago. They're still working on it. He's got some good people down there."

Still playing the role of the innocent, I asked, "What about the feds? Aren't they interested?"

"Very much so," Derby said. "But they're not getting anywhere."

"The mayor said he heard they had two stoolies knocked off."

"That's what I understand."

"So it appears the cops and the feds both are not getting anywhere," I pointed out.

"Oh, this is a big outfit," Brigadier said, shaking his head, "real big. Maybe the biggest we'll ever see."

We spent another hour or so going over the details of the league, particularly the dinner which seemed to interest Derby as much as the aims of the league itself. I noticed he wore a groove in the rug walking to the bar; by the time we left he was glowing.

"Stu," he said fervently as if he were delivering blessings from on high, "we're going to make the league the best weapon this damn city ever had against narcotics!"

I shook hands with Brigadier, who gave me a patronizing pat on the back.

"Watch out for those sharpies downtown, young fellow, they'll steal your eyeteeth."

Perhaps, I told myself, I should now count my fingers.

On the way back to the hotel Stu asked me, "Well, what do you think, Trev?"

"They're both slightly full of bullshit."

"Perhaps," he said musingly, "but there's one thing I can't understand."

"What's that?"

"They don't sound like the guys who wrote that report."

By this time we were sharing the same suspicions.

The next morning about ten the phone rang in my office at the hotel. It was Betsy Van Lyden Derby. It might have been a put-on, something she had practiced for years, but the moment I heard her voice I thought of a good-looking woman in a clinging negligee, smiling, waiting.

"Mr. David?"

"This is he."

"This is Betsy Van Lyden Derby. I'll be working with you on the league. George suggested we get together."

"Anytime."

"How about this afternoon. Are you free for lunch?"

"That will be fine with me. At the hotel?"

"I hate hotel food," she said firmly, "it's like eating plastic. Why don't you come up here at two? Nothing elaborate. Just a sandwich."

"Okay, it's a date."

"One thing . . ."

"Yes, Mrs.—"

"That's just what I mean," she said with a throaty laugh. "Let's make it Betsy and Trev."

"Okay, Betsy, I'll see you at two."

"Good-bye, Trev."

The damnedest thing. All morning I kept trying to visualize her until I had my secretary dig through the hotel's publicity picture files and find a few shots of her. I spread them out on my desk. There she was at a Kips Bay Ball, stunning in a low cut clinging gown, another had her dancing at the Russian Ball, head thrown back, laughing, and still another of a debutante cotillion bowing low in a curtsy to show a breathtaking cleavage.

Then I turned over the photographs; most of them were fifteen years old.

When she met me at the door that afternoon it was obvious she was desperately trying to preserve her fading beauty. A skillful makeup job helped to hide the pouches and wrinkles and the expensive dark blue slacks and shimmering low cut blouse revealed a very interesting figure. But she had also taken a few morning pick-me-ups; I could smell the booze.

"Hi, Trev," she said with a bright, theatrical smile. "Isn't it a marvelous day?"

She waved me into a room across from the one where we had met Derby and Brigadier. It was smaller, less formal, with a desk, portable typewriter, some hunting prints, a fireplace and a leather couch.

"This is George's office," she explained, "we can work here. Stella is just finishing making our lunch."

The door opened and a stout black woman carrying a tray edged into the room.

I took the tray and Betsy leaned over to open a folding table. I was sure she did it on purpose; she wasn't wearing a bra and her breasts were creamy white, full, and damn tempting. It appeared the afternoon might be interesting . . .

There was a cocktail shaker of martinis, chilled, dry and perfect. As she filled my frosted glass a warning gong clanged in my mind; this didn't look like a working session. We made small talk over lunch then the maid took away the dishes but left the shaker.

We went over her list of guests for the party. There wasn't a thing I could quarrel with; it included names from labor, the theatre, politics, city government, Washington, society, every religion.

"I'm leaving the press coverage up to you," she said. "George told me you were a newspaperman."

"I've worked for AP," I explained.

"Do you like politics, Trev?"

"Not particularly. By the way, talking of politics, may I ask you something?"

Those deep blue eyes suddenly became guarded. "Of course," she murmured.

"Does your husband intend to run for the mayoralty?"

"Oh, I don't know about that," she said vaguely. "People are always asking him to run for something or other."

But Brigadier had said they were pushing Derby to the brink.

The maid suddenly appeared as if summoned by an invisible bell, carrying a new shaker of martinis. I was startled, I hadn't realized we had finished the first one. I can usually hold my grog, but martinis are delayed action and I was beginning to feel them. I wondered when Betsy would start showing some effects.

"Want to know something, Trev?"

"What's that, Betsy?"

"I think Stu is off his trolley giving away a hundred grand to get junkies off the street. It's a problem for City Hall. Where are the cops?"

"Maybe the job's too big for them."

"You're damn right it is," she said fiercely. "I knew Dwight Kerr when he was going to Harvard. I always thought—well, I could never see him as mayor. And he's let the city go to pot!" She turned to the desk and I quickly flipped my drink into the ashes of the fireplace; I wanted a clear head for what I suspected was coming.

"Have you any idea of how much money the city gives to the cops every year to make buys from drug pushers?" she asked in a low, conspiratorial voice as she shook a sheaf of papers. "Have you any idea?"

"Not the slightest, Betsy."

"Two million four hundred thousand dollars a year," she said triumphantly. "And all of it to help the police track down the source of drugs. If they can't do it with that kind of money, what's Stu's hundred thousand dollars going to do?" She threw the papers back on the desk. "I tell you, Trev, there's something wrong—something goddam wrong in City Hall. George says it's all out of whack somewhere and he's right. Don't you think so?"

"Where the hell did you ever get those police figures, Betsy?"

"Ever since he was in the U.S. attorney's office George has been interested in the narcotic situation in the city. He and Chuck have put together a lot of stuff like this."

But they never included this in their report . . .

"Now let's get back to our dinner."

It's funny what booze does to women; one moment they're poised, glacially attractive, then they seem to dissolve, makeup oozes, beads of sweat appear on their upper lips, strands of hair break free, their eyes so clear and luminous become watery and out of focus. They giggle and keep tossing back their mane of hair, a gesture that could be winsome but usually looks like a pony fretting at his bridle. I remember the actress I interviewed when I was a kid reporter; she was a well-known lush desperately attempting a comeback. In the beginning she was the beautiful woman who had bewitched me for years, but by the time the interview ended she was nodding in the chair and the press agent was begging me to forget the whole thing.

Betsy wasn't nodding, she was knocking over glasses with cute apologies; but there's nothing cute about trying to pick up slivers of glass from a shag rug. I endured it only because she was talking.

94

"What we need is some damn good publicity. George thinks you're great, Trev."

"Thank you. I think we'll get enough coverage."

"How about that guy at City Hall wanting to give out his report just before the dinner? He's got a damn nerve!" The words came out, slurred but deadly. "The bastard!"

I told myself never to put them at the same table.

"I'm glad George told him off. . . . How about that report? Wasn't it great? God, I'm glad I don't have any kids!"

"I was thinking of calling Inspector Miles, Betsy . . ."

"Sure," she said enthusiastically, "Sonny's a great guy. He just loves George."

I threw the shaft into the darkness.

"As long as he wrote the report I thought he might have something in the trunk we could use for a release. Maybe a good case history or something like that . . ."

It hit home. . . .

"Oh, did George tell you Sonny wrote the report? He was up here for weeks. Chuck Brigadier got him. You wouldn't believe the stuff he has. This city's under siege, Trev. The junkies have taken over. And that idiot down at City Hall just ties the cops' hands! You ought to talk to Sonny about that. You tell him I said for you to call him. Meet him somewhere outside of headquarters. He'll give you loads of stuff."

"But isn't he zinging his own department, Betsy . . . ?"

She gave me an owlish look as she slowly held up her crossed fingers.

"He and George and Chuck are like that." She giggled. "I don't know who the hell's on the bottom."

The way I laughed you would have thought she was a combination of Berle and Youngman.

"Maybe Chuck will make him his number one man when George makes Chuck his commissioner . . ."

She winked at me over her glass. I decided not to press anymore; there would be other meetings.

She tossed back her mane of hair. "I think I'll take a little nap. We have an opening tonight. Some people will be coming . . ."

I was only too happy to get out of there.

"By all means, Betsy. I'm sorry I took up your whole afternoon."

"Don't be silly. We're going to have lots more meetings." She leaned over and clasped my hands. "Let's make this league the damnedest, best league in the whole United States! Right, Trev?"

"Right."

Hand in hand we walked to the foyer.

"I think we're going to get on just great," she said, fuzzy with booze.

"I think so too."

She didn't have a damn thing under that blouse and for a moment I was tempted. It was there for the asking and Betsy might have been interesting on that leather couch, but drunken women turn me off. In the few minutes we were there the foyer smelled of gin and cigarettes. No thanks. I wasn't carrying a torch for Leslie, whom Sam Hoffman once called my Georgia Peach, that girl a shimmering dream when I left and a mother of two when I returned. I couldn't help but compare the two—there just wasn't any contest. It would be far less complicated to call my one-night stand from the Madison Avenue advertising agency who was enchanted by the newspaper business.

Betsy appeared disappointed and pouted a bit, but I whispered she looked enchanting and I had better leave before I would get in all kinds of trouble and that seemed to please her. This was a pipeline I intended to cultivate.

That night when I laid it out for Stu he looked thoughtful.

"Well, there it is. Miles wrote the report, not Brigadier or Derby." He looked at me.

"Why?" I said.

"Miles must be going for big stakes. He's taking a hell of a risk. If City Hall or the PC gets a hint of what he did he'll be out on his ass."

"Then why would Miles take such a risk? What's in it for him?"

Stu looked thoughtful. "I don't know. I wish I knew."

"Look at it this way, Stu; what's in it that's big enough to make him risk getting kicked out of the department or demoted and in addition to put his own bureau on the pan? When City Hall gives out that report, the reporters are certainly going to ask the PC and the mayor what the hell have Miles and his narcs been doing about this mob?"

"I know that. I haven't the faintest idea of what he's up to. Why don't you meet him for lunch, Trev? Try to feel him out. Let's see what you think of him."

"I hope they don't screw us."

His voice grated like a saw cutting ice.

"It will be the sorriest day of their lives."

The next day I called Madam Langford and told her I had heard Derby was interested in running for the mayoralty.

"Keep your ears and eyes open, and I'll do the same," she said. "Maybe we can keep those hustlers in line."

Before I hung up I decided to contact one of Madam Langford's hustlers—Inspector Frank Miles whom everyone called Sonny. . . .

We met in a small sedate French restaurant off Broad Street. I was surprised. I had thought he would have suggested one of those meatball and spaghetti bars around Foley Square that seem to be the traditional meeting places for cops, DAs, and anyone connected with law enforcement.

From the way the maître d'hôtel greeted him it was obvious he was a cherished customer. As Stu had said, his thin handsome face was more like a fine actor's than a cop's.

When we sat down he said, "George tells me you were a newspaperman. What paper did you work for?"

"No paper, a wire service, Associated Press." I briefed him that I had worked in New York for a few years, then transferred to the Atlanta bureau. "I come from a small town near there."

"Weren't you with Harlow?"

"Seven years."

He whistled softly. "That's a long time. I had a buddy in Korea who was a POW for only a few months, but he looked like hell when I saw him in the hospital." He suddenly snapped his fingers. "Wait a minute. Didn't I read something about you guys? What did they call you?"

"The Hounds," I said as he groped for the word. "That's what Charlie called us."

"You guys had guts."

"There were other camps that were worse."

When the drinks came we raised our glasses.

"To the league," I said and we drank to that.

"The old man said I could level with you," Sonny said.

"The old man?"

"Brigadier."

"I hope so. By the way, that was a great report you did."

"Oh, that one belongs to Derby and Brigadier," he said quickly. "I didn't do much."

"It was not only well written but expertly put together," I said, hoping the praise would flush him out.

He hesitated but his ego was too strong. "Thanks."

Now it was on the record.

"What can I do for you, Mr. David?"

"Trev," I said.

"Okay. They call me Sonny." He gave me a faint smile. "Isn't that a hell of a name for a cop?"

"I had a DI in basic whose name was Sweetboy. You were dead if you smiled. By the way, anything we say here is off the record." I handed him copies of the releases. "We hope to get as much coverage on the dinner as possible. One is for the AMs and the other for the PMs."

He read through them rapidly.

"You know what would happen to me if the PC or City Hall knew I had anything to do with that report?"

"But City Hall ordered the report!"

"It's a game. The mayor appoints a committee and lights a candle they don't come up with anything. Most of the time they deliver a crock of shit. Like the one City Hall gave out last week on prison conditions. What did it say? Nothing. Don't send any more people to prison. That's the kind of report they like at the Hall. This one set the mayor back on his heels."

He leaned across the table and lowered his voice.

"It's hard to explain to an outsider but the department's like any other big organization—business, the Pentagon, newspapers"—then he remembered—"Associated Press. They're all made up of cliques, cabals, baronies. All the chiefs have their braves. In the department everybody's maneuvering, from the cop on the beat to the PC. And God help you if you make a mistake. They slit your throat so neat and easy you never know it until your head falls off. If any snitch knew I had a hand in that report and spilled it to the Hall or the PC, I'd be a headless wonder."

He handed me back the releases.

"As far as I'm concerned I never saw them. Okay?"

"Of course."

When the waiter appeared I noticed Miles ordered his *gratin de pommes de terre aux anchois* in what definitely was not high school or even college French.

"You have a good accent."

"My mother was Corsican. I had to learn everything in two languages. It comes in handy. A couple of years ago one of those sheiks who own all the oil in the world came to the UN. He wanted someone who could speak French so I was put in charge of his bodyguards." He shot back a jacket sleeve to show me the heavy gold cuff links. "He gave me these. He wanted me to go back with him. All the wives I wanted. You could screw your life away."

"I know a few guys who would like that."

"Not me." He made a grimace of distaste. "They smell like they bathe in whale oil. I like Oriental women, preferably Chinese."

"Any reason, Sonny?"

"I told you my mother was Corsican, my father was Italian. His family had an importing business in San Francisco's Chinatown for years. I grew up with them, lived with them, went to school with them." He shook his head. "Chinese women are superb. The man is always the boss. No questions, no arguments. You want something and it's done. Maybe I'm a male chauvinist pig but that's the way I like it."

"You sound like an expert."

He grinned. "Let's say I've done a lot of research on the subject."

"How did you come east?'

"My mother died when I was in Korea. It broke up my father. He merged his firm with another and came to New York to take over their main office. I joined him here and went to Fordham. I wanted to be a lawyer. But my father couldn't stand Manhattan, so he went back to the coast. I stayed in Fordham for two years, then tried out for the cops."

"I find it curious that a guy going to college should try out for the cops."

"I took the test with a couple of guys as a gag. I passed, they didn't. The more I looked into it, the better it sounded. So I dumped Fordham and joined the department."

"What year were you in?"

"Sophomore."

"Don't you think you should have gone on for a degree?"

"I got it at night. In fact I have thirty credits for a master's in political science. That piece of paper means something in the department." He eyed me over a glass of wine. "Now that I told you my life story, how about you, Trev? How did you get to work for Harlow?"

I told him about Stu, Tong Le Mai, the reunion, and how Stu's father had been active in community affairs.

By this time I felt we had reached an understanding, so I returned to the business at hand.

"Now that we're leveling, Sonny, I'd like to ask you a question."

"Be my guest."

"Your report certainly didn't make your narcotics bureau look good. After this story breaks the reporters covering headquarters will certainly be all over the commissioner asking him what the hell have you guys been doing."

"The first thing you learn in this department, Trev, is to protect your ass. My explanation is right in the commissioner's files."

"Oh? What's that?"

"I was the first one to get wind of this new mob."

"So Brigadier told me."

"And I put in a hell of a lot of hours before I even sent in my first memo to the first deputy."

"And what did the first deputy do?"

"What all first deputies do—took it to the PC. In every memo I detailed a phase of our investigation."

"Didn't it ever go to the DA?"

"Not enough hard evidence. We had meetings, I put what I had on the table, but we all agreed it wasn't enough."

"So after the report comes out—"

He finished the sentence. "Fitzgerald will ask me to make a report to release to the press. It will certainly show we've been working."

"It could become a campaign issue. You know, the police department with its thirty-three thousand cops and billion dollar budget can't break up a gang of drug merchants."

He gave me a faint smile.

"I wouldn't be surprised if it was."

Then I got it. Derby could clobber Kerr and City Hall with failure to protect the community and its children from this drug mob. Derby wins. And Miles becomes—?

"How about a refill?" he asked.

"No thanks."

He impatiently ground out his cigarette.

"I've got to cut these things out."

"You look in good shape."

"I play handball a couple of nights a week at the NYAC."

"Are you a member?"

"For years."

"That could be expensive."

"Expensive enough. Great for making contacts. The market is down—but I made some money."

"Contacts?"

He studied me through the haze of smoke.

"The old man said to level with you, Trev, and that's what I'm doing. The department's only a small percentage of my life. To me the future is more important than the present. When the time is ripe I'll put in my papers, collect my pension, and start to live. In the meantime I give them eight hours."

"You knew the risks, why did you stick your neck out for Derby and Brigadier?"

"I had only one rabbi in the department—Chuck Brigadier. He's Old Iron Ass to a lot of stiffs but he pulled me up with him. When he left, I said the hell with all of them. I don't want any friends and I don't want any enemies. I'll go it solo until I toss it in."

"Where did you work with Brigadier?"

"I was his lieutenant when he was inspector in the three-four-one precinct. He ran a tight house but I had no squawks." He tapped the releases. "When he asked for this stuff I gave it to him."

"Have you known Derby long?"

"Ever since he was chairman of that watchdog committee in Albany. The old man introduced us."

"I covered those parole hearings. He had developed some good stuff."

There was a note of pride in his voice. "Do you know where he got it? Right here."

"Wasn't that dangerous?"

"I always protect myself. Brigadier was deputy then and I was a captain in intelligence. He gave me the okay—in writing—just in case."

"It looks like you have a habit of going out on a limb."

"I guess I'm a realist," he said evenly. "Derby looked like he was going somewhere and I wanted to go along with him. You'll never get to sit behind Teddy Roosevelt's desk in the PC's office unless you know someone. Like the mayor."

"But it never happened with Derby."

"He's had a few tough breaks but I wouldn't count him out."

"Do you think he'll run for mayor?"

He shrugged. "Who knows?"

"We're leveling, Sonny . . ."

"I really don't know and I don't think Derby knows. Chuck's pushing but there are things to consider."

"Like what?"

"Timing." He paused. "And money. Lots of money."

"I thought Derby's wife was well fixed?"

"That's the story."

He was answering all my questions eyeball to eyeball but he was too neat, too pat. "Have you met his wife?" he said.

"Betsy? A few times. She's helping us with the dinner."

"She has great connections."

"Oh?" I let it hang there.

"I met her once at their place. George needed some statistics, so she called the majority leader in Albany! It was like two in the morning. She said she needed the stuff right away. The next day someone from the New York office hand-delivered what we wanted!"

It was good for a laugh.

"What's with this guy Harlow?" he asked abruptly.

"What do you mean?"

"Putting up a hundred thousand to get some junkies off the street."

"Pushers—not junkies."

"Okay. Pushers. Half the time they're both."

"Five thousand is a lot of money."

"Oh, you'll get calls and mail, mostly on street people, nuts, that sort of thing."

"Doesn't anybody know anything about this mob? Who's the head of it? How do they get the junk into the city?"

He shook his head. "We spent a fortune making buys but you reach a certain level and that's it."

"How did you get what you have? The mayor told Stu the federal people had two stool pigeons killed."

He laughed. "I told that to Chuck and he told the mayor. We had a Cuban bartender as a stoolie. Then the feds made him believe he was a G-man and he dropped us. They found him in a trunk. They also got another guy who was making buys for the feds."

"Who do you think fingered them?"

The waiter brought our coffee and cleared our table.

"It's a funny thing," he said quietly, "how the public—anyone who's not in law enforcement—has fixed ideas on the underworld. To them the mob bosses are all old Sicilians with moustaches who grow tomatoes while they order guys killed. Everything is stereotyped. It's all part of our culture, like those idiotic gunfighters in the TV westerns. Maybe it's Hollywood's fault, I don't know. This I do know, the guys who run today's syndicates don't play with tomatoes. Today's bosses are like U.S. Steel, General Motors, Du Pont, with one difference—you don't get fired, you get killed. They don't have time for mistakes. They're like bloodhounds, they can smell out anything that can make a buck. Junk is the best because the profit is fantastic. So they invest millions, like in this operation. Then they can pick the smartest guy to run it. All the cops have to do is find that guy, get the evidence, and arrest him." He added wryly, "A job that's as easy to do as finding a handball court at the North Pole."

"You're not what I would call an optimist."

"I told you I'm a realist." He hesitated. "There's one thing about Harlow's plan—"

"And that is?"

"There's a chance you may score, just a chance. George the Greek would tell you the odds are a thousand to one. What the hell, it's worth trying as long as you guys are putting up the loot. Let me explain something about investigations. You can go on for a year and nothing happens, no matter how much money you spend or how many man hours you put in. Then one day you get a call or a letter. It's like a stone dropped in a lake. The ripples never seem to end." He finished his coffee and neatly folded his napkin. "Who knows—you guys may drop that stone."

"And if we do?"

"You give it to us and we follow the ripples."

"Do we turn everything over to you?"

"Everything." I recalled later how emphatically he said it. "I'll assign two men to pick up the mail and collect the phone stuff."

"This mob must be ruthless, selling junk to kids."

"Why? It's nothing new," he said calmly. "Drop in on any precinct in Harlem, Bed-Stuy, or the South Bronx and talk to the beat men. They'll tell you. Ten-year-olds push horse like it's breakfast cereal."

"How does a kid keep up—say a seventy-five-dollar-a-day habit?"

"They steal. Christ, how they steal! From their parents, neighbors, friends—anybody and anything. I've seen tenements ready for demolition stripped clean of every copper pipe—they even rip off the tin roofs. They can strip down a parked car within minutes. Then if that doesn't work they can always go down to Times Square and look for a chicken hawk . . ."

"What the hell is that?"

"A homo ready to buy a kid. For ten bucks he takes the kid to an Eighth Avenue hotel. Sometimes the kids aren't lucky. Last month a friend of mine who works out of the West Fifty-fourth Street house got a call from a night clerk of one of those flophouses. He found a thirteen-year-old who had picked up a sadist. After he tied and gagged the kid he used a four-inch leather belt to beat him. The kid was in a hospital for two weeks. He had a fifty-dollar-a-day habit. The doctor said if he keeps it up he'll never reach fifteen. The girls? Pimps can easily get Johns who'll pay a couple of hundred for a young kid. She gets ten, maybe fifteen dollars. They always wind up in the hospital with VD, pregnant, or something else."

"Christ, don't these guys pushing this stuff have any conscience?"

"I guess they believe in the law of supply and demand. As long as the demand is there, they intend to supply it—or someone else will. And don't talk to me about the conscience of the city, that's a lot of crap. I remember when I was a lieutenant and reading how the board of education denied there was any junk in the school system while we

102

had more than a page of beefs from parents that pushers were selling in the schoolyards. Finally we bagged a couple, but when they got to court the judge practically gave them a medal and denounced the cops who made the arrest. The guy on the bench had announced he was going to run for the Senate. It was popular then to be anticop, so I guess the bastard thought it would make him popular."

"You make it sound almost hopeless, Sonny."

"To repeat, I'm a realist, Trev. When I came on the job I was Don Quixote with a nightstick. A couple of years on Fox Avenue in the Bronx taught me a few things."

"For instance?"

"Never let the gumshoes from headquarters catch you with your collar unbuttoned and be sure to give the desk sergeant a fin so he'll check you in when they call the roll in case you're sleeping over with something nice in the nearby project. To survive in this department, Trev, you have to know a lot of little tricks." He paused. "And some big ones."

I signaled the waiter but he waved me away impatiently.

"It's taken care of—I have an account here."

"You live good, Sonny."

He gave me a cold smile.

"It's a life-style, my friend."

We walked up Broadway through the thinning late luncheon crowd.

"Do you think Kerr will run again?"

He nodded. "There's no doubt of it—at least in my mind."

"One of your pipelines?"

"You don't need one. Just look at the guy. He has an ego as big as all outdoors. He could never bow out now."

"What do you think his chances would be?"

"If he gets good opposition that can spend a lot of money? No contest. Money's the answer. Saturation television. That sort of thing."

"Could Derby—"

He cut me short. "I told you I don't know."

The thin handsome face was set, his cool green eyes steady, almost detached.

"I guess I'll see you at the dinner."

"That's right. The fifteenth."

"I'll be there."

We shook hands and he waved down a cab. In a minute he was gone.

Sonny Miles, inspector of the new and expanded narcotics bureau—a man who didn't like losers. . . .

I saw Betsy Van Lyden Derby several times after meeting Inspector Miles, to wrap up the details of the dinner. She was as friendly as ever but curiously, after the first meeting, she didn't hit the bottle as much. Oh, she drank, but at a certain point, as if a gong clanged a warning, she stopped.

When she was sober she was smart; she appeared to have a multitude of friends in politics, society, the theatre. And she was on first name basis with some monsignor in the Powerhouse and seemed to have the private number of every big-time actor on the coast.

I also discovered she was, as Madam Langford had said, a bitch. An actress turned her down, not personally but through a secretary, and within an hour Betsy had given two Hollywood TV columnists a different, scandalous tidbit about her.

"She'll be there," Betsy promised me with a bright smile.

In a few days the actress called back, it had all been a mistake of her appointment secretary, she said fervently, she wouldn't miss such a wonderful dinner for anything. . . .

We saw Brigadier, but not too much of Derby; once I spotted a phone number scrawled on Betsy's telephone pad and gave it to Sam to check out; it was a hotel in Las Vegas where he was listed as a guest.

I decided not to say anything to Stu; he was engrossed in making plans for the dinner, which was shaping up as a glittering tribute to his father, and, after all, I kept telling myself, it was all voluntary, a sincere civic attempt to fight the plague of narcotics. Outside of some publicity how could it benefit anyone? If there were political maneuvers going on in the background, well, the hell with them . . .

The night of the dinner finally arrived and it was soon evident that Betsy had been a valuable asset. There were enough stars from Hollywood and television to collect a screaming mob behind the police barriers; well-fed labor leaders who looked like plumbers at their annual ball; the haughty, reigning queen of models who had been on *Time*'s cover and who constantly flashed her plastic smile and automatically turned her best side whenever she saw a camera; our venerable aging senator who reminded me of a windup toy that could speak on any subject and his preening wife who liked to boast she was part Cherokee when actually, as Tom said, he had discovered in D.C. she was an Armenian from Chicago's South Side; the religious greeted each other like successful partners while the political leaders, wary as jackals, gathered in formal groups.

The mayor looked, to recall Madam Langford's description, like Mr. Collar Ad. He drew a burst of expertly delivered Bronx cheers, but he also received applause from the women spectators.

While Derby and Brigadier checked their coats, Betsy greeted me at the door. A long time spent at her dressing table had cosmetically encouraged a resemblance to an early sultry Ava Gardner.

"How do I look?" she whispered.

Her heavy, sensual perfume started to give me ideas, but I remembered the calls she had made to the Hollywood columnist and decided to cool it.

104

"Like a dream, a beautiful dream," I whispered back.

But I should have known she wasn't interested in me.

"Isn't that Sonny Miles a handsome son of a bitch?" she asked softly.

Miles, a singularly poised man, perfectly tailored, had just come into the reception room.

I warned her, "Be careful, Betsy . . ."

She gave me a cool smile. "I was taught never to mix business with pleasure."

Miles joined us and I left after a few minutes to talk to some newspaper people. As I pushed my way through the crowded room I wondered about this strange triumvirate . . . an aging society beauty who apparently would do anything to become the city's First Lady; her husband, a habitual loser who was desperate to win one more chance, and the cold-eyed, self-styled realistic police inspector who was determined to make the present pay for his future.

I had two press tables, one for print, the other for TV. The releases had been hand-delivered so we would catch the first edition. I had also set up a side room for interviews and made sure Stu was at the mayor's side when the press conference started. The reporters were strangers to me except a weary, bored veteran who had drifted in and out of the Federal Building pressroom when I was covering that beat years ago. I quickly filled him in, and he agreed to ask Stu a few pertinent questions so it wouldn't be all City Hall. But Kerr was generous, he outlined the league's purpose and gave both Stu and his father full praise.

Television took their usual bland shots and quotes but instead of the crews leaving, they stayed, which puzzled me. Usually they give a dinner a fast brush to go on to spot news. I would have preferred seeing them go, that would mean Stu was locked in for the eleven o'clock news spot. After the interview I maneuvered my old friend to the bar.

"What's up?"

He looked about, then whispered, "Our guy at City Hall tipped the desk to have someone hang around. That's all I know, Trev."

A tiny chunk of ice began to form in the pit of my stomach.

I talked to Derby and Brigadier in the crowded reception room, but it was evident they didn't know anything. Betsy was in a corner with Miles, engaged in a low, serious discussion. On the surface the reception appeared normal—noisy, smoky, alcoholic. Sam and Arnie were still in Washington but Tom, Star, and Rudy had their own assignments and the evening looked as if it was off to a smooth start. There was one more guest I had to see, one I considered more important than any of the others, Madam Langford. I had checked several times but she and her brother had not arrived. Then Tom appeared at the door and pointed outside, the signal they were coming in.

I greeted them as Jay was checking his sister's wrap. She looked like someone out of the Czar's court, an imperial old lady in severe black, a handful of feathers, and a gathering of diamonds at her throat. But this time there was no gold jigger or jaunty cigarette holder, she looked tired and had a deep, racking cough.

Jay, a worried little man in an old-fashioned tux, protested, "She shouldn't be out. An old woman with a bad cold socializing?"

"We promised Stuart," she said stubbornly.

"Suppose I put the two of you at the end of the dais?" I proposed. "In that way you can slip out anytime you want."

"Good. Good. Jay, go get us a drink."

He gave her an indignant look and left.

"Where can we talk?" she said.

"There's a room across the lobby we used for interviews."

I ushered her into the room now littered with plastic cocktail glasses and overflowing ashtrays.

"This is something you should know," she said, "the mayor's going to announce he'll run."

"Tonight? At the dinner?"

"So I understand."

"That son of a bitch!"

"Why get excited, Trevor? They're all alike."

"Why the hell did he pick tonight?"

"Could he pick a better time? Look at the people here. He has a perfect audience."

"How did you find out, Madam?"

"What's the difference? I found out, that's all."

I started for the door. "I'd better tell Stu."

"Will it stop anything? Why make him upset?" She stifled a cough with her handkerchief. "Maybe it's not all that bad."

"But this is one thing he didn't want, Madam—"

"Tell me," she said, "you're a newspaperman. Won't this give us more publicity? Isn't that what we want, to let the people know?"

"There's no doubt we'll get the publicity but it's the politics Stu is trying to avoid."

And then with a smile she repeated Brigadier:

"Everything in this city is politics, my dear young Trevor, even dinners like this. You have to live with it." She slipped her arm into mine. "Now take me to the reception."

On the way I gave her a brief description of my luncheon with Miles. "I think the guy's bad news. Stu was wondering if we should ask Fitzgerald for someone else to deal with."

"And start the problems?"

"How about Derby? Have you heard anything more about him running?"

"He's going to run," she said flatly.

"How do you know this?"

"How do I know this? How do I know that?" she said impatiently.

106

"I'm a businesswoman, young man. I see people. I sell to them. I buy from them. They tell me things. Politicians need money. The people who are my friends have money. Is it such a mystery?"

The reception room was emptying when we arrived. The mayor and his frowning police commissioner were about to enter the ballroom when Kerr spotted us. He waved and hurried across the room.

"Already he's starting to campaign," Madam Langford observed dryly.

It was the most elaborate dinner in the history of the Eldorado. I know Stu had warned his banquet manager that if the food and his staff weren't the best there would be a job open. As far as I was concerned the dinner was superb and flawlessly served.

Looking back I realize how Stu had become consumed with the idea of devoting not only the dinner but the entire league to the memory of his father. Over the dais hung a silken banner proclaiming the Five Boro Anti-Narcotics League with his father's portrait in gold thread, while the menus bore the same picture. Also at every plate was a booklet printed in letter press and on heavy coated stock which I knew must have cost a fortune, containing a capsule biography of the senior Harlow and describing his dream of a private citywide organization which would rouse the communities and end the plague of narcotic addiction in the city he loved so deeply. All I had done was copyread the galleys. Stu had written it with an intense devotion, evident in every line.

He had planned and worked on the dinner for months—I suspected long before I arrived—and it was obvious he intended the glittering affair as a posthumous triumph for his father. I comforted myself with the thought that even if he was startled and dismayed by Kerr's announcement, the afterglow of the evening would not be diminished.

I was glad we had agreed that I would sit at one of the press tables; I was sure my uneasiness would have been apparent on the dias, which literally overflowed with celebrities. Stu was in the center flanked by the mayor and his police commissioner on one side and on the other by Derby and Brigadier. Betsy was seated next to Miles. I had changed the Langfords' seats to the end and sent a note up to Stu explaining why. Star, Rudy, and Tom were posted about the hall as sort of troubleshooters; even Rudy, a solemn giant in a tux that threatened to burst its seams, seemed awed by the dazzling evening.

Dessert was finally brought in, coffee cups were pushed aside, a haze of cigarette and cigar smoke began to rise above the hall, there was a stirring on the dais as the microphone was adjusted, then a beaming George Horatio Derby took over.

He was an excellent MC and I was glad he had volunteered. He knew enough inside political jokes for his introductions to produce constant waves of laughter while his definition of the league's purposes, its aims and hopes as set forth by Stu's father, was grave and impressive; in fact he managed to sound like Moses revealing God's laws.

It was obvious that Derby's disclosure of the mayor's drug report had startled both press tables.

Stu's speech was brief, pointed, and sincere. Again I had nothing to do with it, he had written it himself. Then came the mayor, the keynote speaker of the evening. There was no doubt the guy had charisma, and they gave him a good reception. I sat on the edge of the chair and waited.

The mayor said what was expected of him, he recalled his long friendship with the Harlows and the place they occupied in the business leadership of the city. The league, he promised, would have the city's complete cooperation—then he sprung a surprise—and if the league proved to be successful he would seek to support it with municipal funds as a permanent part of the city's drug-fighting facilities. Of course it was unadulterated crap; he had as much chance of getting the city council to vote funds for a nonmunicipal organization as I had of becoming president.

Mr. Collar Ad also had a keen sense of timing and drama. One of his efficient young aides suddenly appeared with a large package wrapped in tissue paper. Kerr, smiling, slowly unwrapped the package to reveal a large handsome plaque. As he told Stu, it was a humble tribute from the city to the memory of his father for the great work he had done in civic and business affairs.

It was a clever coup for what was coming.

I could see Stu had been caught off guard but looked pleased. It was then Kerr kicked over his political landmine.

"I hope," he said slowly, emphasizing each word, "that I can work with all of you at City Hall combating this dreadful peril during the next four years to come."

A moment of stunned silence was followed by wild applause. One of the reporters said, "Hey! That's his announcement," and with the others rushed to the dais. TV crews hurried forward with their gear and reporters thrust their mikes up to the mayor.

"Well, he's going to run," my old reporter friend said.

"Did you have a hint of it?" I asked.

"The guys in Room Nine said there's been something cooking for the last few weeks. I think he was just waiting for the right time." His wave took in the huge audience. "And what would be better than this?" He got up and slapped me on the back. "I'll see you around, Trev. Kerr's announcement and that drug report will probably put you on page one tomorrow."

I waved good-bye, but my attention was on Derby. He just sat there staring at his folded hands. Once Brigadier leaned over and said something but he didn't answer. Betsy got up, called out to him, and when he ignored her she left the dais. Inspector Miles, I noted, was gone.

There wasn't any need to close the dinner formally, it had broken

108

up into small groups with a crowd swirling after the mayor as he left the dais, surrounded by a group of reporters and TV crews. I made my way to Stu who was moving down the dais thanking his guests.

"Get them all together," he whispered.

"How about the room where we had the interviews?"

"Fine. But get them before they leave."

I told Tom to see if the Langfords were still in the hotel, while I searched for Derby and Brigadier. I found them in the deserted reception room talking to a short stocky man I recognized as the Queens leader. They broke off their conversation when I appeared and did not bother to introduce me.

"Stu would like to see both of you before you go," I told them. "He'll be in the room where we held the interviews."

They nodded silently.

The mayor and Fitzgerald were hemmed in a corner, surrounded by the press. Both were being interviewed on the committee's drug report and Kerr on his announcement and plans. When he saw me he waved and I pointed to the lobby. Then Tom told me the Langfords had left early.

Kerr, Fitzgerald, Derby, and Brigadier finally joined us in the pressroom.

There were no amenities. As soon as the door closed Derby said harshly, "I thought there wasn't going to be any politics?"

Stu looked at Kerr. "That's what I thought."

"Oh, I heard George was going to make his own announcement tonight," Kerr said easily, "and I thought it would be nice if we did it together."

The blood mounted in Derby's face. "I had no intention of making my announcement."

"Then I guess someone misunderstood you, George," Kerr said calmly. He turned to Stu. "He had a meeting a few days ago and told some people he would have an important announcement to make tonight." He smiled at Derby. "Right, George?"

Derby's voice rose. "Goddammit! I told you I had no plans to make any announcement!"

"Then the only reason is you didn't get what you hoped to get at that meeting."

"All that is none of your business," Derby shouted. He turned to Stu. "Didn't you tell me there wouldn't be anything political about this thing?"

Kerr gave him an amused look.

"Do you deny that you want to run for the mayoralty, George?"

Stu broke in. "It's none of my business what you or George plan to do. But dammit, the last thing I want is to get the league involved in politics!"

"And you used it tonight as a political forum," Derby intoned. "It's a disgrace, what you did!"

Kerr ignored him.

"I think the league had a fine beginning tonight, Stu. You're going to get all the cooperation you need from us. I intend to make that clear at my press conference tomorrow."

"I instructed Inspector Miles to be in touch with you," Fitzgerald put in.

Kerr glanced at his watch.

"Well, tomorrow's a busy day. Goodnight, gentlemen . . ."

In a moment he was gone.

I had the strange feeling that the threads of this newborn organization were slipping through our fingers.

"That son of a bitch!" Derby burst out.

"Oh, knock it off, for Christ's sake," Stu said wearily, "it's over and done with. Let's get on with the business."

"Yeah. Tomorrow you won't find a line about us, it'll be all City Hall."

"No it won't," I said. "We'll get space—maybe more than we thought."

"The next thing is to meet Miles and work things out," Stu said. "Call him tomorrow, Trev." He turned to Derby. "George, are you going to run for the mayoralty?"

"I haven't decided."

"When you do will you let us know?" Stu asked.

"I feel like resigning now," Derby said. "I think I've been had—"

"Don't be a damn fool," I told him. "Do you know what would happen?"

"Suppose you tell me."

"Kerr's people will leak a story he outmaneuvered you, so you picked up your marbles and ran home. It won't look good in the political columns."

"Forget it, George," Brigadier said, patting him on the back.

"Why don't you, George?" Stu said. "You'll get your licks in."

Apparently my warning had sunk in and he nodded sullenly.

"Okay. Let's forget it. What's next?"

"Trev will meet with the cops and we'll start rolling."

"When do you want to meet?"

"We'll be in touch."

I guess there's nothing so desolate as a ballroom after the last guest has gone. The stripped tables, waiters hurrying off with armloads of linen, busboys wheeling away the last of the china, maintenance men unhooking the mike and podium, electricians dimming the lights, the stale smell of smoke and the squad of elderly cleaning women waiting on the perimeter to launch their shuffling attack with vacuum cleaners, mops and pails. We took a table in the corner and ordered drinks.

110

"How do you like that guy?" Stu asked as he placed the heavy plaque on a chair.

"As Madam Langford said, you just can't trust any of them," I said.

"I didn't get a chance to talk to the Langfords. What did the old lady have to say?"

"I met her when she came in. She told me the mayor was going to make his announcement."

Stu gave me a look of surprise.

"Why the hell didn't you tip me off?"

"She said not to, it wouldn't change anything."

"What else did she have to say?"

"Derby's running. I guess, as Miles said, it's all a question of money."

"How does that old woman get all this inside stuff?" Tom asked.

"She knows more people in this town than any ten politicians." Stu replied. "I believe Kerr, don't you, Trev?"

"I do. I think Derby told some people he was going to make his announcement tonight, but he had to change his mind because he didn't get the dough he needs."

"Can you imagine the two of them making their announcements at the same time?"

"Politically it would be stupid and they're not stupid. I think Kerr got wind of what happened and beat Derby to the draw."

"I couldn't care less what they do," Stu said. "All I want is politics left out of the league. Once you get tarred with that brush no one will take you seriously. That always worried my father."

"At least we control the PR . . . I'll make sure every handout goes through me."

"I wondered why the old lady insisted you handle the publicity," Stu mused. "You must have an honest face, Trev."

"I spark the mother instinct."

Tom pointed to the plaque. "It's a beauty, Stu."

"I guess that was to make it go down easy."

"All in all, it was a terrific evening. Couldn't have been better."

"Best time I ever had, Major," Rudy boomed. He nudged Star. "How about you, Injun?"

Star nodded. "Great, Major. Real great."

Because we knew how much it meant, we wanted to please him so we reviewed the evening while he smiled and studied the heavy bronze shield with the bas-relief portrait of his father.

When the conversation died down we were like backers of a play waiting for the notices. When a bellboy appeared with a bundle of the morning papers from the hotel's newsstand, we each grabbed a copy. Rudy let out a yell and held up the split page of the tabloid. There were two pictures, one of Stu, the mayor, and the police commissioner standing under the big banner and another of a pretty young actress holding up one of the placards we had made up. The paper had obviously replated its first edition to make the mayor's announcement, but while the dinner was only briefly mentioned as to where it had taken place, there was a story on page three about the league and the mayor's report on the new drug scene. The *Times* had split their stories; we were mentioned in the page one story above the fold, with a long side bar on the jump which described the league, its origin, and purposes, along with a two-column cut of Stu receiving the plaque from the mayor.

All in all, good coverage.

"This is great, Trev," an enthusiastic Stu told me. "Now we're off and running!"

Chapter **6**

Sam Hoffman-
Kate's Call

After the call from Kate, Arnie and I flew down to Washington the next day. No train, this time I couldn't wait to reach D.C. I thought I was going to scoop up some big inside information and get back to the city in time to make the mayor's dinner. Forget it. I had forgotten my number one rule—never but never depend on a chick in any investigation. Somehow there's always a foul-up.

At ten minutes after nine I was on the phone with Kate's office. But instead of Kate a strange voice answered her extension to tell me Kate would not be in, her mother had had a stroke during the night and she had rushed home.

When would she be back? Indefinite.

I left my name and hotel number and looked up Chickie McCarthy while Arnie met his CIA contact.

After dinner Chickie took me down to his rec room where he turned up the TV, led me into a small laundry, turned on the dryer, and closed the door.

"Who's going to listen, Chickie? Your kid?"

"Look, this makes me nervous, Sam."

"Why nervous? You haven't told me anything."

"You know that agent?"

"The one who gave you the stuff last time?"

"Yeah. That one. He's just back from New York and we had a few drinks. The bastard's got a hollow leg and never springs."

I knew this was a pitch for how hard he worked for me and how much cash he put out.

"So you had some drinks—"

"Okay. Not so fast. We kept talking and talking and finally I asked him what was doing in New York? He was getting stiff by this time and he started complaining about the guy he works for and how stupid he was."

"Did he tell you anything?"

"Yeah. Yeah. Take it easy, willya? What I got out of him was that a big load of junk came in and started to hit the streets a couple of weeks ago. Jack, that's his name, said they estimated maybe a hundred pounds of smack and forty-five pounds of coke."

"How good?"

"The best. Jack said they busted a place that had pure gold. Uncut. Right from Indochina. It gave them an idea of what was around."

"Any estimate of the load?"

"Ten mil." He looked triumphant. "And that's not all, baby."

"Well, come on—give."

He lowered his voice. "Since the load came in there's been two ODs. Kids. Jack said the kids just starting to shoot up can't handle this pure stuff. One kid's from Staten Island—the other one is from Queens. They're both about twelve."

"How about the strike force—are they getting anywhere?"

"Nothing. Jack said they're going nuts down there. The pressure is starting to build up from here."

"Are they working with the cops?"

"Not any more than they can help. It's all single-o. They made the medical examiner list the postmortems as incomplete so the cops wouldn't get a report."

"Anything else?"

He gave me an indignant look.

"What the hell more do you want?"

"Okay, Chickie. That's good stuff. My man will eat it up. Why don't you go upstairs?"

"Thanks, Sam."

114

"Will you be seeing this guy again?"

"He comes in every few weeks. I'm his drinking buddy now, so he'll give me a call."

"Will you let me know if you have anything?"

He solemnly raised his right hand.

"Thanks, Chickie. I'll see you upstairs."

I put a wad in his kid's dollhouse and flushed the toilet as an excuse for lingering, then joined Chickie and his wife.

The next day I called my contact in the New York ME's office and asked him to check out the information I had that two kids had been brought in, ODs. He knew that after every telephone call he received an envelope with a fifty-dollar bill, so the affairs of the city waited while he worked for me. A few hours later when I called him back he had the information; the postmortems on two black kids, one twelve, the other fourteen, were listed as incomplete. And what did that mean?

"They're waiting for the toxicologist's report."

"Could it be OD?"

"No doubt."

"Why are they listing the PM as incomplete?"

"The medical examiner is only accommodating the feds," was his reply. He promised to get in touch with me when the full report came down and I told him it was a good idea to watch his mail. I like to leave my contacts happy.

A few days later I read a telephone note I had just received from the desk clerk:

"Kate called. 3:40 P.M. She is back in town and would like you to call her as soon as possible."

I didn't bother to return to the room but called her from the lobby.

She sounded low and melancholy and I promised to be over as fast as a cab could get me to Georgetown. She was waiting at the door, her eyes brimming with tears, just yearning to be comforted. That's what I did for the rest of the night. I was so considerate I didn't bring up my favorite subject until we were having breakfast. Then she got out her shorthand notebook and read me what she had. It was dynamite. What she had copied were messages between the strike force in New York and the main headquarters in Washington, summaries of telephone conversations, yellow sheet requests, confidential reports from its own agents, the Brigade Criminelle of the Police Judiciaire in Paris, Scotland Yard, and various out of town and out of country police intelligence units.

Kate read for a long time and I wrote until I had a cramped hand. As she explained she had come back early in the afternoon to find her boss in conference in New York. The girl who had filled in for her returned to her own office, so Kate had the afternoon to rummage through the files and copy what she thought was interesting.

115

I was only too happy to drop her off at the Department of Justice Building and get back to the hotel where I hired a typewriter and put the notes into some kind of sequence.

Before I begin I would like to emphasize one fact: the Mafia, Cosa Nostra, Confederation, Organization, or whatever you want to call it does not issue an annual report describing its profits and losses and projection to be published in the end-of-the-year Business Section of *The New York Times*. The stuff Kate had taken from the files was actually bits and pieces dug out of the underworld at great risk, many man hours and the expenditure of a large amount of government money. It had been refined, analyzed, assessed, and gone over by the world's best experts on crime, so that a picture, even if vague and shadowy, could be formed.

Put the material in that perspective and this is what came out of my typewriter:

By the time the war in Nam was in sight, the heads of the various Families of organized crime in the United States had been badly shattered by the series of arrests of its top men, inner betrayals, and extensive grand jury investigations conducted on the east and west coasts. However, while they were at their lowest ebb, they were still a dominant factor in the structure of American crime. It would take at least another generation of constant harassment by the law, using every facility at its command, to completely erase the influence of the Families, many solidly entrenched in local or national politics and in established business firms including Wall Street. Yet for the first time since the Mafia took over the New Orleans waterfront in the 1880s its foundation was crumbling.

This realistic picture did not belong exclusively to the government. The elder Dons—the crime families' traditional leaders—were trying to do something about it when the war in Vietnam finally ground down.

A number of interoffice messages incorporated a great deal of underworld gossip and meeting with stool pigeons but what gradually came through to me was the struggle between federal agents and the shrewd underworld bosses; the hoods desperately needed to hold another Apalachin-type meeting without the law bugging their rooms or copying down their license plate numbers, while the feds were just as determined to keep every known mobster under the closest scrutiny to prevent such a meeting.

Sometime in the winter of 1972 messages began to fly back and forth between Washington and New York that a conference of major criminals in the States and a few from overseas would be held at a ski hotel in western Canada. Then in the week of the supposed meeting the messages from Canada had a puzzled air; a few minor criminals had appeared but they weren't exactly keeping in the shadows; in fact they were seen at the bar and in restaurants.

116

I could almost hear the sigh of relief when a flurry of phone calls placed by the force agents from the cooperating Royal Mounted Police's Intelligence Bureau alerted New York and Washington that several important *caporegima*, or underbosses, had arrived with their bodyguards and finally the top man, the *consigliere*, or counselor, was on hand.

Terse messages reported to D.C. that plans had been completed for the raid, photographs were on their way for identification, rooms had been bugged. Then came private dinner and the raid: it was a disaster. The hoods they grabbed were second string and they couldn't find either the underbosses or the consigliere. Alarms that went out alerted the border patrol who of course notified their headquarters in Washington. Queries hit the strike force headquarters from all sides and they had to reveal what they were doing. Soon everyone was in the act.

The New York County district attorney's office finally came up with the answer to the puzzle; a DA's investigator recalled that one of the arrested hoods had worked for a makeup department in a TV station before he was made manager of a chain of mob-operated porno massage parlors. After they were closed he became a shylock in the theatrical district. Apparently he was also an amateur artist; once when he was arrested by this investigator he had proudly given him a portrait he had sketched while waiting arraignment in night court.

This information was sent to Canada. The agents quickly found his makeup kit, wigs, putty noses and moustaches hidden in the trunk of a car. The furious embarrassed agents and their red-coated buddies were not only forced to admit they had been outwitted but had to release the gangsters for lack of evidence. The best they got was a deportation order. The hoods were delighted; the Mounties had to drive them over a hundred miles to the border during a raging blizzard to fulfill the court's order to officially escort them through customs.

It was clear, as one report put it, that this clever diversionary move had allowed the heads of America's organized crime, and perhaps their overseas partners, to hold a meeting somewhere in the United States at which an entirely new agenda of activities had been adopted. The material also gave me an insight into the bitter feuds and interagency rivalry that existed between law enforcement groups after Watergate, principally in Washington and New York but also in many other states. The reason for this official suspicion was this: the details of Watergate had demonstrated to all law enforcement agencies the danger of alien ears listening to wiretaps or the indiscriminate distribution of confidential surveillance reports. Gangsters have an affinity for tossing around names of politicians, and a detective or investigator shadowing a suspect might find him lunching or dining with a well-known businessman, powerful legislator, judge, or senator. For self-protection he might include the information in a report that his superiors would make sure never saw the light of day. However, if these reports were inadvertently or mistakenly loaned to another law body and the incriminating political dynamite came out or found its way to a political opponent, scapegoats would be found and dismissed, superiors broken, and promotions delayed indefinitely.

From the transfers and turnovers discussed in one report, the Canadian comedy had terrific reverberations; everyone was scampering all over the place. I felt sorry for the guy who had been in charge of the Canadian group; he probably found himself counting reindeer in Alaska. . . .

Months were devoted to recovering lost ground, of trying to find out where the real meeting had taken place, who was there, and what had been accomplished. A tremendous task and the reason is this:

As any veteran detective on a fair-sized urban police force is quick to agree, hard work, intelligence, common sense, and manpower are necessary for any important investigation into organized crime but what he may not readily admit is the importance of his informers. Believe me, stoolies are a crafty breed, slimy as eels and deadly as cobras. There is no such thing as a stand-up stool pigeon, they're like glass under a torch, they bend at the slightest pressure and will sell out to the highest bidder. The only oath they recognize is the Tammany Hall Oath—the one you take with your right hand solemnly raised and your left behind you, palm out. Their language is the whispered doubletalk, and it takes an expert to separate the wheat from the chaff; nine out of ten times it's mostly chaff. Yet they are important to any law enforcement organization, from the smallest police force to the army of FBI agents; they are a pipeline, a conduit for information. A squad working together can milk its stable of stoolies and from the gossip, lies, rumors—sometimes purposely planted by the mob leaders to flush them out—experienced lawmen can put together the kernels of truth to form the picture I spoke about earlier.

The finest source of information in an investigation is the ordinary citizen who finds himself in a unique position to funnel facts to the law. They are rare—one reason is guts. I hate to say it but a good number of our citizens just don't have the courage or the motivation to take this chance.

The next best informer is someone on the periphery of the underworld who is willing to trade a favor for a favor. Any detective or agent is jubilant when he can make this kind of deal. From the summaries of the phone calls and reports which flowed through the New York and Washington offices during the winter, the federal agents believed they had made a big score when they called on a maid who worked for an independent and pretty call girl named Susan Dennison, who from the feds' description could be classed as the Tiffany of Manhattan's whores.

Her customers came from Hollywood, Wall Street, the theatre, even the opera, but the agents were interested in an old-time racketeer who was devoting all his free time begging Suzy to split from the racket and entertain him exclusively. He was identified only as "Stash."

What did the agents have on her maid? Her brother was up for parole and they put it on the line—either let them into the apartment so they could bug the bedroom—the hustler was too smart to use a phone for business—or her brother would rot in prison. She agreed and a bug was placed in the bed. Summaries of the tapes were fascinating. Not only was this Stash an elderly guy with enormous sexual prowess but he was a great *tummler.*

Every time he went *shlepping* uptown to the whore's layout he told her a new story. A lot was melodramatic fantasy to impress her but there was enough underworld gossip to help the feds reconstruct that secret underworld meeting.

They confirmed the Families were back into junk, stronger than ever, but instead of eliminating the "spics" and "niggers" who had moved into the vacuum after organized crime abandoned narcotics in the 1960s, they were making deals, offering concessions, so to speak. Those who tried to continue to operate independently were quickly eliminated.

When I came to the series of summaries which had to do with the meeting and its purpose, I became so excited my hunt and peck system had a hard time keeping up.

It was agreed the meeting of the top men was held somewhere on the east coast in a restaurant which featured a cocktail lounge fashioned like a western-style stagecoach.

The owner was in debt to a bookie who in turn was owned by a loan shark who was financed by a *capo* in one of the Families. The owner was ordered to close his place, contracting trucks were parked outside, scaffolding was erected and workmen started to make "alterations." The nervous owner provided the place, the food, and the liquor and in return the bookie returned his markers, the bookie got a bonus from his shark, who in turn was allowed to keep all he could collect in a month. The baseball bats that must have been used!

The two-day conference was attended by the recognized leaders of America's organized crime on the east and west coasts and their international contacts. What made this meeting more important than any Apalachin was the adoption of a new goal: the organized Families would return to the smuggling and selling of drugs in the United States for a period of two years. At the end of that time another meeting would be held to decide if the venture had been profitable enough to continue.

One man was selected to head the new syndicate and he was entrusted with a staggering amount of money to finance it.

The most terrifying aspect of the plan had to do with the potential customers—

Kids.

This was the new agenda—the smuggling and distribution of illegal drugs, chiefly heroin, throughout the United States to juveniles everywhere. No ID card necessary, only the few bucks for a bag.

Apparently at the height of the feds' investigation, the mobster named Stash was either tipped by his suspicious whore or by the frightened maid who tried to walk both sides of the street. The agents following him lost their tail when he went out the back entrance of the building. This was a ball game in which you couldn't make a mistake; both agents were transferred to Montana. Stash disappeared and a short time later the whore left for a trip to Paris while the maid stoutly denied she had betrayed the government.

The big question was still left unanswered—who was the leader of this new syndicate?

To try and get the answer I saw Kate every night, met her when she had finished work, took her to dinner or had it by candlelight in her apartment, suffered through more concerts and prowled through more antique shops than I care to remember—and slept over. For a mousy little chick who looked like Louisa May Alcott, she certainly was a terror in bed; Leah would just have to wait until I recuperated. . . .

Twice Kate's boss went to New York for conferences but did not take her along. Each time on his return he held a closed meeting with his assistants. I began to get nervous that perhaps they suspected Kate but she assured me there was no reason for alarm—it usually happened when they received highly classified material from other agencies, especially European. It turned out the Paris Brigade Criminelle of the Police Judiciaire was reporting that the New York whore appeared to be only on a shopping trip.

Kate tried her best but nowhere in the files was the name of the new syndicate leader. It was clear he was still a mystery man to both the federal strike force and New York police. After ten days of this furious business I crawled back to the hotel; that's where Arnie found me in the afternoon, sleeping on the bed.

"Hey, you look like you just spent a day in the Snakepit!" He pointed to the typewriter. "What's this for?"

"I've been typing up the stuff I got from Kate."

"Any good?"

"Sensational. It's down in a safety deposit box."

After I got my notes and the résumé of fifty single-spaced typewritten pages, we found a park bench and I read it to Arnie. He had also been working and dug out scraps of paper, torn menus, even napkins which he used to make notes. As he explained, the best way to make an agent, even a friend, clam up is to bring out a pencil.

What Arnie had was more on the Indochina operation. It went like this:

Two generals from Chiang Kai-shek's old 93rd Kuomintang Army who had fled to Thai from the mainland in 1949 had taken over the

Indochina drug trade. Arnie's friend had told him they were now running an army, mostly criminals and deserters from Burma, who were armed with M-16s, grenade launchers, and mortars—supplied by the Chinese just across the border or stolen from the American ammo dumps left behind for the Saigon government. They had also established several large cutting factories and warehouses on the outskirts of Tachilek on the Thai and Laotian borders.

Arnie's friend said that before he left it was obvious the Chinese generals were paying large bribes because the Thai narco cops suddenly lost interest in making arrests, conducting investigations, or following leads developed by the American agents. They ignored mule and packhorse caravans winding their way to the coast where Thai trawlers took the cargoes to South Vietnam and Hong Kong. It appeared Arnie had made a good guess at our first penthouse meeting; the junk was refined in factories in or around Marseilles, then turned over to representatives of the Union Corse who took it to their headquarters near Ajaccio, capital of Corsica.

The agent said what really concerned them was the appearance of a new American syndicate, well financed and professional, who arranged to smuggle the junk into the United States. They used two methods: small planes from Mexico flying so low the Border Patrol's radar could not pick them up, or using boats along the 1,500-mile Canadian border between Erie, Pennsylvania, and the Maine coast. Arnie drew a crude map to demonstrate why the risk was small, there were scores of waterways, more than a hundred unguarded border roads and countless unknown or abandoned airstrips in the desert.

"Did he have any names?"

"Plenty—in Indochina."

"How about over here?"

He hesitated. "It's only an instinct, but I think the Agency knows the name of the guy who is heading this new syndicate."

"Did you ask him?"

"Sure I did."

"And what did he say?"

"He just smiled."

"Does that mean anything?"

"Could be. Maybe he wants something from me."

"What could you give him, Arnie?"

He shook his head. "I haven't the faintest idea, Sam."

He studied some notes scrawled on the margin of a newspaper.

"I got this out of another guy who works for Customs. I have a hunch all this stuff ties in with the same mob. A couple of months ago a border patrol pilot spotted this plane coming in low through the mountain passes. He contacted his base and was told to follow it to a strip or airport and keep in close contact. It was getting dark and the other plane wasn't using running lights. The pilot thought he had lost the plane when suddenly he spotted a strip outlined by flares. He contacted the base and they told him they were following him on the scope and had alerted other border patrol planes and the highway police. Evidently the other pilot spotted him because he went in for a landing. Apparently he was an amateur, he overshot the strip, flipped over and crashed.

"The government pilot went in low and saw a car shoot out of the darkness. Three guys ran to the plane. Two came back to the car carrying some packages. In a minute the third guy joined them. As they drove off, the plane burst into flame, then exploded. When the highway police and Customs reached the plane it was a pile of coals.

"They traced the tracks of an ATC on the highway where it was probably driven onto a trailer."

"Did they ever find out what happened to the pilot?"

"He was skeletonized. The cops said one leg had been caught in the wreckage."

"So he never had a chance?"

"Well, he never had a chance when those guys from the car ran up to him . . ."

"Couldn't they get him out?"

Arnie folded his notes and carefully put them in his wallet.

"The coroner said he had been shot in the head."

"Jesus! They couldn't get the guy out so they shot him!"

"Like I said, this is a tough mob . . ."

A few hours later we checked out and returned to New York to report to the major.

Chapter **7**

Trevor David-Toni

The league was a failure. Sure, we had agreed it could not succeed, but secretly I hoped we would be proven wrong. After all it was a viable concept—a five-borough civic organization supported by City Hall, the police, politicians, and community leaders not only dedicated to get the pushers off the streets but willing to pay five thousand dollars for legitimate information which would lead to their arrest and conviction.

God knows we all did our best; Star, Rudy, and Tom monitored their telephones twenty-four hours a day, seven days a week, with Spanish-speaking volunteers standing by. Sam and Arnie were still gumshoeing in Washington, while I tramped about the city distributing handouts to newspapers, TV stations, wire services, magazines, even out-of-town media, in addition to setting up interviews, writing speeches, and overlooking the advertising copy. And Stu? He put out both energy and money.

We had an impressive beginning: a full-page ad in the afternoon and morning newspapers—I cringed at the bill—and continuous spots on radio and television. We had rallies in neighborhoods, put sound trucks in the neighborhood of schools, joined street people theatres, distributed placards, even got graffiti "art" groups to spread our plea. During those first few weeks the phones never stopped ringing, and we happily turned the information over to detectives assigned to us by Miles only to watch it vanish into the machinery of the police and the law. In six months we spent over fifty thousand dollars, not counting our salaries, maintaining the telephone and mail service and bringing the league before the public. The peak of the calls was about a hundred a day, but gradually fell to twenty or less. Not all were about narcotics, some were from the mentally disturbed, cranks, and the city's army of the anonymous lonely who only want to talk. Out of the thousands of calls only a few hundred "referrals," as the police called them, were turned over to the narcotics bureau. In a report to the mayor, Police Commissioner Fitzgerald described fifty to sixty percent as "meaningful." He also noted no arrests or convictions had resulted from the league's activities, pointing out the information was usually incomplete and confined to "low level" or pusher addicts. Nonetheless he warmly praised the league and called it "very useful to the police in their untiring struggle to eliminate the drug problem from this city."

In one of our meetings Fitzgerald, frowning more deeply than ever, insisted that the "referrals" would require considerable investigation to make them "productive."

Of course the old days of busting in doors without a warrant because some stoolie tipped a cop were over, but still I just couldn't reconcile the amount of good material we had given the police and the lack of arrests. Fitzgerald insisted Miles was doing his best but the reports he showed us were only progress sheets telling how hard the narcs were working. But Miles gave damn little detail. I was wondering if we were slowly being pushed into the center of a political battleground.

Miles was also curiously unavailable. He had been extremely friendly after our initial luncheon, but as the weeks passed I had difficulty in getting him. Fitzgerald seemed puzzled when I told him this; Inspector Miles, he said, "always has an open door."

Perhaps, I told him, but nobody's inside. . . .

Now our phones began to ring for a new reason; where was our money? informers demanded. They were patiently told that each case was being judged on its own merits but all we got were curses and accusations. The mail was about the same.

I also sensed the media had become weary of us, we were do-gooders without news. Politicians are particularly sensitive as to what the press wants and when their antennae warned them we were no longer the "in" people, they became bored. It was a chain reaction, even reaching the cop who answered the phone in the narcotics bureau; from a fawning buddy he turned into a surly, impatient bastard.

It was clear to me that Kerr, a suave, shrewd politician, had welcomed the league as a dramatic setting for his announcement he would run again. The league wasn't a risk: if it produced, fine—it was his creation; if it failed, it died bravely and well. What was important he could boast it wasn't a burden to the taxpayers and had attracted good names. For Derby it was window dressing, a reason why he should appear on television or radio; he didn't have to mention politics, he was a concerned Lochinvar, girded to fight the dragon of narcotics threatening his beloved city.

The mayor's report? It had been issued from City Hall the day after the dinner, by coincidence and not by design, minutes before a major air disaster. After a few shocked editorials and follow-up stories, it was forgotten.

Frankly I was bewildered by this irrationality and by a violent changing world where even a plague that endangered the lives and future of its children was regarded as commonplace. How much of this chaos, cynicism, and daily assault could our society take? I was shocked to find myself once again considering the observation Stu had made on the day of our reunion that life in the Snakepit had been more vivid, more meaningful. Was the only solution either the demolition or complete devastation of this city, any city—our country?

At lunch one day Madam Langford answered my question with a question.

"Is it anyone's fault, Trevor?"

"The league is a flop, Madam."

"Isn't that what you and I and Stuart had agreed would happen?" she gently reminded me.

"I was hoping we were wrong. And dammit, we should be!"

She tapped a copy of our last report which she had just finished reading.

"But this shows we were right. We all know money is not the answer."

"Then what is?"

She silently held up her hands, palms out.

"There must be some solution."

"Yesterday's poor are today's middle class. When they get there, they move out. What remains? Those who can't make it. No more hope. In a cold water flat, my dear Trevor, you can smell despair. Is that what makes junkies? I don't know. But what I do know is this—there is more fear in this city than I have ever felt. And I have been around a long time, young man, a long time." She finished her tea. "So we leave that problem for the *meshugenehs* in City Hall."

A cough racked her slender body and her hand shook when she reached for a glass of water.

"Is that the same cold you had the night of the dinner, Madam?"

She sipped the water. "It's nothing."

"You should see about it." Then, half in jest, half-serious I asked her, "Tell me, Madam, just what the hell did you people do to this country while we were away?"

"What did we do?" she repeated slowly. "I wish I knew. But we did do something, didn't we? Perhaps we lost something—all of us. Pray God we find it again." She glanced at her wristwatch. "Now I must get back. Thank you for the lunch." She laughed. "The tuna fish salad was a disaster, but the company was divine."

"I always look forward to it, Madam. By the way, what's with Derby?"

She had started to get up but sat back.

"So what about him?"

"When is he going to make his big announcement?"

"To run for mayor in this town, my dear Trevor, you need a lot of money. He's asking but he's not getting."

"Why not?"

She shrugged. "Maybe money's tight."

I pressed, "Why, Madam?"

She arched her eyebrows in mock surprise. "My young friend is still the district attorney!"

"Money may be tight but that's not the whole answer."

"The businessmen in this town are not the bunch of dopes some politicians believe they are. Of course, a good part of what we hear is trash, gossip—sometimes vicious gossip—petty jealousy, outright lies. But many times there is truth, shocking truth. You listen to all this and you judge for yourself."

"Do some of these stories, gossip, or whatever you want to call them, have anything to do with Derby? Or Miles? If so, I think you should tell us, Madam. It's only fair. . . ."

For a moment she hesitated, and I thought she was about to tell me something but then she shook her head.

"Yesterday I heard something," she said. "It was a little thing that maybe could lead to something big." She held up her hand. "No, no, Mr. District Attorney, don't press me. I'm looking into it. If it is true I will tell you, if not"—she shrugged—"then it will be forgotten and no one will be hurt."

"May I call you, Madam?"

"No" she said firmly, "I will call *you*."

"Is this fact, Madam, or is it intuition?"

"Maybe a little of both," she said grimly. "I will know . . . maybe tomorrow, maybe in a week . . . who knows?" She patted my hand. "So be patient, my dear Trevor. Now I must go. Give Stuart our love and tell him if he needs money for his league to call us."

I put her in a cab and before the door closed she squeezed my hand.

"When you get as old as me, you know when the milk is watered and the sugar is sanded. Don't trust Derby, his wife, or Miles. They are up to no good."

The lunch left me depressed and my mood matched the sullen afternoon. About this time I usually met one or two detectives at the branch post office to pick up the league's mail. If there was anything they considered worthwhile, I would take it back to the hotel and give them a Xerox copy. Lately they had not been showing up and once when I called the narcotics bureau that surly sergeant abruptly told me to "mail it in."

This was too much, even the goddam cops were deserting us. After some hot words with the lieutenant who had been put in charge of our project, I told him to shit in his hat and punch it and slammed down the phone. A short time later a disgruntled plainclothesman appeared.

This afternoon there were no detectives, so I picked up the mail by myself. In a way I couldn't blame the cops, the haul was an unimpressive four letters and a flyer for car insurance. One crudely printed note identified a bartender who was running a gun-for-hire racket, another gave the address of a policy drop, a third enclosed a miniature Bible but the fourth, unsigned, was neatly typed on an index card. It read:

Dear Sir:
I have seen your ads on television offering a five thousand dollar reward for information leading to the arrest and conviction of any drug pusher or dealer. I believe I have such information. If you are interested please call this number, DRydock 4-1103 at exactly four o'clock on any day except Saturday or Sunday, and I will answer the phone. This is a public telephone and should it be busy please continue to call.

I reached for the phone to tell the narcs to pick up their stuff but something stopped me. I pushed the card to one side and started to read proofs of our next magazine issue. It wasn't any use, I couldn't concentrate, that damn card intrigued me.

Promptly at four I dialed the number, twice it was busy but on the third try it was picked up on the first ring.

"I am calling in reference to a card which was sent to a box number," I said very briskly. "Are you the writer?"

"Yes, I am."

It was a girl.

"Could we meet and discuss your information?"

"Would four o'clock tomorrow be convenient?"

"Fine. Where shall we meet?"

"Could you come here?"

"Where is here?"

"Oh, this is a luncheonette."

I intoned like the Archbishop of Canterbury, "Are you aware that it's a Class E felony to give false information in a bid to receive a reward?"

"I assure you there is no such intention," she said stiffly.

"Is this luncheonette crowded?"

"Yes, but we can go somewhere else if you wish."

"Are you a student?" I snapped.

A pause. "Yes . . ."

"I want to make sure you know what I'm talking about when I say it's a felony."

The voice was now indignant.

"I am not in the habit of doing this. If you think—"

"Okay," I said, interrupting her, "what's the address?"

"It's called Smitty's. It's directly across the street from the entrance to Bellevue on First Avenue."

"Who shall I ask for?"

"Toni. Can you describe yourself?"

"Nondescript."

She laughed and sounded a bit relieved.

"Don't worry," I assured her, "I'll find you."

Smitty's turned out to be a typical New York lunchroom, long and narrow with a counter on one side and booths on the other. It was crowded with two countermen calling out orders while a harried waitress hurried to serve her dishes. Some of the customers were young and wore white coats like butchers. For a moment I was puzzled then I remembered it was across from Bellevue—they were either doctors, interns, or med students.

"That's right," a soft voice beside me said, "most of us are medical students."

When I turned, I saw that she came up to my shoulder. Her thick black hair was drawn back in an old-fashioned bun and she wore those large fashionable glasses that always reminded me of World War I aviator's goggles. She should have looked like a prim schoolteacher but couldn't; she had a wide mouth, beautiful lips, and when she smiled I saw a dimple. Her short white coat had an NYU patch on one sleeve.

"I've been saving a booth back there," she said.

We slid into a rear booth and I pointed to her empty cup.

"Coffee?"

"No thank you." She bit her lower lip. "I suppose this place is too crowded—"

"I think so."

"Can you wait for about a half hour? I have a few things to do in the hospital . . ."

"Take your time. I'll be here."

She gave me a smile and slid out of the booth.

"Hey, Toni, what's happening?" a young guy in one of those smocks called out as she passed.

She waved and was gone.

I drank a cup of the colored dishwater they called coffee and decided to wait outside. I can't remember when I've been so impatient. I studied the dusty furniture in a nearby antique store until the owner began to eye me suspiciously, then I walked about the neighborhood. Finally I returned to Smitty's as Toni was crossing the street. There was a certain elegance about her, though she was wearing a simple dress and a raincoat.

Her hair, now loose, fell to her shoulders and the late afternoon sun, which had finally found a crack in the clouds, momentarily turned it to burnished copper. She wasn't wearing those ridiculous glasses which had hidden her marvelous dark eyes, large and expressive. The open raincoat revealed a model's figure. She was carrying an incredible number of books.

"I hope I haven't kept you waiting too long," she said.

"My God," I said taking her books, "do you take these home every night?"

"Every night," she said wearily. "I have to review the tests for juvenile rheumatoid arthritis—"

"It sounds grim."

"It's only grim when you see the little kids who have it." She added briskly, "Suppose we talk in the park?"

"Madison Square Park? I haven't been there in years."

"You sound like a southerner."

"Georgia. But I didn't think my accent showed anymore."

"Just a bit." She smiled. "It's nice. What part of Georgia?"

"Near a small town named Jonesboro." I told her about our farm and *Gone with the Wind*.

"I find history very exciting," she said.

"How about medicine?"

"Oh, that's my first love."

"Do you intend to go into general practice?"

"Pediatrics."

"You must love children."

"Of course."

The streets had become crowded and I took her arm as we made our way to Madison Avenue.

"How long do you have to go?"

"I'm in third year."

We reached the park and found a deserted bench.

"Let's introduce ourselves," I suggested. "I'm Trevor David."

"And I'm Antonia Angeli—Toni, please."

"Suppose you start from the beginning, Toni."

She took a deep breath. "Well, as I told you, I'm a medical student at NYU. I saw your ads on television—"

I suddenly decided I didn't want to continue on a park bench with this lovely creature.

"Look, Toni, I think it's silly holding our conference on a park bench. Why don't we have dinner?"

She pointed to the pile of books. "I'm a medical student, Mr. David—"

"Trevor."

"Trevor. One hour away from these books—"

"It's up to you. Obviously you have something you consider important enough to write us."

"Oh, it is important!" she protested. "Very important!"

Happily the street lights went on. "It's going to be dark soon. However, if you're married and have to get home—"

"Married! she said. "A third year medical student? This last month I haven't gone to bed before two."

"What will it take? Less than an hour? I know a nice quiet place a few blocks away."

Actually I didn't know a damn thing about the area, but while walking around I had spotted this restaurant, Boyd's Steak House. It looked clean, unimaginative, and had booths. I was surprised at the sense of relief I felt when she said she wasn't married.

"Boyd's probably has the best steak in town," I said as casually as I could. "Look at it this way, Toni. You have to eat anyway. When you get home that's one thing less you have to do before hitting the books."

"You know you're a very persuasive guy? Maybe Smitty's would be faster. We can get a sandwich."

"Jim Boyd would never forgive me," I said as I led her out of the park.

The place had booths but to my dismay the menu was exclusively Italian; meatballs, spaghetti, lasagna—you name it, they had it. No steak.

"It looks like your friend Jim Boyd must be part Italian," she observed dryly.

"It's the meat prices," I told her. "Do you know that sixty-eight percent of all New York restaurants have changed their menus because of inflation?"

"Very interesting," she said solemnly. "Of course you read that."

"*Wall Street Journal.* Column eight with a long jump."

"A jump?" she said quickly. "Isn't that a newspaper term?"

"Yes. It—"

"Oh, God, you're not a newspaperman, are you?" she said fearfully.

I underscored the word. "*Was.* A long time ago. Now I work with the league."

"Will you please tell me what you do?"

"Well, I take care of a great many details."

"And you have something to do with the letters people send in?"

"That's why I'm here."

"Do you have an arrangement with the police?"

From the very moment I met her I had decided that Miles's sullen narco cops would never meet her. She had to be completely protected.

"I make the recommendation as to what is to be turned over to the police."

"But you protect the identity of the person who gives the information?"

"Definitely. Of course the information we give to the police must be legitimate."

"Oh, I realize that," she said almost reverently.

I leaned over the table and became aware of a fragrance, her own, like the clover at home in the early morning dew.

"Look, Toni, there's no reason to be uptight."

"I keep asking myself what I'm doing here."

"Let's have a drink and talk about anything else in the world except narcotics."

"I wish I could," she whispered. "Oh, so much."

"What will you have?" I asked firmly. "How about a champagne cocktail?"

"Are you crazy?" At least she smiled. "May I have a daiquiri?"

"Right. He's famous for his daiquiris, you know."

"Jim Boyd," she said with a straight face.

"My friend and buddy."

It was good for a quiet laugh and she seemed to relax. The drinks came and I touched her glass.

"To you, Toni."

She shook her head. "To your league."

The spaghetti and meatballs was surprisingly good and Toni said her lasagna was excellent. Even the house wine was full bodied and tangy.

"It tastes like the stuff my father used to make when we were kids," she said. "The whole house smelled like a winery for weeks."

"Are your parents alive?"

She shook her head. "They're both dead. I live in Canarsie with my sister . . ."

We silently watched the waiter take our plates and serve us coffee.

". . . And I guess that's why I'm here."

"Why don't you start from the beginning."

"This makes me sound awfully stupid but actually I don't know where to begin!"

"It must be about narcotics."

"Yes."

"And you have information about a pusher?"

She waited until a couple passed.

"I think he's a dealer."

"And you know him?"

She hesitated. "He's my brother-in-law."

"Shall I continue throwing questions at you?"

"No. Let me try to tell you the story."

I reached out and gently squeezed her hand.

"Relax, Toni. It's not all that bad."

"Oh, pray God that it isn't!" She toyed with her wineglass. "After mother died six years ago, my sister, Teresa, married a man named Frank Cardillo. Our family was against the marriage and I know if my father had been alive it would never have happened."

"You say your family . . ."

"I have three brothers who own a trucking firm upstate. The four of us tried to persuade Teresa it was a bad choice but she's the youngest"—she shrugged—"and Frank was handsome and had money and cars—you know, the usual bit." She smiled. "I guess I never realized how strict my parents were with me. Teresa was thirteen when my father died. My brothers were away most of the time, I was at school and my mother couldn't handle her, so by the time she was in high school we were having our headaches. After my mother died she met Frank. They have two children now."

"Did you know anything about him?"

"A friend of one of my brothers said Frank had been in prison. He admitted it when I asked him but insisted it was only a teen-age thing, stealing a car."

"Was that true?"

"No. After they were married we found out he had a long record. Once he went to prison for shooting a man. I wanted to get the marriage annulled, but my brothers told me to mind my own business. They're typical second generation Italian males—in marriage a woman is a chattel, if a man beats her that is part of the contract. She stays home, takes care of the kids and, whenever he wants her to, joins him in bed."

"And you're not in favor of that arrangement?" I said jokingly.

She looked annoyed at my flippancy.

"I'm sorry. It was only a joke," I said.

"I'm not joking, Mr. David—"

"Trevor."

"This is deadly serious, Trevor. He's an animal. Last month he broke her nose and knocked out a tooth. In high school my sister could have been a model. Now she looks like a middle-aged woman."

"Didn't you call the police?"

"I wanted to, but my brothers kept warning me it was none of my business—it was between a man and his wife."

"Did you talk to Cardillo?"

"I did better than that," she said, "I moved in with them."

"Moved in with them? But you said he was an animal."

132

"Teresa is a sick woman. Last winter I spotted the symptoms, pale gums, listlessness, excessive thirst. I had her in for tests and they found slight anemia but also diabetes. The only reason I moved in was to help her. I don't have much time but I do what I can. The kids are darling but they run her ragged."

"How did this sit with Cardillo?"

"He still thinks he's God's gift to women and of course he began making passes. I called my brothers and they paid him a visit." Her eyes darkened. "He stopped making passes. But I guess he took it out on my sister . . ."

"What happened?"

"I was at an immunology and virology lecture one night, and when I came home Teresa was in bed. In the morning she complained of pains in her abdomen. Only then did I find out that he had come home drunk and beat and kicked her. Another thing I didn't know was that she was two months pregnant. She not only had a miscarriage but they found kidney damage. She was in bed for two weeks."

"My God, Toni, that guy should be arrested!"

"You don't do that in an Italian family," she said earnestly. "My brothers would disown me if I went to the police on a personal matter. They came down from upstate, but he insisted Teresa had fallen and of course she went along with that story." Her eyes brimmed with tears. "I feel terrible telling this to a stranger."

"I wish you wouldn't regard me as a stranger, Toni."

"You're very kind."

"Do you want to go on?"

"Of course." She dabbed at her eyes with her napkin. "I promise no more tears."

"I read an article once that claimed that sometimes tears are as good as medicine."

"*Wall Street Journal?*"

"No. *Ladies Home Journal.* I wrote the article, 'Tears and What the Alaskan Woman Does about Them.' Gloria Steinem denounced me as a chauvinistic polar bear."

"You really are sweet—Trev."

"You just made my night, Toni. If you want to continue . . ."

"This is the reason why I wrote to you. It's been on my mind for months. I can't sleep and my grades are suffering. I spoke to my brothers but as usual they warned me to mind my own business." There was iron in her voice. "Not this time." She hesitated, then said, "May I have some more coffee?"

"Of course."

After the coffee was served she continued.

"My sister has a large one-family house. There are three telephone extensions, one in the bedroom, one in the hall off the kitchen, and one in what Frank calls his office."

"Does he have a business?"

"He claims he works as a salesman for a steel company in Yonkers. He has stationery and business cards." She searched her purse and handed me a card. "This is one of them."

The card read: "Meridian Steel Company, Franklin and Bainbridge Avenues, Yonkers, N.Y. Specialists in Construction Steel."

"He once told me this company does a lot of work with racetracks and fairs."

"Does he know anything about steel?"

"I doubt it. But racetracks—yes. He bets heavily every day. Bookmakers are always calling him up."

"Please go on."

She took a sip of coffee. "Lately he's been drinking heavily. I suspect he's under some kind of tension. He also appears preoccupied and stays in his office a good deal, sometimes very late. One night I picked up the hall extension to make a call when I heard him talking to someone. He was discussing what he called 'a load' which had been delivered to a 'mill.' For a moment I thought he was talking about steel and was about to hang up when the other man started speaking. I knew this was no steel company executive. He was pure Brooklyn and it was soon plain they were talking about a shipment of drugs."

"Is that the only phone call you overheard?"

"No. There were several more. I would wait until he was drinking and then listen. My sister goes to bed with the kids and I'm always alone. Once he and this man discussed where they would meet someone who was bringing in a shipment from Arizona. There was some talk about a plane crash and something about the pilot. I couldn't get all of it."

"When do these calls come in?"

"Between eleven and midnight."

"Do you know if any come in during the day?"

"I'm sure they don't. Once Frank told this other man to make sure he called only at that time. He said he wanted to make sure there would be no interruption from Teresa or the kids."

"How about your sister? Does she know what her husband is doing?"

"I'm coming to that. When I first brought up the subject, Teresa became almost hysterical and begged me never to mention it again. I didn't but then she came to me confessing a little bit each time. I know she feels guilty about what's going on."

She took a piece of paper from her wallet.

"Before I wrote to you I put it all together."

"This is from the conversations you overheard?"

"And from what my sister told me. Apparently the drugs are taken to a warehouse on Water Street near the Williamsburg Bridge. Teresa said she thought it was next to a big auto junkyard. I found out she's right."

"You didn't go down there, Toni?"

134

"I had to convince myself. During the last San Gennaro feast I simply walked around the area. No one noticed me. There were many visitors." She spread a napkin out on the table and sketched a street. "The warehouse faces Water Street. The yard is directly behind it. On the corner is a sanitation garage. From what I can get out of Teresa, they cut the drugs on the top floor of the warehouse. I believe they are using quinine to ward off any malarial effects."

"Do they mention the warehouse in their conversations?"

"Yes. They both call it 'the warehouse' or 'the mill.' "

"Did you ever find out who Cardillo talks to?"

"From what I can gather his nickname is Stash. He has a harsh voice and sounds older than Frank. He's always warning Frank about drinking too much. It is very difficult to understand them. They talk in monosyllables—almost a code." She tapped the napkin. "There's something about the warehouse . . ."

"Oh? What's that?"

"Well, Frank boasts a lot to Teresa when he's drunk. One night he told her they had a way to escape if the police ever raid the place. He told her all they had to do was drop off the roof of the rear extension into the junkyard and get to three cars that are parked by the gate. Keys are on the sun visors and every day someone in the yard makes sure the cars are in running condition. But I'm sure the police have their own way of checking these things."

"Of course. Did Frank or Stash ever mention a pickup?"

"Once Frank said, 'The bird is flying in,' and Stash asked if it was a big one and Frank just grunted but that's the way they talk."

I held up her sheet of paper.

"It's dangerous to make notes like this, Toni. Please don't do it anymore."

"It's a habit, I guess. In med school notes are as important as food. But I realize it's stupid and it won't happen again."

"I can't believe you have all this information, Toni."

"It's been on my mind for months. I was first tempted to go to the police, but decided not to after I overheard something."

"What was that?"

"The man Stash asked about some policeman and Frank just laughed and said some of them are his partners. I realized that not every policeman you see is crooked but I decided I couldn't take the risk."

"Thank God, you didn't."

"For a moment when I picked up the phone yesterday and heard your voice I was tempted to hang up."

"That would have been a catastrophe."

"I must know one thing," she said.

"Anything. Just ask me."

"Am I doing what's right? Is this the best way? Or should I have gone perhaps to the FBI? I'm not sure. I keep asking myself—"

"Let me assure you, Toni, this is the best way. We are in direct communication with the police commissioner and the mayor. You can't go any higher."

"Now that I've told you I feel so exposed—he's a horrible man and I want to see him arrested, but I don't want anything to happen to my sister."

"Please believe me, nothing will happen to either you or your sister."

"I can take care of myself, it's Teresa I worry about."

I took both her hands in mind. They were slim, feminine, but strong.

"From now on you must leave everything to me."

"Please tell me, Trevor, if you think I'm making a mistake—"

"I repeat, this is the only way, Toni. Neither you nor your sister will be involved. It's a sure way to get him behind bars."

She glanced at her watch. "I really must go. I have all this reviewing to do tonight, then I have clinical rounds tomorrow at seven—"

"What's that?"

"Making the rounds with my chief in pediatrics."

"It's hard to believe you'll be a doctor in a few years."

"More than a few. Internship, then two years of residency." She gathered her books and stood up. "Well, thank you for a lovely dinner." She gave me a dimpled smile. "And please give my compliments to Mr. Boyd."

I couldn't let her get away, now I knew I had what Sonny Miles had called the tossed stone which could produce the unending ripples. Toni could lead us to Cardillo, his mysterious partner, Stash, and possibly our main target—the man at the top.

I asked casually, "By the way, when can we meet again?"

The dimple quickly disappeared. "Why? I gave you all the information I had."

"This is only the beginning, Toni," I said gently. "You have given us excellent information but it must be developed. Questions may come up that only you can answer."

She slowly slid down in the seat and gave me a worried look.

"But what questions can come up? I gave you the location of the mill in the warehouse."

"A raid on the warehouse isn't going to put Cardillo in prison, Toni."

"Why not? It's his mill. He's bringing in the drugs, isn't he?"

"The law is not that simple. A lot goes on between when a man is arrested and when he comes to trial before a jury. During that time he's not just sitting back waiting to go to prison. He has his own case to prepare. To put Cardillo behind bars the prosecution must have a stronger, more convincing case—one he can't talk his way out of . . ."

"But can't the police follow him and arrest him in the mill?" she demanded. "It doesn't seem that difficult to me."

136

"Cardillo may be a brutal drunk, Toni," I told her, "but I doubt he's stupid when it comes to the law. He's had enough personal experience. He also knows it's not healthy to make mistakes when you're dealing with millions belonging to a drug syndicate. Before he visits that warehouse I bet he has a cut and dried alibi. Maybe he's the legitimate owner. Do you know that?"

My heart went out to her. She looked defeated as she shook her head.

"Then again we know he works with the police. There could be a tip-off, warning him not to go there."

She gave a deep sigh and slowly stacked her books back on the bench.

"Very well, what specifics do you need?"

"When does he go to the warehouse? Who is Stash? Who are the policemen he's paying off? Who is he connected with beyond Stash? What telephone numbers does he call? Get the license plate numbers of any car that calls on him. Try to get his phone bill so you can copy down any out of town numbers he has called. If you can get into his office, try to memorize anything you find in his scrapbasket. Don't put it into your purse. If he walked in on you . . . ."

"I'll do what I can," she promised, "but some things are not possible."

"Like what, Toni?"

"One night he was watching a TV special on Watergate and saw how confidential material can be shredded, so he bought himself a shredder. He pays all bills—including the telephone bill, which Teresa never sees. I guess now that bill goes into the shredder. By the way, I'm glad you mentioned the telephone. Warn the police not to try and wiretap his phone."

"Why? Has he talked about it?"

"He told Teresa the old Dons were caught because they let the government or the police tap their wires. He bragged he would never get caught like that because he has his line checked regularly. I believe him. For a long time I've noticed a small truck in the neighborhood. One of my neighbors told me it was a telephone man checking the lines. Obviously they work for Frank." She looked at me. "I guess I'll have to keep listening."

For a moment—a brief moment I might say—I had a twinge of conscience.

"If you think there's any danger, Toni . . . ."

"He's not alert when he's drinking and that's almost every night."

"Please be careful. How about your sister?"

"I haven't spoken to her in weeks about Frank but I will."

"Can you trust her?"

"She's my sister," she said indignantly.

"That's true and I'm sorry, Toni, but from what you said she still loves this man."

"No more, not after the last beating," she said firmly. "She's frightened to death of him, but love"—she shook her head—"she only wants to see him in prison."

"There's one thing we didn't discuss—there's a reward of five thousand dollars for information like this."

She rebuked me quietly. "Last year there was a fifteen-year-old pregnant girl on my floor. Her first name is Josephine, the last I never found out. I first met her in the clinic with her mother. Rather than have her daughter shamed for life, as she put it, she forced the kids to get married. The boy was sixteen and a heroin addict. The only way this poor girl could relate to her husband was through drugs. One night he mainlined her with the usual results. He left her before the baby was born, and she became a two-hundred-dollar a day addict; she satisfied her habit by prostitution and shoplifting. When I first saw her she was a plump, healthy, blue-eyed blonde kid, full of life. When she was admitted last week she weighed seventy pounds and didn't get out of the fetal position all the time I was with her."

She slowly crumpled her napkin into a tight ball.

"I saw her newborn baby go through withdrawal; hyperactive, screeching cries, irritability, and even when a nurse touched the crib"—she raised her hand about a foot from the table—"the baby had such startled reflexes it bounced this high."

"My God, that poor kid."

"Kids," she corrected me. "She's pregnant again. They're both on Methadone which is only a crutch. At four o'clock in the afternoon they have tremors waiting for a dose. And she isn't the only one. Multiply that case by the thousands. Not only in New York—all over the country. Last week I checked the morgue records—four hundred drug-related deaths—some were kids." Her voice was so tight it cracked. "A reward? I couldn't care less. I'm concerned with saving life—not destroying it!"

She busied herself with carefully tearing up the napkin without looking at me.

I felt a sense of shame, but far more than that, of pride for her courage and concern for the pathetic young couple and the embittered, helpless mother who had sentenced her daughter to purgatory to avoid not "shame" but a wounded pride.

"Now I must go."

"I'll call a cab," I said as I paid the bill.

"Please don't, the subway's faster—"

"But not as safe, Toni."

She smiled. "I'm a city girl, Trev."

I felt an absurd tug at my heart to think of her on that crummy subway going out to Canarsie, which I will always maintain is just this side of the Great Wall.

It had rained but the air was clear and chilly. The streets glistened in the glare of the streetlights. Only a few stores were open, most were

138

dark behind their heavy iron grill doors. When I held out my arm she hesitated for a moment, then took it.

"Everything has changed," she murmured. "Even in my first year at school the stores were always open, now everyone disappears when the sun goes down. There was a story in the newspapers some months ago about a report on drugs—"

"The mayor's report on narcotics?" I blurted out. "The one about the pushers selling drugs to schoolchildren?"

She shuddered. "My God, how can they do that?"

"Actually that's one of the reasons why the league began."

"I think it's wonderful that someone cares. What's the name of the man who's the head of it?"

"Harlow. Stu Harlow."

"He must be a fine man."

"The best. I wish more people were like you, Toni."

"What did I do? Listen by accident to a phone call?"

"But you did something about it."

"People are afraid in this city, Trevor."

I remembered what Madam Langford had said only a few hours before. "I had lunch with a marvelous old lady who said she feels more fear in this city than she has ever felt before in her lifetime."

"Come to Emergency some night," she said grimly, "and you'll see what she means."

"How can I get in touch with you?" I asked when we reached the IRT.

"You can't," she said firmly as she took her books. "I'll call you." She thought for a moment. "Would you care to meet me on Friday? I'll let you know the time."

"For dinner, I hope?"

"I really can't stay too long."

"I promise to make it short."

I watched her go down the steps. At the bottom she turned and waved, then was gone.

I returned to the Eldorado both jubilant and uneasy: jubilant that we had our first important lead, uneasy that I was risking this girl's life to make sure the league was a success. . . .

Lately I had been waking with a sense of depression knowing there was no other course for the league but to go down with a downward pull, as they say in the backcountry; just another bunch of do-gooders who tried to cure a deadly virus with an aspirin.

But the next morning I awoke, amazed at how little our happiness depends on; a typed paragraph on an index card, a twenty-minute subway ride, and a pretty girl with a dimple and hair the sun turned to a copper waterfall. As I looked out on Park Avenue traffic I suddenly became aware of the trivial things that make life exciting on a bright

New York morning; the dazzling sunshine, the scrubbed skies, and the window washer across the street who nonchalantly leaned against his belt to read the Green Sheet. The one tiny cloud was Miles. But I quickly dismissed him. Neither he nor his narcs would ever know about Toni. She had to be protected. In fact I decided I would be her only contact—there was no reason for Stu or any of the others to meet her.

As usual when I was in town, I had breakfast with Stu. I guess my excitement showed.

"You look chipper this morning," he observed. What happened last night? Miss Madison Avenue drop by for a quickie?"

"I haven't seen her for a couple of months."

"Well, something happened," he said with a smile. "Give."

I quickly described the index card, the meeting with Toni, and the information she had given me.

He listened intently. "Great!" he exclaimed when I had finished. "Now we have something. When will you see her again?"

"Next Friday. It took some talking to convince her she must continue to listen on that damn phone."

"That sounds dangerous, Trev. If that bum ever catches her eavesdropping—"

"I warned her not to take any more notes."

"Christ! She made notes?"

"Before she met me she wrote out all she remembered. She said it was a habit from medical school, where notes are a way of life. I warned her not to do it anymore. She doesn't seem to scare easy."

"I wouldn't want her to get hurt."

"And I certainly don't. I put it up to her and she agreed to continue. Let's face it, Stu, the moment she wrote that card she had a tiger by the tail."

"You know you can be a cold-blooded bastard?"

That irritated me and I showed it. "You would be the first one to demand that I get her to go back and pick up that telephone."

"I guess you're right. In the last few days I would have done a lot of despicable things to get this lead." He filled our coffee cups. "Now that we have this information what do we do with it?"

"Go to the cops—what else?" I raised a hand in warning. "But there's one thing we have to agree on right now, Stu, and that is to protect Toni and her sister. Her name is only between us. It goes no further."

"Okay. That's a promise. How do we explain her information?"

"An anonymous caller."

"Who isn't interested in the reward? That doesn't sound logical, Trev."

"It's logical if it's put in the context of a competitor of Cardillo's who is tipping off the police. It's done all the time. The cops know they're being used to help create a monopoly for some mob but they don't care as long as they can make a big score."

"Cardillo is in a very important position, he's probably the man

140

who takes charge of the big loads when they arrive in the States. Wouldn't he be in contact with the man who runs this syndicate?"

"I would think so. But I think Cardillo and his mill is our principal concern right now."

"Don't forget, Trev, you bust one mill and another will open. The guy behind Cardillo is the guy I want." He slowly sipped his coffee. "What do you think of one of us, like Sam or Arnie, tailing Cardillo?"

"It would be too much of a risk, Stu. This guy's been around. If he spots a tail, that's the ball game."

"Maybe you're right. Do you think we should set up a meeting with Kerr and the others right away?"

"I would. The stuff's hot. Let's not wait too long. Who knows what can happen? Some cop may accidentally get a tip and the place will be raided as simply another large cutting mill."

"Fine. I'll call Kerr. But I think we should wait until this afternoon to see what Sam and Arnie have. They called early this morning."

"Did they come up with anything?"

"You know Sam. He always sounds like a foreign agent on the phone. He claims they made a big score."

Sam and Arnie did have something. We all gathered in the penthouse and sat fascinated while Sam read his account of that hilarious underworld meeting in Canada, the made-up gangsters and the new syndicate leader who was becoming more shadowy, more deadly. Sam is an enthusiastic and excitable guy, but Arnie, a true agent, underplays everything and his soft, almost indifferent voice made my attention wander. Toni's smile, Toni's face, the big dark eyes with tears ready to spill over, her last wave, kept flashing in between pictures of caravans moving along jungle trails, the mobster named Stash who wooed high-priced whores, the border patrol pilot peering down in the thickening desert dusk at the fiercely burning plane.

I almost leaped out of my chair. Stu gave me a puzzled look.

"What's the matter, Trev?"

"Arnie just mentioned a guy named Stash and a plane crash."

"Yeah," Arnie said.

I turned to Stu. "That's what Toni overheard!"

He snapped his fingers. "Christ, that's right! I forgot. You did say that."

"Who the hell is Toni?" Sam asked.

"Let Arnie finish," Stu said with growing excitement, "and then Trev will pick it up. Some things are starting to make sense."

After Arnie finished I described Toni, our meeting, and the information she had given me.

"Trev's information seems to tie in with some of the stuff we got, Stu," Arnie said.

"Are we going to give all of this to the cops?" Tom asked.

"No," said Stu flatly.

Frankly, I was surprised. "Why not?" I asked.

"I don't trust them."

"But Stu, somebody has to make a case for the grand jury! That's been the big holdup. The police brass keep telling us how much investigation they have to do to make a case. Now here's one we can give them on a gold platter."

"We'll give them everything on Cardillo so they can make a bust on the warehouse, but the stuff Sam and Arnie are getting we'll keep for ourselves."

I was exasperated. "What the hell are we going to do with it, Stu?"

"I don't know, but something tells me to keep it on the shelf. Let's see what they do with the warehouse."

"Up to the time Trev talked to this girl," Arnie pointed out, "we only had what the feds and the cops are doing. But now we have more than they have."

"You mean the fact that Stash is linked to Cardillo?"

"Exactly. He and Cardillo can be a link to the guy who's running this thing."

"And remember what Brigadier said at our first meeting, Stu?" I reminded him. "This syndicate could be the biggest of all time."

"I could bug Cardillo's phone," Sam suggested.

"No way," I said and repeated what Toni had told me about Cardillo regularly checking his lines.

"I agree with Brigadier, Stu," Arnie said. "I have a feeling this is a big one. It must be, working with the Union Corse and those two Chinese generals! They have millions invested even before a load hits the States."

"Let's leave it like this," Stu said firmly. "We'll give the cops what we have on Cardillo. Arnie, you and Sam go back to D.C. and keep digging. Trev will see Toni—"

"I have to check something," Sam said suddenly and walked across the room to the phone.

"These people are ruthless, Trev," Arnie warned me. "Look what they did to that pilot. I don't think that girl should continue intercepting Cardillo's phone calls."

"That's what I said," Stu replied.

"Look, Miles told me the only break we would ever get is if we found someone who can throw a rock into this investigation and let the ripples do the rest," I told them. "Well, I think Toni has that rock. Why shut her off now?"

"It's dangerous," Arnie said.

"What would you suggest? Turn her over to Miles?" I asked them. They looked at each other.

"Hell no," Arnie said. "But if Cardillo ever found out she fingered him . . ."

"Okay. So what do you want to do?"

Stu said, "What do *you* say, Trev? You found her."

"Let her continue to listen for a while."

We were preparing to break up when Sam hurried across the room and rejoined us.

"Remember those two kids we told you about?" he asked.

"The kids from Staten Island and Queens? The ODs?"

"Right. The feds had the medical examiner list them as incomplete for a cover so it wouldn't get out. Did Miles or anyone else mention these two kids?"

"No," Stu said.

"Then the cops aren't leveling with us," Sam said triumphantly. "I just called my contact in the ME's office. He tells me Miles was tipped off about the two kids, they think the leak came from an assistant ME who has a nephew in the narcotics bureau. Miles raised hell with the ME and City Hall called and warned the ME it would be his ass if the story got out to the papers."

"But isn't that a public record?" Tom asked.

"It's a public record only when they want to make it a public record," Sam said.

Stu looked at me. "Well, we've been shafted again. A story like that could have shaken up this goddam city!"

"That's what they don't want," I pointed out.

"It only underscores what we've been finding out in D.C.," Arnie said. "There's a hell of a lot of competition on this one, not only between the federal agencies but also the cops. I guess they all smell how big it is."

"The cops are fighting the feds. The feds are fighting not only the cops but among themselves," Tom said, shaking his head. "And kids die of OD. Like everything else in this city, it just doesn't make sense."

"You white men are really in trouble," Star said.

Rudy said, "Politicians. They'll screw you every time."

"I can leak the story about the two kids, Stu," I said. "We can get quite a ride in the papers and on TV. It will be sure to help the league but they'll start asking questions."

"The cops will make the leak more important than the two kids," Arnie said.

"No, we'll do it this way," Stu ordered. "Sam and Arnie go back to D.C.; Trev works with Toni; Tom, Star, and Rudy will remain on the phones and I'll continue with the league as if nothing happened . . ."

"When do you want to turn the info over to the cops, Stu?" I asked.

"As soon as I can get Kerr to call a meeting of the board so we can hand it over—"

Arnie said evenly, "But not everything."

"Only what we get on Cardillo and his mill," Stu said firmly. "The stuff on that guy Stash and his link to the big picture, we'll keep to ourselves."

"Do you have any idea of what you're going to do with it, Stu?" I asked.

He looked at me. "Not yet. When I do we'll all know. . . ."

Stu discovered Kerr was at a mayors' convention for a week so we voted to wait until he returned. Meanwhile I kept seeing Toni.

To the old waiter at Boyd's it was now routine that we were first for dinner and had the rear booth away from the window. He accepted us as lovers and made sure there was a candle on the table. He suggested the best the menu offered and brought the bill with our coffee so we could leave immediately. In the beginning he protested that we ate too quickly and was indignant when we refused his desserts, but was mollified when I silently pointed to the pile of books on the seat next to Toni.

"Mama mia! For such a little girl!" he exclaimed. "You teach?"

"First grade," I assured him.

"Ah. Like my little granddaughter."

After that he gave us fantastic service.

I found Toni charming, intelligent, with a great sense of integrity—and very stubborn. She wasn't a pushover to get into bed like my advertising friend from Madison Avenue. There was just no time for chance encounters in her busy, crowded world of medicine and books. That was fine with me. I didn't need or want any emotional entanglements. We didn't draw a battle plan, it was left unsaid, but we understood each other and got along fine.

We shared a common goal—to put Cardillo behind bars and make sure his cargo of drugs never reached the streets. But Toni had a strong sense of moral outrage, while I was only seeking a way to pay back a friend for scores of debts owed—to make sure Stu's league would not suffer an ignominious end.

Gradually a picture of Cardillo's operations began to emerge from the information she provided.

There were between seven and ten cutters working in the warehouse "mill" or "factory," as Cardillo called it. Stash, older, with a harsh, gravelly voice, appeared to be either a courier or liaison man between Cardillo and a connection in New York City.

Then one night Toni said Cardillo and Stash were discussing a large cargo of "goods" which was ready to be delivered to the United States.

"Do you want me to continue, Trevor?" she asked.

For the first time I detected a trace of nervousness in her voice.

"Why do you ask that, Toni? Is anything wrong?"

"Well, not really—"

"There is something wrong. What is it?"

"It's nothing to worry about."

"Suppose you let me be the judge of that, Toni."

144

"Well, Frank was talking to Stash last night and told him to hang on. He wanted to get a pencil. Teresa was out with the kids and I was using the phone in the bedroom. I told you I have the smaller bedroom that has an extension. Teresa never wanted a phone in her bedroom because Frank gets calls at all hours and it wakes up the kids. I don't know what made me do it, but I carefully hung up the phone. The stairs have thick carpet, so I didn't hear him come up. My door was slightly open and suddenly, before I realized it, Frank was standing in the doorway. He had been drinking but wasn't drunk as usual. He said he was looking for a pencil. I gave him one but he just stood there, looking from me to the phone. Finally he asked me what I was doing. I was sitting on the edge of the bed and I told him I was about to make a phone call when he walked in. Then he began cursing and yelling that he didn't want anyone using the phone while he was conducting business. I put on a show of being angry, too, and went out to the corner booth to make a call. To make it real, even for myself, I called a friend of mine who had the night rounds on the ward where I work." She smiled. "It was a bit scary."

"Of course if you feel frightened, Toni, that's enough for me."

She corrected me. "I said it was scary, I didn't say I was frightened. We need more information." She looked at me. "Don't we?"

"Well . . ."

I deliberately left it hanging. I knew it would make her feel guilty.

"Well, that's it," she said briskly. "I'll get everything I can."

"Toni, perhaps the police should take over now."

"No," she said, shaking her head. "We have to know when they're ready to bring in the drugs."

I reached over and squeezed her hand.

"You're a brave girl, Toni."

She ignored the laurels. "Trevor, I'm depending on you more than ever."

"In what way, Toni?"

"That I'm doing the right thing."

"Please believe me, Toni, it's the only way. We're working with the police—they'll bust him."

"God, I hope so. It makes me sick to see those kids come into the hospital for their Methadone. What a waste!" She gave me a sharp look. "I must have your assurance on something else, Trevor."

"Anything, Toni, you name it."

"That my name or my sister's will never come out. You did promise me that on our first meeting."

I solemnly raised my right hand.

"We'll never give it out, I take an oath on it, Toni."

"You say *you* won't give it out but what about the others? The police?"

"We won't disclose your name, Toni."

"But will the police accept that? Won't they think that's peculiar?"

"They will have to accept it. They're only interested in information—not the source."

I'm not a very good liar and I hoped it didn't show in my face.

"I never knew there was so much trouble connected with being a good citizen," she said ruefully. "I'm beginning to realize why people hesitate to go to the police."

"It will be worth it, Toni."

This time she leaned over and squeezed *my* hand. "You've been very patient, Trevor. Thank you."

"Let's talk about something else, Toni. Let's forget Cardillo, drugs, the hospital—"

"I'd love it. Tell me about—well, about that farmhouse."

"Riverview?"

"Yes. Do you have horses?"

"Why, do you ride, Toni?"

"We had a riding club at Hunter. Twice a month we went over to Staten Island for an afternoon. Ever since I was a little girl I've wanted to own a horse. Didn't you once tell me the house is on a river?"

"Flint River. In the morning you can see . . . ."

I went on, describing the old place, the mares and foals, the mist along the river at twilight, and the crisp, clean dawn breeze. Maybe my love for the place came through; she didn't say a word, only sat and listened.

I guess for the first time I really looked at her.

"Toni, maybe you shouldn't be doing this anymore."

She looked startled, as if she had been suddenly yanked out of a reverie.

"Do what, Trevor?"

"Keep intercepting Cardillo's calls."

"But I thought we had decided I would continue?" she said in a puzzled way. "It's important. You said we need more information. So I'll continue to listen. It's as simple as that."

"Well, I changed my mind."

"Well, I didn't," she said firmly. "We still have to know when they're bringing in the drugs and that's what I intend to find out. Now you said you wanted to talk about something else."

"Toni, I want to talk about Cardillo's phone calls."

She ignored me. "In medical school you eat, think, study, and talk about medicine twenty-four hours a day, seven days a week, fifty-two weeks a year." She gave me a dimpled smile. "I love to listen to you talk about that old house and your family, Trevor. Maybe it's because I can only go back to my grandfather. He had a little shop on Madison Street in Little Italy. The San Gennaro feast was held right outside his door. My mother and father would take me and my sister over there for a whole day and we would eat until we got sick."

"I remember the feast. When I worked as a reporter covering the courts we would walk over there for pizza . . ."

"I make very good pizza," she said. "Some night I'll make some for you."

"And maybe someday you'll visit Riverview."

She said quietly, "Would you like me to?"

"Of course."

"When was the last time you were there, Trevor?"

"When I came out of prison—"

I stopped but it had slipped out. She looked startled.

"Prison! My God, what did you do, Trevor?"

"Not that kind of a prison, Toni. In Vietnam. A camp called Tong Le Mai. Maybe you saw it on television when we were released."

"Of course," she said. "I cried when those fellows came off the plane." She added accusingly, "You never said anything."

"I happen to find war heroes very boring."

"Well, I'm very proud I know you," she said with a toss of her head. "May I ask how long you were there?"

"A little over seven years."

"Seven years!" she repeated incredulously. "My God, Trevor! It must be like returning to a new world."

"Something like that."

"Do you like what you found?"

"The girls are prettier—especially medical students. And I love the short skirts."

"Your reflexes are normal," she said dryly.

"In that department? I hope so."

"But you missed all of the things that went on," she said. "The man on the moon, the peace demonstrations, the riots, Bobby Kennedy's death—there was so much! I was just going into Hunter as a freshman when you were captured!"

"I suddenly feel ancient."

We went on like this for a long time with Toni recalling events while I tried to tell her how it was in the Pit. Then suddenly she remembered the time and how much she had to study! I took her to the subway and she was gone with a dimpled smile and a wave.

A few days later she called to tell me a drunken Cardillo had boasted to Stash how the incoming "goods" would be the biggest load they ever received. She promised to call with any new developments.

But I was no longer so interested in Cardillo, Stash, or the cargo of drugs—the league didn't seem as important as it had. After our last meeting a tiny voice of conscience had begun to nag me. I kept hearing Arnie's warning that these people were ruthless. I kept asking myself what would happen to Toni if Cardillo found her on the phone intercepting his calls?

I decided she had more than fulfilled her obligation to both medicine and her morals, so when she called again I insisted I meet her; she reluctantly agreed to walk with me up First Avenue to University

Hospital, then back to Bellevue's entrance. It was a big ten minutes. She insisted that was all the free time she had between rounds. During that brief walk I ordered her to stop intercepting Cardillo's phone calls. She listened to my arguments, then calmly told me she intended to continue to listen until she discovered when the drugs were actually on their way to the warehouse.

She said very calmly:

"Trevor, you convinced me how difficult it is for the police to make a criminal case. I don't want any mistakes in this one. I consider Frank Cardillo a menace, and I intend to do everything in my power to see that he is put in prison." We reached the entrance to Bellevue. "Take care of yourself, Trevor," she said looking up into my face. "You know you've been looking very tense lately. Would you like me to get you a few tranquilizers?"

Just what the hell can you do with a girl like that?

That evening we saw Kerr interviewed at LaGuardia on the TV news and Stu said he would call the Hall in the morning to make an appointment. He still insisted on holding back what I considered vital pieces of information: the link between the mobster named Stash and Cardillo and the conversations that connected them to the deadly group who had killed the trapped pilot in the Arizona desert. Obviously they were all part of the syndicate dealing with the Union Corse and the Chinese generals in Thai. I had the curious feeling that, perhaps unconsciously, Stu didn't want the league to work. I didn't care—I only wanted Toni out of it. . . .

The meeting was held late the next afternoon in Gracie Mansion. Present were Stu, myself, Mayor Kerr, Police Commissioner Fitzgerald, Brigadier, Derby, and Inspector Miles, who I suggested should be invited to sit in. The Langfords were absent; Kerr told us privately that Madam Langford was ill.

Stu gave them a detailed briefing of what we had, including a blown-up photograph of the area he had ordered from a helicopter service; the Water Street warehouse, squat and ugly, was ringed.

"That's quite a story," Kerr said.

Fitzgerald said, "You people are to be congratulated."

"You got yourself a great informant," Miles said. "You have his name, of course?"

Stu gave him a flat no. "The information came from an anonymous caller."

Miles looked incredulous. "You mean the guy wasn't interested in five grand?"

"Apparently not. He gave us the information and hung up."

"How many times did he call?"

"Twice."

"You should have called me."

"Why?" Stu snapped. "We even have trouble getting your cops to pick up the mail."

148

"Is this true, Inspector?" Fitzgerald asked.

"I believe it did happen one or twice, Commissioner. I ordered Lieutenant—"

"How many times did it happen, Trev?' Stu asked.

"Six times. I called the lieutenant, then the sergeant."

Fitzgerald said, "I want a full report on this, Inspector."

"What's so mysterious about an anonymous informant, Inspector?" I asked Miles. "As I understand it, that's standard procedure for a mob that wants to get rid of competition. Is that right?"

"That could be," he grudgingly admitted.

"I just don't see why the informant is more important than this information," Stu said.

"Your informant could be a disgruntled member of the syndicate," Miles explained with elaborate patience. "Potentially he could be a People's Witness."

"Why don't we leave that for the DA?" Stu said. "What I want to see is Cardillo arrested and his operation busted."

"I have to agree with Inspector Miles," Derby said. "I can tell you as a former prosecutor that a good arrest helps the state to get a conviction, the bad one goes out the window."

Brigadier said, rubbing his crewcut, "This could be a big one, Harlow. We can't blow it."

"Okay. How long is it going to take you to make what you call a 'good arrest'?"

Miles said, "you just don't go in and bust down doors."

"I'm aware of that," Stu said, "but I don't think it should take a year and a day to find out when Cardillo is at his factory."

Something flickered in Miles's eyes. "If it will take us a year and a day to make a good arrest, Mr. Harlow, that's how long it's going to be."

"Then maybe we should do it ourselves," Stu said.

Kerr said, grinning, "Oh, come off it, Stu."

"I'm goddam sick and tired of excuses, Mr. Mayor," Stu said quietly. "Every report, everything we've heard from the police is how tough it is to make a case of the stuff coming in. Granted some of it was hearsay and investigations had to be made but here you have the complete *modus operandi*, the name of the principal, the address of his cutting factory, and the time span when a large load will be delivered. What the hell more do you guys want?"

Kerr exchanged a quick glance with Fitzgerald. The police commissioner cleared his throat and frowned deeply.

"Inspector, I want every man available put on this investigation."

"There are eight continuing investigations from the referrals of the league's phone calls, sir. Shall we—"

"I don't think anyone is as important as Cardillo," Stu said.

"Give it your highest priority," Fitzgerald said.

Miles snapped shut his notebook. "I'll be very happy to, sir."

"You'll continue to give us what information you may get, Mr. Harlow?" Fitzgerald said.

"Of course. Trev will liaison with Inspector Miles."

"Don't try the Con Ed bit on his block," I warned Miles. "The informant insisted Cardillo has his wires checked regularly."

"It's like a big numbers setup," Derby said. "The whole area's on the mob's payroll."

"One step at a time," Fitzgerald said, glowing with confidence. "We'll get 'em."

"But you will start immediately, Inspector?" Kerr asked.

"Yes sir. Just as soon as I get back to headquarters."

"You can ride downtown with me, Inspector," Fitzgerald said in a grave voice.

Miles looked over at me with a thin smile.

"Thank you, gentlemen, for the information."

Derby said, "If your informant calls again—"

"We'll get back to you immediately."

"This looks good, Stu," the mayor said heartily. "It should give the league a big boost."

"It won't be long before we'll be running out of money," Stu said.

"Maybe I can get the council to move," Kerr said hastily.

"I wouldn't want to hang that long."

On the way out Kerr asked Stu in a low tone, "Let's have lunch next week, Stu. I have a few things I want to talk to you about."

"Make sure I'm in China when he calls," Stu said in the cab going downtown. "What do you think, Trev? Will they move?"

"The look Kerr gave to Fitzgerald said, 'Get off your ass.' "

"The more I see of that guy Miles the less I like him."

"You and Madam Langford."

"By the way, remind me to send her some flowers. Kerr said Jay's worried."

"Why don't I go up there this afternoon?"

"Good idea. Let me know how she is."

But Madam Langford was not at her Park Avenue apartment; the maid said she had been removed to Lenox Hill Hospital. No visitors were allowed; she had pneumonia. Jay was with her so I sent up a note, ordered flowers, and when I got back to the hotel assigned my secretary to check the hospital daily.

Several days passed without any word from Toni. After she failed to show up for our last meeting, the cashier at Smitty's had handed me a terse note from her which said she was studying fiercely and would be in touch with me. Time dragged until finally she called one morning before noon: Could I meet her in an hour? She had a few minutes between classes.

I fairly flew down to Smitty's and staked out a rear booth by drinking numerous cups of vile coffee before she appeared. She was wearing her hair in a bun and had on those idiotic glasses along with her butcher's coat. She looked thinner and the skin around her eyes seemed drawn.

"Just coffee, Rose," she told the waitress.

"What have you been doing with yourself, Toni?"

"Studying like mad. I only have a few minutes—"

"You look tired."

"Please, Trevor. Please listen."

"I'm sorry."

She leaned across the table. "There haven't been any calls in a week but there was one late last night."

"Stash?"

"Yes." She quoted: "Frank told him, 'It's coming in. I'm waiting to hear from the girl of the bells.' "

"The girl of the bells? Does that mean anything to you, Toni?"

"Nothing."

The waitress put down two cups of coffee.

"You never heard that phrase before?"

"This is the first time."

"But he did say the stuff is coming in?"

"The exact quote is 'It's coming in. I'm waiting to hear from the girl of the bells.' Right after he said that he hung up. Have you spoken to the police?"

I described the conference at Gracie Mansion.

"I have goose pimples. Do you think the police are watching the house?"

"Possibly. I warned them about putting in a tap."

"Frank was drunk the other night, and Teresa said he kept talking about how smart he was and how the police would never get him."

"We'll see about that. Has your sister given you anything more?"

"No. She's been busy with the kids. They both have colds." She looked at her wristwatch. "I have to go. In fifteen minutes I'm making the rounds with the resident."

"Will I see you next Friday night?"

"I hope so . . ."

Her voice was weary and there seemed to be an almost invisible burden on her slight shoulders.

"Now that the police have been brought in I'm frightened. I hope I did what was right."

"Of course you did."

"I wish we didn't have to share a guilty secret. I wish it was something happy."

"Before you know it Cardillo will be in jail and out of your life, Toni."

She smiled. "We won't be partners in a conspiracy anymore."

"We'll see each other again, Toni. I'll be your first patient."

At least it made her smile.

That afternoon when Stu returned from a business appointment I told him what I had learned from Toni.

"Girl of the bells," he said, puzzled. "What the hell does that mean?"

"Take a guess."

"She never heard it before?"

"Never. It's probably a code."

"I wouldn't give it to Miles," he said after a moment's thought. "We'll only tell him the load's on the way in."

"Nothing about the girl of the bells?"

"No. It would only complicate things. We'll keep that on the shelf with the other stuff. They say they want to get Cardillo; well, here's their chance. Let's see what excuse they come up with this time."

Miles refused to discuss anything on the phone, he insisted on meeting me outside headquarters, this time it was a small bar off Madison Avenue. He was sitting at a rear table and waved me over when I came in.

"Will you have a drink?"

"J&B and water," I told the waiter.

"This is a good time, there's nobody around," he said.

"Don't tell me they're tapping your wires at headquarters!"

"Cops gossip like old women. You said you got another call?"

"This morning. Our contact said simply, 'The load's coming in,' and hung up."

He was starting to lift his glass but stopped in midair.

"When? Today? Tomorrow? Next week?"

"He didn't say. The entire message was 'The load's coming in.'"

"Still no name?"

"Nothing more."

I remembered Madam Langford's warning as he studied me over the rim of his glass.

"I'd love to talk to your informant, Trev."

I felt a cold chill and hoped my eyes wouldn't betray me.

"I'm with Stu on that. What the hell is so important about the informant? Isn't the information—"

"True," he broke in, "but you'd be surprised how much you can milk out of them."

"Well, we don't know who this one is."

"Not even a nickname?" he suggested.

"Not even a nickname. You sound as if you don't believe us."

"Oh, sure. But you know how people get messages, they sometimes leave things out. Little things, but put together they can be important."

"We gave you all the information we have."

"Okay." He carefully ground out a cigarette. "Anything more just call me."

"What have you gotten so far?"

"There's a mill in that warehouse—a big one."

"So our information is good after all."

"I never said it wasn't," he protested gently.

"What about Cardillo?"

"We checked his neighborhood. Your man was right. It's tight. He's got quite a record." He pulled a sheaf of yellow sheets from an inside pocket. "You name it, he's done it."

"Is he big time?"

"I wouldn't call him 'big time' but he knows a lot of people. He's been in junk before with the Genovese Family."

"Do you think he's working for himself?"

"Not a chance. He's fronting for somebody."

"Who?"

"That's the sixty-four-thousand-dollar question."

"What do you plan to do?"

"Your boss wants action so we'll try to give it to him. If the load comes in and we spot Cardillo going into the mill, we'll knock it off."

"Any idea of how big it will be?"

"There's no way of knowing. We counted thirteen to fifteen inside, weighing, cutting and wrapping. We have every one of them covered."

"How about the escape route? You know what the informant said, they could go out a back window, down a roof, and into a car lot where there were three cars ready to go."

"We checked it out."

"Was it true, Sonny?"

"Everything was as your man said it would be, right up to the cars and the keys on the sun visors."

I persisted, "I hope you don't mind the stupid questions."

"No questions are stupid, the best of us can miss the obvious. Don't worry, Trev, we have every one of the cutters covered like a blanket. When we hit, the place will be surrounded—back, front, sideways."

"It's a big one, right?"

A glance summoned the waiter and he gave Miles a refill but I waved him off.

"It is a big operation, no doubt about it," he said. "Maybe the biggest we've ever seen." He paused. "What do you think of the campaign so far, Trev?"

"Kerr's working at it. Every time you turn on a news broadcast, he's part of it. I think he's running scared. What's with Derby?"

I was mistaken if I thought I might catch him off base.

"I wouldn't know," he said. "I'm living with this investigation. You guys got the commissioner so excited he's on my back day and night. Christ, the calls start at six in the morning!"

"Well, I guess that's it, Sonny."

"You'll call me if you get anything more?"

"Definitely. Will we know when you move?"

"I imagine the mayor will be calling your boss," he said.

Four days later, in the early morning, we met Fitzgerald and Kerr at the Mansion for breakfast. The police commissioner, bursting with good humor, informed us that the teams of detectives watching the warehouse reported a small panel truck had made a delivery of several boxes. The truck bore no name; a check of the license plates revealed they had been legitimately turned into Motor Vehicle several months ago by the widow of a man who had owned a small hardware supply company. Pictures taken by a team hidden in the hanging ceiling of a nearby building had been blown up; two of the delivery men were identified as longtime drug traffickers. One was believed to have been living in Brazil, the other was a soldier in the Genovese Family. A few hours after the truck left, Cardillo appeared and stayed in the warehouse for several hours; he had made three visits since, and the cops had a pictorial record.

"We believe he is personally supervising this operation," Fitzgerald said. "When he returns again, the place will be raided. Every team is on the alert."

"No phones to tap in the place?" Stu asked.

"There are no phones. Everything has been visual."

Kerr broke in, "They've done a fine job, Stu. As I understand it, the guys with the camera are squeezed in a cubicle no bigger than a phone booth."

"There are also rats," Fitzgerald said proudly. "One of the men killed a bugger as big as a cat."

"How about copies of the films?" Stu asked. "Is there any reason why we can't have one? Just for the record."

"Do you see any reason why they can't, Fitz?" Kerr asked.

"I'll have a copy sent over this afternoon," Fitzgerald said magnanimously. "Of course, they will be only for your records—not for the press."

"How will the story be released?" I wanted to know.

"Do you have any objection to Fitz announcing it at headquarters after the bust is made?" Kerr asked.

"Not if you mention the league," I said. "I think it's only fair."

"Oh, of course," Kerr said. "I plan to incorporate that in the statement I'll be giving out at the Hall. It will demonstrate what I've been saying all along—if we can get the community to work with us, we can lick this narcotic problem."

And it will also be great television coverage for you, my friend, I thought. Free television time. And in a campaign for reelection. It was the old story—politicians with their backs to a wall have less ethics than a whore faced with a trick's wallet on the floor.

"When do you think they'll hit the place, Commissioner?" I asked.

154

"In the next few days," Fitzgerald replied.

"But Cardillo hasn't come back so far?" I pointed out.

Fitzgerald shook his head. "We are confident he will return. He was there three times on three consecutive days, Monday, Tuesday, and Wednesday."

"This is Saturday." I ticked off on my fingers, "Thursday, Friday, and today. Three days he hasn't showed up. Is that right, Commissioner?"

Fitzgerald looked uneasy.

"That is correct."

"Why didn't you raid the place in the three days he was there?" Stu asked.

"The panel truck was still delivering," Fitzgerald said. "They had a set time. Three deliveries on three consecutive days—and each time Cardillo showed. If we had hit the first day we might have lost the load."

"And they haven't delivered anything since Wednesday?"

"No."

"Have your men tailed the truck?"

He gave me an indignant look. "Of course. To an apartment in Yonkers. Both drivers have been kept under strict surveillance, day and night. We take them from Yonkers to the warehouse and back again. There's also a man assigned to anyone who enters or leaves the building."

"And the drivers are the two guys in these photographs?" Kerr said, pointing to the blown-up prints.

"That's right, Mayor."

"If Cardillo doesn't show, what will you do, Commissioner?" Stu asked.

"We'll still raid the place," Fitzgerald said. "It's clear they're preparing the load for street sales."

"How big do you think it is, Fitz?" Kerr asked.

Fitzgerald shrugged. "There's no way of knowing. But the men believe it's very big. I don't want to raise my hopes at this point, but it could be the largest in many, many years."

"That's great news, Fitz," Kerr said. "Congratulations. We'll have a fine ceremony."

"First we have to get whatever's in there, Mr. Mayor," I pointed out.

"I can't agree more with Mr. David," Fitzgerald said. "We have no way of knowing what was delivered to that warehouse. It was drugs, but how much . . ."

"I don't like the business of Cardillo not coming back," I told Stu in the cab returning to the hotel.

"I don't either but you must admit Fitzgerald's reasons for not raiding the place when Cardillo was there seem reasonable."

"I'm not a lawyer, but I think no matter how many pictures they have of Cardillo entering and leaving that warehouse, it won't mean a damn unless he's caught inside with the junk."

"Well, goddammit, what the hell can we do, Trev?" Stu said impatiently. "Raid the place ourselves?"

"We can't do anything."

"They can't blow this one!" He shook his head. "Trev, I just can't see them doing that!" He brooded in silence for a moment. "Any way of getting in touch with Toni?"

"No way. I've been through that route with her."

Stu said grimly, "I'm going to get on Kerr's back."

Kerr oozed confidence on the phone, but he knew no more than what his police commissioner had told him. And Fitzgerald only knew what Miles had told him. I tried to get him several times at the narcotics bureau but each time I was told he was "in the field." I was reminded of the excuse reporters covering old police headquarters would give the city desks when they called for their philandering man, "He's across the street."

However, Fitzgerald kept his word, he not only sent us a copy of the police films but also copies of the blowups of the frames. In the darkened penthouse we watched Cardillo, dark-haired and husky, dressed in slacks and sport shirt, enter and leave the warehouse. Then came the cutters and finally a nondescript panel truck pulled up to the curb and two men got out and casually carried in many loads of boxes; they could have been delivering a shipment of machine parts.

The next roll, clearly taken with a telescopic lens from a nearby roof, showed what looked to be a car junk lot ringed by a high cyclone fence topped with barbed wire. There were several general pan shots, then the lens zoomed in on the back of the warehouse where two windows overlooked a sloping shed, then the camera slowly moved to one side of the shed where three cars were parked.

"The escape route," I said. "There are the cars Teresa told Toni are checked out every day."

"Well, we can't complain they haven't covered everything," Stu said when the roll ended.

"There's one more thing I want to do," I told him. "And that is to check the building plans for the warehouse."

"What brought that up?"

"Nothing special. But in the middle of the night I woke up remembering an old homicide detective I knew as a kid reporter when I filled in for the regular beat man at police headquarters. I covered the lobster shift—that's two A.M. to ten A.M. The old guys who worked for the A.M.s hated to leave their poker game but I used to wander around and talk to the cops. This old guy was fascinating. In the summer we would sit outside the old tenement the reporters used—remember when Brigadier at our first meeting called it 'the Shack'?—and he would go on for hours recalling the murders he had worked on. One thing he told me, and this is what I woke up with, in any investigation you must check out everything, from the contents of a wastebasket to the building plans. I don't know what good it will do . . ."

"Why not?" Stu said.

Curiously, the plans were not in the archives of the Building Department. Even the old clerk was puzzled and disturbed that his precious files were not in perfect order.

"They should be here," he said over and over but they weren't. Then finally he added brightly that perhaps they were over at the Landmarks Commission. Of course Landmarks wasn't interested in preserving a dingy, weatherbeaten warehouse built back in 1922. Back I went to Buildings and went through the procedure with another clerk. The plans were just not there.

The following day I was about to go back to the Municipal Building and continue my search when Stu called and said he had been advised by the mayor's assistant to be "available at any hour" for an important call. We decided to wait in the penthouse. I had the television on, watching some inane midday talk show when the MC suddenly broke off to read what he said was a wire service bulletin:

"Narcotics bureau detectives today raided a lower East Side warehouse which they said was the cutting factory for a major drug syndicate. Paraphernalia used to cut drugs was found but no drugs.

"Simultaneously, Frank Cardillo, alias Frankie Carr, was arrested and charged with conspiracy to sell dangerous drugs. Police identified Cardillo as a member of organized crime. He was arrested at his home in Brooklyn and will be arraigned later today. Now back to the program and Jennie Frost, our guest panelist, who was discussing the question of whether or not hospitals refusing to perform . . ."

I stared over at Stu. His face was set with tiny bunches of muscle tightening along his jaw line.

"They blew it," he said softly. "I can't believe it."

"Let's try to get Kerr."

He dialed City Hall. "The mayor's office, please. This is Stuart Harlow." He waited a moment, then said, "I understand. You have my name? Thank you," and hung up.

"Is he ducking?"

"His secretary said he's with Fitzgerald."

The phone rang and he picked it up.

"Oh, yes, George, how are you?" He motioned to the bedroom, where there was an extension. When I picked it up Derby was talking.

"Teddy Fitz is with the mayor who went clear through the roof when he heard it. I tried Sonny but he's down at the warehouse."

Stu was surprisingly calm. "What happened to the load?"

"They must have gotten it out some way."

"Trev is on the phone now, George. Trev, George says they didn't find any drugs."

"Hello, Trev," Derby said, "I was just filling in Stu. Teddy Fitz

157

called the mayor after Sonny Miles and his boys hit the warehouse Chuck Brigadier is with me now. We both feel like hell. But anyway they did get Cardillo.''

"For what?" I said, "Spitting on the sidewalk? You know as well as I do, George, he'll walk out."

A deep sigh.

"I know, Trev. What the hell can you do? Fitz got nervous and didn't want to wait any longer . . ."

"And they let twelve or thirteen cutters and a couple of million dollars in junk get away from them? How could it happen? Did they leave by magic carpet?"

"Trev, I don't know," Derby said earnestly. "I'm only calling to let you guys know what happened. Chuck is on the other phone now trying to find the mayor and Fitz. I'll call you back. Okay?"

"You do that," Stu said and we hung up.

When I came back into the room he was staring out the window.

"What do you think?" he asked without turning around.

I joined him. It was a grim, gray day with a threat of rain. Across the river clouds stretched along the horizon like a towering wall of dirty cotton batting.

I said, "I think we were sold out."

"I think so too."

The phone rang and he answered it.

"Oh, yes, Mr. Mayor. Yes, we heard it on television."

He listened for a moment in silence.

"I'm sure you will. Right. I'll wait for your call."

"He's with Fitzgerald," he explained. "They're waiting for Miles to come in. Kerr said Fitzgerald ordered Miles to hit the place after none of the cutters showed up this morning. They have detectives out trying to pick them up—"

"What do you mean 'trying'?"

"Every place they hit nobody's home. It looks like they all blew. Even the two guys with the truck. The cops grabbed the truck outside the apartment house in Yonkers but the two drivers are gone. The cops claim they had the place under twenty-four-hour surveillance but they got away."

I repeated, "We were sold out, Stu."

"There's no doubt about it. But by whom?"

The phone rang. This time it was Derby. Brigadier had finally reached Miles who told him the same story, they had no choice but to move in.

It was a neat perfect betrayal.

Then Toni called and in a small, fearful voice asked if I could see her at once. I told her I would be outside Smitty's in fifteen minutes.

As I was leaving, the phone rang. It was the mayor asking us to join him and the rest of the committee in an hour at the Mansion.

"You'll have to shovel your way out of that one by yourself, Stu," I told him.

"Don't break it off with her, Trev."

"I don't think it's our decision anymore, Stu, it's got to be up to Toni."

He explained, "I only want to keep her on our side."

"After I tell her what happened, I doubt if she'll talk to me."

"Trev, try like hell."

"I'll do my best, Stu. But we've been sold out. It's over—finished."

"It's not finished," he said in a taut, cold voice, "not by a damn sight, it isn't."

Toni was crossing First Avenue as I was getting out of the cab. She looked pale and worried.

"I heard it on the radio when I was having lunch," she said, "and I called my sister. She said the police came in and arrested Frank. It was awful. They tore the place apart. Then they started digging up the backyard and ripping out the walls of the garage. The two kids were screaming—Teresa's on the verge of hysteria—my God, what have I done?"

"I hate to tell you this, Toni, but you'll only see it on television. They blew it."

She looked stunned. "You mean the police didn't find the drugs!"

"Not an aspirin."

"But they arrested Frank!"

"On conspiracy, it's a nothing charge, doesn't mean a damn!"

"How could this happen? I gave you all the information—where the warehouse was located, when the drugs were coming in—"

She searched my face for an answer, but I didn't have any and I felt heartsick.

"Stu's with the mayor now trying to get some answers."

She was stiff with anger and fighting back the brimming tears.

"Who cares about answers from politicians? You assured me this was the right way, the only way to stop these gangsters. And I believed you. You said the mayor and the police commissioner were the highest a citizen could go to. Well, I went to you and what happened? Nothing! Now you tell me Frank Cardillo was arrested on what you call a 'nothing charge.' And this is the man who is dealing in *God knows how many millions of dollars of drugs!* Selling it to children."

"You must continue to believe in me, Toni. When we meet the mayor—"

"Please call me a cab," she said. There was a slight quiver in her voice.

"Let me take you home. I can drop you off a block from your house."

She looked at me.

"Dammit, will you call me a cab?"

Cursing every cop and politician in the city I waved down a cab. It swung into the curb with a screech of brakes.

159

"Will you call me later, Toni?"

"I want to go to Canarsie, driver."

"Toni, will you listen to me?"

"Close the door, buddy," the driver said.

"Toni—"

"Buddy, will you close the door? The lady wants to get going. Canarsie's a long trip." He peered at Toni. "You sure you want to go to Canarsie, lady?"

"Definitely," she snapped.

I leaned inside the cab and said softly, "Call me and I'll meet you in Brooklyn. I'll have the whole story by that time."

She ignored me and told the driver, "Will you please get going, driver."

The cabbie looked bored. "Buddy, I can't take the lady to Canarsie where she wants to go unless you close the door."

"Toni—"

"Buddy, don't make me call a cop—"

There wasn't any use. I carefully shut the door. She stared straight ahead as the cab pulled away and merged with the growing afternoon traffic.

Later in the penthouse Stu described the meeting at Gracie Mansion.

"They were all there, the mayor cursing up a storm, Fitzgerald looking like a fool and Miles as if he couldn't care less."

"How about Derby and Brigadier?"

"They came in after the meeting started. George said they had a good case against Cardillo, but I told him he was full of shit. Just like that. Then we got into a shouting match. God, it was awful."

"What's the story, Stu?"

"There's no doubt they did have a twenty-four-hour watch on the warehouse, the people working in it, and the panel truck. They still don't know how they got the stuff past the cops and out of the warehouse. The detectives who were down there swear no one went in or left this morning and frankly I believe them. The last action was about five last night when the cutters left, as usual, one by one. Each one was covered by two narcs, who took them home and never moved all night."

"But they were gone when the dicks went into their apartments to pick them up?"

"Right. The cops believe they were ordered to go home as usual and sometime during the night get out of their building by going over a fence, a rear door—who knows?"

"But what happened to the junk?"

He shrugged. "You got me, Trev. It's a sellout from the inside. Fitzgerald was so nervous he couldn't talk straight."

"And Miles?"

"He put the whole thing in Fitzgerald's lap. He had the log of every detective who covered the warehouse and the people inside. He said he called the PC when his detectives warned him no one was showing up. That's when Teddy Fitz ordered him to hit it."

"What about the mayor?"

"You won't believe this, but all he's worried about is a possible police scandal. I got the impression he's afraid of the cops."

"And he's the guy who promised us all that great cooperation. What about Cardillo?"

He gave a short laugh. "You're a pretty good amateur lawyer, Trev. He was arraigned in Supreme Court and the DA asked for high bail, but Cardillo's lawyer pointed out his client was miles from the warehouse."

"What about the films the cops got?"

"The lawyer said Cardillo rented the lower part of the warehouse to store steel scrap he sold to smelting plants. You know the bastard had leases and bills to prove it!"

"There's either some honest cops who are mad as hell or somebody's putting on a big show. Toni said they took their house apart."

"I saw it on television. From the way it looked, they were honest cops who were really mad. How did Toni take it?"

"Not good. She was furious."

"That's too bad. I had plans for her."

I looked at him. "What kind of plans?"

"As far as I'm concerned this thing is far from over, Trev."

"I don't get you, Stu."

"The way I see it, we gave them their chance and they blew it. Now maybe we should look into it."

"You're kidding!"

"No, I'm not kidding. I'm deadly serious."

"You mean play cops and robbers?"

"Not 'cops and robbers,'" he said sarcastically, "but perhaps an intelligent investigation can turn up some interesting facts."

"And where does Toni come in?"

"She will still be our source of information."

"I don't like that."

"What are we going to do, let them laugh at us?"

"My God, Stu, we can't ask her to go back and start picking up that phone again! Cardillo will be suspicious as hell, he must know he's been fingered."

"Sure he does. But he'll never suspect Toni. Another thing to consider is what Toni told you about his blind ego. Can't you see Cardillo patting himself on the back and boasting to his boss how he outsmarted not only the entire New York City Police Department but the mayor? This will make him a big man. And I also believe it will make him vulnerable."

"I don't think Toni should be involved anymore, I really don't."

161

"Will you let me talk to her?"

"No."

"Why not?"

"I think we would be endangering her life for a ridiculous scheme."

"All we can do is ask her. If she says no, the hell with it. How did you leave her?"

"She feels we sold her out."

"Toni strikes me as someone who won't sit back and take it. You went into great detail about how horrified she was that this mob is selling drugs to kids. You also told me she wasn't interested in any rewards—only humanity. Right, Trev?"

"Don't con me, Stu."

"I'm not. I'm only repeating what you said."

"That was before she knew we were dealing with thieves."

"That's my point, we don't have to deal with them anymore; this time we'll do it our way."

"You know I suddenly have the feeling you wanted this all along."

He shrugged. "Maybe you're right. But you'll have to admit I did everything to make the league a success."

"You didn't give the cops everything, Stu. You know that."

"In view of what happened? Thank God I didn't."

"Well, leave me out of this one."

"Whatever you say."

"Do I formally hand you a written resignation?"

"You know I'd ignore it." He mixed us both a drink and handed me one. "Let's put it up to the others."

"They'll never say no to you, Stu."

"Not always. Arnie is talking about leaving for China. He has a job lined up with a company that's going to build a steel plant in Manchuria."

"Is this something for the Agency?"

"No, he only wants to see what's inside. You know Arnie. Sam is getting more business than he can handle. He's making plans to expand and open an office on the west coast. Tom is rushing a girl he met at an air force dinner in Washington. Her old man runs a cargo plane outfit and Tom smells a flying job. Star got a letter from a cousin up in Canada: they're building a bridge outside of Montreal and he can get on high steel again, Rudy will go along with him. That's the way I hoped it would be; after everyone settled down and got that stinking stable out of their systems, they'd take off on their own.

"I meant every word when I said at Clark that you guys were the greatest. I told you before, Trev, the six of you are my family. I don't have anyone else. If the others go, fine and good luck, but I'd hate to see you take off. Christ, we've been through a hell of a lot together . . ."

"I have no plans to leave, Stu, but dammit I don't like what you have in mind."

He smiled. "What exactly do I have in mind?"

"The cops or someone sold us out and you want to take over and investigate this goddam mob. That's insane! These bums are killers! They'll cut your throat and throw you into the river without thinking twice."

"Oh, come off it, Trev, what the hell are they? Supermen? No, they're a bunch of stupid tough guys with the mentality of apes who happen to have lots of muscle and money. I don't go for folklore when it comes to mobsters! Compared to Charlie, they're amateurs."

"Maybe so, but I don't want to find out."

"Well, I'm still going to put it up to the other guys."

"Fine, Stu, but I'll pass."

We had two more meetings with the mayor, Fitzgerald, Miles, and the others but they were all the same, the usual recriminations, Stu and Derby ending up in a shouting match, poor Fitzgerald offering his resignation, which Kerr refused to accept because it would only raise questions, while an impassive Miles, seemingly bored, listened to it all. City Hall was successful in keeping the lid on the story of the sellout—at least for a time—and while the *News* had a story hinting police brass was looking into the raid, the media's coverage was perfunctory.

At this point the league died without even a whimper or a death notice; for $100,000 we got one pusher sent away for parole violation, hundreds of "referrals" which the police said would require "months and months to determine whether they are productive," a glowing letter and press release from the mayor's office praising the league as a great "community and civic effort," a daily caller who lectured Star and Rudy on the virtues of the Bible, and ten parking violation tickets. Heroin and cocaine addicts and pushers still moved freely on the streets and police admitted it was business as usual for the addict-pusher and the big-time dealer in drugs. The league had failed.

Then Toni called; she was between classes and was very brief.

"I feel I owe you this, Trevor," she said in a tense voice, "I overheard it last night—"

"Toni, let me meet you in Smitty's."

"I'm sorry. I can't, I only have a few minutes before I make my rounds." She added hurriedly, "I want to tell you what I heard between Frank and that man, Stash. This is the first time he's called since Frank was let out on bail. They were discussing the case and Frank said he didn't have to worry, he was going to walk away, as he put it. Then he said, 'The man with the finger said to give Sonny what he wanted because he's a guy who knows how to get things done.' He also called Sonny 'a stand-up guy' and told Stash that if things went right, they could be wearing the mayor's hat."

It was stunning news and I was silent so long Toni said hesitantly, "Trevor?"

"I'm sorry, Toni. What you heard is very important. More important, when can I see you? Tonight? Tomorrow? I hate to think you're angry."

"I'm not angry, just, well, disgusted."

"I hope not with me, Toni."

"No, and I'm sorry for what happened the other afternoon."

"I must see you if only for a few minutes."

"I can't, Trevor, not now. I have to go. Good-bye."

There was a click and she was gone.

I found Stu and described Toni's message.

"Miles!" he said. "That son of a bitch!"

"I was stupid. Maybe this is what Madam Langford was trying to tell me."

"But she admitted she didn't have any evidence."

"Do you remember what I told you after I had lunch with her? She was trying to check something out . . ."

He walked to the phone.

"What are you going to do?"

"Call Kerr. We're going to see him as soon as possible."

Within the hour we were at Gracie Mansion and being ushered into Kerr's bedroom as he slipped on an evening shirt.

"Pam and I are going to the PBA dinner tonight," he said jovially. "Want to come along and hear them boo me?"

"That's certainly like walking into the lion's den," Stu said. "Why we came here was to—"

"Hey, toss me that box of cuff links, Trev," he said, "the one on the dresser. Thanks. I don't want to rush you guys but I want to see a few people before the dinner starts."

"You cultivating the cops, Mr. Mayor?" I asked. "That's a switch. How come?"

"To coin a phrase, politics makes strange bedfellows. Tonight we're buddies."

"I guess then you wouldn't be interested in listening to what we have to tell you," Stu said.

Kerr slowly turned away from the mirror.

"You sound serious, Stu."

"I am. Our informant called."

"Oh? What did he have to say?"

"Miles sold us out. Possibly to get enough money for Derby to run."

Kerr stared at us as he slowly tied his bow tie.

"That's hard to believe. I know Derby has hot nuts for this job but taking . . ."

". . . Money from a mob? You know better than we do it's been done before. It will come in clean as a laundered shirt."

Kerr carefully put on his cummerbund and slipped into his

flawless jacket. If looks were all that was required, Dwight Kerr would be the nation's greatest mayor.

"You don't seem excited. I thought you'd be breaking out the champagne," Stu said. "This could kill Derby before he starts his campaign. All we have to do is—"

Kerr calmly interrupted him. "Let's look at it this way, Stu; we don't have any proof. You know, hard evidence."

"What do you think we should do?"

"This belongs in the DA's office," Kerr said quickly.

"The DA's office! What the hell can we give the DA? An anonymous phone call? I think you should call in Fitzgerald, start an immediate departmental investigation of Miles and—"

"Take it easy, Stu," Kerr said soothingly. "You mean bust a guy who's head of our new narcotics bureau on the basis of a call from an unknown informer?"

"Wait a minute," I broke in, "this unknown informant gave us the warehouse which your own police commissioner said was one of the largest drug factories in the country!"

"And your cops blew it and now we know Miles is the reason," Stu added fiercely. "Miles would be forced to resign if Fitzgerald gave out the bare facts!"

"That would be just great," Kerr said. "You'll have me starting a campaign for reelection along with a major police scandal and the PBA on my ass! And on what basis? You got a call from an unnamed informer! I agree the guy's information and past track record have been great, but now we would be making sensational charges . . ."

"Dammit, they're true!" I protested.

". . . that a high-ranking official of the police department sold out our investigation of a drug syndicate for money to finance my opponent's mayoralty campaign! What the hell would the police commissioner charge Miles with? Where are the witnesses?"

"You just said it belongs in the DA's office," Stu said, fighting to keep his voice under control.

"And I mean it," Kerr said fervently. "Let them handle it. They can put it all together, get Miles before a grand jury if necessary."

"By that time the election will be over," I reminded him. "Maybe Derby will have your job . . ."

"I would rather take my chances running with him neck to neck," Kerr said firmly, "than running with a bonfire hanging to my ass. Look, Stu, let's do it my way. I'll call the DA first thing in the morning and—"

"And you had the goddam nerve to offer me a job," Stu said in a low deadly voice. "If you win, I'm sure you'll run the best whorehouse in the country."

"It's very simple. He doesn't want to make waves with the cops," Stu said as we walked to the car. "Maybe one of his polls told him he's in trouble."

Two days later on the six o'clock news, George Horatio Derby announced his candidacy for the mayoralty. Hearty, good-humored, and bursting with confidence, he announced his law and order program to rid the city of street crime. The drug problem headed the list of problems he promised to solve.

He told an overflowing press conference that to bring this about he had obtained the services of what he called one of the nation's leading authorities on drugs—Inspector Frank Miles, head of the police department's Metropolitan Bureau of Dangerous and Controlled Drugs. He cited Miles's impressive record and revealed that a few hours before the conference Miles had put in his retirement papers to head his advisory staff.

Miles, looking as if he had just walked off a Warner Brothers musical sound stage, then joined him. From the other side of the wings came Betsy; they stood there before the cameras, a smiling, beaming trio almost tasting City Hall.

Stu and I watched in silence as they faded out, holding their linked hands aloft.

"Judas incorporated," Stu said grimly. "I've asked the guys to be here Saturday night. Do you still want to pass, Trev?"

"Deal me out this time."

"No problem. Let's get some dinner."

A tense three days passed, then on Saturday about noon Stu called me.

"Could you drop by the penthouse, Trev? There's someone here who wants to see you."

I thought it might be an old newspaper friend looking for a job but it was Toni. She was standing with Stu by the windows, the bright sunshine picking out the copperish tints in her hair as it had done the first time we had met. She looked stunning in a skirt and sweater, and I noticed with a pang there were a pot of coffee and two empty cups on the cocktail table. I looked over at Stu but he made a defensive gesture with his hands.

"Toni called *me*, Trev."

She said, "I called Mr. Harlow this morning, Trevor."

"I also have a telephone, Toni."

"I wanted to discuss something with him."

Stu glanced at his wristwatch. "The president of the Downtown Association is on his way to see me. I'll head him off and get back to you later."

"Will you have a drink, Toni?" I asked when we were alone. "I make a pretty good daiquiri."

"No thanks, but I will have some coffee."

I poured us each a cup and we sat on the couch.

"Mr. Harlow told me the whole story. I want to apologize for the other day, Trevor."

"There's no need to apologize, Toni."

166

She sipped her coffee. "It was stupid of me but I was upset." She shook her head. "You wouldn't believe the mess I found when I got home. Frank and his lawyer were back from court, and they were shouting at the police who were ignoring them as they ripped down walls and dug up the garden. I asked one officer what he was looking for and he said, 'Anything we can find, lady.' Newspaper reporters and TV cameramen were all over the house. Then Frank got into a fight with one of them and the police took Frank to the local precinct to charge him with breaking an expensive camera. His lawyer paid the damages and they let him go. It was a nightmare living with him for the next few days. He was drunk most of the time. Once when I came in from school I found he had beaten Teresa. The kids were terrified, my sister was crying most of the time, and all I could think of was that the police has missed the drugs and Frank would go free!" She added disgustedly, "My total reward for trying to be a good citizen."

"Does Cardillo suspect anything, Toni?"

"No. He told that man Stash he thinks the informant was someone in the junkyard or in the Sanitation Department garage." She shuddered. "He said that when he finds him he will kill him."

"Why did you come here, Toni?"

"I told you I wanted to meet Mr. Harlow. I've been doing a lot of thinking—"

I prompted, "And?"

She said determinedly, "I'm not going to stop now . . ."

"Is that why you're here?"

"I wanted to find out from Mr. Harlow if the league was still operating. I saw something in the papers—"

"The league is dead, Toni."

"So Mr. Harlow told me."

"What else did he tell you?"

"He intends to do something independent of the police."

"Did he tell you I don't want anything to do with it?"

"Yes, he did."

"Do you know why?"

"I guess you have your reasons, Trevor."

"He wants to continue to use you as the source of information."

"Yes—he asked me if I would be willing."

"What was your answer?"

"I told him I would do anything to help put Frank Cardillo behind bars. It almost makes me physically sick to hear him brag how he's too smart for the law and that people like me are stupid." She pulled up a sleeve of her sweater. Near her elbow was an ugly bruise. "I was in my room studying when he came in and grabbed me. Fortunately he was so drunk Teresa and I could push him out. I called my brothers and Julio, he's the biggest, got Frank on the phone in the morning. I don't think he'll do it again."

"For God's sake, Toni—move out."

"No," she said firmly, "that would be running away and I don't believe in running away from problems."

"You crazy wonderful girl, don't you see what this could lead to? We can't make arrests. It's an insane idea!"

"Mr. Harlow told me that at the proper time he intends to turn all the information we get over to the proper federal agency."

"What about medical school? You keep telling me you don't have any time for anything except your studies."

"All I will do is simply listen in on Frank's phone calls and report what he said."

"Report to whom?"

She studied my face.

"To you—no one else. I told that to Mr. Harlow."

"Dammit, will you stop calling him Mr. Harlow? Call him Stu or Stuart."

"Are you angry with me?"

"Of course I am. I don't want you to get involved. You've done enough. Toni, you can't be the conscience of the world. This is a police case. They blew it and it's their responsibility."

"I guess that's what wrong with medicine," she said with a sigh, "there are no other worlds. You can't cope with a thing like this. I once read an article in a medical journal that physicians are the most gullible of any profession. Am I being gullible, Trevor?"

"You certainly are if you don't realize how dangerous Stu's plan can be."

"I have a technique now," she said. "I first wrap a handkerchief around the mouthpiece and then pick it up very slowly so there's no sharp click. The handkerchief muffles my breathing and outside noises. A telephone repairman working in one of the halls told me how to do it."

"I don't know what the hell I'm going to do with you. Suppose that bum found you listening?"

She gave me a wide-eyed look, full of innocence.

"I'd say, 'Oh, I'm sorry, Frank, I was about to make a call.'"

"And he'd believe you?"

"You don't know him, Trevor, his egotism is incredible. He insists they don't have a case against him. His lawyer told Teresa the same thing. He said they will probably indict him to save face, but he doubts the district attorney will ever bring Frank to trial." She added fiercely, "That's what I find shocking. A man who is distributing drugs to be sold to children can operate as if he owned a candy store!"

"Toni, Cardillo is dangerous. You heard what he said, he'll kill whoever informed on him. And I believe him."

"If I ignored what he's doing I couldn't live with myself."

"Don't ignore it then. Give it to—well, give it to the law. But don't get involved with us!"

"The law will get everything I hear—through you," she said with that relentless, infuriating logic. "I had one experience with the police.

168

I am sure there are honest policemen but I am also sure that if I went to any law enforcement agency it would only mean trouble for me and my sister. When I came home from school, the police were talking about taking me and Teresa to a precinct for questioning."

"Send them an anonymous letter."

"And have them back on our doorstep in the morning looking for Frank? No thanks. Isn't it strange how you must plot to be a law-abiding citizen? You're either afraid of corruption or the effect it might have on your life. I've thought about all this, Trevor, it's been on my mind for days. Something must be done about this man—but what? Should I go to the FBI or one of those other agencies and tell them what I know about Cardillo? And if I did, what would happen to us?

"Would they take us in for questioning? Force us to testify before a grand jury? Is Frank Cardillo a liar when he boasts of his friends among the police? The judges? I don't know, Trevor, it's hard for me to believe that a drug peddler can manipulate the law. Yet from what has happened you must admit he has influence somewhere . . . maybe I've been too close to books and medicine but it's bewildering. I didn't know what to do. I had to go somewhere—so I came here . . ."

"But we failed you, Toni."

Except for the light filling her eyes, the composure in her face never changed.

"I'd rather trust you than anyone else."

Looking back, I believe it was at that moment I began to realize Toni meant something more to me than a diversion, a part of a conspiracy. I had no clear idea of what I wanted to say to her. I tried to do what I had always done in the Pit, look at my feelings objectively, paw over them, examine them again and again. But when it came to thinking about Toni the cold, calculated emotionless reasoning was for the first time lost in a jumble of confused thoughts. This could hardly be love, I felt. Could it be infatuation? Strange, now even her slightest habit mattered.

All I could say was, "You know you can be very infuriating."

"Why?" she demanded. "Because I'm determined to see Frank Cardillo in jail?"

"I know how you feel, Toni, but Stu's plan is dangerous. Cardillo's a thug. A killer. His police record is as long as your arm."

She reminded me gently, "You thought it was all right for me to do the same thing a few months ago, Trevor."

"I was stupid," I admitted. "If I knew then what I know now, I never would have allowed you to join us."

She said stubbornly, "It's my duty as a citizen—"

"For God's sake, Toni, don't go patriotic on me! You're beginning to sound like Stu. You did your part for God, country, and community, now forget it. Let someone else take care of Cardillo and his gang of drug runners. We probably scared them off for a while anyway."

"No we didn't."

"What do you mean?"

"Stash called late last night. He asked Frank, 'When is the boid flyin' in?'" Her voice became deep and guttural. "'The boid, Frankie, when is the boid flyin' in?'"

Her mimicry was amazingly good and despite myself I had to laugh.

"What did Cardillo say?"

"He told Stash 'the goods' would be in any day now. They will know for sure when 'the girl of the bells' calls. Then they talked about what Frank's lawyer was doing and hung up."

"That's the second time he's used that phrase. Do you have any idea of what it means?"

She shook her head. "No, but it seems important to both of them."

"How about Teresa? Does she know?"

"She doesn't have any idea of what it means. She's very upset. I had the doctor give her a tranquilizer. She's worried about the kids. Now she tells me Frank is talking about a divorce and how he'll take the kids away from her. He claims a phone call to a judge who is a friend of his will do it. She's all mixed up."

"When I think of you with Cardillo in that house—"

"I'm not afraid of him. He knows that."

"And you're determined to keep listening to that damn phone?"

"Yes."

"And there is nothing I can say that will change your mind?"

"No."

"Well then, I guess I'll have to join this crazy plan. Dammit, Toni, why don't you just work at being a doctor instead of trying to save the world?"

"Because it would not be right" was her simple answer. Then she added, "By the way, we'll have to skip our Friday nights."

"Now what is it?"

"I'm spending every possible minute on the floor. I can call you or perhaps we can meet outside of Smitty's for a few minutes—"

"What's so important?"

"An adorable six-year-old boy who isn't going to make it."

"What's wrong with him, Toni?"

"He has a teratoma, and it will soon kill him. We're doing everything we can." She paused. "I guess that's what I've been talking about, Trevor."

Toni's quietly spoken words and impenetrable calm were like accusations. I was relieved when the phone rang. It was Stu.

"Everything okay, Trev?"

"Sure, sure, everything's fine."

"Please believe me, I did not call Toni."

"Toni explained everything. She insists on continuing. So count me in. I feel responsible for her."

"That's good news. Don't worry about her, Trev, you'll be her only contact."

"You know about the load coming in?"

"How do you like that? The bastard's out on bail but it's business as usual. Now you can see how big a sellout it was."

"Cardillo and that other guy Stash are still talking about 'the girl of the bells.'"

"So Toni told me. Obviously it's a code. Maybe Arnie and Sam can figure it out."

"When will they be in?"

"Everyone's coming in today. We'll meet tonight about eight. Do you think Toni should be there?"

I hesitated. Perhaps it would be better for the others to see what they had to protect.

"I'll ask her." She looked up questioningly as I crossed the room. "Toni, Stu is on the phone. Would you care to meet the others tonight? They all worked with us on the league."

"If you think I should, Trevor."

"I really do."

"I don't want to sound like a broken record but it can't be for long. I have a few hours now but tonight it tight."

"What time will you leave the hospital tonight?"

"About seven, when the child's parents usually arrive. I wait for them. They know there's no hope, but they like to talk to me."

"And after that?"

"I plan on going home and studying for the whole weekend. I have to give a review of the case on the Monday rounds."

"Can you come right after seven? You can meet the others and leave right after that."

She agreed and I told Stu.

"Wonderful. I'm with this guy from the realty board. We're on our way to the Waldorf for their monthly meeting. I'll be back in a few hours."

We met an hour before Toni arrived. Stu factually and candidly described how and why we had been sold out and offered us the alternatives of forgetting what happened and charging it to experience or continuing our investigation of Cardillo independent of the police or any other law enforcement agency.

"I don't know about you," he said in a tight voice, "but I'm concerned about this goddam society of ours. I think it's facing the biggest crisis in our history, certainly as bad as the Civil War. It doesn't seem to be one single problem, like civil rights, Prohibition, or any of the single concrete issues which we always had. It looks like a conglomeration of problems, most of which we can't seem to define. But whatever the reason, the way of life we knew before we left is gone. Forget it. Drugs are no longer a 'problem,' as they called it, but a plague. Yet the largest police force in the nation has cops so corrupt they stole enough junk from their own offices to satisfy the habit of half the junkies this side of the Mississippi! Honest cops are so frustrated they don't care or are afraid to do their job. In courts turnstile justice is routine.

"The streets? You need fifteen Wyatt Earps to escort you across Central Park, yet an idiotic police commissioner once told the city there wasn't any danger—in fact he would walk in the park any day or night. He forgot to add he was six foot four, weighed two hundred and fifty pounds, and had bodyguards twice as big. We had a presidential crisis, prices are out of sight for the ordinary family, and while we keep shouting what must be done, it remains status quo as the country continues to slide downhill."

"You palefaces seem to be in trouble," Star said with a grin. "Why don't you give it all back to us?"

"That's one of our problems, Star," Stu said grimly, "we didn't know how to take care of what we stole. When we left for Nam this country was one of the giants of the world. We came back to see a couple of sheiks in a medieval nation the size of Rhode Island snap the whip and change our economy. Americans are killed by terrorists who blow up planes with bombs and what is done about it? Nothing. We kiss their asses in an international window and beg their forgiveness.

"We've come back to a society of crumbling institutions, half-baked causes, and self-deception. You can't turn on television that you don't hear someone crying over the rights of defendants. Fine. I'm all for that, but what about the victims? The poor bastard who's mugged or beaten for a few bucks lies forgotten in a hospital—or is many times buried, with his wife and kids the only ones who will grieve for him, while the guy who beat or killed him for a few bucks is treated like a celebrity. Reporters pushing mikes into his face as if he was a man who had done something important instead of what he really is. Remember the bank stickup last week? The bums killed one guy and took several tellers and customers as hostages so they could bargain with the cops and make a "public statement," as they called it, to the press! And while they were reading this goddam rambling crap to a national television audience, behind them cops were bringing out the body of an innocent guy who had just come in to make a deposit. Remember the bastards grinning and giving the victory sign?"

He stood up and faced us. His eyes were cold and he continued in a harsh, dry voice I'd never heard him use before

"At first when we came back I couldn't believe it. Then I found myself accepting everything as a new way of life. The friends and businessmen I spoke to said the same thing, 'You can't fight City Hall,' or some other stupid cliché. It was almost like a conspiracy to keep up pretenses. Now we have some well-heeled hoods bringing in millions of dollars of junk to sell to kids and what the hell is being done about it? Nothing. Why? Because a top cop hopes to be police commissioner someday and a two-time loser with a smart-assed bitch for a wife wants to live in Gracie Mansion.

"We have a mayor, who thinks he can win back his job and maybe go on to Albany or Washington, too busy trying to win cop votes to be concerned. He's afraid a scandal in his administration will ruin him so he tells us to go to the DA when he knows damn well the DA will only hold out his hand and ask for the evidence that we don't have or can't give him. And the federal people? They've been outsmarted by this mob at every turn . . ."

"Why don't we—" Tom started to say but Stu held up his hand.

"Let me get this off my chest, Tom, it's been gnawing the hell out of me for weeks. Believe me, I could become the most bored man in New York City and all of you could go your own way, but I don't think we could sleep nights knowing what's going on . . . we didn't spend all those years in the Pit for this! Hell no!"

He paused, then continued.

"After we took care of those bums in that bar I knew there wasn't anything we couldn't do—if we did it together. We have a load of know-how right in this room. Now it's up to you. Anything you agree on is fine with me."

"I agree with Stu," Arnie said quietly. "It's a stinking world."

"Change one thing and you must change everything," I pointed out.

"Fine," Stu snapped. "Let's start with Cardillo."

"You mean go after him like we were narcs?" Tom asked.

"I mean to continue as we were doing," Stu said. "I don't think it takes superintelligence to do the job of a detective or a federal agent."

"They have a hell of a lot more manpower than we do," Sam pointed out, "and besides they're the law."

"Actually we would be helping the law, a sort of new vigilantes," Stu pointed out. "When we agree we have reached our limit, then I propose we turn everything over to the feds. Sam, you must know people in Washington you can trust."

"In the Department of Justice?"

"Anywhere. Any federal law enforcement agency. All we want is Cardillo and his gang in jail."

"This is like that barroom bit all over again, Stu," I warned him. "You realize the chance you're taking? All of us?"

"As I told you, Trev, I'm more than willing to take the chance. Anyone who feels it's too much of a risk . . ."

"In other words we'll be vigilantes."

He shrugged. "There have been vigilantes before in this country. You're good on history. What about California? Montana? Didn't the vigilantes bring law and order? Weren't they the best people in the community?"

"Hell, that was a hundred years ago and on a frontier."

Star said, "I bet more damn murders, stabbings, and robberies are committed in New York than in any five towns in the old West." He reached inside his jacket, there was a tiny click and he held a deadly looking blade in his hand. "Know when I bought this? Right after I came back from the reservation. Man, this Indian is scared!"

"Do you know how many vigilante groups there are in this country, not a hundred years ago but right now?" Stu asked me.

"No, I don't."

"At least a hundred. They may call themselves security or local crime preventive outfits but there's a smell of vigilantes about all of them. One of the largest cities in the Midwest has a group of cops in plain clothes," Stu went on. "In one year they killed fifteen pushers. They carry heavy duty pistols and M-1 carbines."

"Cop vigilantes! How did that come about?" Tom asked.

"Six cops were killed, and there were so many stabbings, muggings, and shootings the local paper just bunched them all together in a column headed, "What Happened in our City Last Night . . .""

"I know from my own business," Sam said, "people are not depending on the police anymore. If they don't hire attack dogs or guards they get together to protect themselves."

"Christ, give them all guns and it will be worse than Nam," Tom said.

"Nobody wants to arm a bunch of Archie Bunkers with rifles or handguns," Stu said. "But as you can see, it's symptomatic of what's happening, there's a feeling of betrayal, of having been screwed—"

"Do you think we have enough to go on, Stu?" Tom asked.

"I believe we've made a hell of a good start. We know Cardillo is linked to some guy with the nickname of Stash, that another big load is coming in, we have the Yonkers steel company's address and the code phrases, 'the man with the finger' and 'the girl of the bells,' whoever they mean. We know at least four little kids have died of OD since this mob began operations, but more importantly we have something the narcs or local cops don't have—a pipeline right into Cardillo's phone! Trev and I talked to Toni this morning and she's willing to continue. She'll be here at seven. Trev thought you should meet her."

"As I understand it," I said, "we won't be working with the law—"

Stu interrupted me. "Only up to the point where we all agree it would be useless to continue by ourselves."

"Then we turn everything over to a federal agency?"

"Right. Sam will make the contact."

"And you don't think we're too amateurish, Stu?" Tom asked.

"Who gave the cops the warehouse, Tom? That's what I mean about Toni."

"Can't we do anything about Miles or Derby?"

Stu made an angry gesture. "What can we do? We went to the mayor. He wanted us to go to the DA. With what? An anonymous phone call and no corroboration?"

174

"If you gave out Toni's name—"

I quickly broke in, "Stop right there, Tom! One thing we have to remember, Toni and her sister must be protected. Her name stops here."

"If the DA subpoenaed either one of them," Arnie said, "they would never live to testify." He picked up the morning paper beside him. "There's a story on page one of how they found the remains of a guy who agreed to testify against some hoods in a narcotic case."

"Arnie is right," Sam said. "We'll be mixing with some tough bastards. Does Toni realize what she's getting into, Trev? If Cardillo finds out she fingered him—"

"I tried to talk her out of it all morning. She's determined to do something about Cardillo."

"Toni's quite a woman," Stu said. "Wait until you meet her." He gave us a slow appraising look. "Well, anything else?"

"Let's take a vote," Arnie said.

Of course the vote was unanimous. It would have been the same if Stu had asked us to climb the Matterhorn. I guess down deep I knew that even if Toni had refused to continue, I could not have said no to Stu and the others. In Tong Le Mai, when I was hungry we were all hungry. We were scared together. We hoped together. We shared each other's dreams and fantasies. If peace had not come I am sure we would have died together. Stu made sure the ties which bound us remained when we returned to civilian life. Looking back I guess that's the way he planned it. Now we were the New Vigilantes. . . .

Toni captivated them as I knew she would. While they stood around the fireplace and sat next to us on the big semicircular sofa, she described from the very beginning the contents of Cardillo's phone calls.

"Any idea of who this 'girl of the bells' might be, Toni?" Tom asked.

She shook her head.

"Don't forget 'the man with the finger,' " Arnie said. "Obviously they mean a connection. Toni, tell me this, does Cardillo's steel plant make anything ornamental?"

"Not that I know of. He once told my sister they supply steel for racetracks, fairs, and amusement parks."

"Well, one of the first things we should check out is that Yonkers company," Arnie said.

Stu said, "Suppose you do that, Tom."

"Look up their corporation papers," Sam suggested. "You'll find them in the county clerk's office in the White Plains courthouse. Then check with the Better Business Bureau." He looked over at Arnie. "Maybe he'd better drop by on some pretext and see what's doing?"

"Have some business cards made up," Arnie said. "Tell them you represent a syndicate that bought some land in Jersey and plan to put up an amusement park. Take along Rudy and Star as your construction men. Let them handle the technical stuff."

"Be careful," Sam warned him. "If it's a mob operation, they'll really look you over."

"Use a hired car but not from up there," Arnie told him.

"Will do," Tom said.

"Let's also check Cardillo's background," Arnie suggested. "Sam, you have a contact on the parole board. Maybe you can get something on Cardillo. It's possible he may have worked for some company even remotely connected with bells."

"How about the guy with the finger?" Star asked.

Arnie shrugged. "You got me. Has he any friends with a deformed hand, Toni? Perhaps a cripple?"

"Not that I know. In fact his friends never come to the house. He's always meeting them on the outside."

We went on like this, trying to find clues and leads from everything Toni had overheard. We all made suggestions which Tom, Star, and Rudy would check out but we knew it was only groping.

I tried to persuade Toni to let me drive her home or at least put her in a cab, but she was adamant about taking the subway.

"You're the damnedest, most stubborn woman I've ever met!" I told her. "Now I'll be worrying about you more than ever . . .."

We paused at the IRT entrance. "Don't worry about me, Trevor," she said with a smile. "I can take care of myself. You have to know how when you're in a family where you're outnumbered by brothers. When I was ten I was playing ring-a-levio with them. When I was thirteen I was playing one-for-one in the backyard, where we had a basketball court. When I was fifteen Julie, who was in the Golden Gloves, was teaching me how to box." She kissed me lightly on the cheek. "So watch it, Rebel, if you're thinking of—"

"We can do better than that," I said and pulled her close.

"There are an awful lot of people around, Trevor," she whispered.

"The hell with them," I said and kissed her, her arms holding me about the shoulders. There was a great deal of street noise, but for one delicious moment we seemed to be in the middle of an enormous quiet. There was a steady, singing silence. Then she slowly pulled back, her eyes full of cool secrets.

"We have an audience," she said.

There was a grinning cabdriver at the curb.

"I better say good night," she said. She smiled, ran down the steps and as usual when she reached the bottom she turned and waved. This time it seemed important. She was gone in a second. As I turned away the driver gave me a lazy smile and the V for Victory sign. I gave him one in return and crossed the Avenue on stilts ten feet tall.

No one even looked at me and I was reminded of a line from Alice Duer Miller:

Strange that in Broadway no head should be turning,
To watch one gentlemen quietly burning.

A week passed. Then one morning Stu called to tell me Madam Langford had died in the hospital. I had only known this fascinating old lady a short time but I felt a sense of personal loss.

The *Times* started her obit on page one and like all *Times* obits of notables, it had a multitude of facts but completely missed her personality. And the formal file stock cut didn't help. The funeral was crowded but we managed to say a few words of condolence to Jay, a frail, subdued, frightened old man who clung to Stu and whispered, "What will I do without her, Stuart, what will I do?"

As we were about to leave the funeral home an elderly brisk woman dressed in black hurried after us to tap me on the shoulder.

"Pardon me," she said, "are you Mr. Trevor David?"

"Yes, I am."

"I'm Mrs. Foreman, personal secretary to Madam Langford. I was with her the last few days taking dictation. One letter was to you. I've been trying to get them all off but with the funeral . . ." She handed me an envelope.

"That's quite all right, Mrs. Foreman. Thank you."

"From the way Madam Langford spoke I know she thought a great deal of both you and Mr. Harlow."

I gestured to Stu. "This is Mr. Harlow."

"She talked a lot about your league, Mr. Harlow."

"Thank you. She was a fine lady."

I opened the envelope in the cab. Inside was a brief note:

Dear Trevor:
The flowers you and Stuart sent are beautiful. I told my nurses they were from two very handsome young men, both bachelors, who would soon be visiting me. Now I have more nurses than anyone else on this floor. Wasn't that clever of me? My secretary reads me the newspapers and the doctors let me watch a little television so I know what has happened. I guess an old woman's intuition was correct this time.
You and Stuart should look into the background of this company. When the meshugeneh of a doctor allows me to have visitors we will talk about this.

Then was added:
"The International Amusement and Vending Machine Corp."
There were three addresses: New York, Las Vegas, and Miami.

We turned it over to Sam and Arnie to check out. In a week we had answers. This corporation manufactured, sold, and repaired gambling equipment, jukeboxes, and slot machines. A contact in a federal agency told Sam the company equipped casinos in Vegas, Europe, the Caribbean, and South America. Both the government and McClellan's committee had investigated it as a possible underworld conduit for cash but, although the corporation's books had been examined and its officers subpoenaed and questioned, no illegal activity had been uncovered. Curiously, in the last several months the company had been reorganized. The corporate structure was a maze of holding companies on the east and west coasts with Swiss bank references; Sam and Arnie had checked them out, all were postal drops.

But one listed the new corporate officers—a secretary and an attorney; Betsy Van Lyden and George Horatio Derby . . . .

"Well, now we know what he was doing in Las Vegas," I said. "Trying to get money for his campaign. Anybody's money."

Stu said savagely, "How does that old baseball expression go?"

"Tinker—to Evers—to Chance."

"That's the way it happened. You don't have to be Sherlock Holmes to figure it out—Cardillo to Miles to Derby—dough enough to run his campaign. As Cardillo said, when he wins they wear the mayor's hat."

"What does Miles get out of it?" Tom asked.

"Brigadier is appointed police commissioner. After the old guy gets his ego trip, he steps down and Miles takes over. Meanwhile Betsy is queen of Gracie Mansion."

Arnie said, "Now all we have to do is prove it."

"That could be a hell of a job," Tom said dubiously.

"We got this far," Stu pointed out.

"Proving is another ball game."

"We'll prove it," Stu said confidently.

"Well, now that we have this information what are we going to do with it, Stu?"

His smile was curved and deadly as a sickle blade.

"Keep it in our own collection, Trev. We may need it someday."

Then Sam called bursting with news and so excited he forgot to play his foreign agent's role. He and Arnie had learned the name of the leader of the syndicate, Cardillo's boss.

When I recall that morning with Stu smiling triumphantly at me from across the room as he listened to Sam, I become so infuriated I could drive my fist through a wall. Instead of taking Toni, kidnapping her if necessary, and fleeing to the remotest village in Alaska, I did nothing.

I curse that day.

BOOK TWO:

SIEGE OF GRAND VISTA

Chapter **8**

Sam Hoffman-Del Morenci

On the way back to Washington, Arnie and I discussed at length Stu's plan of continuing on our own. Frankly I wasn't too hot over this vigilante idea, but Arnie surprised me; he was actually enthusiastic about tracking down Cardillo and his mob. My old man always said he was never afraid of big talkers but quiet guys gave him chills. That's the way I felt about Arnie. Me, I'm not the hero type. Then again, I'm no coward. But the killings in Nam bothered me; after I came back from a patrol I found it hard to sleep. No matter how many patrols I went on, taking a body count made me almost physically ill; to see a buddy ripped to pieces made me want to cry. When we hit that bar and took care of Whitey, it was to teach some bullies a lesson. I could take it. But this business of trying to track down Cardillo and his boss made me uneasy. They were not backwoods bums lording it over a log cabin bar; big-time narcotics means money, power, and guys who view murder as simply a job that must be done quickly and efficiently.

There was another thing to consider, we all knew we might not be together much longer.

For some time I had realized Arnie was getting restless. He'd be heading for China. And the others had plans, so before long it looked like most of us were going to leave Harlow Realty. I hated to think of it. Arnie pointed out it was going to be tough for Stu when that day came around. Arnie claimed that for Stu anything after Tong Le Mai would always be anticlimactic, that those prison years were the peak experience of his life and through us he subconsciously relived them. It sounded complicated, but I felt I knew what he meant.

Yet if Stu wanted it, that was good enough for me. I would have cut off my arm for the guy; I know Arnie and the others felt the same. I recognized this when we were taking the vote in the penthouse. We seemed to automatically move in a tight protective circle around Stu, and I had the impression we all felt very close—maybe it's corny, but like a band of brothers.

I guess we were still a long way from forgetting Tong Le Mai.

I also saw that Toni was starting to get to Trev. He had never talked about it but I think he was hurt more than he admitted when he came home to find his Georgia peach had two kids, a house, mortgage, a station wagon, Friday night trips to the supermarket, and was no longer the slender blonde beauty he had described for us so many times in the Pit.

I thought a good-looking guy like him would be sweeping them out of his bed every morning, but it didn't happen like that; at the reunion cocktail party he left with something nice in green which he kept for the weekend, and there were a few others Stu brought around, but not one of them grabbed Trev. He was like Arnie and Tom, there was something dead inside. I hoped Toni would bring it back to life. . . .

The night we returned to D.C., Arnie and I had dinner at Kate's place in Georgetown. She's great for cooking offbeat dishes and when she heard Arnie liked Chinese food she cooked something with saffron rice, pork, and all kinds of vegetables topped with a spicy sauce that was delicious even though I tasted it the next day. Arnie flipped over the dinner; his evening was complete when he found Kate knew a hell of a lot about China. I was amazed listening to them bat it back and forth for hours. Oh, that Kate is a shrewd one. A couple of days later she confessed that before she invited us, she asked a girl friend who worked as an editor in the Government Printing Office to get everything they had on China; an Oriental girl who worked in her office was recruited to teach her how to make that dish.

Arnie grinned when I told him all this; his only comment was that Kate had me, I didn't have a chance. I told him the woman who hooked me would have to know how to make lentil soup rather than some

Chinese dish, but then I suddenly remembered I had taught Kate the secret of making that goddam soup and now she was better at it than my old man.

Well, a few nights after we had this dinner at Kate's, Arnie disappeared and I started to dig. Kate continued to come up with material but it appeared the strike force still did not have the name of the leader of Cardillo's syndicate.

Chickie fouled out with me. I know he was trying, but there wasn't anything in his Washington office. His lush agent friend had not returned to D.C., which left Chickie offering me rumors but no facts.

Then one night or rather morning—it was about four o'clock—the light was turned on in my bedroom and there was Arnie with that twisted grin and calm as if he was coming in to tell me it was raining.

"What the hell is this?" I demanded.

"Get your ass out of bed and make some coffee," he said, "I have something to tell you."

"It's four o'clock! Can't it wait a couple of hours?"

"Sure," he said casually and switched off the light.

"You *klutz*," I shouted, "put that goddam light on."

He switched it back on.

"I'm going to take a shower," he said.

"Give," I pleaded.

"Make the coffee. Do we have any English?"

So I got up, made coffee and toasted English muffins, and waited until he came out of the shower. I knew the moment that light switched on Arnie had something big. He did—the name.

Del Morenci, leader of the syndicate.

I sat there like a stone man as he dumped crumpled napkins, match covers, folded pieces of notepaper, even margins of newspapers, on the bed.

"Does the name mean anything to you, Sam?"

"No—but how the hell did you—"

"I'll tell you everything after I eat. I'm famished. Then I want you to sit at that typewriter and take down everything I say. Okay?"

"Okay."

I sipped at a cup of coffee while he wolfed down the muffins. That *putz* knew I was busting with impatience but no, he had to have two more and even complained I had set the toaster to make them darker than he liked. But finally he pushed back the plate, poured himself another cup, got together the garbage he called his notes, and waved me to the typewriter.

"Okay, Sam, let's go."

It appeared Morenci had put together his drug syndicate with a great deal of planning and expertise not only in Indochina but France, Corsica, and this country. It surpassed earlier groups such as the so-called French Connection mob or the South American organization that used a diplomat's yacht. There was evidence that loads valued in

181

the millions had already been smuggled past our borders; a Corsican informer working for the Brigade Criminelle of the Police Judiciaire in Paris claimed a cargo of narcotics, possibly the largest ever moved out of Indochina, was on its way to the United States. There were so many kilos, the informer said, that three caravans were used to bring them out of the jungle. Delivery date was vague, but Morenci had sent word to Corsica that the American end of the syndicate would shut down for an indefinite period after the cargo arrived.

Arnie guessed this was to allow Morenci to call another meeting and let the bosses of the crime Families vote as to whether or not they wanted to stay in junk. Undoubtedly they would continue their operations after making such a big score.

I marveled at the Agency's tenacity in gathering bits and pieces from law enforcement groups and informers all over the world to put together a personality and background portrait of Morenci.

There was only one thing—no rogues' gallery picture.

"Doesn't he have a record?" I asked Arnie.

He silently held up a copy of Morenci's yellow sheet.

"No picture," he said.

"Why not?"

"Somehow it got out of the police files," he said. "It's the old story—like the prints of the old-time mobsters that are always missing."

"Dammit! We need a picture, Arnie!"

"Keep your cool, baby, we'll come to that. Now let me get on with this stuff."

As Arnie had suspected from the very beginning Morenci had spent most of his adult life abroad. He had been born in East Harlem of Italian and Corsican parents. His early crime history was American classic—he had graduated from petty thefts into policy where his organizational skill had been spotted by a *capo* who brought him inside. He had a record of several arrests mostly for policy and drugs and two felony convictions. He did time on Rikers' Island but miraculously was granted unusually early paroles.

Evidently he was a cool hand even as a kid. A team of detectives working on a policy bank bust kicked him out of bed one morning in the house where he was boarding. A search revealed a handgun in a closet.

"I guess the people who own this house are criminals" was his explanation.

He was eighteen.

He also started a gun-for-hire business, leasing or selling stolen weapons to stickup artists, burglary rings, hijackers—anyone who could pay his price. He became known as an expert in firearms, and one informant told a New York City detective he had witnessed Morenci testing some guns stolen from a sporting goods store and swore the guy was ambidextrous:

"Informant states he had been in a cellar on Trogart Place when

Morenci was examining the load of stolen firearms. A target had been placed at one end of the cellar. Morenci fired each handgun and once tossed a gun from his right to left hand and fired, each time hitting the target. The informant later said his friend Tommy Glaze, alias 'Tommy the Sheriff,' told him Morenci 'had it down to a science' and used to win bets he could hit a target with either hand. He also said Morenci had killed two men, both Hispanic, on West 117th Street on orders of the numbers mob, after the men tried to work the Avenue independently. Morenci, he had said, bragged how he had killed one with the right hand, the other with the left, 'for practice.'. . ."

From policy Morenci went into narcotics. During the Korean War he ducked the draft by going abroad. From Sicily he made his way to Paris, West Germany, and finally to Corsica where he lived with his mother's relatives. He was well heeled, and information from the Brigade Criminelle insisted he had been active in the international drug traffic. He disappeared for three years, then showed up on an Interpol confidential communication as a big buyer of drugs in Hong Kong, where he maintained a legitimate exporting office. The Interpol flyer claimed he had established an extensive network of drug dealers in Indochina to supply his American contacts.

He next returned to Paris, then Corsica where the French police said he became close to important members of the inner council of the Union Corse, that many law enforcement agencies believe is the most powerful crime group in Europe. Compared to the Corsicans, the Mafia of Sicily is an ancient band of bandits, extortioners, and gunmen. While the Corsicans are as ruthless as the Mafia they have more finesse; to them crime, power-politics, and international diplomacy are one.

Morenci lived in anonymity, he shunned publicity and was known to only a few experts in the French and British police. Ironically one of the best sources of information was a Hong Kong police captain; his father-in-law owned the building where Morenci had his exporting firm. He had a duplicate key for Morenci's office. Every weekend the captain made a leisurely inspection of Morenci's files and during the week collected contents of the scrap baskets.

Then one day a young gunman walked into a restaurant where the captain was having lunch and shot him three times. The dying police officer, using his table as a shield, exchanged shots to kill his assailant. Hong Kong's organized crime groups would have paid the killer a small fortune to polish off the captain, but they both died over a pretty young whore; the captain had set her up for himself, the killer was her disgruntled pimp.

That's what I mean when I say the unexpected can change any investigation—from a stolen car to an international drug syndicate.

This wrapped up Arnie's report. I pushed back the chair and just looked at him. He filled his cup and silently toasted me.

"Just where the hell did you get all this?"

"From the Agency." He yawned. "Christ, what a night."

"The Agency. You mean you just walked in and they gave it to you?"

"Come on, Sam, you know the Agency won't even tell you if you're on the right street."

"Well then, how the hell did you get it?"

"A little horse trading." He gestured with his cup. "I wanted something they had and they wanted something I have."

"Arnie, I can't believe an outfit like the CIA would open their files to an outsider."

"First of all I'm not an outsider. I gave them ten good years in Indochina and almost six in a goddam prison camp without opening my mouth and they know it. Of course they wanted to know why I wanted the information and I told them I was going to turn it over to you to pay back some favors."

I almost leaped out of the chair. "Me! You told them we were working together?"

"Of course, there's no use in lying, Sam; they'll find out about you."

"What story did you give them, Arnie?"

"That you ran a private detective agency in New York and had been hired by a writer to gather new and authentic information on the international drug traffic. Of course they checked you out and found you had a good reputation. Then they made you my responsibility—I had to vouch for you."

"Okay. So they swallowed that story, but the CIA giving out any of its information—"

"Sam, it's been done countless times," Arnie said wearily. "The Agency has never been immune to leaking or trading peripheral material if it will help them. I believe I told you this before: by law the CIA is not interested in our domestic crime, they couldn't care less. In fact their charter specifically forbids them from interfering with a local investigation. That's why the Agency got its ass burned in Watergate and doing that domestic spying in the sixties. They're concerned with international espionage. However, from the very nature of their business they collect a hell of a lot of information from their agents' reports. And a few of them just happened to include Morenci's name and something about his activities."

"Now let me get this straight, Arnie," I said, trying to put my head together. "The Agency had Morenci's name and something about his drug running and gave it to you in trade for something they wanted . . ."

"That about sums it up, Sam."

"Well, what in the hell do you have that's so important to them?"

He pushed back his cup and put his feet up on the bed.

"When the CIA wants something real bad, Sam, they'll move heaven and earth to get it. They don't care how, with them the battle is the payoff—getting what they want is all-important. Ford's committee brought that out. Let me try to tell you how it works . . ."

184

For more than an hour Arnie lectured me on the CIA, an outfit he claimed was run by men who could only be described as hard-nosed realists mainly concerned about two things: the People's Republic of China and the USSR. Arnie called China the last espionage frontier; only a witless *nahr* would insist there is nothing to worry about as long as we have a working agreement with the Chairman. Arnie pointed out that if the Chinese discovered an American agent moving around their country in disguise, there would be no formal arrest and subsequent international outcry which could hurt the fragile understanding between our countries; maybe instead a simple fall from a balcony or something slipped into a cup of tea. . . .

Arnie said he had great respect for the Chinese counterintelligence agents, he said you could be sure they would kill you with class.

"Always remember, Sam," he said, "the Agency has a Machiavellian philosophy, expedience, not morality. The 'how' is not important—that you get what the Agency wants is all-important."

"You still haven't told me what you have that the Agency wants."

"Okay, let's start off with this premise—the Agency is desperate to get someone into China—"

"I would say that's obvious."

"Then I come along. I want to go to China. I speak the language. I have an excellent record. There's only one thing—I don't want to work for the Agency. However"—he leaned back and yawned—"I want something they have and I want it very badly. And that thing is not important to them—but getting me back and off to China is. Comprende?"

"Si."

"That was when they began feeding me this information on Indochina."

"Do you mean they actually set you up?"

"Exactly. The first guy I met tipped off the Agency what I was after and they primed him as bait, feeding me that information on Indochina."

"But Arnie," I protested. "Why should they go through all this playacting? Why didn't they just ask you if you wanted to go?"

He sighed. "You're not listening, Sam. I told you they had asked me to come back and I told them I was up to here with their operation. Then when they discovered I was interested in getting into the mainland, they decided I was their boy. The next thing was to get me back into the fold."

"But what about the steel guy? The one who offered you the contract to go to China?"

He laughed.

"It's an Agency firm, Sam! That was only a little sweetening! They do it all the time. Remember the coup in Chile? I can't prove it, of course, but I'll bet the Agency helped to dump Allende by using private American-owned companies."

"Just how could they do that?"

"American banks shut off credit while American businesses slow vital deliveries. That means economic problems. Then technical help is drained off. Oh, the Agency has lots of tricks up its sleeve, Sam."

He added bitterly, "That's what I mean about our society."

"Well, if you feel that way why make a deal with them?"

"For a couple of reasons. I owe a lot to Stu. I happen to agree with him that Morenci is a menace. Also I want to get out of this country for a while. It's a bad scene for me, Sam."

"So the whole thing—this CIA guy giving you this stuff on narcotics, the introduction to the steel man—this company, your contract—everything was arranged by the Agency?"

"Right. I smelled something the first time I met that guy. Remember when I told you I thought the guy didn't click right with me? But what the hell, Sam, we're getting what we want. I'm going to China, and somehow we'll take care of that son of a bitch Morenci. You can't beat that combination!"

"Stu will crawl through the phone."

"I'm going to love telling him"—he gave me a sly grin—"just like I'm going to love telling you, you're going with me to Paris."

I could only stare at him. Sometimes Arnie is unbelievable.

"Paris? What are we going to do there?"

"It's a little extra bonus the Agency gave me for signing up immediately. Right after we get Morenci, I'll be on my way to China. To get back to Paris, Sam, we're going to see a Colonel Simon Bouquet, Deputy Chief of the Intelligence Division, Brigade Criminelle, Police Judiciaire. The colonel and I are also going to do a little trading. You're going to be my assistant."

"You're going too fast for me, Arnie. What do they have on Morenci? And what do you have that they want?"

"As I understand it, Paris has quite a file on Morenci and is well acquainted with his drug running. The Agency has been in touch with Paris and it's all set."

"That name Colonel Bouquet is ringing a bell somewhere in my mind, Arnie."

"It should, Sam, you dug him out."

"I did?"

He was mentioned in one of Kate's first contributions. Do you remember—"

Then it came to me. "Dammit! Sure I do! Somebody on the strike force in New York wanted to contact a Colonel B in Paris!"

"That's it. Bouquet is the liaison officer in Paris for all the intelligence bureaus in Washington."

"Now what in the hell do you have that someone in Paris wants?"

"Seriously, Sam, I don't know. The people I spoke to in the Agency said it has to do with China and our relationship with Paris but that's all they would give me. They said I would get the whole story from Bouquet."

186

"And Bouquet is going to sit there and open up with me in the picture? He must want you awful bad, baby."

"Your guess is as good as mine. I'll find out soon enough."

"This is getting bigger every day, Arnie."

"And it all began because one day Toni picked up a telephone . . . ."

"I think she should bow out."

"I said that a long time ago," he pointed out.

Kicking off his shoes, he said, "God, I'm tired . . . give me an hour, Sam, before you put in the call to Stu."

Within seconds he was in a deep sleep and I was rereading the notes I had typed—still finding it hard to believe that at last we were on target.

Morenci . . . Del Morenci. . . .

As I predicted Stu was overjoyed at hearing the news and insisted we fly to Paris immediately.

It was no sightseeing tour. After landing at Orly we had a few hours' sleep in a hotel, a fast breakfast, then a cab delivered us to Colonel Bouquet's office in the enormous headquarters of the Police Judiciaire on the Quai des Orfèvres.

Bouquet turned out to be a fastidious little guy with a scalpel-sharp mind and a long horn of a nose he kept wiping. I told myself he either had a chronic cold or was allergic to Americans. In perfect English he told us he was a Corsican and the brigade expert on that island's drug smugglers.

I have a habit of making notes after every important conference so my statements are not all from memory. This was Bouquet's deal:

It seems an old Frenchman whose name is not important had worked for a French company for many years in Harbin, Manchuria. He had been there during the Japanese occupation of the thirties, the Russian control during World War II, their withdrawal, and finally when the Chinese Communists drove out the Nationalists and established the control which rules Manchuria today. Harbin is an officially closed city. Even though the United States is on good terms with the Chinese, only a few Americans have been permitted to pass through the area—and no Europeans.

Now what should a colonel in the Paris office of the Brigade Criminelle want with an old man who has been living in Manchuria for over forty years?

Get this:

For over forty years the old Frenchman had been working for his country's counterespionage bureau, funneling information to Paris by way of a listening post in Hong Kong.

Arnie said the CIA had had an excellent relationship with the French counterintelligence since the early days of the Cold War.

After Arnie had agreed to accept the assignment of working as an agent in Harbin, Manchuria, under the guise of an employee of the steel company, Washington notified the director of the Police Judiciaire that he was going and was eager to make a trade for anything that had to do with Del Morenci, a Corsican drug smuggler.

Now why did Washington notify Paris that Arnie would be going to Manchuria? Simple. The old Frenchman had been married for many years to an American; for years they had shared their intelligence—the husband reporting to Paris, the wife to Washington on military and political moves in Manchuria during the post World War II years.

After his wife died and the Chinese took over, the Frenchman found it impossible to get his reports through to the French agent in Hong Kong. The last Paris had heard from him was in the mid-sixties when a White Russian came back to Paris to die.

Since 1969 the Russian military threat poised less than three hundred miles from the Manchurian border made the Frenchman an extremely important listening post; Harbin, as the major rail and industrial center in Manchuria, would be the first objective of a Soviet sweep into northeastern China.

Arnie would be employed by the steel company in Harbin, where the Frenchman lived. Both Washington and Paris were drooling over the possibility of getting reports out of Harbin through Arnie.

"So you see, Monsieur Harper, you would be in a splendid position to visit my countryman," Bouquet said with an attempt at being jovial. "Of course there are details we will be discussing with Washington. . . ." He gave us a thin smile. "There are times when we find each other very helpful." He added with a grimace, "And now Monsieur Morenci . . ."

A practiced swipe of the big handkerchief took care of that French horn. Then he opened a file and began reading as Arnie took notes. Their stuff on the Indochina drug syndicates was in greater detail than what Kate had found in the Washington files; he had incredible details of the internal politics of Burma, Laos, and Thailand along with the names of the officials who were accepting bribes from the two Chinese Nationalist generals who controlled the largest part of the opium crops and the interior refining factories.

Then he reached a series of reports from their Corsican informer which showed a side of Morenci that made me wish I had never left Bensonhurst.

Once one of his lieutenants had committed the error of selling a load of junk to a Sûreté undercover agent. Morenci had him bailed out, then invited the guy to dinner. The poor guy was strangled over dessert.

Another time Morenci was sitting with a girl in a seaport village near Ajaccio, the island's capital; the local schoolteacher was with a group playing darts. Morenci claimed they were making too much noise and ordered them out. The others left, but the schoolteacher, who had been hitting the wine all afternoon, told him to drop dead and continued to play darts. On the way home he was jumped and later found wandering along a country road; both his eyes had been gouged out.

The French police came from the "Continent," as the Corsicans call France, to question Morenci but all they got were shrugs. Although Morenci couldn't be found, a police artist made a portrait sketch based on the schoolteacher's description.

Bouquet placed it on the desk before us as carefully as if he was unveiling the Holy Grail.

It showed a man in his early fifties with thick black wavy hair, jowly, thin lips, a battered nose and pouches under his eyes. I will never forget the evil in that face.

There was another sketch of Morenci's right hand; a fingertip was missing.

Clipped to that sketch was an affidavit from a West German doctor who identified the portrait as that of a French exporter whose hand had been caught in a car door. He had amputated the mangled tip of the middle finger of the right hand. The sketch was taken from his X rays.

The colonel casually pointed out that now we had the only known portrait of Morenci and his hand. Later Arnie said that was for his benefit, the Frenchman wanted to underscore the value of what they were offering in trade.

As for me, the moment I saw that hand I recalled Cardillo's phrase, as overheard by Toni:

"The man with the finger."

When I handed the sketches back to Arnie, a slight flicker in his eyes told me he had spotted the same connection.

"Do your people know where Morenci is at present, Colonel?" Arnie asked.

The tip of the big nose temporarily disappeared in a whirl of handkerchief.

"We have a report that Monsieur Morenci left for Canada some time ago. Exactly when we do not know."

"Do you have the alias he was using?"

A Gallic shrug.

" 'e uses many, Monsieur Harper. All common Corsican names—like your Smith or Jones—Colombani, Nicolai, Mariani. Morelli, Forelli, take your pick."

"Do you think he crossed over into the States?"

A wry smile.

"We do not believe Monsieur Morenci has any business interests in Canada."

"The United States is a big place, Colonel."

Another shrug.

"That is the extent of our information, Monsieur."

"But didn't you contact Canada, Colonel?"

I watched fascinated as a pearl slowly formed at the slightly reddish tip of his nose. But before it could drop it disappeared into the handkerchief.

"France always cooperates with its friends, Monsieur Harper. Your people in Washington will tell you that."

"We were hoping we could meet with your Corsican informer."

He gave us an outraged stare.

"If he were alive that would be impossible. Surely you know that!"

"Alive? You mean he is dead?"

Bouquet nodded sadly.

"Unfortunately. Shortly after he sent us his last report on Morenci leaving Ajaccio his body was found in the harbor. His tongue had been cut out. It is the traditional Corsican warning to informers. Too bad, but these people are always vulnerable." He added softly, "Like your two informers in New York."

"What specific warrants and charges are there against Morenci?" Arnie asked.

Bouquet shook his head.

"There are none."

"But didn't the police look for him after the schoolteacher—"

"For questioning, Monsieur," Bouquet interrupted. "There is no evidence he committed the crime. Or that he killed his associate. Or that he is even in drugs." He shrugged. "He could walk in tomorrow and walk out within a few hours." He gave us a contemptuous glance. "You don't think he would admit to anything?"

Arnie's reply was smooth and soft.

"Of course not, my dear Colonel, but we had hoped the magnificent Brigade Criminelle had found a way to get the evidence to send this thug to prison."

Bouquet flushed. "This man is not a simple thug, Monsieur, he is extremely clever." He added coldly, "In fact, monsieur, we welcome the opportunity to permit you to find the evidence to put him behind bars."

He closed his folder with a snap.

"Indochina to Corsica to the United States! It is a big operation, Monsieur Harper. We wish you luck with Monsieur Morenci!"

Back at the hotel we went over Bouquet's material and studied the portrait of Morenci and his right hand.

"He's a rough-looking guy," Arnie observed.

"That could be the understatement of the year. As for me, I'd just as gladly not find him."

"We will," Arnie said cheerfully. "He's somewhere in the States."

"What do we do—go from state to state?"

"A guy like this doesn't hide out in Montana or Wyoming, Sam. He's in the metropolitan area."

190

"Why there?"

"That's where his junk is coming in. Besides, he's a city guy—he may not be in Manhattan, maybe on the Island or in Jersey. Somewhere near, so he can get a smell of the city."

"I can't believe there's no warrant out for the guy."

"As Bouquet said, he's clever. You can't put suspicion before a grand jury."

"Don't you think this is getting too big for us, Arnie? We're looking for a guy who is somewhere in the United States under an assumed name. He's supposed to be the head of an international drug syndicate. There's no warrant or charge against him. I might add the federal people and the NYPD haven't had much luck either."

"You're forgetting something—we have his name and his portrait. A little something the others haven't got—yet."

"But you said now that they leaked it to us, the Agency will probably turn it over to the others."

"They gave us a head start."

"I say it's a million to one we don't find him."

"I'll take those odds."

"Let's suppose, Arnie—just let's suppose we do find Morenci. What the hell will we do with him?"

"As Stu said, turn him over to the feds."

"What can they do with him if there isn't a charge against him?"

"By that time maybe we'll have enough to make a charge."

"And if we don't?"

"He can always be a political expediency."

He said this with an air of challenge, almost defiance, as if he expected me to question or rebut it.

For a moment I didn't get it—then I did.

I said, surprised, "You mean kill him?"

He picked up the portrait of Morenci and studied it for a moment.

"When they write the history of our generation, Sam, they'll probably blame Nam, Watergate, corruption, crooked politics, the recession, and lack of leadership for the erosion of our society, but they'll also have to include drugs. I think it will be years before we realize the damage narcotics have done to us." He tossed Morenci's portrait back on the bed. "As far as I'm concerned a rattlesnake is more important than this son of a bitch! Kill him? Definitely, if we have to. Does that answer your question?"

It did.

We made return reservations, but because I had never seen Paris Arnie gave me a quick one-day tour. It's lucky he did, on our return to the hotel we had a call from Bouquet; back we went to the Brigade Criminelle.

The colonel told us something had come up shortly after we left; the agent assigned to investigate the murder of the Corsican informant had returned to Paris. His report was incomplete, still in the agent's raw notes. There was only a brief mention of Morenci but he thought it might be of interest.

He gave his nose a wipe, then began reading from a yellow legal pad. This section of the full report concerned the activities of a New York prostitute who had been put under surveillance because of her known relationship with drug merchants in Marseilles, Corsica, and Hong Kong. He rattled off a list of shops she had visited and the hotels where she stayed. A stoolie had informed the agent an American gangster named Morenci, living in Corsica, had briefly visited her; he assumed it was for sex.

Bouquet pointed out this was shortly before Morenci left France for Canada. The whore had only recently returned to the United States. Her pile of luggage indicated how extensive her shopping tour had been. French customs, advised to examine her carefully, found nothing.

"And her name, Colonel?" Arnie asked.

Bouquet glanced down at the sheet.

"Renee Talbot," he said. "But that is only one of many aliases she used in hotels and shops. I assume you are aware, Monsieur, that this is a common practice for prostitutes."

"And her port of entry in the States?"

He flipped through the records.

"New York."

Again we said good-bye and returned to the hotel.

"Did you get it?" Arnie asked.

"Of course. This must be Stash's whore whose bedroom was bugged by the feds. But didn't Washington ask Paris to keep an eye on her?"

"Right. And Kate gave us the report Paris sent back—"

"That she was on a shopping tour."

"Right again. But that was three months ago. This is all new stuff. You heard what Bouquet said, the agent hadn't even finished his formal report."

"But why didn't Bouquet tell us this was the whore Washington was interested in?"

"Why should he? It's not in our deal he must reveal their confidential messages."

"Wasn't the whore in Kate's stuff named Suzy?"

"Susan Dennison. But as Bouquet pointed out, traveling whores use different names."

"So we have another leg up on Washington. They don't have Morenci's portrait, the fact he's lost a finger, or that Stash's whore is back in New York."

"Do you think your contacts at headquarters can dig her up, Sam?"

"I'll certainly try. What are you planning? Getting Stash through her?"

"We know she's a link. Any whore who comes back to set up her

192

business calls every John in her trick book. We know Stash really had hot nuts for her. He'll probably be the first she'll call. Now all we have to do is find her. . . ."

He went to the kitchen and returned with two cups of coffee.

"Morenci's next load, the big one, should be coming into the States any day now. That's where Toni comes in—she's going to be damn important in the next few weeks." He sat down on the edge of the bed and sipped the coffee. "I hope that guy Cardillo never gets wise."

We looked at each other.

"Arnie, all I can think of is that Corsican schoolteacher . . ."

We returned to New York and spent a day with Stu, Trev, and the others going over the Washington and Paris material. Tom made a sort of divisional map on which we listed our goals and priorities:

A—Find Morenci

B—Identify and find Stash

C—Identify and find the whore

Trev reported he had briefly met Toni who gave him the contents of three phone calls, all from Stash; one discussed what Cardillo called the "locations," the other two were about his lawyer's attempts to set up a meeting with the assistant district attorney handling his case before the grand jury. That's usual with hoods, they're so naturally crooked they will try to fix a case even though they are assured by their lawyers it will be thrown out of court.

It was decided that A and B objectives were too hard to take on until we had more intelligence, so the location of "Renee Talbot" or "Susan Dennison" was given top priority. These were the facts we had to go on: She was a professional, once had an apartment on East Seventy-seventh Street, had only recently returned from Paris, and did not work with a pimp, which made her a loner—and harder to find.

I went to the first obvious source, the apartment where she had lived at the time of the bugging by the federal agents—we had the address from Kate's early report. She had voluntarily left the building without a police bust so that indicated the super was on the pad. He had one of those short upper lips that exposed his teeth and gave him the look of a rodent. Before he would talk it cost me five tens and a frisk for a service revolver to prove I wasn't a cop; he was a professional, he looked up my pants legs for a holster. I identified myself as a researcher hired by an author doing a serious study on prostitution in New York City; it was so original it intrigued him. After answering a lot of stupid questions he whispered his answer—Suzy was in Paris.

I was so mad I could have kicked this *schmuck* in the ass, but I played it cool and promised another fifty if when I called he had some specific information.

Then I had dinner with my inspector friend in Morals—he called the Bureau of Identification and came up with two Susan Dennisons, one a whore, the other a seventy-year-old shoplifter. The whore was reported out of the city. It was negative on Renee Talbot.

After a week I had nothing; a friend in the garment district went down the numbers in his little black book but all the girls insisted they had never heard of a Susan Dennison or a Renee Talbot. Of course they were lying, Macy doesn't tell Gimbels, even in whoredom. . . .

We continued plugging, then on a hunch I called my rat-faced friend, the super. It paid off, he wanted to see me right away. This time it cost me a C note to say hello. Suzy had come back with a Paris tie for him and a request for an apartment; she was now back in business at her old address. An introduction would cost another fifty bucks. I told him my author-boss would want to be in on the interview and I'd get back to him.

At a penthouse meeting we all agreed it would be foolish to sit down and *tummel* with this bitch; the first mention or indication we were interested in Stash might blow the whole project. There was an alternative; check the license plates of Suzy's customers in the hope that Stash would appear. This is standard cop procedure but terribly time-consuming. How would you know her customers? Suppose they arrived in a cab or just walked into the building? Cops could put the arm on the super but we had to tiptoe around this creep.

We were all arguing and making suggestions when the phone rang. It was Toni, who wanted to see Trev right away. He flew out of the penthouse and we waited.

Toni had come up with a weird piece of information she got from her sister; Teresa told her that she had accidentally learned Cardillo had bought a small business some time ago named "Adolph's Lunch Boxes"; she had no location or details but told Toni she believed it served coffee and sandwiches to construction workers.

The Brooklyn telephone book gave us the full name—Adolph's Traveling Lunch Boxes. Arnie and I found the office in an old building on Fan Street near Borough Hall. In the garage under the building were a number of small aluminum trailers, all shaped like lunch boxes. On the sides was the name Adolph's Famous Traveling Lunch Boxes, Est. 1948.

There was only one other office in the building; The Happy Valley Wine and Liquor Company and The Happy Valley Catering Company were on the door.

Both the Lunch Box and the other offices were locked.

We walked over to the Kings County clerk's office in Borough Hall and checked out the lunch box firm. Only a partnership agreement between a man we quickly determined to be an accountant and his wife were on file. Obviously it was a blind.

We temporarily put the whore on the shelf; Star and Rudy were assigned to tail one of the traveling lunch boxes while Arnie and I *shlepped* up to Albany to do some digging in the secretary of state's office. We found the corporation resolution for both Happy Valley concerns; they had the same accountant and his wife as president and vice-president but also a new name as treasurer, Michel Forelli.

It immediately clicked with both of us—Forelli was one of the Corsican names Bouquet said was like our Jones or Smith.

I ran the names through my contact at headquarters and came up negative on the accountant and his wife but got plenty on Forelli:

Michel Forelli, alias Mike Fortunato, alias Mike Stash; twelve arrests, mostly for narcotics and usury (shylocking), two convictions, one for violation of the usury law, the other for assault with a deadly weapon. He spent sixty days on the island on the usury charge and two and a half to five in Sing Sing on the assault rap.

The sheet gave the names of the arresting officers for the two arrests so Arnie and I spent a good part of the next day looking them up. One guy was dead, but the detective who had locked up Fortunato—that's the name he was known by for the assault—was a tough old-line cop who first checked with my friend the inspector before he would accept our invitation to lunch.

My interest was simply explained; I had a client who was about to make a business deal with Fortunato.

"Better tell your man to stay away from that bastard," the old cop warned us.

"He's no good?"

"You got his sheet."

"How about your collar?"

"I was in the One-O-One in Harlem when I grabbed him. He was putting out muscle for the shylocks. He clobbered this guy with a pipe. The poor jerk still dances instead of walks. Me and my partner got ahold of him on the Avenue and gave him a rememberance before we booked him."

"Was he ever connected with a Family?" Arnie asked.

"He was always small-time, good with a pipe but no brains. After he got out he went into junk." He polished off his drink and I signaled the waiter who quickly refilled it. "I don't go for that marky-larky stuff about crime Families and Soldiers. To me they're all bums, especially them in junk. Me, I'm glad I'm gettin' out of the job. You throw 'em in at ten, they're out by two. In a couple of months I pitch in the tin and me and the wife'll go down to the Keys. My old partner has a charter boat. We're gonna buy into it and sit around seein' how much Miller's we can drink and how many lies we can tell. . . ."

He gave us all the details he could remember about Fortunato and called a retired detective who had also arrested him. The hood was now about fifty-five, a bachelor, and known to patronize whores.

The detective gave a short laugh. "The bum's a pushover when it comes to pussy. He even romances whores."

The retired West Harlem cop recalled Fortunato had a known eccentricity; in an age when a Cadillac was a gangster's status symbol he never owned a car or learned how to drive. He did all his traveling in cabs.

A routine call to the Better Business Bureau produced a gripe sheet on Happy Valley, a beef for slow payment which was not unusual, but the second was from a Flatbush liquor store owner who charged "harassment."

Posing as a credit checker I phoned the owner who floored me by praising the company as among the best. I reminded him of his letter to the BBB but he called it a "misunderstanding." When Arnie and I paid him a visit we found a very nervous middle-aged guy who insisted Happy Valley was a joy to deal with; it was evident Cardillo's boys had answered his letter.

There was one more item to look into, the name of the original owner of the Lunch Box mentioned in the partnership agreement.

As my old man told me many times, neighbors can be an important source of information. Nine out of ten will slam the door in your face, but the tenth usually turns out to be a neighborhood gossip or a guy with a grudge. We started looking for that jewel when we discovered the original owner, an Adolph Steiner, had returned to Germany after he sold the business.

The people in the apartment house all gave us the same answers, either they were new in the neighborhood, they didn't know Steiner, or they couldn't care less. Then, halfway down the block, this woman answered the bell. The moment I saw her I knew we had hit the jackpot. I can't explain it, I guess it's just instinct.

She invited me in, I whistled to Arnie who was across the street and we settled down to coffee, cookies, and gossip.

At one time she could have been called good looking in a brassy sort of way. She was in her fifties with a fairly good figure, tired, bleached hair, and a pinched face that warned the world she was mad about something. There wasn't a thing out of place in her apartment; it looked as if she had made dusting a career.

She and her late husband had bought the two-family house during the Depression so we had to listen to stories of those hard days. Then came a denunciation of the city's services, the energy crisis, Watergate, and the idiots in Washington, inflation that was making us all poor—I agreed to that—and how, if it weren't for her two sons' contributions and her tenant's rent, she could not survive.

A litany of woes about tenants followed. We were almost mesmerized, sipping coffee, munching cookies, and nodding. Finally when she appeared exhausted, I returned to Adolph.

She certainly knew a lot about him. He came out of the army to work in the corner deli for a while, then started his Traveling Lunch Box idea. Her husband had been killed in the war, leaving her with two kids. She was looking for part-time work when Adolph, who lived on the block, suggested she help him prepare the sandwiches; he would provide the meat, bread, butter, mustard, lettuce, and tomatoes and she

196

would deliver the finished product. I gathered they did a little cheating between orders but it looked like Adolph had sidestepped anything permanent.

"I guess he did a good business at those construction jobs," I said.

"Construction jobs? He only went to schools."

Arnie and I gulped.

"Schools?"

"Oh, he was a smart Dutchman," she said, shaking her head. "Ad—we'll call him that—said right from the beginning the kids would rather buy food on the outside than eat in the school cafeteria. This way they had more time for playing. He had a good head on his shoulders, that guy. Now mind you, I'm not saying he didn't give the kids good food because he did. Every sandwich I packed was loaded with meat. More than most of them got at home, I can tell you that. He had soda, chocolate milk, and coffee because after a while people in the neighborhoods would drop by and get their lunch from him. In a couple of years he had three trucks." She added proudly, "We served the biggest schools in Brooklyn."

I pointed out, "With only three trucks?"

She shook her head. "He knew he couldn't cover them all in the lunch period so he had an army buddy who lived in Fort Hamilton make little vans out of plywood and shaped like lunch boxes. We spent a whole weekend painting them silver. I think in a year we had ten. They were like trailers. He attached three or four to each truck and just dropped 'em off at the schools. Everybody in Brooklyn knew him.

" 'There goes the German's lunch boxes,' they would say."

Arnie said, "I guess he had a great business."

"None better," she said firmly. "I had three women from the neighborhood helping me. Do you know we worked sometimes until midnight? Even on the holidays like Christmas, we had plenty to do with bills and paper work."

"How about vacations?" Arnie asked as if he was really interested.

"That's why he went into the catering business," she said bitterly. "He couldn't stop. He couldn't take a day off. He was never satisfied, he always had to have more . . . no vacations . . . no holidays, just work, work, work. . . ."

We waited while she silently cursed Adolph.

"I worked my fingers to the bone in those days!"

She angrily selected a cigarette, tapped it sharply on the table, and took the light Arnie offered.

"But he wasn't a good businessman?" I put in.

She gave me an indignant look.

"Adolph? The best! He had the first nickel he ever made. You know how Germans are. It wasn't catering that ruined us, it was that wine and liquor company! I told him he was a fool to get into whiskey but no, he had a chance to buy this fellow out and nothing I said meant anything."

"That's the Happy Valley Wine and Liquor Company on Fan Street?" I asked.

She nodded. "He had his office downstairs. They were one flight up. Happy Valley was owned by another German fellow—he died of cancer and his wife sold out to Adolph." She conceded, "It was good for the first couple of years, then he got in with some bad people." She lowered her voice. "Eyetalians, real gangsters."

"How did that happen?"

"It was his gambling," she said furiously. "I warned him but he wouldn't listen. Two, three nights a week he was gambling. Sometimes he stayed up all night and went right to work. That's no way to run a business! I tried to talk to him but he just waved me away."

And she waved her hand.

Arnie sighed. "That's the trouble," he said to me with a solemn face, "people don't listen. They just don't listen."

"You're right, mister," she said, "people should listen to their friends, that's what friends are for—right?"

"Right," Arnie echoed.

"I guess he lost everything?" I asked.

"Not right away. He kept selling pieces of the business to those people and one day, maybe because he finally started to listen to me, he refused to sell them any more . . . and . . ."

She hesitated.

Arnie prompted gently, "And then what happened?"

"They put a gun to his head." She fashioned her hand into a gun and put it to her temple. "One day they did this in his office and made him sell them everything. They gave him money but not what the business was worth. He took a big loss."

"Did he go to the police?"

She licked her lips and her hand quivered as she filled her cup.

"One night two of 'em came to his apartment with a ticket to Germany. They told him it would be good for his health to take a long vacation. He came down to say good-bye and told me. He said it didn't make much difference anymore, he was sick of this country with all the gangsters and was going back to Germany to live with his sister." She pointed. "I looked out that window when he left and saw him get into the car with two tough-looking Eyetalians and drive away."

"Did Adolph say who bought him out?"

When she started to shake her head Arnie asked, "Was it a man named Forelli or Fortunato?"

"That's it!" she said triumphantly. "Fortunato. Adolph used to call him the Italian fortune cookie. He said he was a very tough man. Ad was afraid of him."

"Are you sure Adolph went to Germany?"

"I'm sure. He sent me a letter telling all about the business and how that fellow—"

"Fortunato?"

"Yeah. That's him. The Eyetalian fortune cookie. How he made him sell out and how the hoodlums brought him to the plane. He said he was planning to make a run for it at the last moment but they took him to the entrance—right to the entrance where you get on the plane—and one of them had a gun in his coat pocket. Ad said the guy made him put his hand in his pocket once to prove he really had a gun . . ."

"Do you have that letter?" Arnie asked quickly.

She rummaged around a drawer.

"It's here somewhere," she said apologetically. "Maybe if you come around again sometime, I'll find it by then. Here are two postcards he sent me—they're both from Stuttgart—now he's living with his sister." She tossed a photograph on the table. "There's Ad, you can have it if you want, my son works for a photography studio and made me several copies."

The glossy print showed a smiling, round-faced man in his forties, who, to me, looked as if he liked fun and games and no permanent bicycle built for two. I wondered if Ad was just as happy to have gotten out from under and return to homemade schnitzel and bock beer.

"He always wants me to write to him," she said.

"And did you?" I asked her.

She shrugged. "Maybe he would want me to come over. But what could I do over there? Learn to make sauerbraten?"

"Did Mr. Steiner have a route sheet by any chance?" Arnie wanted to know.

She nodded. "I got one here," she searched in the drawer and came up with a mimeographed sheet. "That's the last sheet we made up. It has all the schools." She ground out the cigarette in an ashtray and carefully dumped it into the wastepaper basket. "That damn fool!" When she looked up her eyes were glittering as she nervously patted her hair. "If he had only been satisfied—there would be Lunch Boxes all over the city today."

"Now we have the picture," I told Arnie on the way back to Manhattan, "Cardillo and Stash muscled in on the German's business."

He began, "More important," but I stopped him.

"I know, the schools. They're using an established business."

"A bag of horse with your sarsaparilla and sandwich! How do you like these guys?"

Stu was alone in the penthouse when we returned. He listened to our report in silence.

"What's our next target, Stu?" Arnie asked.

I pointed to the divisional map.

"Stash or the whore?"

Stu said, "We agreed you can't go to her."

"It would be risky. She would probably call Stash to warn him some guys are asking about him."

"What about Stash? We know who he is, we know where he lives." He looked up. "Any suggestions?"

"We put the snatch on him," Arnie said.

"Okay, we grab Fortunato," I said. "Where do we take him?"

"That's no problem," Stu said, "I'll rent a place on the Island, one that's isolated. It's not unusual to take over a shore house for the winter."

"We get him there and he tells us to drop dead."

"He'll talk," Arnie said quietly.

"It's kidnapping, Arnie," I warned him, "a class A felony."

"It's a business deal. We want to buy into Happy Valley."

"Stop kidding yourself. A couple of strangers? He'll run like a thief."

"Nicotine sulphate," Arnie said. "It will knock him out in seconds." He grinned. "The last time I used it was on a Charlie informer. He was a hundred miles from his village when he woke up."

We looked at each other.

"This guy is a thug, someone who's selling drugs to kids in a schoolyard with sandwiches," Stu said slowly.

"I say let's snatch him," Arnie said. "He's not that tough."

"Sam?"

"I don't want to sound like a broken record but it's a big, big felony . . ."

Silence. They looked at me again. Like a fool I nodded.

"We'll bring in Star and Rudy on this part of the operation," Stu said, "but I don't want Trev or Tom to know anything about it—for a while at least."

That shook me up.

"Wait a minute, Stu, we're all in this together! We never did anything unless we all—"

He leaned across the desk.

"Trev and Tom might not go for this, Sam. The only alternative would be for them to leave. I don't want that to happen, so let's not give them a reason. When it's all over I'll do the explaining."

"What will they be doing in the meantime?"

He held up the sheet listing Steiner's school route.

"Each school will have to be checked out. You found those lunch box vans in the garage so they must be in business, probably selling junk to the kids."

I didn't like this arrangement but I went along.

Again I recalled what my old man said many times as we were tailing some *klutz* in a matrimonial case. Maybe in the beginning for him it was only once, then before he knew what was happening, more lies, more deceptions turned what he had thought was a hello and good-bye date into a regular performance. My old man said sex wasn't the only reason, it was a combination of things: excitement, the sense of danger, escape from the humdrum, variety—and just plain stupidity. That's what happened to me, in a matter of days I was caught up in the machinery of planning for what I know now was plain craziness. I was just plain stupid.

One thing I remember is how quickly we all slipped into a military frame of mind—discipline, technical terms, planning, and execution—it could have been an operation in Nam instead of Brooklyn. Hell, some of us were even calling Stu "Major." Even in my best days I had never been a gung ho grunt, but something got under my skin, maybe it was the thought of those bastards selling a bag and a sandwich to some kid.

It was difficult tailing Stash because his street was short, quiet, and residential, any strange car or unusual movement would have attracted the attention of someone in the neighborhood. Fortunately Arnie and I were able to rent a furnished apartment across the street from his house. I also hooked up a car relay so we could communicate with Rudy and Star who cruised nearby.

In a week we had Stash pinned down to his routine; the pictures we took showed a short, dumpy guy in his mid-fifties; he looked like a retired vegetable store owner. He left and returned in the same cab—a check showed it was an independent.

As that old detective had told us, Stash loved his pussy. Star and Rudy tailed him to Suzy's place three or four times a week. They reported he had a funny habit, after the cab left he would remain outside the building for a few minutes, carefully counting the bills in his wallet. Star said you could see his lips move. He appeared to be a very careful guy with a buck.

The only other places he visited by the same cab were two bookmaking joints, a small bar named Barco's in the east twenties that had the smell of Mafia, and a sister on Cherry Street. Curiously he didn't go to the Happy Valley Wine and Liquor Company. In Arnie's opinion Stash or Cardillo couldn't care less about the day-to-day operation, only the loot from the sale of drugs counted. How it was picked up and where it went were still unanswered questions.

Meanwhile Tom and Trev were kept busy checking out the lunch box vans. Incredible as it may seem, there were sixteen grammar, vocational, and junior high schools on Adolph's route. They reported back to Stu that it was difficult to determine if junk was being passed to the kids along with their sandwiches, but up close a couple looked high and it wasn't from celery tonic. I didn't like this double-dealing, Tom and Trev were close to me, especially Tom. Arnie and I argued about this but he agreed with Stu—it just had to be this way. So I made my toss and went all the way. That's how it is with me.

We voted to snatch Stash on a Sunday night when he never failed to visit Suzy. It was the best time, the street was usually deserted, the few minutes he stopped to count his money would be enough for Arnie to hit him with the tranquilizer and for us to get him into our car.

Stu and Arnie had it planned to the last detail. We had blown-up map sections of the areas and each one knew his assignment. Arnie pointed out political kidnappings are done swiftly and successfully because each move is executed with the finesse of a ballet corps, let one dancer trip and the whole thing might collapse. It was evident this would not be his first snatch. We made three dry runs; all went smoothly. The house Stu had rented near the Hamptons was perfect, beautifully furnished, and on the ocean. When I was there the light was fading and all you could hear was the measured boom of the surf. It was like a movie setting but it gave me the chills.

I was wound up like a clock that Sunday night, but professional kidnappers could not have done a better job. The cab left and Stash began counting his bills. He was so engrossed he never heard Arnie come up behind him. He gave a surprised grunt when the tranquilizer barb hit and started to shout: "What the hell are you—" but then he slumped over. Rudy caught him, the car door opened, and we had him in the back seat and were moving carefully within minutes.

It was an uneventful trip to the Hamptons, we made it without incident. Stash sat in the corner of the back seat, snoring and peaceful. Close up he didn't look healthy. He had a pudgy face, cheeks lined with a network of tiny veins, and a W. C. Fields nose. He was a far cry from the pipe-wielding hood I had imagined but, as Arnie pointed out, that was years ago.

He was starting to come around when we got him into the house and down to the large rec room where Stu had coffee, sandwiches, and booze waiting. He waved away a cup of coffee and pointed to a scotch bottle.

Arnie shook his head. "Wait a while on that. The sulphate's still in his system."

"How about some coffee, Stash?" I asked.

"How do ya know me?" he asked in a gravelly voice.

"We've seen you around."

"Yeah. Where?"

"Barco's Lounge on Twenty-eighth—"

"You ain't never been in Barco's," he said accusingly, but this time he accepted the coffee.

"Sure, we were up at the end of the bar near the window," Star said.

He studied Star for a moment.

"You Eyetalian?"

"Siciliano," Star replied with an impassive face, "from the boot."

"Yeah." He looked around at all of us. "Whadda you guys want?"

"Not money, Mr. Forelli," Stu said quietly, "just some information."

202

"This no snatch?"

Arnie spoke rapidly in Italian.

"I told him this has nothing to do with the Families. It's something personal—something we want to know," he translated.

"Hey! you speak Eyetalian!" Stash said. "Where'd ya learn? You're not Eyetalian."

He seemed to relax and started to show less signs of belligerence.

"Mr. Forelli, we don't want to waste our time and we certainly don't wish to waste yours," Stu said quietly. "All we want from you are some answers."

"Oh yeah," he rasped. "Whaddaya wanna know?"

"Anything and everything about Del Morenci," Stu said. "To start, where is he now?"

Stash tried to look blank but he didn't succeed. With his mouth open and his protruding green eyes, he resembled a big dead flounder.

"Waddaya talkin' about? I don't know no Del Morenci. What is he, a bookie?"

Stu repeated slowly and emphatically. "I'm asking you for the last time, Mr. Forelli, where is Del Morenci?"

Stash shook his head vigorously.

"I swear, fella, I don't know no Del Morenci. If I knew I'd tell ya." He looked to Arnie for support. "Right, *pisan*, wouldn't I tell 'em?"

Stu placed a candle and a small plastic bag on the table. When he opened the bag I thought a hand had reached inside to clutch my stomach.

There were several long bamboo splinters.

"What the hell's those things?" Stash said quickly. "What's that?"

"These are bamboo splinters, Mr. Forelli," Stu said, calm as if he were explaining the best way to get to Times Square. "When inserted under a fingernail the pain is excruciating. When they are passed across this lighted candle—"

"Hey, wait a minute!" Stash cried. "What are you guys, crazy or somethin'? Like I told you, I don't know no Morenci."

Stu picked up a sliver and nodded to Rudy and Star who jumped Stash. For an old guy he put up a battle, but they easily forced him back into the chair, taped his mouth with surgical tape, and clamped one hand on the table.

I was like a chicken hypnotized by a snake. Stu slipped the splinter under the highly polished nail and pushed it in hard.

Stash's bull neck expanded like a rubber hose under pressure and turned dark red, his eyes bulged until they seemed ready to pop out.

Stu carefully pushed in another. Then a third. A dark stain appeared around the hood's crotch. I could feel sweat covering my face and bile rise in my throat.

Then he groaned and slumped over.

"He fainted," Arnie said.

"So this is the great big tough guy?" Rudy said. "The guy who busted people's heads with pipes?"

Arnie felt inside the shirt. "We don't want to scare him to death, Stu."

"Take out the slivers," Stu ordered.

Rudy and Star removed the splinters and blood ran out on the table.

When I went to clean it up with a paper towel, Stu waved me away.

"Let him see it."

Stash came around in a few minutes. For the first time I saw fear in his eyes as he held his bloody hand.

"I would like you to know, Mr. Forelli," Stu said, "that we intend to do this all night until you talk. If this doesn't work we have a few other methods which I'm sure your own people don't know about."

"I keep sayin', fella, I don't—"

He broke off as Stu lighted the candle.

"What's that for? Hey, fella, what's that for?" he asked Arnie.

"Heat increases the pain," Arnie replied in a flat voice. "I don't think you can take more than two of those."

"That's for Mr. Forelli to decide," Stu said.

The silence was almost unbearable as we watched Stu slowly pass the deadly looking sliver back and forth through the steady flame. Then he nodded to Rudy and Star. Stash struggled frantically but they again taped his mouth and held him fast.

"If you want to talk just wave your hand," Stu said.

I closed my eyes and my flesh cringed as the sliver went home. I wondered if Arnie was recalling how it felt when Charlie was doing it to him to try to get the location of that jungle relay station . . .

One was enough, Stash began waving frantically.

Stu, who had another ready, ordered Star to rip off the tape. Stash moaned with pain and clutched his hand.

"Goddam fools!" he rasped. "I got sugar, you know that? You could hurt me real bad."

"We don't want to hurt you anymore than is necessary, Mr. Forelli," Stu said soothingly, "all we want is information on Morenci."

"Waddaya wanna do—get me kilt?" he pleaded. "Look, maybe we can make a deal."

"Tape him up," Stu snapped.

"Wait! Wait!" Stash cried. He stared down at his bleeding fingers and the sliver sticking out from beneath the nail.

"Maybe I know a guy named Morenci."

"You not only know him," Arnie shouted, "you work for him! Now give!"

Stash closed his eyes and moaned.

"I got in the hands of crazy people. Crazy!"

Arnie looked over at us and winked.

204

"Why waste time?" he said loudly. "He's not going to talk."

"We'll give him one more chance," Stu said. "You said you knew a man by the name of Morenci, where is he?"

"I swear I don't know him," Stash said fervently. "I never saw the guy."

"How about Cardillo, does he know Morenci?"

"Maybe. Frankie. Maybe he knows him, but I don't."

"This is bullshit," Arnie cried. "He's not giving us anything!"

"This I swear on my mother's grave," Stash cried. "I never met the guy!"

Stu leaned closer to him.

"You're selling junk from those lunch vans—right?"

"Well, maybe a little bit—"

Arnie slammed the table with his fist.

"Not a little, goddammit! A lot! Where are you getting it from? How does it come in? Talk, you son of a bitch, before I ram one of these—"

He grabbed a sliver and Stash almost fell off the chair. I thought Arnie should carry an Actor's Equity card.

Stu said quietly, "How do you get it, Mr. Forelli?"

"You guys cops or somethin'?"

Rudy shook him. "We're not cops—just keep talking."

"I dunno. Some dame calls up Frankie and she picks up the load."

"What dame?"

"Dunno. She's somethin' to do with bells, that's all I know."

"What do you mean, bells? Does she sell them?"

He shrugged. "Ya got me. All I know is, she calls Frankie."

"And what do you do, shitface?" Star asked.

"I only collect," Stash replied. "Believe me, that's all."

"Collect what?"

"The vans."

"In other words you collect the money from the sale of drugs to the school kids?" Stu asked.

"Yeah. That's right."

"You filthy bastard!" Rudy said and shook him until I thought he'd break his neck.

"Hey, big fella!" Stash gasped, "take it easy—"

Star said, "You're selling junk to kids!"

Arnie threw a pair of pliers on the table. Stash stared down at them, then looked pleadingly at Stu.

"You know what this is?" Arnie said, pointing to the pliers.

"Yeah. Pliers."

"You know what we can do with them?"

Stash shook his head.

"Pull out every one of your goddam nails. Get it? One by one." He picked up the tool and leaned across the table until he was only a few inches from Stash's dark red mottled face and frightened eyes.

"Do you want me to try it?"

"I'm tellin' ya everythin' you ask me—"

"You're not telling enough. Now give! And fast. We haven't got all night." He slammed down his fist. "How does the junk come in?"

"They fly it in from out where the cowboys are," Stash said in his rasping voice. "I don't know any more. What would I do out there? I ain't been outside of Brooklyn since the army and then I was in Atlantic City. I swear on my mother's grave!"

"Okay. Now where does it go when it comes into the city?"

"Frankie says they have depots."

"Where are they located?"

"Dunno. Frankie never told me."

"How about the Yonkers steel company? Doesn't Cardillo have something to do with that?"

His eyes widened. "Jeez! You guys know a lot!"

"Is Yonkers a depot?"

"Dunno. All I know is Frankie goes up there. Once, maybe twice I drove him."

"Who did he see? What did they say?"

"Dunno. Frankie told me to wait outside."

"You're his partner—"

He shook his head. "No. No. I only collect. That's all, fella, just collect. I know Frankie from the old days. When he ast me to help I said sure."

"How long ago was that?"

He paused. "Maybe a year, a little more."

"And all you do is collect?"

"That's right, fella."

"Collect where?"

"A joint on Fan Street, near the Hall."

"Not a joint on Fan Street," Stu said disgustedly. "Isn't it the Happy Valley Wine and Liquor Company?"

Stash blinked. "That's right."

"When?"

"The last Friday of the month. They have a bag ready—"

"And it's filled with money?"

"That's right."

"And where do you take it?"

Before he could hesitate, Arnie thoughtfully weighed the pliers in his hand.

"Fifth and Forty-fourth—"

"What's at Fifth and Forty-fourth?"

"He's the guy I deliver to."

"What's his name?"

"Bernie—"

"Bernie what?"

"Lennis—Bernie Lennis."

206

"And what does Lennis do?"

"He's a lawyer."

"Where does he live?"

"I don't know. He never tolt me."

"What does he do with the money?"

A shrug. "Maybe he brings it to Del."

"Do you know?"

"No."

"You don't know an awful lot, do you, stupid?" Arnie shouted.

"Take it easy, I'm sure Mr. Forelli wants to cooperate," Stu said.

They were playing the old cop game, one guy is the villain, his partner, easygoing, understanding.

"Sure, sure," Stash said, eyeing the pliers. "I'm talkin', ain't I? Maybe I'll get dumped in the river for this."

"When you leave here you will receive compensation for your cooperation," Stu told him. "If you ever come back or tell Morenci what happened, you will be killed." He picked up the barbs. "After we use every one of these."

Arnie pointed to the pliers. "And this."

Stash's eyes widened. "You'll take care of me?"

"That we will."

"You're not kiddin', fella?"

Stu walked into the next room and returned with an envelope. He tore it open and crisp new thousand-dollar bills along with a plane ticket poured out on the table.

"When we are assured you have given us all you know about Morenci and his narcotic operation"—he picked up the bills—"you will be compensated, along with a one-way ticket to Los Angeles. You will be driven to the airport and put on the plane. I told you what would happen if you tip off Morenci or anyone else."

Arnie said low and menacingly, "You play stoolie and I'll follow you to the end of the earth! Do you understand that?"

"Okay. I take your dough and that's it," Stash said, nervously. He held up his hand. "Hey, this hurts like hell."

"Take it out," Stu said.

I thought Stash would keel over again when Rudy and Star pulled out the sliver. It was in deep and the pain must have been awful. I started to feel sorry for this guy, but then I remembered the four kids who died of an OD and poor Adolph who had a gun pointed to his head.

"What the hell, I was gonna get out anyways," Stash said.

"Why?" Stu asked.

"The doc said I have sugar. I got to watch my diet. No wine. No nothin'."

"Only pussy," Star said. "Like four, five times a week. How does an old guy like you get it up so often?"

"Yeah, the dames go for me," he said proudly, "they like me."

"You don't know who this girl of the bells is?" Stu asked.

Stash shook his head. "I never seen her. That's what Frankie calls her."

"Does Cardillo know her?"

"He never seen her either. She just calls and says she will pick up the junk and bring it to the mill."

"And where is the mill?"

"I don't know. Frankie don't know either."

"Who tipped you about the warehouse raid?"

Stash whistled. "Hey, how did you guys find out—"

"Who tipped you?" Arnie bellowed.

Stash licked his lips and gratefully accepted the cup of coffee Stu offered.

"Frankie said a guy named Miles. I seen him on television with that guy who's runnin' for mayor."

"What did Cardillo tell you?"

"He said if we played our cards right we could be wearin' the mayor's hat."

Arnie looked at Stu and nodded, Stash was repeating what Toni had heard.

"What did Cardillo give Miles?"

"Money. What else?"

"How much?"

"I dunno. Frankie said they gave him a pile to make the race for the mayor's office."

"Who are 'they'?"

"I guess he meant Del. Frankie never does anythin' except that the Boss okays it."

"And the Boss is Morenci?"

"All the way, fella."

"How many cops do you have on the pad?"

"I don't handle that. Frankie takes care of the bulls."

"Are there many?"

"Enough. Frankie always tells me cops is no problem. If you give 'em enough grease, they won't squeak."

"What do you do about honest cops?"

"Avoid 'em. Frankie said when you smell a straight arrow you run like a deer."

"Tell us about the International Vending and Amusement Machines Company."

He looked as if he had been kicked in the stomach.

"I told you we know everything," Arnie said in a cold, menacing voice. "You damn well better play ball with us."

"I don't know too much about 'em," he said fearfully.

"Just tell us what you know, Mr. Forelli," Stu said soothingly, "we don't expect you to know everything—"

"But we expect you to know something," Arnie growled. "Start talking."

"Jeez, I know it's in Vegas."

"Jeez, I know it's in Vegas," Arnie mocked. Then he roared, "We know that, fathead! It's in Vegas, LA, and New York. Do you think we're stupid? What does it have to do with Morenci? With Cardillo? Who's the head of it?"

Arnie certainly had scared the old guy. He rolled his eyes fearfully and talked directly to Stu.

"All I know is that when Frankie went out to Vegas, two, three years ago, he tolt me he was gonna see the guy who was the head of this company. He said it had to do with gamblin' equipment, like wheels."

"Let me work on this bum," Arnie said pleadingly to Stu. "We're not getting anything out of him."

Stu raised his hand as if to hold him off.

"I believe he's trying. Now, Mr. Forelli, we know what this company manufactures and sells, what we want to find out is what connection does it have with Cardillo and Morenci."

"From what I understand," he said, licking his lips, "they handle the money."

"What do you mean when you say 'they handle the money'? In what way?"

"I think, maybe I'm wrong, they take the dough to the laundry."

"In Vegas?"

"Once I heard Frankie say 'they cleared it in the islands.' "

"By 'they' he meant this amusement company?"

"That's what I think."

"And the islands?"

He shrugged. "Frankie flew down to the Bahamas last year. He says they—this company—was gonna have a meetin' about makin' a laundry deal."

"Let me get this straight, stupid," Arnie said. "You pick up the dough, this attorney takes it somewhere, maybe to Morenci, and then it goes to this company in Vegas, and they send it to be laundered in the Bahamas. Is that right?"

"Yeah. Yeah. That's right, fella," Stash replied. "When it comes back it's clean."

"You're doing fine, Mr. Forelli," Stu said softly. "Now let's get back to the lawyer—Bernie Lennis."

"Yeah. Bernie."

"You said the last Friday of every month you take the money from the sale of the junk to his office on Fifth and Forty-fourth. Is that right?"

"Yeah. You got it."

"What do you know about Lennis?"

"Not much. He's a kind of a jerk."

"In what way?"

"He's kinda jerky . . . you know what I mean? Jerky."

"Do you think he deals with Morenci?"

"The way he talks maybe he does."

"What do you mean, the way he talks?"

"Well, like I said, he keeps callin' him Del, and he tells me what a big man he is and how we're all gonna make a lot of money with him as the big boss."

"Did he mean you?"

"He kept tellin' me how Frankie told him I was doin' a great job and he said he told this to Del."

"And what did Del say?"

"He says Del said for him to say thanks and he won't forget when a good territory is open."

"What did he mean, a good territory?"

"Shylockin'." A whine crept into his gravelly voice. "I worked hard but they never gave me a good spot."

"You just busted heads," Star suggested.

Stash looked genuinely surprised. "Hey, fella, you can't give money away for nothin'. When they can't get the vig up, you gotta coax 'em!"

"The vig?" Stu asked.

"Yeah. The interest," Stash explained.

I asked, "How thick a pipe do you use?"

"Naw. I never hurt 'em much. Just a little thing."

"One of your old customers dances instead of walks. Right?"

He looked thoughtful. "That may be little Danny the Bookie from Hundred and Tenth Street. He took an awful lot of money without payin' back." He said jovially, "We're good friends. I see him all the time."

"Let's get back to Lennis," Stu said impatiently.

"Yeah. Bernie."

"Where does he live?"

"That I don't know, fella. He never tolt me."

"And you don't know what he does with the money?"

He shook his head.

"Tell us exactly how you collect it and what you do with it."

"Well, I goes over there at four o'clock on the last Friday. The boys have the bag ready. Then Louie, the cabdriver, picks me up. Every Friday he takes a different route—"

"Why?" Arnie broke in. "Are you afraid of being hijacked?"

"Nobody takes Del Morenci's money," Stash said slowly. "But nobody."

"He's a big man."

The old hood nodded almost reverently.

"And you take it to Lennis's office?"

"That's right."

"What floor is it on?"

"Second floor."

"And you give it to him. No one else?"

"Only Bernie. Then I take the elevator and go downstairs and Louie takes me home or to Barco's or maybe my sister on Cherry Street near the project."

He hesitated and we waited.

"One day I didn't take the elevator right away . . ."

"Oh, why?"

"A couple of times I see Bernie coming out of the chink's place—"

Arnie interrupted, "What chink's place? A restaurant?"

"No. A chink's place that sells chink stuff. Sorta like you see in Chinatown. This store I know on Mott Street, they have 'em in the window. Little fat guys with their belly buttons showin' . . ."

"Buddhas?"

"Yeah. Yeah. Stuff like that."

"An importing company?"

"Yeah. A couple of doors from Bernie's office. They sell all kinds of chink stuff. There's this young chink broad who works there, and Bernie's always foolin' around. I think he's tryin' to make her. This Friday I come down the hall and he's got her up against the wall and he's talkin' real low—"

"What did he say when he saw you?"

"He just looked surprised, so then we went into his office."

"Did he say anything about this girl?"

"He just said she was one of the dames that work next door and he's been tryin' to bang her for a long time but she won't put out. That's all he said and then he took the bag."

"But you said one time you didn't take the elevator down right away. Why?"

"Yeah. This time I walked to the end of the hall and waited. Just to see what happened. After a few minutes Bernie came out with the bag and went into the chink's place."

"How long did you wait?"

"Ten, fifteen minutes."

"And he didn't come out?"

"No. Then I took the elevator and Louie drove me downtown and I went to my sister's—"

"Do you know the name of this importing company?"

"No. It's next to Bernie's office on the second floor."

"You don't know what connection it might have to Lennis? Or Morenci?"

"No. I swear."

"Did you ask Cardillo?"

"Yeah. But he only said Bernie's a jerk and don't pay any

attention to him."

"Did you tell him you saw Bernie take the bag into that importing office?"

"Hey, fella," he protested. "I can't ast Frankie things like that. He'd bust both my arms!"

"Why did Cardillo select you as his collector?"

A note of pride edged into his voice. "When Frankie was workin' the numbers in Harlem and I was shylockin' I usta give him sums. No six for five, only dough between friends. He always paid me back. Then we went into junk together. We didn't sell on the street, we let the other guys do that. We had a good thing goin', then Frankie got the draft and took a long run to beat Uncle. Like I said, he came to me with this proposition and I said, 'Sure, why not?' I wasn't doin' much because of the sugar. What the hell, it's only a cab ride with Louie into the city with a bag for Bernie . . ."

"And Cardillo has been your only contact?"

"The only one."

"You trying to tell us you don't know Adolph, the German?" I asked him.

He looked uneasy. "That German guy? Yeah, I know him."

"You put a gun to his head, you creep!"

"I swear on my mother's grave, fella! We paid him."

I said, "You put a gun to his head and made him turn over his business for peanuts." Arnie leaned over and grabbed his shirt.

"That's what I mean, you fat tub! You're not talking!"

"I'm talkin', fella. I'm talkin'. You didn't ast me about the Dutchman—"

"We don't have to ask. You tell us. Understand? Tell us—everything. Now start!"

Stu warned him, "I advise you to tell us everything you know, Mr. Forelli."

"Whose idea was it to buy out Adolph?"

"Frankie's. The Dutchman was goin' heavy with crap and laid off a lot of markers. Frankie bought 'em up from this guy that runs the game and then bought the Dutchman out—"

"You put the poor guy on a plane with a gun to his head," I said.

"Not me," he protested loudly, "it was Marty and Ginger. They're a couple of Frankie's boys."

"But the reason why Morenci wanted this lunch box business was to sell junk to school kids. Is that correct?" Stu asked.

Stash explained in a rush of words. "Like Frankie said, 'What's the difference?' The little bastids are drinkin' wine in the stairwells and they're buying hash to shoot up. Frankie said it was just like givin' 'em a butt to sell 'em cigarettes. Only we give 'em a 'catch 'em bag'—"

"Wait a minute," Stu interrupted him. "What is a catch 'em bag?"

"A little free hash so they come back to the van to do business."

"You no-good son of a bitch!" Arnie said slowly. "You killed a couple of kids with those bags! The kids couldn't handle it. Did you know that?"

Stash looked uncomfortable. "Yeah, I read about it in the papers. I guess it was too strong. I kept tellin' Frankie I didn't like it, but one day he was drunk in Barco's and gave me a bust in the face, so after that I kept my mouth shut."

Arnie observed, "So you think Cardillo's a tough guy."

The bulging eyes studied him.

"Maybe you guys should meet—"

"I hope to—someday," Arnie shot back. "Does he still have the finger missing?"

"Who, Frankie?"

"No, Morenci."

Stash's surprise was genuine.

"How do ya know that, fella?"

"I told you before we know everything." Arnie jabbed Stash with the pliers. "Now fathead—answer this. If you never met Morenci, how do you know his finger is missing?"

"All I know is this: One night Frankie is talkin' about Del, and I says, 'What kind of guy is he?' and he says, 'A real classy guy with lots of moxie and brains.' Then he goes on to say Del never has any trouble with women. Then he calls him 'the man with the finger,' and when I ast what he means he says, One time Del got his hand caught in a car door and they had to cut off the tip of his finger. I swear on my mother's grave, that's all I know about the guy. After that when Frankie says 'the man with the finger,' I know who he's talkin' about."

Stu asked, "What about the new shipment coming in?"

Stash shook his head in amazement.

"Jeez! You guys know a lot!"

"What about it?"

"All I know is what Frankie told me."

"Isn't it a big one?"

"The biggest. Frankie said they'll have to hire more cutters."

Arnie leaned over to tap Stash on the wrist with the pliers.

"Think real hard. What exactly did Cardillo say to you?"

"He just says the boid is flyin' in and it will be the biggest—"

"What did he mean?"

"Ya got me, fella. Maybe he means a plane."

I put in, "What about the pilot?"

He frowned. "What pilot, fella?"

"The one that was shot after he crashed."

Stash nodded. "I remember. We were havin' dinner in Barco's and Frankie told me about it. He says they were runnin' the stuff in and the plane crashed, so they kilt the guy because he couldn't get out, but they got the load."

"Why did they kill him?"

"Frankie says dead men tell no tales. Like me. If he knew I was sittin' here he'd cut my throat."

"Suppose we called him right now and told him?" Stu suggested.

Stash almost leaped out of the chair, his face drained of blood and his hands shook.

"You wouldn't do that, fella! I'm takin' your money. I'm talkin'! Right? You give me the dough and I'll blow. When I get to the coast I'll go to a hospital and take care of my sugar. Okay? Nobody will ever hear of Mike Fortunato. Okay? We got a deal?"

"I still think you haven't told us everything." Arnie said.

"Tell you?" Stash cried. "What more can I tell you? Ast me, for crissakes. Ast me . . ."

"When a big load comes in, it's not only for New York, so where does the rest go?"

"Frankie says they split up the goods in the mill. Then it goes to Chicago. Detroit. All the big cities. Even on the west coast. All over. Frankie said the last time they had so much goods they hit maybe twelve, thirteen cities—"

"When you say goods you mean drugs?"

"Yeah. Frankie says it's the best stuff. The pushers love it because they can cut it so much. Frankie says it's strong."

"So the entire load goes to the mill, is that right?" Stu asked him.

"Yeah. Right to the mill. Then the cutters work on it."

"And you insist you don't know where the mill is located."

"No. I tolt you, Frankie wouldn't tell his mother."

Arnie worked the pliers and they closed with a cold, vicious snap.

"I swear it, fella," Stash said frantically. "I swear it!"

Stu nodded to me and Arnie.

"Give him a drink," he told Star and Rudy, and we followed him into the next room.

"What do you think?" Stu asked.

I said, "I don't think he knows much more."

"I don't think so either," Arnie said. "But now what do we do with him?"

"Give him the money Stu promised and put him on the plane," I said.

"Suppose he calls Cardillo?" Arnie asked.

"I think he's scared shitless," I said. "I don't think he'll go near Cardillo."

Arnie shook his head. "He could make a big score with Morenci if he went back and warned him some guys were looking into his operations. Remember what he said about hoping to get a good shylocking territory? Both Cardillo and Morenci would love him. They would both drop out of sight and nobody—us, the feds, or the cops—would ever get a smell of that junk. This big cargo is probably worth millions and they'll do anything to protect it." He added in a cold, flat voice, "I say we dump him."

214

I stared at him.

"You mean kill him? You're kidding, Arnie!"

"No I'm not, Sam. If that slob talks the project is not only blown but we could be in trouble."

"I have what he said on tape," Stu said.

"It doesn't mean a damn," Arnie said. "It would never hold up in court. It's a confession obtained by force and duress."

"I didn't mean it for a court,' he said in a strange mild way.

"What then did you mean it for, Stu?" I asked, surprised.

"Perhaps we could use it in some other way."

"What we do with the tape is neither here nor there," I said. "But Arnie's suggestion is out! I'll do anything for you, Stu, but not murder. That son of a bitch in there deserves to be cut up into little pieces—but not by me."

Stu said briskly, "I don't think he'll talk. We'll give him the money and the ticket. Star and Rudy will drive him to the plane. We'll just have to take a chance."

"I meant it when I said I'll find him if he talks," Arnie said shortly.

"He won't," I assured him. "The guy's glad to get out alive."

"Anything more we can ask him about?" Stu said.

"Let's have a couple of drinks with this *schmuck* and just talk," I suggested. "Maybe the booze will help."

That's what we did, we fed Stash scotch until he almost finished the bottle. I got a basin and found some peroxide and Band-Aids and took care of his fingers. The nails were dark red with congealed blood and starting to swell. One thing, he wouldn't be feeling Suzy's knockers for a while . . .

The combination of whiskey and relief at the thought he would walk away from this one made Stash very talkative. He told us a number of stories about Cardillo which confirmed the old detective's opinion that he was a ruthless, vicious thug. Once we froze when he mentioned Toni's name.

"Who's Toni?" Stu asked casually.

"His sister-in-law. She's a schoolgirl. Nice kid but won't give Frankie the time of day. He says he's gonna make her if it's the last thing he does. He's got hot nuts for her. He says he tried one night when he was drunk, but she and his wife got him out of the room. Then the kid called her brothers—"

"What did they do?"

"The big guy's name is Julio. He was in the Golden Gloves, then fought pro. A good welter. He came down and told Frankie he'd break his arms and legs if he ever touched his sister."

I pointed out, "But you said Cardillo's a big man. Couldn't he take care of this guy?"

Stash gestured with his bandaged hands.

"It's the rule."

"What rule?"

"You can't have nothin' personal to make trouble for the organization. If Frankie does anythin' it's on his own."

"What does he intend to do about the girl?"

"He says that after this big load comes in he's takin' a vacation. First he's gonna bang her, then if her big jerk of a brother comes down, he'll have a couple of his boys drop him in the river."

Christ, was I glad Trev wasn't listening to this. . . .

We talked all night and finally toward morning Stash fell asleep. We left Star and Rudy with him while we played the tape recordings of the whole night. It was a detailed account of Morenci's drug operations. Along with Cardillo, we now had the lawyer Lennis and the pretty and mysterious Chinese girl who worked for the oriental importing company next door to Lennis's office.

"If these tapes had been obtained by a law enforcement agency through a court order," Arnie said, "it could help to convict Morenci, Stu, but they're worthless!"

"I don't think so," Stu answered. "We'll make use of them in some way."

It was still dark when I left. Rudy and Star were preparing breakfast for Stash who had awakened, still half-drunk and rambling on about Morenci and Cardillo.

Traffic was light going into the city and I had a lot of time to think. I tried to tell myself that Stash was nothing, the scum of the earth, but somehow there was a hollow ring to it. I felt weary, depressed, and dirty.

We got three good leads from Stash:

The name of the lawyer, who could be a direct contact to Morenci, the vending outfit that laundered the syndicate's money, and the Oriental girl who worked in the importing company that had some strange connection to the whole drug operation.

The following Monday, while Arnie flew out to Vegas to look into the vending company, I paid a visit to the lawyer's office. The entrance to the building was on Fifth, deliveries were made on Forty-fourth. The hall directory and the name on the door were the same, Bernard A. Lennis, Attorney at Law; there was no firm name. Next to it was a vacant office then the importing company, The Indochina Trading Company.

The New York County clerk's office didn't have anything on the Chinese but the City Sales Tax Office and Customs showed they had offices in Hong Kong and Marseilles. Very interesting. The Bar Association's files produced Lennis's record and home address; he was a New Yorker, graduated from NYU Law School with an unimpressive scholastic record, lived in Riverdale, was married, and had two kids. He was thirty-eight. Telephone information provided the news he had an unlisted home number, rather unusual for a working lawyer.

Over a cup of coffee I debated using three possible maneuvers to

216

get a look inside those offices; I could hide my topcoat and jacket in the stairwell, roll up my sleeves, put a pencil in my pocket and walk into the trading company, posing as a guy who worked in the building—I had a choice of firms from the directory—and was interested in buying an oriental gift. Or using the same dodge, to drop in on Lennis with the story I was thinking of starting divorce proceedings and ask his advice. Or visit the delivery entrance with a pound note in one hand; freight elevator operators can be excellent sources of information.

I discarded all three ideas. My instinct warned me this was a delicate phase of our operation and needed a perfect cover. At the time I had no idea of what it could be.

That night we had a meeting in the penthouse. Tom and Trev reported they had seen at least two kids walk away from one of the Lunch Boxes, open a glassine envelope that had been concealed in a sandwich, then run down into the basement of a nearby house.

Stu suggested that they make a movie of what they had seen at as many schools as possible. In fact from now on, he told us, it would be a good idea to start a file of evidence including pictures, tapes, and photostats of documents which could be turned over to the federal people along with Morenci. I agreed it was a good idea and supplied Tom, who liked photography, with one of my small, powerful cameras. Arnie and I also obtained photostats of the material we had found in Albany and the Kings County clerk's office and went back to see Adolph's old blonde girl friend who willingly repeated her story on tape. She also gave us the letter Adolph had sent her from Germany in which he described how Stash had forced him to sell at pistol point and how two of Cardillo's gunmen had escorted him to the plane. The letter was an excellent bit of evidence, overflowing with Adolph's bitterness and self-pity but providing details on names, places, and dates.

By the next morning we had gathered an impressive file to show how Morenci's syndicate got started and how it was operating.

Meanwhile I returned to Forty-fourth Street, but no matter what I came up with, it didn't click.

At our next meeting Stu explained for the benefit of Trev and Tom that the tailing of Stash had produced the name of Bernie Lennis and the importing company at the Fifth Avenue address.

After I outlined the physical layout of the building, I sketched the three plans I had abandoned of getting in to see Lennis and the company.

"Why did you discard them, Sam?" Stu asked.

"Something tells me you can't use the usual gimmick to get into these offices," I explained. "It should be something that fits in with the picture, something natural, or we could blow the whole thing. I'm open for suggestions."

"How about the building's cleaning company?" Star suggested. "Fatso and I could be great as porters."

"I checked them, they use only women at night."

Trev said, "Last month I happened to go into a building on Fifth Avenue to get a part for my aunt's hearing aid. As I walked down the hall I noticed the door of an office was open. It was a canoe company and they had a display of canoes. In fact it was so eye-catching I walked in and picked up some literature . . ."

"You mean use that vacant office to get their attention and make a contact?" I asked.

"Exactly," Trev replied. "We can make them come to us—if we can get something eye-catching—"

"The lawyer has kids?" Tom asked.

"Two small ones, I would say about eight and ten."

"And there are girls in the importing office?"

"We know there's one—maybe more."

"Well, what would catch the eye of a father of small children and some Chinese girls?"

"Do you have ideas, Tom?" Stu asked.

"Toys," Tom said. "A big, eye-catching display."

"I like that idea," I said, "but I don't know anything about toys."

"I know a little," Tom said. "My uncle owned the oldest wholesale toy house in New England. Every time he paid us a visit it was Christmas morning. I had more trains and my sister had more dolls than all the kids in our town put together. When I was in high school and college, I worked every vacation in his Boston warehouse and twice a month I went on the road with him as far as Quebec."

"Is he still in business?" Stu asked.

"He died before I went into the service, but his sons still run the business. They were up home when I came back."

"Can we work it with them so I can set up an office?" I asked. "It must be legitimate, these guys may check us out."

"Tom, why don't you and Sam run up there tomorrow?" Stu said.

"I'll tell them Sam's a friend who wants to go into the business," Tom said.

"That's a great idea, Tom," Stu said enthusiastically. "Stock the whole damn office, Sam . . ."

"Hey, will you have any trains?" Rudy wanted to know.

"We're gonna let you demonstrate the hoola hoop, Fatso," Star told him.

Tom and I spent a week in Boston talking to his cousins, three young guys who ran the family toy business. They gave us a tour of the factory and I was fascinated. When I was a kid a glove or a bat was the extent of my presents; on one unforgettable birthday, a bicycle. This warehouse was a fairyland inhabited by a million different toys. One section was devoted to trains, they ran in tiers and I was sorry Rudy wasn't along; in fact I had a hell of a time dragging myself away.

Tom's cousins didn't question my story of wanting to take a try at the wholesale toy business; when Tom told them I had been a fellow prisoner in Tong Le Mai, they couldn't do enough. I felt a pang at lying to these three nice guys, but Stu's check guaranteed they wouldn't lose a dime.

They also gave me a week's cram course on the business and suggested I work in a local toy department for a few months, but Tom told them he would be my advisor and we left with their fervent wishes for success.

Renting the office was easy, all realty wanted was a month's rent and a signed lease. First came the display racks which Tom, Rudy, Star, and I put together, then boxes and boxes and boxes arrived. I had games, trains, dolls that walked, wet, nursed, crapped, and did everything but fornicate. They were from every country and were really cute. Rudy set up the tracks and we soon had a chugging, smoking locomotive and line of cars racing around on one side of the office. When we were finished it was so damn eye-catching I seriously considered the business as a sideline.

Now the stage was set; one morning I opened the door and waited.

By noon Lennis was inside.

"What the hell is this?" he asked, looking around in amazement.

He was slender, medium height, and losing his hair. He had thick lenses in his glasses, a dark beard that needed a razor by three o'clock, expensive clothes, and gold cuff links big as manhole covers.

"Toys," I said. "Hoffman Toys. The name will be on the door in a few days."

"You Hoffman?"

"Sam Hoffman. And you?"

"Bernie Lennis, Sam. I'm your next-door lawyer. If you need anything legal give me a call."

"Do you have any kids?"

"Two. Sarah, seven, and Josh, five."

I was so confident I had put aside a few dolls, cowboy and indian sets, and a yellow tractor. I gave him a doll and the tractor.

"With my compliments," I told him. "Tell your kids to play in good health."

"Hey, that's wonderful!" he said. "Thanks a lot. My kids will appreciate this. I don't have to ask, you're a New Yorker, right?"

"Bensonhurst."

"The community on Ninety-second Street, right?"

"Hey, you know the place!"

"I had a cousin who lived in Bensonhurst. We used to play basketball over there when I went to visit. Maybe you know him, Davey Schwartz, a little guy with red hair?"

"The little red-haired guy who was a great dribbler?"

"That's him," he said delighted. "Wasn't he great? The *putz* could have gone to City College on a scholarship but he knocked up his girl friend and had to get married. He's got three kids and works as a salesman in the garment center."

"A fantastic dribbler," I said.

"Fantastic. I don't have any appointments until this afternoon. I'll take you down to the deli and introduce you. Okay?"

"Great. It's on me."

"The hell it is. It's welcome to our second floor."

We had lunch in the deli next door; I returned to my toy office agreeing with Stash—Lennis was a jerk. They had one thing in common—pussy. That subject occupied most of the luncheon period.

This is one thing I will never understand about organized crime. The guys on the top, usually all gifted with great organizational ability, establish a racket with finesse and skill, but when it comes to the periphery people they manage to find only dimwits like Stash or jerks like Bernie Lennis. By the way, I didn't know a redheaded kid named Davey Schwartz who was a great dribbler. That's what I mean when I say Lennis was a jerk.

The following morning Lennis dropped by to tell me how his kids loved the toys. Over his shoulder I saw three Chinese girls stop by the door, hesitate, then cautiously enter to admire a large doll—an American Indian woman complete with braids and beaded buckskin skirt, which I had set up on a table in the center of the display. It was one of the most attractive I have ever seen—not that I'm a connoisseur of dolls, the plastic kind—and one I knew would catch any female's eye.

Lennis followed my stare and turned around.

"Hey, how do you like that?" he said. "Isn't it a beauty? What's her name, Sam?"

"Hole-in-the-Sky," I said. "She was made by Cherokee women in North Carolina. Everything is authentic. The bead design means she's a chief's daughter."

Sam Hoffman, American Indian expert. I had taken it down, word for word, as Tom read it off the brochure in the Boston factory.

"No kidding," Lennis said. "Made by real Indians?"

"Right down to the braids. The hair is real, from Cherokee women."

"I got to get Sarah one of these," he said. "Do you know these girls, Sam?"

"I haven't had the pleasure."

Lennis introduced them with a flourish. "This is Gloria, Tina, and Lucy. They're all looking for boyfriends with Cadillacs . . ."

The three girls looked shy and giggled. They were about eighteen.

Then framed in the doorway was another Chinese girl, but this one was older and a knockout. She was small, less oriental-looking than the others, fine boned, and prettier than any doll on display. A knit dress showed every curve of her terrific figure. This had to be the one Lennis was drooling over. I didn't blame him. In one swift, sure glance she had taken my measure. Then she turned to the other girls and said something in Chinese. With eyes lowered they slipped out.

"This is Mary," Lennis said. "She's the boss next door. Mary, this is Sam Hoffman, our new neighbor."

220

She gave me a faint smile, but then those dark slanted eyes took in the room. I had the feeling she was wound tight, although she was polite.

"How do you like this doll, Mary?" Lennis asked. "It's made by real Indians."

Her reply was edged with contempt. "As compared to plastic Indians?"

"You know there's a restaurant called Geronimo's?" Lennis said with a snicker. "They got guys dressed like Indians making pizzas."

"I think that's disgusting," she said.

"But there are Indians in Brooklyn," I said.

Lennis gave me a look of disbelief. "You're kidding!"

"No, I'm not. They're Mohawks. I know one of 'em."

"There's a community of Mohawks," Mary said. "They're mostly steelworkers and come from the Six Nations Reservation in Canada."

I was amazed. How the hell would a Chinese girl know about Star's people?"

"Not many people know about that," I said.

"My thesis was on the various communities in the city," she said.

"Mary knows something about everything," Lennis said, slipping his arm around her waist. "She got her master's from Columbia last year. What was it for, baby, history?"

She pushed him away. "Political science," she said shortly. Then to me, "You have a nice display, Mr. Hoffman."

"Sam," I said. "If you're married and have children, Mary, I can give—"

Lennis broke in with a laugh. "Married? A million guys want to marry Mary, but she's only crazy about me. Right, Mary?"

He was about to slip his arm around her again, but those cold unwavering eyes stopped him.

"Do you sell wholesale, Sam?" she asked.

"Only wholesale."

"Have you been in the business long?"

"About a year."

She was asking the questions as she moved about the room. They were casual but direct. Like she was Mrs. District Attorney. She seemed restless, picking up this toy, then another. Once I reached to the top shelf to get a game, but it slipped from my fingers. When it hit the floor I thought Mary would leap through the roof. She spun around, the pencil in her hand held like a dagger. Then she gave a short, nervous laugh and quickly asked Lennis a question that had him drooling all over her.

She continued to walk around, throwing me those questions with Lennis following her like a dog after a bitch in heat. It was a good thing I had done my homework with Tom and his cousins.

I told her I planned eventually to have a line of over two hundred toys, featuring dolls like the Indian doll and the familiar ones, Raggedy

Ann, Smokey Bear, Lassie, the Flintstones, and Bozo the Clown. I also spun a fictitious story of how my father had owned a doll hospital for years and produced dolls for carnival prizes—one of Tom's uncle's sidelines.

I even rattled off an impressive knowledge of toymaking; how the factory in Boston, where I bought most of my items, uses nearly two million yards of cloth and over two hundred tons of stuffing plus a million yards of yarn for "hair" in their dollmaking, while other toys use over six hundred thousand board feet of maple, birch, and beech a year. Then I went into the shortages and how we were getting away from plastics.

Lennis looked impressed at my knowledge.

"I never knew it was such a big business."

I casually rattled off the figures.

"Last year's wholesale toy volume was two point eight billion. We had over a six percent gain. This year at the toy fair we expect about seven hundred and fifty manufacturers and nine thousand buyers . . ."

Mary asked, "Is the fair something like the garden show at the Coliseum?"

"Something like that but not as big. We usually hold it in a hotel."

"Maybe you'll take me this year?" Lennis said.

"By all means."

"Suppose the three of us go? How about that, Mary? Maybe you'll meet the Indian who made this doll."

Mary shrugged, wished me luck, and left.

Lennis whistled softly and rolled his eyes.

"How do you like that piece of goods, Sam?"

"Terrific! Have you scored yet?"

"Any day now," He lowered his voice. "One thing I don't like, she's a Commie."

"A Communist?"

"A real red-hot. The Chinese kind. The bitch is a bomb thrower. You should hear the arguments we have."

"She's not all Chinese."

"Her mother. Her father was a navy captain."

"What's her name?"

"Mary Chang Winslow. She comes from California."

"What does she do next door?"

"She's the boss. It's an importing company. The other girls work for her."

"The real boss?"

"The real boss," he said emphatically.

"What do they sell?"

"Oriental stuff. Some of it is junk, but they have good stuff. Antiques they sell to museums. She goes over once or twice a year to buy—"

"To China?"

"No. Burma. Laos. Thailand. Maybe one of these days now that they opened up, she'll buy in China."

"What the hell is she uptight about?"

"Aw, that's her way. She's all business."

"She seems to be a smart dame . . ."

"Smart? Like a whip. Last year, three nights a week she went to Columbia. If I was still in the office, I'd drive her."

"But no score?"

"I'm trying, baby."

We laughed like two chauvinist pigs.

Lennis and I continued to be buddy-buddy, and I made it a point to drop into his office as much as possible. I had spotted this private phone he kept in a drawer and once when he left it out I memorized the number. Late one afternoon I had Star and Rudy deliver some dummy packages to me, and when the building was deserted we put in a tap with a recorder.

The first results were excellent, they showed a link between Mary and Lennis. She called him at least twice to ask about me. Lennis insisted I was only a *nudge*, while Mary said while that might be true she insisted I be checked out.

Mary Chang Winslow. The Indochina Exporting Company. Bernie Lennis, the attorney, and bagman who Stash said received the money collected from the sale of the lunch box drugs and who claimed to be on intimate terms with Morenci.

Now we had determined they were connected, but how and why . . . ?

Fortunately I had established an airtight cover; the Boston toy factory had my credit rating, name, and home address and I had told them to release all information concerning me to anyone who called for business reference. Although I was temporarily living at the hotel, I had placed seals on my apartment door and on my desk drawers which contained a file of my factory and inventory toy orders, credit slips, freight delivery dates, paid bills, a phony letter from a girl friend wishing me luck in my new toy venture; there was no address on the letterhead and only a signature, "Fran," so it could not be traced. I had also included numerous brochures and pamphlets from toy companies.

Several days later I found the seals broken. The doorman swore no strangers had inquired about me but I knew this *putz* sneaked down to the garage to play cards with the car jockeys so anyone could have slipped in and out.

I explained all this at our next penthouse meeting and offered a suggestion:

Why didn't Arnie come on as a radical and see if he could make the Chinese girl . . . ?

They all thought it was a good idea, so Arnie's new role was a bomb thrower with a knapsack. Like I said, he should have carried an Actor's Equity card. When he appeared at the showroom he was dressed like Serpico, complete with a beard and moustache and carrying a knapsack. He said his handle from now on would be Clint Fontaine from Chicago.

"What the hell kind of name is that?" I asked.

"It's an old cover I once used," he explained. "Everything about it can be checked out, school, business, family, home address, bank references, arrest record . . ."

Then he gave me a folded, torn newspaper photo that showed him, beard and all, attacking a cop with a broken signboard. He was bleeding from the head, and a cop lay sprawled at his feet, out cold.

"When the hell did this happen?"

"It never happened, it's a prop. Tell her you tore it out of a paper. If she asks which one, say you forgot the name."

To complete the stage arrangements I put a beautiful Chinese boy doll next to Hole-in-the-Sky; when Mary passed down the hall on her way to the Ladies Room I called out. Arnie, sprawled out in a chair on the far side of the room, was seemingly lost in a newspaper.

"I gave Hole-in-the-Sky a boyfriend," I said when she came to the doorway.

She smiled and walked to the table. I saw her catch Arnie out of the corner of her eye, but she gave no sign she saw him.

"He's cute," she said. "What's his name?"

"I give you the honor, Mary."

She thought for a moment. "We shall call him Chang Jung-chu."

"Who was he?"

"Chang Jung-chu was a great poet in the early days of the Revolution," she explained. "The Chinese people loved him very much."

"He was just another academic intellectual who would have been shot if he hadn't died." Arnie said quietly, not even looking up from the paper.

She looked startled but quickly regained her poise.

"Your friend seems to know something about China," she said to me.

"Mary, this is Clint Fontaine, a very old friend of mine from Chicago," I said. "He stopped by to borrow some money which I will never see again."

Arnie carefully folded the paper and flung the knapsack over his shoulder.

"Thanks for the key," he said. "I'll see you later."

"Put the towels in the hamper," I told him.

"Always a bourgeois," he said disgustedly and left without giving Mary a glance.

"Don't mind him, he's a great guy," I said, "maybe a little weird but okay."

"Does he really know something about China?"

"I would say Clint is a genius," I said solemnly, "outside of his politics."

"What's wrong with his politics, Sam?"

"Everything as far as I'm concerned. Do you remember those peace demonstrations?"

I opened my wallet and took out the clipping.

"For one thing he doesn't like cops."

"When was this?"

"Oh, one of those peace demonstrations . . ."

"Is this the *Times*?" she asked with an innocent look.

"I forget what paper it's from. I happened to recognize him and tore it out."

I carefully retrieved the clipping and put it back in my wallet.

"I guess your friend is a radical."

"He's a Maoist," I said. "He tried to explain it but I'd rather talk about toys. Maybe someday you can talk to him. He's a very interesting guy."

Then I quickly switched the subject, and a few minutes later she left.

I don't care what kind of a female you pick—Maoist, Marxist, Republican, Democrat, Socialist, Catholic, Jew, or Holy Roller—they will always be intrigued by a handsome guy who looks right through them. . . .

I should teach a course in female psychology; the next day Mary dropped in and asked me a lot of stuff about toys but the key question came as she was leaving; she tried to make it appear as an afterthought as she paused at the doorway:

"Oh, how's your friend, Sam?"

I deliberately played dumb and made her come to me.

"Friend?"

"The fellow who was here yesterday . . ."

"Oh, Clint? He's coming in this afternoon. I know it's going to cost me money."

Ten minutes after Arnie sprawled out in the chair Mary passed down the hall. Arnie winked and I called out to her.

"Look who's here, Mary," I said. "I was right, it cost me money."

"Ah, the academic intellectual," he said with a grin.

"Please don't call me that," she said with a flash of irritation.

"You like Chang Jung-chu."

"He was a poet of my people," she said coldly.

"His works were denounced at the celebration in the Papaoshan Cemetery for Revolutionaries last July," he said evenly.

"How do you know? Were you there?"

"No, but I read about the celebration."

"Where would you read a thing like that, Clint?" I asked.

"The *Guardian*—where else! Certainly not in the capitalist press," he shot back. "When are we going to lunch?"

"I'll be stuck here all afternoon," I said. "Why don't you take Mary?"

"Maybe I'll let her take me," he said. He yawned, stretched, and walked over to her, then said something softly in Chinese.

Mary stared at him, genuinely startled, then burst out laughing.

"I told her she was beautiful as a Fenghuang," he said without a smile.

"What the hell is a Fenghuang?" I asked.

"It's the new bicycle that was recently presented to Chairman Mao," Mary said. "The people are very proud of it."

"Chairman Mao called it a beautiful Chinese jewel," Arnie said.

"How do you know about that?" Mary asked with a puzzled look. "Are you in importing?"

"I'll tell you all about it at lunch," he said. "I'll meet you in the lobby in ten minutes."

After he left Mary looked at me.

"He speaks Chinese perfectly."

"I told you he was a genius. Why don't you have lunch with him? You'll find he's a great guy. A little crazy maybe . . ."

She did have lunch with him and that's how Arnie started romancing Mary Chang Winslow, who he said looked like a beautiful Fenghuang.

But she was no fool. After a week Arnie checked Washington and found out someone had looked into the background of Clinton Wilson Fontaine, a graduate of the University of Chicago, who came from a middle class family in Berwyn.

Arnie explained it was a standard Agency cover that could be used by an agent in an emergency. . . .

For the first few weeks the tap on Lennis's phone produced nothing, mostly legal talk with other lawyers and routine chitchat with friends. Star and Rudy followed up some of his cases and reported he was good in a courtroom. We made a pattern of his clients and found ninety percent were in organized crime, numbers, shylocking, truck hijacking, and cigarette smuggling. He received his cases from anonymous callers who only gave him the defendant's name, the charge, names of arresting officers, and when and where the arraignment would take place.

Then one day he was talking to an old school friend and gave us what we wanted—his home phone number.

He lived in an expensive Riverdale garden apartment complex with fountains, flowers, and a doorman. I outfitted a telephone company panel truck I had bought used and went up there with Rudy and Star. There is only one way to put in an illegal tap; be casual and efficient, remember every New Yorker has a bitch about the phone service.

"There's trouble on the main feed," I told the doorman. "We have to check every phone. Where's the terminal box?"

He was an old guy who never suspected that three guys with wide leather belts, tools, and work phones were anything but Ma Bell's troubleshooters. He took us down to the cellar and even had a cigarette while he repeated the tenants' complaints about the phone service.

We put in the tap and hid the recorder behind a pile of dusty trunks with a prayer that their owners wouldn't suddenly get the idea to move out. Would you believe it, we went back three times to retrieve the tapes and each time the old *meshugeneh* had a complaint about the phone service!

Bernie's wife turned out to be a talker; she was never off the phone.

In a way I felt sorry for the guy. She was either running to a beauty salon, backgammon club, Hadassah meeting, or to visit girl friends or mother; we finally scored in one of her calls to mommy. I kept a log of every call so I can quote accurately:

IN: So maybe you and Bernie will come for dinner on Saturday? About six. Stanley and Minnie will be here. They just came back from Miami. Cold, they said, like the North Pole.
OUT: Okay, Mom, but not six. Maybe seven or a little after. Okay?
IN: Why so late?
OUT: Bernie has to see a client in Jersey. You know, the man from that company—"
IN: What company?
OUT: You know, the one that makes gambling machines. Remember when we went out to Vegas? When Bernie bought me the sable? You remember.
IN: Do I remember? What a coat! This man is a good client?
OUT: We should have five like him. When he comes back from Europe, Bernie sees him in a golf club.
IN: In Jersey?
OUT: Yeah. The Black Oak Country Club. Very exclusive.
IN: Maybe like Lakewood where Aunt Fay lived? In the country. Remember how I took you there in the summer?
OUT: No, not there, Mom. Some place called Cidertown.
IN: Who goes *shlepping* to a place with a crazy name like that?
OUT: Don't knock it, Mom. The fees are terrific.
IN: So we'll see you when Bernie gets back from that crazy Jersey? You can bring the kids. Minnie and Stanley haven't seen them in two years. They have a present.
OUT: Naturally.

Arnie and I didn't wait for the next meeting but immediately went over to Jersey to have a look at the Black Oak Country Club. It was beautiful, a small but stunning clubhouse set in a grove of trees, pool, tennis courts, and the golf course in the distance. Lennis's wife was correct when she said it was exclusive; we started to turn into the driveway when a uniformed guard jumped out of a sentry house and held up his hand.

"Are you guests, sir?" he asked with a smile, but his eyes were anything but merry.

"Why no," Arnie said, "we thought—"

The guard didn't let him finish.

"I'm sorry, sir," he said, "this club is for members only and their guests."

Arnie asked, "Could we apply for membership?"

"I'm sorry, sir, the list is closed for this season. Perhaps next year . . ."

We did some local digging and found the club was owned by a corporation; corporation papers in Trenton only showed members of a law firm as the officers. The village of Cidertown, a few miles from the club, was colonial looking and expensive. We stayed in a motel overnight and chatted with the bartender who turned out to be an old marine. Of course Arnie immediately became an old marine, First Division; they were soon buddies. Black Oak, he told us, was strictly membership and very difficult to get in—unless you got close to the mayor, a guy named Decker Reynolds who also happened to be Cidertown's only realtor.

"Deck's on the board of trustees of the club and I think maybe he owns a piece of it," the fighting marine told us.

"Would it help if you bought property around here?" I asked.

"From Deck?"

"Naturally."

"It would," he lowered his voice, "along with some shekels. It costs plenty to get in."

We arrived back in New York to find Trev and Tom ready to show the films they had taken and reporting on their preliminary investigation of the Dutchman's Lunch Box wagons.

The 16mm films were not exactly Fellini, but they proved Adolph's Lunch Boxes were selling junk to school children in their sandwiches. The opening frames showed two kids as they came up alongside the car. As they hurriedly opened one of the sandwiches something dropped out and a kid picked it up. The camera zoomed in on what lay in the palm of the kid's hand—a glassine bag of white powder. They had other surprises, a large envelope contained a worn leather belt, a hypodermic needle, a pair of tweezers, a soot-black metal bottle cap and a pack of matches.

"The junkie's equipment—the 'works,' as they call it," Trev said. "I'll explain after this next roll."

The films this time were both hilarious and grim; we were

228

introduced to Trev, looking like a bum as he lounged around the area of the school. It was a crummy neighborhood, and he certainly blended in with the scene. Then we saw him walking up the street to the Lunch Box and returning with a sandwich. Tom's camera followed him for a few blocks to a deserted factory area where they met. The camera showed Trev uncovering the sandwich and holding up the glassine bag.

The following day—at my suggestion they marked each date by Trev holding up a daily newspaper's front page—Trev followed the same procedure of buying a sandwich. The second seemed larger than the first.

After the blinds were pulled back Stu produced the sandwiches. Each was carefully marked for identification. Both would be wrapped in a box marked "Mr. Harlow's venison steaks" and placed in the hotel's freezer. Under a scant slice of meat in each sandwich lay a glassine bag.

"Good score," I said. "How did you guys get it?"

"I did the photography, Trev did the gumshoeing," Tom said.

"I got an old pair of pants and a jacket from the porter's storeroom, and didn't shave for a few days," Trev explained. "While Tom made his movies I moved around the neighborhood. I found one kid nodding on a stoop. For ten bucks he gave me the code word, another ten bucks bought the works. In the Lunch Box wagon there's a price list posted over the grill for the usual hamburgers, ham and cheese, liverwurst, and so on. There's also a special, a Big Daddy Sandwich that has everything but the front wheel mount thrown in. But this is not it. You ask for what's not on the list—a Super Big Daddy." He pointed to the glassine bag. "That's heroin. Then there's another one called 'The Scarlet Creeper Special.' That's supposed to have spicy meats and red peppers and this. . . ." He picked up the second bag. "It's cocaine—coke. Each bag is ten bucks a throw. The kid I talked to had a seventy-five-dollar-a-day habit. When I left he was starting on a bottle of what they called 'Candy-jag' wine—a quart of cheap sweet wine."

"How old would you say he was?" I asked.

"We have a few shots of him," Trev said.

The camera panned down a littered street lined with rotting brownstones and wooden three-family houses. Suddenly a black boy in dungarees, T-shirt, and sneakers came down a stoop. He stopped for a moment to try laboriously to stuff a bottle in a brown bag into his hip pocket. When it wouldn't fit he tilted the bottle and tossed it into the street. Then he walked toward the Lunch Box wagon with slow, almost exaggerated steps, as if he were imitating an actor in a slow motion movie. As he came alongside the car the camera went in tight on his face. He was smiling vacantly, his lips moved as if he was whispering or singing to himself, his eyes were dull. He was shockingly young. Adults standing about a panel truck or sitting on stoops took no notice of him.

"That kid can't be more than fifteen!" Stu said.

"That's the average age of the Lunch Boxes' customers," Trev said. "Some look younger."

"I guess I'm square, but how do they use this stuff, Trev?"

"The junk is put in the bottle cap and mixed with water," Trev explained. "You hold it with the tweezers while you heat the fluid with a match." He picked up the leather belt. "This acts as a tourniquet to raise the vein. The dissolved heroin is then injected by the hypo."

"What about the coke?" Rudy asked.

He tapped the imaginary powder along his finger and slowly drew it under his nose as he sniffed.

"We all know it's horse and coke, Trev," I pointed out, "but how would it hold up in court?"

"I took the bags to a private lab to be analyzed. They gave me notarized reports. The chemist said the drugs are mixed with quinine but are still very powerful. In his opinion this is not the weak stuff usually found in street sales."

"You fellows going out again?" Stu asked.

Trev glanced at his watch. "We have to get moving. We're going to see what action is going on in a school in South Brooklyn.

"Trev and Tom plan to hit every van with the camera," Stu said. "I think it will be an impressive record for our files. What do you think, Sam?"

"If you can score at the other schools like you did at this one we'll have some damn good evidence," I told them. "Get an affidavit from whoever develops them that the films were original and not doctored in any way."

"Will do," Trev said. "You're going to have a freezer load of Super Big Daddies, Stu."

After Tom and Trev left, we told Stu how the tap on Bernie's Riverdale home telephone had supplied us with the name of the New Jersey golf club which we had pinpointed as the place where the attorney met someone who runs a gambling supply house.

"International?" Stu asked quickly.

"It could be the same firm and maybe it's Morenci's. We have no way of knowing."

"Did you look over the club?"

"You can't get inside the gates, it's very exclusive. We got cozy with the bartender at a motel who told us one way to get in is through the town's mayor who also happens to be the only real estate broker."

"What will it take—money?"

"You may have to buy a piece of property over there, Stu, and pay off this bastard . . ."

"Okay," he said calmly, "buy the property."

"This won't be an eight by ten lot, Stu!" I pointed out. "The homes out there go for maybe a hundred thousand! Christ, Stu, we've been pissing away your money like it's going out of style! Maybe we can get around it some other way . . ."

230

"If the only way to get into that club is through buying property," he said, "pay off that guy. I don't care what it costs, we have to get inside that club. We've come too far to stop now. I can almost taste Morenci."

I said, half-jokingly, half-seriously, "I'm getting worried about you, Stu."

Stu gave me an inquiring look.

"Worried about what?"

"You seem bugged by this guy Morenci."

"I'm going to get him," Stu said quietly. "Come what may, this is no longer a matter of just looking for a big-time drug operator . . . a thug. I am going to get that son of a bitch if I have to do it myself. But I'll get him."

At that moment, for the first time, I detected a change in Stu. Slight, nothing important. I told myself he was more intense, more determined. But in a—I wouldn't think it then but I will now—a paranoid sort of way. . . . Nothing seemed to matter anymore—except Morenci. I felt uneasy and tried to argue him out of spending a small fortune for a piece of property over there but he wouldn't listen; he waved aside our objections. He said in an inflationary period, property was a good investment and he could always charge it to his corporate expenses.

Arnie wanted to make another visit to the Agency's headquarters in Langley, Virginia, so I returned to Jersey.

Before he left I asked the question which had been on my mind for days—did they put Stash on the plane without any trouble?

"Oh sure, nothing to it," Arnie said casually. Too casually, I thought.

When I asked Rudy, that big *nahr* only looked uneasy and didn't answer.

Something told me not to ask any more questions about Stash.

Decker Reynolds, the mayor and Cidertown's only realtor, turned out to be a squat bald-headed guy with a mechanical smile that turned on and off at the sound of money. He had an office in a pseudocolonial building next to an antique shop that featured a number of old toy iron banks in its window. You put a penny in one and a donkey kicked a farmer in the ass. I bought the damn thing for a hundred bucks, which is ninety-nine dollars more than my old man ever paid for a toy. But anytime I get mad I put a penny in and watch this farmer get his ass kicked, it never fails to make me feel better.

We were soon on first name basis—Deck and Sam.

"Are you a Jew, Sam?" he asked bluntly.

In this day and age? Frankly the guy startled me.

"Well, I remember a few words of Yiddish," I said. Like you're a *shmuck*, I thought.

"What the hell, Hoffman could be German," he said.

"Sure, I'm German," I said. "Eins, swei, drei, vier."

"You don't have any Latin friends?"

"Only the woman who cleans my apartment, but she's Mexican. I won't bring her."

The smile flashed on.

"The club dues are three thousand a year. But everything's included—carts, green fees, the pool, locker, discount at the gift shop and the dances. You married, Sam?"

"They haven't caught me yet."

"You'll enjoy the company. There's a few widows who could go for a good-looking young guy like you."

He winked. I winked back. Buddies.

"Now let's see about a house." He frowned. "I have a few, Sam, but they're all too damn big. You'd be rattling around by yourself—"

"How about a condominium?"

"Not one for sale. Wait a minute!" He paused and looked out the window. "Could you live at the club for a couple of months?"

"No reason why not."

"My son, Roger, is putting up some townhouses over where the old Towers farm tract was. There'll be occupancy in two months . . ."

"What's the price?"

"Eighty thousand," this pirate said without blinking. "But they are beauties! There's only six left and when they go, that's it."

"Do you have a model?"

"Sure. Want to look?"

"Let's go."

Out of the five thousand Stu had ordered the hotel cashier to give me before I left the city, I put down a thousand dollars' binder on a ninety-day agreement. Deck's smile flashed on and off like a broken neon sign when I told him I wouldn't need a mortgage but would pay cash.

Of course I didn't intend to be around in ninety days; if we didn't find Morenci in the club within that time we had a case of mistaken identity or were following a cold trail.

I refused to spend the kind of money Stu was willing to throw around, I guess maybe my old man's pickle jar with its nickels and dimes was still too vivid a memory.

I checked into the club as a temporary guest with a glowing recommendation from my old pal, Deck, and tried my best to play the decadent wealthy role. I became the last of the big-time tippers; caddies, porters, and bellboys jumped when I appeared.

I'm no Arnie Palmer but I play a respectable game. Deck introduced me around and I hired a smart if talkative kid named Lance as my daily caddy. Between Lance and my golf partners, mostly wealthy businessmen who insisted Nixon was forced to resign by a radical plot and a personal vendetta waged by the media, I learned a great deal about the community and the club members.

Cidertown was very wealthy, dominated by a few old-time local families, like the realtor, Reynolds. They had impressive homes, servants, and a special bus equipped with a bar that went to New York City once in the morning and returned at night, to serve these royal commuters. They were determined to keep out the world and what they considered their inferiors. They had only one requirement, that you be white and wealthy. I concluded it would be a perfect hideout for Del Morenci.

After a week of idle living, I decided to start digging. I passed up my usual foursome and went out early with Lance. He was selecting an iron when I casually asked him if he had ever heard of a friend of mine, Bernie Lennis, a New York lawyer who came out to the club once or twice a year to see his client.

"Oh sure, I know him," the kid replied. "He doesn't play golf. He waits until Mr. Nicolai gets off the green, then they have dinner in the clubhouse."

I was so excited I hooked the ball into the rough.

"Now I remember, that's the fellow he meets, Frank Nicolai. Isn't he an importer?"

The kid corrected me, "Pascal Nicolai, they call him Pat. He's not an importer, Mr. Hoffman, he's an international contractor; he builds dams and bridges in Europe and things like that. My father says he probably has more money than anyone else around here."

"I bet he has a hell of a house."

"You gotta believe it, Mr. Hoffman," the kid said. "My father says it must cost a fortune just to heat Grand Vista."

"Grand Vista is his house?"

"Didn't you ever see it?" he asked with a look of surprise as if I had just zoomed in from outer space.

"I've been promising myself to take a look at the countryside."

"Don't miss Grand Vista," the kid said, "my father said General Grant once stayed there for a weekend."

"General Grant! Is it that old?"

"We have houses in this town that were built before the Revolution," he said proudly. "Our house is from 1820. There's a plaque on the door that says so. Once a year in the fall the Women's Club sponsors a tour of the old houses. They call it House Tour Day."

"How about Grand Vista? Are people allowed to visit that one?"

"Oh sure. Mr. Nicolai opens up his house like everybody else."

"And you just walk in?"

"Only on House Tour Day."

"Oh. He doesn't like visitors any other time?"

"They have guards and dogs and everything around that place. My father says Mr. Nicolai is afraid of kidnappers."

"Did he tell this to your father?"

"One of the gardeners who works there told my father Mr. Nicolai hopes to have his grandson stay with him for a while, and he doesn't want anything to happen like it did to that kid in Italy who had his ear cut off."

"You mean Getty's grandson?"

"That's the one. I saw his picture in the paper." He rubbed his ear. "I wouldn't like that to happen to me."

"My friend Mr. Lennis said Mr. Nicolai is a fine man."

The kid marveled, "What a tipper he is!" He added ruefully, "He never takes me, only Johnny Trent—he's one of the bigger kids."

"If I meet him I'll tell him privately that you're better than any of the two bigger kids put together—"

"No kidding! Will you tell him that, Mr. Hoffman?"

I gave him the scout sign.

"By the way, how could I meet Mr. Nicolai?"

"Every Tuesday afternoon he comes and Johnny Trent is waiting. After his game he goes in for lunch. Then his chauffeur drives up and waits for him."

"What time is that?"

"One thirty. Johnny always cuts lab to be there. He says that after a year of Mr. Nicolai he'll be able to buy a car. What kind do you have, Mr. Hoffman?"

"I'm in between models right now. I think I'll be buying a T-Bird."

"Mr. Nicolai has a blue Caddy. When Johnny sees it coming up the drive he's out there waiting. I told him if he ever gets sick to give me a call! Someday I'm going to buy me a car—"

"I'm sure you will, Lance," I said hastily. "Does Mr. Nicolai have a chauffeured car?"

"Besides the chauffeur another car rides behind him. It parks near the gate and waits until he comes out. My father says when you're as rich as Mr. Nicolai, that's the way you have to live."

"I'll have to get a look at his house someday. When is that historical society tour?"

"The House Tour Day? Oh, that was last month. It won't be again until next year."

When Lance told me he and his father had visited Grand Vista on the last House Tour I pumped the kid to get a physical layout of the place.

"How many rooms does Grand Vista have, Lance?" I asked.

"Twenty-six, there's about ten in each wing."

"That's big! The place has wings?"

"North and south. Then there's the main house between the wings. There's about eight bathrooms. We saw one. Wow! Would I like to take a bath in that! It was like a little swimming pool and the faucets were made of gold! Real gold, Mr. Hoffman!"

234

"Did you go through the house?"

"Only the south wing and the main house. They use the south wing for guests. Mr. Nicolai uses the north wing. Most of the time he spends in the library." He went on, "It must be nice in the summertime. They have glass sliding doors that you can roll back and look out over the valley. Dad said he liked that setup best of all. But I liked the story of the tunnel . . ."

"A tunnel? What kind of tunnel?"

"Dad told my mother it was just another one of those stories that's always told about old houses, but I liked it. It was kind of spooky."

"I guess Mr. Nicolai has a lot of guests?"

"Dad said he looked into the old carriage house and it was full of cars, mostly from New York. He said they were probably Mr. Nicolai's business associates. That's the way to do it, my father says, work at home and make the business come to you."

For a ten-buck tip I was given a wealth of information about Mr. Nicolai, a name Colonel Bouquet had said was Corsican, a good idea of the physical layout of Grand Vista, along with a history lesson.

Was Del Morenci in Grand Vista as Nicolai, the international contractor?

The next day, following Lance's directions, I found Grand Vista. It was like a castle built on the peak of a good-sized hill, overlooking a valley. As the kid had said, the place had two huge wings, north and south, with the main house in between. I didn't need the sign, "Danger—Electrified Fence," to tell me the only way you could get over it was by a pole vault. When I passed the main gate I also spotted the guardhouse, a mean-looking attack dog, and the electric-eye system. I spent the morning exploring dirt back roads and secondary blacktops to end up finally on a hill across the valley that was directly in line with Grand Vista.

It was a glorious day; the summer heat was gone and the air was soft and gentle as a woman's touch. I took off my jacket and sat down in the grass to study that grim-looking old house with its wings, turrets, main house, sloping slate roof, and outbuildings. Tiny figures moved in and out of the woods that edged the gardens. In the center of an enormous lawn was a splashing marble fountain. Once the bright sun bounced off something shiny. I knew a fence surrounded the acres of land and the house, then it came to me—a guard and his attack dog were making their rounds, the sun was reflecting on the chain in the man's hand.

When I had first started my business, someone suggested I look into guard work using dogs so I went to a demonstration. I will never forget the sight of those snarling mutts tearing apart that stuffed dummy. . . .

As I walked back to the car I told myself Grand Vista was going to be a tough nut to crack. Maybe now was the time to go to the feds.

The following Tuesday afternoon I was in the bar when Nicolai came in. I had a camera strapped under my shirt with a powerful lens as part of a brass button on the lapel of my very, very expensive sport jacket. I had selected a table that commanded a clear view of the bar section and the door; if I knew Mr. Nicolai, his table would view everyone entering and leaving.

When he sat down I immediately started clicking but to say I was disappointed is an understatement. Instead of the sullen, paunchy-looking thug in Colonel Bouquet's portrait, the guy who waved a greeting to the bartender and several people having lunch was trim, dark, and handsome. He appeared in his early forties and smiled a lot. His guests looked to be people from the club. I kept snapping but then when he raised his hand to touch glasses with a woman companion I almost choked on my scotch and water.

The tip of the middle finger of his right hand was missing.

To hide the confusion and excitement which I was sure were evident in my face, I buried myself in the big menu and ordered a lunch which I barely touched. I snapped every frame on the roll; he left as my kid informer predicted.

I called Stu from a highway phone and urged him to call an emergency meeting for the following morning.

I knew I had Del Morenci.

In Manhattan I paid triple to get the film developed in a rush and have 18 X 20 blowups made of some of the frames.

There was the missing fingertip, but what had happened to his face? A plastic surgery job?

After I gave a detailed account of the club and my observations of Grand Vista, we passed around the blowups of Morenci with a magnifying glass; Arnie and Tom confirmed my suspicions immediately.

"He had a face job," Tom said. He pointed to Morenci's ear. "You can see the cut with the glass, fine as a hairline." He touched his cheek where that bar-bully's boot had landed. "It's as good as mine."

"That's the answer," Stu said. "It's got to be Morenci."

"Now what do we do?" Trev asked.

"The next thing is to find out how to get inside Grand Vista," Stu said.

"Don't you think we've gone far enough, Stu?"

"No, I don't, Trev."

"That place is like a fort, Stu," I pointed out. "It's one thing to tap the phone of a jerk like Lennis, but it's another ball game to try and crack a place that's protected by electrified wire, probably the best security system money can buy, in addition to guards and attack dogs."

"It was only a short time ago that we were wondering how we could ever find Morenci," he reminded me with a smile.

"That was a lucky break of Toni getting the Adolph Lunch Box tip."

"Maybe Toni will get another one about Grand Vista," he said.

"I think Toni's done enough, Stu," Trev said. I was surprised at the sharp edge to his voice.

236

"Toni doesn't seem worried, Trev."

"Well, I am! If this is Morenci—and I'm sure Sam has him pegged right—then we've done our job. We found the bastard. Let the feds break into the place! They can get search warrants and subpoenas."

"Sure they can," Stu said evenly. "By the time they get finished with the routine business of the law and cut through the bureaucracy, the load could be cut and gone."

"What do you mean? Has it come in?"

"Arnie called this morning. His contact said the junk got over the border. And every hour is in Morenci's favor. Once he gets that load inside his mill, his cutters will work day and night to get it out." He made an angry gesture. "When that happens, it may be too late. In the meantime how many kids will have died of OD? How many more new junkies will there be? How much more street crime? Violence?"

"So what do you propose, Stu?" I asked.

He glanced over at Trev. For a moment I thought I detected a flicker of a challenge in his eyes. Then I wasn't sure, his face was so tight, unmoving.

"I say let's give them a package they can't possibly foul up."

Trev said shortly, "Spell it out."

"Find some way to get into Grand Vista," he said.

"Why?"

"For a few reasons. Do you recall the cases of those stupid agents who raided the wrong houses and scared the hell out of the people?"

"Wasn't there a grand jury investigation?"

"They were indicted but acquitted. Now the agencies are extracautious. Can you imagine them breaking into a mansion owned by a supposedly millionaire international contractor and the town's top citizen?"

Tom protested, "But if the junk is there—"

"We don't know where the junk is, Tom," Stu replied.

"You said it was here."

"I said it was somewhere in the United States—not here."

"How can you be sure?"

"Remember 'the girl of the bells' code? She hasn't called Cardillo yet or else Toni would have warned us. So we can assume the cargo is arriving by easy stages. Arnie agrees with me."

Trev pointed out, "But then all the feds have to do is watch the Yonkers plant and Grand Vista and grab the stuff when it arrives."

"The Yonkers plant closed down over the weekend."

I was surprised. "How the hell do you know that?"

"Toni called just before we started the meeting."

"Goddammit, I'm supposed to be her contact," Trev said angrily.

"She was calling from Bellevue and was in a hurry. When she couldn't get you, she gave me the message," Stu said with elaborate patience. "She said she would call you later. For God's sakes, Trev, let's not argue over formalities."

"But Trev is right, Stu," Tom said doggedly. "Okay, so the

Yonkers plant is closed. But Morenci is still in Grand Vista waiting for his cargo of drugs. Maybe the federal people don't have to bust in but they certainly can stake out the place and pick it up. That makes sense to me."

"To me it doesn't," Stu told him. "First of all it's not that easy. No law enforcement agency on the basis of suspicion can wait outside a man's home and stop every car going in, anymore than they can crash in with a tank. Take it or leave it, gentlemen, that's the law!"

"But what would be the purpose of trying to find a way into Grand Vista?" Tom asked. "After all the trouble of getting the cargo out of Indochina to Marseilles and to here, won't they simply go right through the front gate?"

Stu nodded. "Probably, Tom, but suppose there's another entrance we don't know about? There are at least ten acres of woods surrounding the place. Is there a back entrance?" He turned to me. "Sam, didn't the caddy say there was once a tunnel into the place?"

That was one thing about Stu, his mind absorbed details like a vacuum cleaner picking up dust.

"I took it as a legend, Stu. I remember asking the kid if either he or his father ever saw the tunnel and he said no. In fact the kid said his old man told him it was only a story."

"Suppose it isn't a story, Sam? Suppose there is a tunnel into that place? And suppose they use it to bring in the cargo? We could be sitting here for years wondering what the hell happened to it."

"Suppose we do find this tunnel or whatever it is?" Trev asked impatiently. "What then?"

"We turn everything we have over to the feds," Stu said triumphantly. "At that point I would say we have done our job."

Okay, we went along with Stu. But I could see that Trev and Tom were uneasy, worried. Now I felt the same way. On the trip back to D.C. I recalled that ugly Gothic mansion with its two gigantic wings, turrets, and gray roofs, the bright sunshine glinting on the attack dog's leash, and I felt the hair on the back of my neck begin to rise as if I were walking through a graveyard at midnight instead of watching the Washington Monument appear through the clouds as we came in for a landing.

It would be good to see Kate again . . . maybe she would have some lentil soup ready. . . .

Chapter **9**

Trevor David-
The Way In

I felt Stu's plans were now getting to be like taking a walk in a place back home we called "Devil's Den." On the surface it was an innocent marsh but it contained deadly, hidden quicksand pits.

Tom felt the same uneasiness. We talked after the penthouse meeting, but agreed we should go on in this final phase for Stu's sake.

"What the hell, Trev," he said, "we have Morenci identified and we know now where he lives and where the junk will be delivered. I think it will be only a matter of time before the other agencies hear about the load."

"But suppose they don't?"

"Well, to satisfy him we'll look the place over and see how we could get in." He laughed. "We're not going to get into that place, Trev. Did you hear what Sam said? It's a goddam garrisoned castle!"

Tom's cheerfulness was fine, but I was determined now more than ever to persuade Toni to stop intercepting Cardillo's calls; she had been a partner too long in this dangerous game.

I had spent a great deal of time thinking over what I was going to tell her and I rehearsed it a dozen times. Although by now I knew her to be the most stubborn, determined, exasperating—but wonderful—woman I had ever known, I hoped the combined pressure of her common sense and my arguments would change her mind.

It was a desolate feeling knowing that I had brought her into this terrible situation by manipulating her courage, her integrity, and her deep and intense sense of humanity. If anything happened to her, it would be my responsibility. The very thought made me almost run the last block to Smitty's where I could see her waiting on the corner. . . .

It was a wasted effort.

Frowning and thoughtful, she listened to my account of our last meeting in the penthouse.

"The drugs are now in this country?"

"That's the word Arnie got in Washington."

"But nobody knows where?"

"We're assuming the load is on the way to Jersey."

"But you don't know?"

"No. How could we?"

"But you will know when I tell you," she said triumphantly. "The 'girl of the bells' must call Frank. That's the way it happened last time, Trevor. She will have to call!"

Then she went on very quickly, "I've decided we shouldn't see each other until this mess is over."

"That's the most ridiculous thing I've ever heard you say."

"I have my reasons."

"Well, what are they?"

"There's no need to discuss them. I will still keep in touch with you by phone—"

"Toni, answer me—has anything happened?"

"No. Everything is fine."

"And Cardillo still doesn't suspect anything?"

She hesitated for only a moment.

"Tell me, Toni—please!"

"That man Stash—"

"What about him?"

"He hasn't called in a long time and Frank is worried."

"Tell me everything."

"I was in the kitchen last night and I heard him dial a number and talk to someone. I couldn't hear everything but I did hear him ask, "Where's Stash?" Then he slammed the phone down as if he was angry. Later I heard him stumbling around the kitchen. My sister said she found him drunk on the couch. When I came home he was gone. Teresa said he was out looking for a friend of his."

"Stash?"

"Perhaps. He returned late and went into his office. I could hear him making phone calls but I wasn't in a position to pick up the phone."

"Did your sister say anything?"

"All Teresa talks about is getting a divorce and going upstate with the kids to live with my brothers . . ."

"Thank God someone in Canarsie has common sense!"

"My brothers finally talked her into it."

"But what has that got to do with seeing me?"

"Frank is worried and very suspicious lately. Suppose he got it into his head to follow me and saw you?"

"But why would Cardillo want to do that, Toni, if he doesn't suspect anything?"

"I don't think we should take chances."

"I'll be worried sick if I don't see you, Toni."

She looked up at me.

"Will you, Trevor?"

"Of course."

She persisted with a smile, "Why?"

"Dammit, because I care for you very much. Hasn't that been evident?"

"It took you a long time to say that," she pointed out.

"Well, maybe I could say a hell of a lot more if you gave me the chance . . ."

"My chief warned us in second year—no romance."

"Tell your chief to go to hell. Politely, of course. Now can we be serious?"

"I was never more serious in my life, Trevor," she said. "I'm not going to see you until this mess is over."

"But why?"

"Maybe it's because I don't want anything to happen to you." She glanced at her watch. "I have exactly five minutes to get to class." She raised herself on tiptoe and kissed me. "Good-bye, Trevor."

Then she was gone, beating the traffic light by seconds and disappearing into the long alley of the hospital's entrance.

I stood on that windy corner for a long time debating with myself whether I should follow her and demand that she sever all ties to us but I decided I knew Toni well enough by now to know she would calmly listen to what I had to say, then politely tell me she intended to do it her way. . . .

I walked away wondering who had written that the first stirrings of love in a man's heart can make him a confused hollow shell, empty of all his habitual resources. . . .

It was a perfect description of me.

Later at the hotel when I told Stu about the strange disappearance of Stash he dismissed it with a shrug.

"You know how those bums are, Trev. They're either killing one another or selling out to the highest bidder."

"Didn't Arnie and Sam say Stash was part Corsican, like Morenci?"

"That's right."

"Maybe Morenci sent him to Corsica as a courier."

"I doubt it. Morenci doesn't seem the type to entrust anything important to a jerk like Stash."

"How do we know he's a jerk, Stu? He seems to be able to follow orders."

He looked irritated.

"The way Toni said he sounded on the phone."

"I think you should get in touch with Arnie or Sam and tell them."

"I'll do that," he said shortly.

His obvious lack of interest in Stash seemed strange, but I thought no more about it.

The next day Arnie and Sam returned from Washington with more details but nothing exciting. Tom had hired a helicopter to make a series of airview slides of Grand Vista and color movies which we ran off several times, while Sam showed us with a pointer the very thorough electrical system protecting the grounds along with the guards and attack dogs, which could be seen patrolling the entire fenced area.

"I had to make several runs over the place so they wouldn't get suspicious, but from what I could see there doesn't seem to be a rear entrance or any trails through the woods leading to the house," Tom said.

"We could make a silk raid," Star suggested. "We could get the dogs before they knew what hit them."

"You would have to go in low enough to make a parachute drop," Tom pointed out. "You might as well fire a cannon."

"Suppose someone starts shootin', Injun?" Rudy asked.

"So we shoot back," Star replied.

Tom broke in, "That could get hairy."

"What the hell, we're not looking for a confrontation," Sam said.

"Penetration—that's the problem," Stu said thoughtfully.

Tom looked over at me. "The quicker we know all the entrances to this place, the quicker we can give it to the feds."

As we studied a large blowup of Grand Vista, an idea began to form slowly in the back of my mind.

"How old is this place, Sam?" I asked.

"The kid said his father told him Grant stayed there one weekend."

"Is this the original building?"

"I suppose so. I guess that's why people visit it on this annual tour."

"We have the same thing down home," I explained. "Our

historical society sponsors a tour of the old homes once a year. It's a great tourist attraction. One year they featured the original plans of Riverview—now they're hanging on the wall of the local museum."

"What's the point, Trev?" Stu asked.

"If Grand Vista is an historical landmark, perhaps the local historical society has the original plans. They might show something we can't see from the films or the slides—"

We looked at each other.

"The tunnel!" Sam blurted out.

"At least the plans will show there is one or it's simply a legend," Stu said. "That's a great idea, Trev! How would you go about it?"

"I can say I'm writing a book on the outstanding historical homes of the metropolitan area."

Arnie said, "Wouldn't they ask for credentials?"

"Your interest is your credential."

"Let's give it a try, Trev," Stu said. "Sam, what do you think?"

"The people over there love old buildings," Sam replied with a grin, "so they must love people who love old buildings. While Trev is playing author I'm going back to my toy shop. Arnie, you better come along and check on your chink woman—"

"Chinese, for Crissakes."

The historical society's headquarters was in a small brownstone building. Ten minutes after I entered the place I discovered Sam's tunnel was a fact, not a legend.

"I've run across a number of old homes with tunnels," I said to the curator, an elderly woman, a Miss Foreman. "Many down south were used as way stations for the Underground Railroad. Are there historic buildings with tunnels in this area?"

"Why yes," she said, "in fact a very famous one is in the home you'll be researching, Mr. David—Grand Vista."

A gong crashed inside my skull.

"Oh? Are there some accounts of it?"

"Right here," she said and placed four large folders on the table.

The title of the last one jumped out at me: "Grand Vista and the Tunnel of History."

Grand Vista had been the dream of John McCleary Abbott, swashbuckling Civil War cavalry officer and hero, brawler, Indian fighter, politician, hard-drinking freebooter in steel, railroad baron, friend of Grant, McClellan, and Custer, and legendary lover of many women and kingmaker in national politics.

After the Civil War he returned to his native New Jersey to read law in his father's firm. I felt a strange kinship with this ghost when I read a letter he had sent to his father, resigning from the firm to return to the army because "I am dissatisfied with my unrewarding daily life and the attitude of many civilians who take for granted the victories we won in the field . . ."

Two years in the Indian wars on the frontier apparently changed his philosophy, he returned to his father's law firm, won a degree, and took over the firm following his father's death.

From then on his rise was swift and sure.

Ground was broken for Grand Vista in the spring of 1872. A clipping from Greeley's *Tribune* called it "the beginning of what surely will be one of the great estates in the East."

There was another clipping, brown, brittle, and crumbling, which I carefully put together. It told how a crew working on the foundation had discovered a deep underground creek and tunnel which ran through the property. They traced it for a half mile to emerge on the far side of the hill on which Grand Vista was to be built. A professor from Princeton called it "a natural aquatic, underground waterway with a beautiful underground lake and grotto."

Major Abbott, the reporter wrote, after conferring with the architect and the professor announced he would incorporate the tunnel into his building plans "with a surprise to be announced later."

What Abbott had done was to convert the natural tunnel into a fabulous combination of a wonderland and nineteenth-century Madam Tussaud museum. Entrance was by way of the great kitchen, down a circular iron stairway which led to a wooden deck and a fleet of small gondolas.

A reporter for the *Herald* described how they made a long winding trip in the gondolas, illumination supplied by torches, and were "thrilled to find a series of extraordinary historic scenes" depicted by tin manikins placed in niches carved into the tunnel's rock walls. Major Abbott told the reporter special "artists" from Italy had designed the figures and it had taken more than a year to prepare his "Tunnel of History."

"Is the tunnel still in existence?" I asked as casually as I could.

"I don't know," she replied. "The present owner of Grand Vista, Mr. Nicolai—he's an international contractor—told me when workmen renovated the kitchen they discovered an iron cover in the floor had been cemented over. We believe this was the original entrance."

"Then the new owner—"

"Mr. Nicolai."

"—didn't open the tunnel?"

"Oh, no. He said he had engineers in who advised against it. The house is so old they feared any work on the foundation could endanger the understructure." She shrugged. "Frankly that puzzled me—the place sits on a bed of granite, that's all the hill is made of—rocks and springs. Perhaps he doesn't want to be bothered."

I said, "When was the last time the tunnel was open?"

"During the thirties. Two kids found the old exit on the other side of the hill. It had been filled in with boulders around the turn of the century after Abbott died. Grand Vista remained empty for some time, then went through a succession of owners until Mr. Nicolai bought it. The kids told the police, and Chief Van Gelder and the editor of the *County Leader* traced the tunnel back to the house. They found the place filled with bats and they had a devil of a time."

"Do you remember the editor's name?"

"I think I have it somewhere—just a moment."

She returned in a few minutes with an index card.

"Here it is, I wrote it down for you on this card."

I read: "Warren Hutton, editor, *The County Leader*."

"Perhaps if I dropped by the paper they could—"

"Oh, the *County Leader* went out of business a long time ago—about 1942 or '43, I think."

"How about the police chief?"

"Van Gelder? He died fifteen years ago. His wife told me the story many times but she also passed on about five years ago."

"Didn't the editor write an account of the trip for his newspaper?"

"We never found one. It was about this time that the paper folded. Hutton, as I recall, was a young man who had inherited his family's farm outside of Cidertown. I heard he once worked for a New York newspaper. The *County Leader* was a small paper and people weren't paying for ads in those days and it just dropped out of sight. It also was a bit of a muckraking sheet and the county politicians didn't take to it. Then the war broke out and Hutton sold the farm and, I believe, went into the army. I often wonder what became of him."

"I was hoping I could find the original plans for Grand Vista."

"We don't have them," she said, "but I think I know where you might find them—"

"Oh? Where would that be?"

"The last Abbott in these parts was his grandson who was killed in the Pacific. He gave all his grandfather's private papers to the National Archives." She gave me a frosty smile. "I might say we were disappointed because we consider Grand Vista and the major a part of the town's heritage."

"Do you think the papers might contain the original plans?"

She smiled. "You certainly know the trials, tribulations, and triumphs of research, young man."

I took a late flight from Newark for Washington, checked in at a hotel and applied for a search card minutes after the National Archives had opened.

It was a fascinating maze operated with quiet efficiency. *Civil War Records* supplied me with a small trunk and key with the nameplate: "Major John McCleary Abbott, U.S.A."

Under it someone had inked in the fabric: "June 5, 1840—Sept. 10, 1901."

By late afternoon I had made a good dent in the collection of letters, pamphlets, diaries, magazine articles, and newspaper clippings; Grand Vista apparently had held many sad memories for Mary Sinclair Abbott, Abbott's wife.

> I am sick to death of that horrible tunnel [she wrote her sister]. How many times have I heard our guests applaud my husband's genius after he took them through it. Now the servants tell me rats have been seen in the gardens and the caretaker insists they come from the tunnel. We also have another danger; when the fall rains are heavy or the snow and frost thaw, the creek inside the tunnel rises without warning with the waters reaching the level of the stairs. I have warned my husband but he said he would rather cut off his right arm than close his precious tunnel . . .

There was one last clipping. It showed a large woodcut of Abbott and his architect, Robert Lewis, surrounded by workmen, all standing in knee-high water inside the tunnel. The headline read: FAMOUS TUNNEL SAVED!

The story described how Abbott had hired Lewis and some engineers to construct a dam inside the tunnel which would hold back the rising water during a sudden thaw or heavy rains. His next guest was to be the Prince of Wales, who planned to stop off at Grand Vista on his tour of the United States, and apparently Abbott wanted to ensure the safety of his royal guest. . . .

The following day I came upon a small leather bag with the title in gold letters:

"Original plans for Grand Vista. Robert Lewis, Architect. Ground breaking ceremonies, March 2, 1872. Building finished, July 27, 1876."

Grand Vista appeared to be like two giant Ts joined together, the bars at either end were called the north wing and the south wing. On the roofs of both wings were turrets, like watchtowers.

The wings, about a story higher than the main house which lay between them, contained numerous bedrooms, sitting rooms, and servants' quarters. Two sweeping stairways in both ends of the house led to the upper floors of the wings.

The main house had a large formal dining room, what appeared to be a huge library, a smaller dining room, a ballroom, two kitchens, one at each end, servants' quarters, a billiard room, a "spirits room," storerooms, and winery.

I had the plans, letters, and clippings photostated. When I returned to New York, I found a message from Miss Foreman, the Cidertown Historical Society curator.

"I had some luck, Mr. David," she said cheerfully over the phone. "I found a nephew of that Hutton fellow, you know, the editor of the *County Leader*, who toured the tunnel with Chief Van Gelder . . ."

"I remember him, Miss Foreman."

"The nephew is a young carpenter who lives at the other end of the county. He never fails to get a Christmas card from Hutton. The last one said he's working on the *Syracuse Journal*. I hope this helps."

I left a note for Stu and took the first plane to Syracuse. I found Hutton, a stout, jovial, middle-aged man who chewed on an empty cigar holder as he talked, working on the *Journal*'s copy desk. He seemed amused that I had traveled from Manhatten to talk to him about Grand Vista's tunnel for a book but was eager to help.

"Oh, sure, I remember it," he said, the amber cigar holder bobbing up and down in rhythm with his words. "That morning I met the chief getting in his car—the town's police force in those days consisted of Van Gelder, a tough old Dutchman, and a nightside cop who was more a watchman than anything else—and I asked him what was up. He said some kids had found the entrance to a cave that led to Grand Vista's tunnel, and he was going to take a look before some other kids went in and got hurt. I was running this weekly and thought I'd go along and maybe do a story for the paper.

"The old guy was a hunter and real outdoorsman, and he lent me a pair of boots. On the way he dropped by his house and I helped him tie a canoe on to the roof of his car.

" 'What the hell's this for, chief?' I asked, but the old Dutchman was anything but talkative and he just grunted.

"We found the cave, about halfway up the hill and not far from a narrow road called Apple Run, used by the apple pickers who had worked the hills many years before. Before the Civil War, orchards covered the whole area. I put on the boots and we unloaded the canoe. When we got deep into the cave I could see why the chief wanted the canoe. We had to cross a small lake to get into the tunnel. We had a couple of flashlights and when the light hit that darkness!" He shook his head. "I've never seen anything like it. There seemed to be millions of bats either hanging from the ceiling, flying around, or dive-bombing us. Van Gelder didn't give a damn; he just whacked them away with his hands, but I was petrified.

" 'Gott im Himmel, vilt you paddle!' he kept shouting, and paddle I did, while he fought off the bats.

"The bats didn't go into the tunnel, but then there were rats, big as cats."

He shook his head again and went on.

"It was a weird morning. We were hours in that damn tunnel. We found at least four of the old tin scenes the major—that's what Van Gelder called him—had installed in niches carved right out of the rock. Most of them were so rusty you couldn't tell what they were, but some you could make out. I remember one, Washington kneeling in the snow at Valley Forge. Part of the arm and sword were gone but the face was still very lifelike. Later out of curiosity I read some of the early accounts in the Historical Society. It was very interesting."

"What happened to the cave entrance?"

"Oh, the chief had the WPA brick it up so the kids couldn't get in. He brought the two kids who discovered the cave into his office and warned them that if they told any other kids about the place he would put them in jail. Apparently he scared the hell out of them because word never got around town."

"You didn't do a piece on it?"

"I wrote a feature story on Grand Vista and the tunnel without giving away the location of the entrance but it never got into type," he said with a grin. "I didn't have the money to pay the printer so we had to skip a few issues. Then I was classified 1A. By the time I went into the army I had sold the farm and the paper was dead. I remember I did give my notes to the county WPA team that was working on the state guide."

"I read the state guide in the museum. It only has a few lines on Grand Vista."

"Well, I hope I've been some help."

"I wonder if you could sketch the possible location of the entrance on the hill?"

"I'll be glad to." He borrowed some copy paper from the receptionist and started to make a drawing of the hill, when he paused.

"I'll be going down to the city in a few days to look into a job on the *Daily News* rim," he said. "I'll be staying over with a friend of mine on Twelfth Street. If you want to drive me out there . . ."

I brought Hutton back to Manhattan and after his interview at the *News* we rode out to Jersey. It was almost forty years since the day he and the old chief had climbed the hill, but he finally found the narrow dirt road called Apple Run. We drove through the woods for about a mile as it gradually ascended the hill in the rear of Grand Vista. Hutton explained this land was part of an undeveloped state park; Grand Vista's property line touched the state line on the peak of the hill.

Halfway up he motioned to me to stop and we got out. We clambered about the hill, Hutton puffing and blowing as we climbed over mounds of rocks and pushed through the underbrush.

"As I remember," he said, sitting on a rock and mopping his red, dripping face, "there was an old waterfall course nearby. The chief traced it by the rocks and moss. Just give me a little time . . ."

The sun was going down behind the tip of the trees and the air was edged with a chill when he suddenly shouted, "Here's the old waterfall . . . this way. . . ."

We climbed up the sloping floor of rocks and brush to a point where the hill leveled off for several feet to end up at a sheer cliff.

"The chief said this was the waterfall," he said, panting, and pointing to the cliff face. "As I remember we walked along this ledge to the left."

I followed him for about twenty-five feet along the cliff and then

248

he stopped and began pulling away tangled vines and mountain laurel.

"Here it is," he said triumphantly. "That's where they bricked it up."

The entrance to the cave was about twenty feet in height and ten feet across. The WPA workers had used the native stones and someone had scratched in the cement near the bottom: "WPA 1938."

"Jeez! I haven't had so much exercise in twenty years!" Hutton said, mopping his face. "I gotta take a leak."

When he disappeared into the bushes I picked up something on the ground. It was a small mason's trowel, encrusted with cement. And it was not from 1938. I pulled away more of the vines—at least half of the entrance showed new cement between the stones while the branches of a large laurel bush had recently been broken. I put the tool in my pocket and carefully pushed back the vines.

"Satisfied?" Hutton asked when he returned.

"More than satisfied," I said. "I'm going to come back with a camera and take a few pictures for the book."

He pointed through the trees.

"Now that we found it, you can reach it with no sweat. Apple Run is in a direct line and not too far. We'll put up a marker on the road when we come out of the woods so you can find your way back here."

We reached the road without any difficulty and while I made a mound of rocks, Hutton hammered a fork-shaped branch into the dirt.

"That should do it," he said, "just remember, at the bottom of the hill you turn off the blacktop road by that big apple tree."

As I carefully maneuvered the car down the twisting road he waved his hand in the direction of the hill.

"Have you met the guy who owns Grand Vista now?"

"No. But I plan to."

"His name is Nicolai. He's supposed to be a big contractor."

"Do you know him?"

"No, but my nephew Elmer Timmons does. He's the fellow who gave Mae Foreman my address for you."

"Oh? How does he know Nicolai?"

"He's a small contractor and has done a lot of work on the property. Would you want to drop by his place and say hello? I could use a cold one."

"That would be fine."

Timmons was a younger replica of his uncle, big, jovial, and eager to please.

"If I can get some goddam carpenters, I plan to go over to Grand Vista next week," he said as he took a six-pack out of the refrigerator. "The caretaker called me twice to put up hanging doors in the old

249

carriage house they use as a garage." He tore off the seals of the cans and poured the beer into glasses. "You know, Uncle John, there's a hell of a lot of people comin' and goin' in that house."

"What do you mean, El?"

"When I was over there last time there were about eight cars in that carriage house."

"I guess he's a busy guy," I said.

"He must do a lot of business in New York," Timmons said. "All the cars were from the city." He turned to his uncle. "Frank's Service closed during the gas shortage, Uncle John. I told him I'm thinking of buying a horse and hitching up Dad's old wagon."

They joked about the idea of horses and wagons returning while I waited for a chance to get back to Grand Vista. It came when he offered me another beer.

"Did you ever see the tunnel, Mr. Timmons?"

"Elmer. No, I only knew what Uncle John told us. Did you find the entrance?"

"Yes—after we hiked over the whole damn hill!" Hutton boomed. "You were too small to remember, but your father was mad as hell that day when I told him I had been in the tunnel with the chief. He wanted me to take him back but your mother put her foot down. She said he'd come back with a bat in his hair and he'd have a hell of a time!" He turned to me. "My brother had real thick blond hair. He was dying to get a look inside that tunnel but he knew what was good for him."

He laughed and shook his head. "Those were good days, El. We didn't have a pot but we had a lot of fun out here . . ."

"You and that damn paper, Uncle John!"

"I thought I was a backwoods Horace Greeley," he explained to me. "I had the politicians shaking in their boots. They never knew what the hell I was going to print."

"Are carpenters hard to come by, Elmer?" I asked.

"Damn hard. Even with the layoffs it's hard to get good ones. A couple of months ago I had a big job over there but I had to do it myself."

His uncle asked, "What kind of a job, El?"

"Rip out two or three walls to make one big room. Then I made Mr. Nicolai a long table. He said he needed it to lay out his blueprints. His caretaker told me he just finished building a big dam in Italy. He's certainly a careful man."

"What do you mean?"

"Well, when I got finished he said he wanted new doors for this big room. I said sure, I could put up some nice oak doors, but he said he didn't care what kind they were as long as they were steel doors. I said, 'Steel doors inside a house, Mr. Nicolai?' He just smiled and nodded. 'Something like fire doors,' he said, 'as thick as you can get 'em.' Then he pointed to the table I had just finished and said, 'The

250

material that will be on this table will be worth a fortune to my business. This is a very old house and I want to make sure my property is protected at all times.' "

"You don't have much call for fire doors, El."

"In this county? Hell, no! But I got 'em. A special order. I told him I had to take the truck to Long Island to pick up the doors but he said he didn't care how I got 'em as long as they were put up in a hurry. Then I had to match that old paneling to put over those sheets of iron. He said he was about to start on a big project and he wanted things just so. I put 'em up myself but it was a bitch of a job! Heavy? Those doors must've weighed a ton! Then you need heavy tracks on the floor so they can roll." He shook his head. "That was a job. I gave him a stiff bill but, dammit, I earned my keep on that one."

He crumpled the can in his big fist and tossed it to one side.

"That's not all. After the fire doors he wanted me to put up ladders on either side of both chimneys that would go down to the courtyard. When I asked what the hell he wanted these for, he said they had trouble with the chimneys' draft and they couldn't clean 'em out unless they had ladders to get up and down. He also wants me to repair the roof."

"You seem to be getting a lot of work out of that place," I said.

"One of these days when I get a rigger I'll put up those ladders and repair that roof. That's a mean one! All slate and slippery as hell." He made a swift downward gesture. "You could go down those sides like you were on a kid's slide in a playground."

"You watch yourself, El," his uncle warned him. "You're too damn fat to be climbin' around slate roofs."

"Don't worry, Uncle John," Timmons said. "I won't touch the job unless I get me a rigger. Maybe someday I'll go into the city to one of those big construction jobs and see if I can get some guy to come over."

"Half the job is to get 'em to come over to Jersey," Hutton said with a chuckle. "Funny thing about New Yorkers, they still think Jersey's just this side of Montana. How about another cold one, Mr. David?"

Stu couldn't wait, so the following afternoon we parked on the side of narrow Apple Run and made our way to the cave's entrance. I carefully pulled aside the vines and bushes and pointed to the newly cemented section.

"They rubbed in dirt to try to make it look old," Rudy said as he knelt down and ran his hands over the rocks. He dug out some of the cement with his fingernail and rubbed it between his fingers. "It's prepared stuff."

"What does that mean, Rudy?" Tom asked.

"They used bags of sand and mortar already mixed. That stuff's good for patching but not for a big job." He tapped the stones with his huge fist. "One shot with a sledge and this whole thing'll cave in. But maybe that's the way they want it."

"Well, here is your entrance to Grand Vista, Stu," I said.

"That's it," Tom said. "We're finished."

"I don't think so," Stu said quietly.

"I'd like to get a look inside that tunnel," Arnie said.

"Me too," Star said.

"If we go into that tunnel there's going to be trouble," I said.

"And why should we, Stu?" Tom asked. "Suppose we get into the house, then what?"

"I'm not talking about breaking into the tunnel—now," Stu replied. "To begin with, we still don't know there's anything in the house. I think before we make our move and go to the feds, we should know definitely that the cargo of junk has been delivered. Maybe they don't intend to go in the front gate—maybe they intend to use this tunnel."

"We can't sit out here in the woods day and night waiting for them to show up," Tom protested.

"Sam has an idea," Stu said. "Let's drive over to the other hill and he'll tell us about it."

Hidden by a clump of trees on the peak of the hill across the narrow valley, Sam studied Grand Vista, stark and grim against the lowering sky, through powerful glasses.

"I can set up a laser beam right here," he said, "but I need a couple of relay stations hidden somewhere on the grounds."

"What will a laser beam do?" Tom asked.

Sam passed around the binoculars.

"From the original plans Trev found in Washington, somebody replaced the small windows on the first floor with sliding glass doors so they can walk out on the lawn from the library."

"So what does that add up to, Sam?"

"On the last House Tour Day the guide told my caddy's old man the library was the most comfortable room in the house and that's where Morenci—Nicolai—spends most of his time when he's at Grand Vista. Now a human voice makes glass vibrate, even a telephone conversation, so the reflected laser would be imprinted with the voices which could be picked up by a relay station and transmitted to a parabolic mike up here. The mike in turn collects the beams and amplifies them into intelligible words which are then recorded. We won't have to stay here. We can hang the equipment in a tree so that even if someone comes up here by accident, they'll never spot it. Every day one of us can drive over and pick up a recording."

"Didn't you say this guy Timmons needs a couple of carpenters and a rigger, Trev?" Arnie asked.

"He said he needs them to help him install overhead doors on the carriage house used as a garage."

252

"How about Rudy and Star? Rudy, you know how to install overhead doors, don't you?"

Rudy nodded. "I can put 'em up with my eyes closed."

"And the rigger to work on the roof and put up the ladders he was talking about?"

Star studied Grand Vista through the glasses.

"I could do it with a bosun's seat rig," he said. "No problem."

I protested, "We're getting in deeper and deeper, Stu! There will come a time when we can't turn back! Why go through all this? Having Sam set up this laser beam and Rudy and Star get into that place? Christ, haven't we done enough? We know Morenci is there and now we know a tunnel leads into the building. Isn't that enough to give to the feds?"

"When the cargo of junk is delivered—that will wind up our part," he said in a tone of calm patience.

Arnie broke in, "If he's not caught with the junk, Trev, forget about it. You don't have a case. The gun must not only be smoking but must be in his hand!"

Tom gave him an incredulous look. "You mean all the stuff we dug up doesn't mean anything?"

"Not in a court of law, Tom. It's great for an investigation but can't be considered as evidence."

"Remember, Morenci's not a fugitive from anything," Stu pointed out. "Is that right, Sam?"

Sam nodded.

"No warrants? New York Police? Sûreté? Interpol?"

"No—nothing."

"Why then all the big deal in Washington and Paris over this guy?" Tom protested. "You would think he was ready to blow up the world the way they were investigating him!"

Stu said, "You haven't been reading the papers, Tom. It's not easy to convict someone these days, the laws are tough. Maybe it's good, maybe it makes the cops get off their butts and become better investigators. But sometimes no matter how hard they work the evidence just isn't there—at least within the legal boundaries. They're boxed in, but we're not."

I said, "You mean we're supposed to break the law to help the law?"

"I guess that's it," Stu said. "As far as I'm concerned I'm willing to do anything to make sure Morenci doesn't get away this time."

Arnie said, "I put a lot on the line to make sure we get this guy—"

"It's like the gooks have a hill that we need," Rudy said with a chuckle. "Hey, Major, let's take it . . ."

"Oh, Christ, Fatso," Star said disgustedly, "get out of Nam, willya?"

"I could use a little action, Injun," Rudy replied.

"When will this end, Stu?" I asked.

"When they grab Morenci," Stu said quickly. "But this time with the junk."

"To set a beam and recorder up here isn't that much of a problem," Sam said, "but it won't work unless we get in and plant the relay stations."

"How big are they?" Star asked.

"About the size of a pack of cigarettes."

"Call that hick contractor, Trev," Star said. "Fatso and I will put them in."

"The more stations we have the better the reception," Sam said.

Arnie, who was studying Grand Vista through the glasses, turned around and pointed across the valley.

"There's a tremendous load of drugs coming into that place," he said quietly. "Paris doesn't know when or how, neither does Washington. If it had been delivered, Toni undoubtedly would have caught that 'girl of the bells' code name to alert Cardillo the stuff is ready to be delivered. I agree with Stu—let's make sure the drugs are inside Grand Vista before we contact the feds."

Sam said, "And you think that's the best way, Arnie?"

"The only way."

"And once we know the junk is on the way in—"

"That's it," Stu said.

"Let's take a vote," Arnie said.

What can I say? In the quiet woods overlooking Grand Vista, Tom and I were outvoted in the classic democratic way. To break the law, to help the law. It was going to be Stu's way. Again.

The next day I called Timmons who was overjoyed with the news that two carpenters I knew, one a rigger, were willing to come to New Jersey and work for him.

Later Star described Grand Vista's extraordinary security measures. They were stopped at the gate until the boss of the guards arrived to question Star and Rudy closely. It was clear he didn't like the idea of two strangers, but when Timmons became angry and told him to shove the job, he allowed them in with a warning they were to notify him anytime they wanted to leave or work on another section of the house or grounds.

"Not only did they go over Timmons's panel truck inch by inch," Star said, "but a guy with a dog sat under a tree and watched us."

"Yeah," Rudy said, "he didn't leave from the minute we got on the job until we took off."

When he saw they were competent, Timmons, escorted by a guard and dog, moved to another part of the estate to work on an outbuilding.

Rudy easily hid a relay station under the eaves of the carriage house. Then Star installed others as he explored the dangerous sloping roof, repairing damaged slates, leaders, and gutters. He and Rudy also put up iron ladders leading down from the two massive chimneys to the courtyard in the rear of the house.

He said he took his time caulking the windows but he found each one covered with heavy drapes. There were no sounds of voices or music in any part of the mansion.

They found the carriage house was attached to the south wing with an entrance to the kitchen. Inside were eight cars. They got the plate numbers and Sam checked them out; all were cars hired in New York to a fictitious rug-cleaning firm.

They also discovered the guards worked in teams, periodically inspecting the house or the grounds. When one bent over, Rudy saw the bulge of the gun on his hip.

They were inside Grand Vista for five days; across the valley on the peak of the hill, Sam had finished putting up his laser beam recorder. On Friday afternoon after they were paid off by the grateful Timmons who begged them to return and finish the roof, Star and Rudy drove to Apple Run to pick up the first recording. They were about to turn into the dirt road from the blacktop when a farm truck skidded to a stop alongside them.

"Where you fellows goin'?" the driver shouted.

"We're working in Grand Vista and left our tools there," Star replied. "This is a shortcut?"

"Hell no," the farmer said, "that leads to a dead end on the top of the hill. Follow me, I'll show you how to get there."

They followed him to the main road which led to the country club.

"About five miles up this road, you can't miss Grand Vista," he shouted.

"Thanks a lot," Star said with a wave. After a few hundred feet they made a U-turn and returned to the hill and picked up the recording.

"Next time I'm goin' there at night," Star said. "Too damn many nosy farmers in the daytime."

We gathered in the penthouse and listened to the surprisingly clear voices; the chief of Grand Vista's security forces reporting to someone that their phones were "clean" and the grounds and house secured; overseas calls, two from Paris, one from Ajaccio, capital of Corsica, another from a bank in Genoa, and one in Switzerland.

Stu and Arnie translated the conversations in French which were brief and related to routine business matters. But the call from Ajaccio between Morenci and someone who played the role of a family member had a swift, jocular reference to "the honey...it was delivered to Mama by a Golden Hawk."

We played the recording over and over trying to guess the meaning of the obvious code, when suddenly Tom snapped his fingers and jumped up.

"Wait a minute!"

He hurriedly searched through a pile of magazines, selected one and flipped open its pages.

"Here it is! *Aviation Age.*" He held up a full-color page ad which showed a beautiful private plane. The caption read:

"The Golden Hawk . . . the plane that will take you to your board meeting in record time from Seattle to the Bahamas . . ."

"This job was only put out by Lockheed," he said. "The ads are all over the aviation trade magazines."

"They said 'delivered to Mama,' " Arnie repeated slowly. "That must mean to a central point—"

"Maybe Grand Vista?" Sam suggested.

Arnie shook his head. "No. The 'girl of the bells' makes the final delivery. This must mean the step before it's taken to Jersey."

"How would they use that plane, Tom?" I asked.

"To fly in from Mexico, Canada, or one of the islands," he replied. "It's fast as hell and could easily slip under Customs' radar belt."

"Didn't they use a plane once before in Arizona?" Sam recalled. "When they killed the pilot."

"This is a beautiful ship," Tom said as he lovingly studied the ad, "but expensive as hell."

"Money doesn't count now," Arnie said. "The stuff they're bringing in must be worth millions.'

I was more concerned with Toni than the cargo of junk. She had called only once to assure me everything was fine and there was no cause for worry. But worry I did. Meanwhile Star and Rudy returned to Grand Vista with Timmons to finish the roof and Sam and Arnie went back to their toy shop.

It was the start of the three-day toy fair at one of the hotels, Sam and Arnie were taking the Chinese girl, Mary Chang Winslow, and Bernie Lennis, the next-door lawyer. Partly out of curiosity and because I was getting so tense worrying about Toni that I twanged like a well-tuned E string, I persuaded Sam to let Tom and me meet them at the fair.

Sam warned me that while Lennis wasn't too shrewd, the girl was sharp.

We arranged to meet them ostensibly by accident; Sam would identify us as old friends from the Boston toy warehouse who had come down to look over the next season's products.

Our "accidental" meeting appeared normal but Mary Chang Winslow, an attractive Chinese-American, wasn't at her sharpest; Sam had taken Arnie, Mary, and Lennis to several wholesale and buyers' cocktail parties—Lennis was flying and Mary smiled a lot and clung to Arnie. Both were beginning to have that out-of-focus look.

After a tour of the fair we had dinner. When Arnie gave me the eye I followed him into the men's room.

"I don't know what's with her tonight," he said, "she's really uptight. Usually she has a drink and that's it. She's now on her fifth Manhattan and she won't be able to stand up much longer."

"Any idea what's wrong with her?"

"I think maybe she's had a fight with a boyfriend."

"How do you know that, Arnie?"

He gave me an owlish wink. "When they drink, they talk too much. I don't know who the guy is, only that she met him in San Francisco. I got her on the rebound tonight and that's good."

"Why?"

"I'm going to take care of her tonight," he said firmly. "I'll find out what's wrong." He carefully dried his hands. "Up to now it's been arguing about the principles of pseudo-Gemeinschaft or Debray's mystique of guerrilla action. But not tonight, buddy!"

"You're walking like you have a pocketful of nickels, Arnie."

"I kept up with her but now I have the waiter serving me vermouth. I slipped him a fin to make her Manhattans extra strong . . ."

He ran a comb through his hair. "She's getting stoned . . . she's worried and she's mad at the other guy. That's good. I shouldn't have much trouble."

A short time later he left with Mary. We took Lennis to Grand Central and poured him on the last train to Westchester. Tom and I accepted Sam's suggestion that we walk to the Eldorado, but as we came to an all-night Automat he suddenly said, "Let's get a cup of coffee and do some talking."

We got the coffee and found a table in the rear of the almost deserted restaurant.

"I'm worried," he said bluntly.

"About what, Sam?"

"The whole setup. Okay, the recordings are telling us what's going in the house but I'm getting the feeling Stu won't be satisfied until he takes us into that place."

"Any reason?"

"Well, the other night I went up to the penthouse to see him. Apparently he didn't hear my knock so I walked in. He had a big blowup of the plans of the house, to me it looked like a regular attack plan. He didn't say anything, just folded it up and put it into a drawer."

"He gave his word that once we found out the stuff was going into Grand Vista," Tom said, "that would be it. No more playing cops and robbers."

"I want to see that bastard Morenci get thrown in the slammer as much as anyone," Sam said. He shook his head.

"But we're not the people to do it," I added.

"Exactly. But I'm afraid that's not what Stu has in mind."

"You think he wants us to go in and take the guy?" Tom asked.

"Maybe. What's your opinion, Trev?"

"I believe Stu is making this thing a war. We have found and fixed the enemy—now he wants to go in and destroy him."

"That's one place I don't want to be," Tom said. "If we ever go into that tunnel, it will be a shooting war—"

"And we would be in the wrong," I said.

"Very wrong," Sam added.

"It certainly didn't start out this way," Tom said.

"It never does," I said.

Tom said, "I can't believe Morenci isn't wanted for something."

"Not a thing," Sam said. "I checked."

"Illegal entry?"

"Why? He's an American citizen."

"But didn't he sneak across the border?"

"Where will they deport him to? East Harlem where he was born?"

"And they can't pick this thug up for anything? That sounds incredible!"

"Sure they can pick him up for questioning but he'll hit the bricks in a day on bail. Stu's right on that—to really get this guy he must be caught with the goods."

"That's for the government to do," I said.

"Right. The three of us know that."

"We were outvoted, Sam," I reminded him; "you went along with the others."

"We would still have been outvoted four to three. I thought I could talk some sense into Arnie."

"No luck?"

"He's worse than Stu. He wants to go in and blow the whole goddam place up. Rudy and Star don't care, they'll do anything Stu wants them to do."

"Stu's a persuasive guy," Tom said.

Like they say in the backcountry, I told myself, he can persuade a bull to have calves . . .

"Christ, all those guards are armed," Sam said. "That's what worries me. Morenci's not stupid. He has a perfect cover. His guards are protecting his private property. If anyone crashes that place, even with an ice pick, it's criminal trespassing."

He nervously picked up a saltshaker and moved it back and forth between his hands.

"But that's not what I want to talk about. There's something you both should know."

"What's that?"

Then he told us about Fortunato.

"Yesterday I asked Arnie for the second time if they had put him on the plane and he said, 'Oh, sure,' but there was something about the way he said it that didn't ring."

He slowly pushed the shaker from one side to the other.

"What do you think happened to Stash, Sam?" I asked.

Sam said, "I'm not going to say it, Trev."

I felt sick to my stomach, and Tom nervously rolled a paper napkin into a tight ball.

"Holy Christ," he whispered.

"I have an idea we can kick around," Sam said. "Kate called late this afternoon and left word she wanted to see me. I plan to go down in the morning. Suppose while I'm there I have a drink with a guy I trust—he's an assistant attorney general—and *shmooze* with him. I'll play it by ear. The way things are in Washington I think he'll grab it. If he insists he can't do anything unless he knows the source, I'll tell him it came from someone who liked what the league stood for. And if they want to throw any bouquets, they can toss one in the way of the league. Stu will like that." He shook his head hopelessly. "I don't know what to do! Christ, I don't want to do anything to hurt Stu but—"

I interrupted him, "I think it's too late, Sam."

"Do you have an alternative, Trev?" Tom asked.

"I don't think we should go behind Stu's back. I'd rather lay it on the line with him. Let's find out what happened to Stash. If the guy is really hiding out on the coast, fine. If not—"

"You're talking about murder one, Trev," Sam said softly.

"Who said he was murdered, Sam?" Tom asked nervously.

"Let's not pussyfoot about semantics, Tom!" I told him. "That's what it's all about, right, Sam?"

Sam dumped some salt into his hand and let it slowly trickle down to form a mound on the table. We studied the tiny pyramid of crystals as though it held a mysterious secret.

"Remember, I'm only giving you what I think. I wasn't there," Sam said at last.

"Goddammit! You know it would have been stupid to work that hood over and then expect him to take a plane to LA, keep his mouth shut, and just drop out of sight. That's fantasy stuff, Sam."

"He was awfully scared, Trev. He wet his pants."

"But don't you see, Sam, once he got out to the coast he'd ask himself, 'Who were those crazy bastards? What the hell am I doing here?' Then he'd call Cardillo. In a few hours Stash would be back in Brooklyn. No way, Sam—they killed the guy to keep him quiet."

We looked at each other in silence. Near the entrance a drunk dropped a tray, it sounded like a mortar.

"Well, do we talk to Stu?" I asked.

Sam carefully dusted the salt from his hands.

"Okay with me."

"Tom?"

He nodded.

I said, "Let's go."

We walked into the lobby of the Eldorado about 2:00 A.M. The glass doors were still swinging shut behind us when the night manager came from around his desk to hurry toward us.

"Oh, Mr. David! Mr. Harlow has been trying to reach you all

night." He nodded at Tom and Sam. "And you gentlemen also. He was on the phone only a few minutes ago."

"Anything wrong?"

"I don't know, sir, he didn't say. But it sounded urgent. I'll tell him you're on the way up."

In seconds the elevator took us up to the penthouse. Stu was waiting. He looked strained and tired.

"Close the door," he said impatiently.

"What's wrong?" I asked.

"Toni's been kidnapped."

"Oh, my God! When? What happened?"

"I was about to enter the Conquistadores Room to have dinner with a date when the headwaiter said there was a hysterical woman on the phone asking for you, Trev. I went into a booth and picked up the phone. It was Toni's sister—"

"Teresa?"

"She kept saying she had a message for you but wouldn't give it to anyone else. I finally calmed her down and got her address in Canarsie. I promised you'd be out as soon as possible. I dumped my date and I've been on the phone since then trying to find you. I sent one of our security guards down to the toy fair but he called back and said you had gone to dinner. He's still checking the restaurants in the neighborhood."

"Did her sister tell you Toni was kidnapped?"

"She said Cardillo had taken her, she kept asking for you. As I said, she was hysterical when I first picked up the phone."

"Let's get out there," I said.

"We'll take the Cadillac. I have it waiting out front."

In the elevator Stu asked where Arnie was, and Sam told him he had taken Mary Chang Winslow home.

"Where's Star and Rudy?" Tom wanted to know.

"They went over to Jersey to pick up the recording. They're on their way back by now."

"This late?"

"They didn't want to meet another nosy farmer. Darkness doesn't bother Star."

Tom broke in, "He did his best scrounging at night in the Pit. Remember when he stole that gook's roll of wire?"

I tried to listen to the small talk but a thousand thoughts and fears crowded my brain. Toni . . . Toni . . .

Sam, who knew Brooklyn, drove. Once when we stopped for a light he nudged me and whispered, "Take it easy, Trev, she'll be okay."

We found the street without difficulty, the house was an attractive brick ranch. Before we could ring the bell the door inched open, a woman's pale, frightened face peered out at us.

"I'm Trevor David," I said softly, "Toni's friend."

She opened the door and closed it quickly behind us.

260

She was a thin almost emaciated woman dressed in a housecoat. Her black hair was tangled and uncombed and she had an ugly bruise on her chin. She held a tight ball of handkerchief in one hand as if it were an anchor to reality.

I remembered what Toni had said the first night we met and wondered what happened to the girl who once was pretty as a model.

"You're Teresa?" I asked.

She said brokenly, "He took her away, Mr. David. He took her away."

"You're talking about Toni?"

She nodded.

"Who took her away?"

"Frank. My husband, Frank."

"Suppose you sit down and tell us what happened," Stu said and guided her to a chair. She had begun to tremble.

"I go to bed with the kids. I was asleep when something woke me up, for a minute I thought it was one of the kids, then I knew. I ran into the hall and saw Frank. He had Toni up against the wall and was hitting her with his fist. I grabbed him around the neck and tried to pull him away. Then he turned around and gave me this"—she touched the bruise. "I went flying back almost to my bedroom door." She closed her eyes. "Oh, my God, he beat her terrible! He kept shouting bad things, about how she was working with the cops. Toni tried to get away, but he caught her and this time hit her so hard she fell on the floor. Then Frank ran downstairs to where he has his office."

I closed my eyes and tried to shut out what this woman was saying in that dreary monotone.

"What happened then?"

"I picked up Toni and took her into her bedroom. Blood was coming from her nose and I tried to stop it with a washcloth but she pushed me away. Then she told me to look in her jewelry box, that under the velvet was your name and telephone number. She said I should call you right away and give you this message." She repeated slowly and carefully, "She said, 'Tell him the girl of the bells called and said the delivery will be made tomorrow.'

"I tried to call my brother upstate but Frank met me in the hall. He threw me against the wall and kept shouting that I was helping Toni turn him in to the cops. He wouldn't listen to anything I said, he only kept hitting me, then he opened my bedroom door and pushed me inside. My little girl—she's four—got up and started crying and that woke her brother. I heard the garage door roll up but by the time I got downstairs Frank's car was going out the driveway. I ran after him but I couldn't stop him."

"Was Toni in the car?"

"Earlier in the evening I had taken some sheets and a blanket out of the drier and piled them on a chair. The blanket was gone and there were pieces of torn sheets on the floor."

She closed her eyes and rocked back and forth sobbing.

"Do you have any idea where your husband might have taken Toni?" Stu asked.

Without opening her eyes Teresa shook her head.

"He will hurt her," she whispered. "I know Frank will hurt her. I must call my brothers."

She stood up and held on to the chair. From somewhere in the house a frightened child called, "Mommy . . . Mommy . . ."

"That's my little girl," she said. "What should I do?" She buried her face in her hands. "I told Toni, I warned her! Get out of this house, I told her. Frank gets crazy when he's drunk."

"Have you any idea of what your husband has been doing?" Tom asked, but Stu waved impatiently.

"Forget it, Tom." He said to Toni's sister, "We're going to start looking for Toni right away. We'll find her. In the meantime if you hear anything please call either me or Mr. David."

He started to give her his card.

"There's no use of giving me your number," she said. "Before he left Frank ripped all the phones out of the walls. I had to leave the kids and run down to the corner booth."

"We'll be in touch with you," I said. "Let's go."

As we got into the car Tom asked, "Where do we start?"

"Grand Vista," I said. I turned to Stu, "You've been so damn eager to get into Grand Vista—fine, now let's go."

"I'm just as anxious as you, Trev, to find Toni," he said, "but let's not be stupid. One bad move and they might kill her."

"Bad moves? Didn't we make enough of them? All I want to do is find her. If she's in that house—"

"How do we know where Cardillo's taken her?"

"Goddammit, where else would he take her?"

"Maybe we'll have the answer when Star and Rudy—"

"What the hell do Star and Rudy know?"

"They're bringing the recordings back. They didn't leave the hotel until after midnight. Toni's sister said Cardillo ran down to his office to make a phone call. Who else would he call except Morenci? The call should be on the record."

He was right—the recording Star and Rudy brought back told the story.

The phone had been answered by someone else; Morenci sounded sleepy and angry when he got on.

OUT: Frank—you goddam fool! Didn't I tell you not to—
IN: Del. Del. Wait a minute. I got trouble. I just caught that bitch sister-in-law of mine listening in on my call. This is not the first time.
OUT: You got her?

IN: Yeah. In the trunk.

OUT: Take her to the depot.

IN: Yonkers?

OUT: No, for crissakes, that's closed! The other one, you idiot!

IN: Yeah. Yeah. I'm nervous, Del.

OUT: (soothingly) Don't be nervous, Frankie. Everything's goin' great. They'll include her with the honey. Okay?

IN: Yeah.

OUT: You come out in the morning, you hear?

IN: Okay, Del. Stash—you still haven't heard?

OUT: Forget him. (soft laughter) Hey, Frankie, maybe a pimp ate him. Right?

IN: Yeah. You're not mad, Del?

OUT: Mad? What for? You're my boy, Frankie. Listen—

IN: Yeah, Del.

OUT: One thing. You tell them that if anything happens on the way over—

IN: Like what, Del?

OUT: Like anything.

IN: Yeah. And what, Del?

OUT: Then you got one less sister-in-law. Okay?

IN: Yeah. Okay, Del.

OUT: I'll see you in the morning, kid.

IN: Yeah. Right, Del.

"Now where's the depot?" Tom asked.

"We have to find it," I shouted. "Did you hear what he said?"

Star said softly, "This is a big city, Trev. We can't keep riding around all night. We don't even know what kind of a car to look for."

"I'm going back to Canarsie."

"What for, Trev?" Stu asked.

"I'll find out from her sister what kind of car Cardillo owns."

"Suppose it's a black Cadillac? Will we chase after every black Cadillac we see?"

"I don't want any logic now, Stu," I told him. "I want to do something—anything but sit here." I stood up. "Maybe this is the time for the cops."

"No, it isn't," he replied. "Look at it sensibly. We know fifty times more than they do."

"They can use cops on the beat. Radio cars. Plainclothesmen. Teletype alarms."

"It would take them until morning to question all of us and get the entire story," he said with infuriating calm. "Then they'd check Washington, and Washington would send agents here to talk to us. Trev, I know how you feel but this is no time to call the police."

Sam said, "Stu's right. To call in the cops now would only make it worse. I think the best thing we can do is go over every recording, every piece of stuff we got in Washington and Paris and see if some way we can dope out that girl of the bells code."

Tom asked, "Why is she so important, Sam? Who gives a damn about the drugs now? It's Toni we want to find."

"Play the recording again, Star," Stu said quietly.

The harsh voices of Morenci and Cardillo echoed in the room as Star turned up the recorder's volume. When Morenci was talking about the depot, Stu shut it off and replayed it.

"That's what I mean," he said. " 'They'll include her with the honey.' I think it's plain they're going to bring Toni along with the junk. Morenci must find out all he can about Toni. Why was she listening to Frank's phone calls? Is she working for the cops? The feds? How much does she know? Is she the reason why the warehouse was raided? Toni is now very important to them. They have a load coming in worth millions. If they make Toni talk and find there's a squeal, they can move the stuff out of Grand Vista."

"That makes sense to me," Sam said. "What do you think, Trev?"

"Do we have a choice? But before we begin, Stu, there's one question I want to ask you and I want a straight answer."

He gave me a quiet glance.

"Sure, Trev. Anything."

"Sam told us about Stash. Did you kill him?"

The silence was almost unbearable.

"Yes," he said, "I killed him."

"He's in an ashcan with a blanket of cement," Star said. "Me and Rudy dumped him in the ocean."

Tom gasped. "That's murder, Stu!"

Stu shrugged. "Technically I guess it is."

I said, "Technically? You killed him, Stu!"

"You know something? I haven't missed a minute's sleep," he replied.

Tom began, "I never bargained—"

Stu spun around. His eyes were cold and his lips were in a tight thin line.

"What the hell's so horrifying about killing a son of a bitch like that? Human scum who's making a fortune from selling kids drugs with their lunch sandwiches! Am I making this up? Didn't you and Trev take the pictures? Didn't we see them here in this room? You heard Sam and Arnie. That bastard put a gun to the head of an honest businessmen and forced him to sell so they could peddle those sandwiches with their drugs. You heard the report on Fortunato. He liked to use an iron pipe on people's heads because they didn't pay up. But that's the least of it. He was helping to bring in these drugs. Millions and millions of dollars' worth of drugs.

"He was part of the mob that screwed us last time around. If we hadn't grabbed him we'd still have our hands up our ass!" He swung around and pointed to me. "And don't you give me any bullshit, Trev. Do you know why I killed him? To protect Toni. You don't think I believed that lying bastard. Sure he would get on that plane, but four hours later he'd be on the phone with Cardillo. They could put two and two together—"

"Cardillo didn't need Fortunato to find out it was Toni."

"I protected Toni in every way possible. I would kill ten Fortunatos to make sure she wouldn't be hurt."

"You didn't know when to stop. You kept getting us in deeper and deeper," I said, "and we went along—all the way. But you never said anything about murder."

Tom said, "I wash my hands of—"

Stu interrupted him in a bitter voice. "If you want to play Pontius Pilate, Tom, you need a bowl of water."

"This isn't getting us anywhere, Trev," Sam said. "We're wasting time. Let's go over those recordings and notes instead of arguing." He glanced at his wristwatch. "It's five o'clock already."

Star clicked on the recorder and we started with the first record.

We played the recordings over and over and studied all our notes and reports, arguing, suggesting, trying to read in things that were not there.

It was about seven when we heard the gentle thump of the elevator and the doors slid open.

"Who's there?" Stu called out.

The foyer doors opened and Arnie walked in. He was drawn, unshaven—and slightly drunk.

"Got any coffee?" he said.

"Arnie, we have to tell you something," I said. "It's important."

He gave me a lazy grin.

"Hiya, Trev. We don't have to use Toni anymore." He slumped down in a chair. "She's a great kid . . . real great."

"Arnie, listen—Cardillo found her on the phone and snatched her," Sam said. "We got a recording from Jersey. Morenci told Cardillo to bring her over there with the junk this morning."

"That goddam 'girl of the bells,' " Star said. "She's the key, Arnie. We got to find her."

Arnie rubbed his hand over his face.

"Thank God," he whispered. "Thank God."

"What the hell are you talking about?" I asked.

"Mary Chang Winslow is the girl of the bells," he said. "She's picking up the junk . . . ."

Chapter 10

Sam Hoffman- Operation Hounds

We sat like frozen men after Arnie told us Mary Chang Winslow was the girl of the bells. When we started to throw questions at him he held up his hands.

"Give me a few minutes."

Then he got up and staggered into the john. We could hear water running and when he came out he was drying his hair with a towel and his shirt was wet. I poured him a cup of coffee, and we sat on the edge of our chairs and silently watched him gulp it down. I guess the combination of hearing about Toni, cold water, and the coffee sobered him up because in a few minutes he was shaky but clear-eyed. But that's nothing unusual for Arnie; I've seen him drink all night, take a catnap in a chair, and then bounce back as if he'd had eight good hours in the sack.

"I knew at the fair something was wrong with her," he said as he put aside the cup. "She had never drunk like that before. When we got back to her place she started putting the booze away like it was going to be rationed. Gradually it came out. As I suspected she had a fight with her boyfriend. She kept telling me he's an important guy in the city, but that could be boasting—"

"No chance of finding out who he is?"

"Even when she's drunk she's smart. I didn't press it. She brought out some pot and wanted to smoke but I stalled her. I didn't want her stoned more than she was. It took some doing but I finally got her in the sack. It was a bad scene, she kept crying and saying she was afraid of this guy—"

"Is he Chinese?"

"No. White. I got that much out of her."

"Why is she afraid of him?"

"I don't know, she said she's been trying to break off with him for a long time but he won't let her go."

"Where do you fit in, Arnie?" I asked.

He got up, rubbing his head with a towel as he walked to the window.

"I'm in solid. That's one of the reasons why she wants to get rid of this guy." He went on. "That's not all—she has orders to go to Burma next weekend and she doesn't want to go."

"Burma!" Star put in, "why the hell is she goin' there?"

"She goes there twice a year on a buying tour to find curios—some junk, some real antiques. She says they sell the good stuff to museums."

"Who gave her the orders to go?" Stu asked.

"It has something to do with this ex-boyfriend."

"But why is she worried?"

"The last time she was in Mandalay someone tipped her to get out fast. She said she later learned the government police missed her by minutes."

"Why would the police be after her?"

"She claims it's because she has friends in the party."

"The Communist Party?"

He emphasized, "The Burmese Communist Party. It's getting more powerful every day. The last I heard, it controls the Northern Shan State, east of the Salween River."

Tom gave him a puzzled look.

"I don't get it, Arnie. What does Mary have to do with the Burmese Communist Party?"

"I don't know the full story," Arnie said. "Somehow it's connected with Burmese politics and drugs. The president of Burma, U Ne Win, tried to force those two Chinese Nationalist generals I told you about sometime ago, who now control the drug market, to join his army. There was some kind of fight and they moved into Shan State asking protection from the Commies, who gladly gave it to them; after all it's two thousand more guns and foot soldiers. Now Mary says Chinese regulars are crossing the border to fight with them against U Ne Win's troops."

"What about the drugs? Are they still getting out?"

"Apparently the generals, with the help of their new Commie friends, are having no trouble moving their caravan into Thai. Her story is that now all foreigners going in and out of Burma are suspect."

"Do you believe her, Arnie?" Stu asked.

"About the part of foreigners being suspect in Burma? No. That the police wanted to question her? Yes. I also believe her story of the Nationalist generals moving out their junk under the protection of the Commies in the north. However, she left out one vital part."

"What's that?" Tom asked.

"That she's the courier for the syndicate. The importing company is just another part of Morenci's setup."

"Why do you say that?"

"In the last couple of months Washington has been putting the pressure om Burma to stop drug smuggling. If they don't take some strong measures all aid will be cut off. That's why U Ne Win tried to force the two generals into his army. But they went north for one reason—they'd rather split with the Commies than have nothing. I understand they now have eleven factories outside Lashio and their profits have become so big, one caravan returned from Thai with a million dollars in gold bars. U Ne Win is desperate. While he doesn't want to commit his army, he's got to turn off the supply of drugs to satisfy Washington. Now he has his police putting on the pressure."

Stu said, "Then you think the government found out she's the courier for Morenci's syndicate?"

"No doubt about it. The way it now shapes up is: Morenci's people are dealing with the group organized by the generals. I believe she picks up Morenci's money and delivers it to Mandalay, Lashio, or Rangoon where the deal is made. The whole drug scene over there is loaded with counteragents and government spies. Undoubtedly the last time she was in Mandalay someone tipped the police."

I asked, "And she knows she will be grabbed next time out?"

"I don't blame her for being worried," Arnie said. "I worked with the Burmese Frontier Police and they're rough. They get the information they want whether it's from a kid or a woman they have in custody. They can be as bad as Charlie . . ."

"If she knows she might be grabbed by the Burmese police," I pointed out, "why would she go back there?"

"In Burma she has friends who will help her avoid the police," Arnie said patiently, "but maybe if she refuses to go—"

"You mean this guy—her ex-boyfriend or whatever the hell he is—might drop her in the river?"

"She didn't come out directly and say that but there is no doubt she is scared to death of what this guy will do to her."

Stu put in, "And you don't know anything about him?"

"Not a thing. As I told you, she let slip he's a big wheel in the city government."

Trev asked eagerly, "And you are sure, Arnie, she's the girl of the bells?"

"Definitely."

"How did you find that out?"

"What I told you is the background stuff she gave me. What comes next is important. When I asked her to show me some of the stuff she buys in Indochina she brought out a tray of curios, you know, tourist crap. I laughed at her and said I could find better stuff in the five-and-ten. That got her mad. She went to a closet and lugged out a heavy box. It was teakwood embossed with pearl. It was very beautiful and obviously a valuable antique. Then she opened it."

He poured another cup of coffee with elaborate calm but I knew Arnie and I could see he was tense.

"Inside were bells. Fairly large size beautiful silver temple bells. She said they were more than five hundred years old and part of a collection they had sold to a museum. I asked what museum and she said it was in New Jersey. Then she put the box back in the closet."

He returned to the chair.

"After I heard that I made a show of knocking off. When she went to the john I hit that closet. It was a walk-in and filled with wooden boxes—and not teakwood. They all contained bells, not solid silver like the real ones. Some had bells of different sizes and shapes, there must have been hundreds."

He lit a cigarette, inhaled, and let the smoke curl out from between his lips.

"They were hollow."

"The girl of the bells," Trev said grimly.

"They're using the hollow bells to run in the junk," Tom said.

Arnie smiled a small smile.

"Give the man a cigar."

"Why didn't they fill the bells with the junk in the first place?" Tom asked.

"To go through regular customs?" Arnie said. He shook his head. "Too risky. They probably bought it in by separate loads to a central place. Like they said, it was delivered to Mama by a hawk. There they will fill the bells and bring the load to Jersey." He went over to the map he had used in the beginning to show us the drug routes. "From Burma to Thai by caravan. Then over the mountains to South Vietnam where the trawlers are. It goes on to Hong Kong, where the Corsicans pick it up and bring it to Marseilles. From there it's moved to an entry point near the border—Canada or Mexico, then it's brought in by boat or plane to a central spot—Mama's place—maybe that's the office on West Forty-fourth Street."

He ran his finger from Manhattan to New Jersey.

"This final stretch is where they are most vulnerable; they're out in the open more or less, no friends, no payoffs, no bribes. The Jersey state police have a good track record of picking up junk being moved along their highways. They almost seem to smell it. Then again the narcs may have a squeal or there could be a minor accident. Don't forget that with the high court decision, police can now search a car or truck involved in even a minor traffic violation. Morenci would be a fool to take chances for the last few miles with this load worth millions. And we know Morenci's no fool. That's why he's using an ordinary panel truck and what seems to be a load of silver temple bells from a legitimate Manhattan importing company."

"Do you think they'll use the tunnel?"

"It's a toss-up. She could drive right through the front gates or he may decide to take it in by way of the tunnel."

"If he doesn't intend to use the tunnel, why did he go to all the trouble of reopening it?" Tom asked.

"Maybe they brought the other loads in that way," Arnie replied. "Maybe that's the way he intends to dispose of the junk in case of a raid. It could also be a perfect exit. The cops or agents come in the front door and they slip out across the hill. I repeat, Morenci's no fool. He likes fire escapes."

"And you're sure Mary will make the delivery?"

"As sure as I can be. Before I left she begged me to come back later today. She said she first had to pick up a manifest at the office, then ride over to Jersey with the deliverymen to deliver the bells. When I asked her why she had to go, she explained they were irreplaceable and it was her responsibility to see they were safely delivered. Now what about Toni, Trev?"

Trev described very quickly our visit to Canarsie and the story Teresa had told us of how Cardillo had snatched Toni. Then we listened to the last recording.

"Morenci said 'deliver her with the honey,'" Trev pointed out. "I'll lay odds she'll be in the truck Mary drives over there."

"Then we'll hijack the truck," Star said.

"They'll kill her before we can get to her," Arnie said. "You heard what Morenci said; the last thing he wants is a witness."

"I guess we're not much different from Morenci," Trev said bitterly. "We don't want witnesses either."

Stu said, "Sam told them about Stash, Arnie."

I said, "It was something that was festering, Arnie; it had to come out."

"It's just as well," he said. "As far as I'm concerned we declared war on those bastards. It's either all out or forget it! Remember, Trev, these people aren't addicts willing to sell their shoes for a shot. They're goddam international drug merchants. And they have Toni. Is there any question of what we have to do?"

He dropped his cigarette into the remains of his coffee. It made a loud hissing noise in the silence.

"Well, are we going to go in and get Toni or are we going to sit

270

around and discuss moral ethics in a goddam society that no longer knows their meaning?"

Stu looked at Trev. "You call the play, Trev."

"I told you before, Stu, we have no choice."

Stu told Arnie, "Earlier Trev wanted to call in the police."

"Morenci will kill her and dump the junk before the cops or feds step inside the front door," Arnie said impatiently. "This is a highly sophisticated operation. If anything goes wrong they will make sure there's no evidence or witnesses."

"What about the cutters?"

"Once the alarm goes off they'll dispose of everything. The agents will be lucky if they can get any dust for evidence with a vacuum. The cutters are professionals. Working on drugs is a way of life. They all have yellow sheets, the guards probably have been handpicked. If we gave it to the police or the feds it would take them weeks to devise a strategy. With us it will be over in a couple of hours—that is, if we're willing to toss the dice."

"Go in," Trev said in a voice as rough as a saw cutting through ice.

Stu turned to Tom.

"Tom?"

He nodded.

"Sam?"

This mush-headed *schlemiel* said yes.

Stu said, "I want to make sure we all know what will happen when we enter that house."

"Fireworks," Rudy said happily.

"And we all know what we will be giving up and that possibly we could face criminal charges and jail terms?"

Stu looked at us, one by one.

"Agreed?"

Arnie snapped, "Agreed."

"What about China, Arnie? You'll probably blow it."

"China's been there a long time, it won't go away."

"And the Agency?"

"They've been screwed before and by experts. They have a short memory if they want you bad enough."

"Sam, this could mean the loss of your license. That's the least of it."

"So I'll buy a farm. I'll probably live longer," I said, crying inside my head.

"Tom, it could mean a difference to someone in Washington."

"If she calls it off—" he shrugged. "But what about you, Stu? My God, if anything happens you could be—"

"Nothing they could hand me would be worse than eight years in the Pit," Stu said tersely. "Rudy?"

"Cut one and we all bleed, Major."

"Star?"

"I was always sorry I missed Wounded Knee, Major."

271

Stu slapped his hand down on the desk.

"Agreed. We go in!"

"We'll need plenty of firepower, Major," Star said.

Stu turned to me.

"What do you have on hand, Sam?"

"Handguns, shotguns, and rifles with scopes."

"There's a demolition job to do, Major," Star reminded him. "Didn't Trev say that hick contractor put in fire doors?"

Rudy ground a big fist into the palm of his hand.

"If we had some of that clay we used in Nam!"

"Where the hell are you gonna get a claymore mine in Manhattan at eight o'clock on a Saturday morning?" Star asked disgustedly.

Rudy winked at him.

"Maybe I know where, Injun—"

"You know where we can get explosives, Rudy?" Arnie asked.

"I know someone who's doin' some blastin' in Queens for a high rise," Rudy replied. "Maybe we can make up a little somethin'."

"Would the guy give you a few sticks?"

"I'll kick his ass all over Queens if he doesn't," Rudy growled. "He's my nephew and he still owes me the grand I loaned him to buy furniture."

"Let's get it," Star said impatiently.

"I also got two M-30s and an M-16," Rudy said smugly.

"Where the hell did you get 'em?"

"In a bar last summer. Some kid who just came back needed dough."

"We'll need some kind of boats for the tunnel," Trev pointed out.

"There's a sporting goods store two blocks from here on Lexington Avenue," Tom said. "I passed it the other day. They have a collapsible duck hunter's boat in the window. It folds up like a knapsack. When it's opened the boat automatically fills with air."

"We'll need about four," Stu said. He scrawled something on a piece of his note paper. "Give this to the night cashier. Get what we need."

Arnie broke in, "Don't forget flashlights and ropes, Tom."

"And get me a sledge for that wall," Rudy called out. "C'mon, Injun."

"I better go along with them," Arnie said.

"I'll give you a hand, Tom," Trev said.

"Take the Cadillac, it's out front," Stu said. "Sam, the station wagon's in the garage."

Before the door closed I saw Stu take a .32 out of a drawer and snap on a silencer.

Without looking up he said in a dry, harsh voice I'd never heard him use before, "Try to get back as soon as you can—I want to move out at ten hours."

272

It sounded like Nam. But this time with Cadillacs and station wagons . . . .

Let's face it, we were fools. I admit it. The trouble was that none of us was thinking straight that morning. We were going to go into Grand Vista, bring out Morenci and his fabulous cargo of junk—and, most important, find Toni.

And we were going to do it with guns, blasting powder, dynamite, or whatever Rudy could hustle out of his contractor-nephew.

Don't forget Toni. There is no doubt we all secretly felt guilty—Trev most of all.

Looking back, what I think is most frightening was our automatic refusal to rely on the law enforcement agencies; even Trevor, who was frantic, didn't press his original idea to call the cops. This would not have happened in the world we left for Nam. As Trev once said, we had come back aliens, not heroes. And there were no more institutions to believe in. Maybe that sums it up, but whatever the reason for the events which took place, I find it strange that this point has been lost in all the rhetoric written about us.

It's something to think about.

Once again we were a military unit, we slipped back into the old role with surprising ease. I felt like a goddam armorer as I gathered the weapons from my warehouse and kissed my New York license good-bye; it's lucky I was going to California. An example of our temporary insanity was the reaction when Rudy showed up with his two M-30s and the M-16 all wrapped in greased rags, as new as when they had been stolen from a Nam ammo dump by some souvenir-hungry kid who was about to leave for the States. The only comment was from someone who asked Rudy if he had enough ammo. He held up a bag—that big *nahr* had enough to start a war.

Tom and Trev returned with the canvas boats, flashlights, crowbars, sledges, ropes, and some miscellaneous stuff. At the last minute Stu included a flask of brandy.

But the prize was in the dusty burlap bag Arnie and Star handled gingerly. Rudy's horrified nephew had refused to give him anything—he thought his uncle was preparing to blow up some Queens bar—but when they left the explosives trailer to argue, Arnie and Star slipped inside and took what they wanted.

They had fashioned four crude bombs attached to a blasting cap as a detonator; Arnie said just one was powerful enough to crash in the heaviest of fire doors.

I also rigged up a short wave relay in the cars we were to use in tailing Mary from her apartment house to pick up the junk and gave them a crash course in car surveillance.

We would use three, each had a code call: Car A, Car B, Car C. In

Car A I would take the tail for a few blocks, then let Car B pass me and take over to be replaced by Car C, so it would not be apparent to Mary or her driver that the same car always showed up in their side mirror.

Rudy and Star went on ahead with a pair of my powerful walkie-talkies to stake out a spot near the entrance of the tunnel; our rendezvous point would be on the peak of the hill where I had set up the laser beam and recording outfit.

Stu called it "Operation Hounds" and the name stuck.

Before we left the hotel I spoke to Kate. Only after I promised to come to D.C. the following morning would she tell why she wanted to see me. There was no big secret, she simply was lonely. I would always be Número Uno even if I never married her.

Sam Hoffman, lover supreme from Bensonhurst.

The truth is, I was really upset when I hung up. Kate had become much more than a necessary shack-up. I discovered I liked a lot of things about her, she had class and made me feel I was the most important guy in her world.

Leah? I even forgot where she lived. Anyway, Kate made much better lentil soup . . . .

We had two cars and a station wagon; Arnie and I were in the lead car, Stu and Trev in the second and Tom drove the station wagon. Star and Rudy had taken the guns and ammo to Jersey but Arnie had that goddam burlap bag in our trunk. I drove like a motor vehicle inspector on parade. If we were rammed, there would be some interesting pictures on the six o'clock news.

To make sure Mary was home, Arnie called her. He said she was almost ready to leave for Jersey but begged him to come back later in the afternoon.

She lived in an old brownstone on West Twelfth, just off Fifth. Arnie and I parked halfway down the block where we had a good view of the entrance; the others waited on nearby side streets that headed in the same direction.

"Arnie, what do you think of Mary?" I asked as we settled down.

He shrugged. "What is there to think? She's a courier for a drug mob. Doesn't that answer your question?"

"I know I'm the world's worst judge," I told him, "but I sorta like her. How about you?"

He said shortly. "I can't forget she's helping to bring in drugs that are sold to kids. Christ, Sam!"

"Okay. I know. Do you think if you had stayed longer at her place . . ."

He interrupted impatiently, "She wanted to talk but only to a point."

"She could tell a lot if she wanted to."

He said harshly, "She could blow the whole thing if she wanted to."

274

"What would make her talk?"

"How the hell would I know? What makes anybody talk? Something important."

"Like what? Money?"

He made a disgusted noise in his throat.

"A mink coat?"

"Don't be stupid, Sam."

"I'm just asking. What then?"

He turned to me. "Why the hell are you so interested in her motives?"

"Just curious. What about the guy you said was her boyfriend? Do you really believe he's somebody in the city?"

"After what happened in Washington over the past year, I believe anything, Sam. I read the papers and listen to TV and ask myself, 'Is this really going on?' So if you ask me if I believe her, the answer is yes."

"But why is she afraid of this guy?"

He said with elaborate patience, "Sam, she didn't talk to me like I was Dear Abby, but from the few things she said she has been trying to dump this guy, only he doesn't want to be dumped. When she insisted it was all over, I guess he threatened her. Whatever he did, she would rather go back to Burma and risk a bust there than say no to him."

"Lennis called her a bomb thrower."

"Lennis is a moron," he snapped. "She claims to be a Maoist, a revolutionist. She's not," he said disgustedly. "She's been on the fringe of a lot of freaky groups and has all their rhetoric but not much else. For one thing no true Maoist would be in drugs—instead of working with a pusher, they'd kill him. I told her what Chairman Mao remarked once to a nephew: 'You have never suffered—how can you be a leftist?'"

"You know, Arnie, I really think you like her."

He slowly lit a cigarette and didn't answer me for a moment. Then he said, "Revolution. Any revolutionary struggle is governed by the principle of the transfer of total opposition, prepared for exile, prison, or even death. In other words you can't walk the middle of the road. You must go all out or be considered a compromiser."

"I wonder how many would be willing to die for their revolution, Arnie?"

"Well, that's romanticizing it, Sam. They all say they're ready to die for the cause, but very few get a chance to prove it."

"How can they?"

He said savagely, "By having a goddam gun pointed at their heads."

"What will that prove?"

"It's not the gun that's important, Sam."

"I would say that having a gun at your head can be very important." I added, almost impulsively, "I—we all know that."

"Why was it important to you?"

275

"Because I knew Charlie wasn't playing a game."

"That's exactly what I mean," he said. "The gun isn't as important as the knowledge the guy holding it is ready to pull the trigger."

"In other words that's when you know how much you believe in your cause?"

"Right. If someone put a gun to Mary's head and she knew he was going to pull the trigger, she would cave in."

"With the exception of you and Stu, we're no stronger than she is."

He looked surprised. "What do you mean, Sam?" Then he caught on. "That was another situation . . ."

"The hell it was! When Charlie put that gun to my head, I would have signed a document that said George Washington was a pimp and Lincoln sold out the country. We all gave 'em what they wanted, Arnie, except you and Stu."

"Don't put me in the same class with Stu," he said bitterly. "If they had kept it up one more day I would have given them the location of that relay station. It's like I told Mary—play revolutionist if you want but expect to find a pistol at your head some day. . . ."

"Could you pull the trigger, Arnie, if the gun was at Mary's head?"

"Hey, Sam, you're getting awfully heavy," he said sarcastically.

"I'm just *shmoozing* but I do like her. I wish she was on our side. She could give all the answers to all the questions we've been asking. Dammit, then we wouldn't have to go into this crazy house!"

"I did everything to get those answers out of her, Sam," he said wearily, "particularly the answer to the most important question: Why is she in drugs? I know it's not for money and it's against her political concepts."

"There must be a very important reason, Arnie."

"I'll find the answer someday, probably when—"

He broke off and hastily ground out the cigarette as he leaned toward the windshield.

"Speaking of paper tigers," he said softly, "here she is."

Mary was wearing an attractive green knit suit and matching beret and looked quite a dish. She stood in the front entrance staring up the street as if searching for someone.

"She isn't carrying anything." I asked Arnie, "Where are the—"

A black panel truck passed us and double parked in front of her building. She hurried to the truck and spoke to someone, then two guys got out. One went into the house with Mary, the other remained as if on guard, at the rear doors. In a few minutes the first man appeared, carrying several wooden boxes.

"The bells," Arnie said.

The delivery man made many trips, each time the one remaining behind would open the back door then carefully close it until the next load arrived. I counted one hundred and ten boxes. Arnie said each box contained at least five bells—five hundred and fifty bells filled with heroin or cocaine. . . .

I gulped when Arnie estimated they must have over five hundred pounds of junk, which could be worth a hundred million in street sales.

They drove leisurely uptown to the delivery entrance on West Forty-fourth Street; the heavy iron door swung up, the truck vanished inside and the door came down.

Hours passed before one of the two guys came around the corner from Fifth, carefully looked up and down the street, then rapped on the door. It swung up, the truck came out, driven by the second man. The first one got into the other side and they swung into Fifth Avenue. Mary sat between them.

Saturday traffic was light and we kept a good distance. However, they didn't appear suspicious and headed for the Lincoln Tunnel. I had Tom pass them and wait on the Jersey side. I told him to pull into the disabled car zone, lift the hood as if searching for some motor trouble and to pick us up as we came out.

He was poking under the hood like an amateur mechanic as we emerged; in minutes he was back in line. The truck remained in the far right lane so we played checkers, each taking a turn in passing to move on ahead.

Traffic thinned as we got deeper into the rural areas and we remained far behind. We did this for about an hour and a half, then suddenly the truck swung off the highway into a dirt road that was not familiar. I was in the lead car and warned the others to continue on the highway; for us to follow would have been to obvious.

We gathered in a highway ice cream parking lot. I insisted we all have shakes or cones to make us appear as innocent as possible in case the truck had become suspicious and was doubling back to see if they were being followed.

There was no sign of the truck. The map showed we were at least fifteen miles from Cidertown, the dirt road they had taken would eventually lead them to Grand Vista but by a long roundabout route.

We were faced with many possibilities; were they on the way to the mysterious "depot" to pick up Toni? Was Toni in the truck? And was that the reason why the second man outside Mary's house had carefully opened and closed the rear door each time they put in a load of boxes?

Had she been brought to Grand Vista by some other means?

Had they swung off into the dirt road to lose our tail?

Were they only using this back road route to get to Grand Vista?

We decided Grand Vista was their ultimate goal and we should continue on to our rendezvous spot on the hill. We passed through Cidertown, then sped past my former gold-plated bedroom, the country club, until we came to the road that led to the hill where I had set up the laser beam equipment.

I studied Grand Vista through the glasses. It appeared deserted, the large curtained bay windows of the second floor like hooded, malevolent eyes. The only thing alive was the splashing fountain in the middle of the sloping lawn. From the very first time I saw the place, I thought it was romantic, mysterious, but now I felt a chill at the thought we would soon be in that goddam tunnel.

We contacted Star and Rudy who said they had selected an excellent spot but no one had appeared.

For more than an hour we took turns with the glasses.

Suddenly Stu said, "They're coming up the road now."

We parted the bushes and I could see the truck slowing down as it approached the entrance of Grand Vista. A guard peered out of his house, waved, and the electrified gate slowly swung open. The truck wound its way along the driveway and stopped at the carriage house. The doors Rudy and Star had installed swung up, the truck entered, and the doors rolled down.

"Well, they're in," Stu snapped. "Let's go."

At the cave's entrance we moved like a unit of commandos on a raid; Trev and Tom brought the supplies from the station wagon, Stu and Arnie took care of that dangerous burlap bag, I prepared the firepower, while Rudy and Star worked on the entrance to the cave.

It only took that big Irisher one shot with the sledge to knock a hole in the wall. With each blow it became larger while Star carefully piled the rocks to one side. In a few minutes all the WPA's work lay on the ground.

Air hissed and the collapsible boats quickly resembled fugitives from a float in Macy's Thanksgiving Day Parade. Stu took the safety off his silenced .32 and Star passed around the handguns and rifles. Stu clicked on his flashlight and stepped into the cave, the rigid, white-cold beam stabbing the blackness.

"We'll move up, ten paces between each man."

For a moment I smelled the dank jungle heat, heard the clank of my buddy's gear in front of me, then heard his surprised grunt simultaneously with the crack of the sniper's rifle; mortars thumped and there were cries for medics.

Arnie prodded me in the back.

"You ready, Sam?"

"Ready as I'll ever be."

I repeated to myself what I had heard one night on a cornball old movie about football:

Let's win one for old Gipper . . .

I stepped into the darkness and followed the steady beam of light.

When the reflection of our flashlights lit up the small lake in the rear of the cave, the air was suddenly filled with the weirdest noises I had ever heard in my life, like the meowing of a million angry cats. Something hit me in the face and I whacked it with my flashlight; in the light I could see the tiny devil's face. Bats. Thousands. They swirled about us as we pushed on to the water.

"Get in the boats," Trev shouted, "they won't follow us into the tunnel."

His voice sounded like an echo chamber.

I jumped into one of the boats with Arnie and we paddled out into the water. Behind us I could hear Rudy swearing and cursing, his light making crazy circles on the water and ceiling as he fought off the bats.

"Get into the boat, Rudy," Stu shouted.

Star pushed him into a boat. Halfway across the lake Rudy suddenly raised up and swung. There was a loud splash and his light winked out. Arnie and I pointed our flashlights to see Star and Stu go in after him. Star surfaced, his face glistening in the light.

"He can't swim," he shouted.

"He can't swim . . . can't swim . . . can't swim . . ." bounced off the walls, gradually diminishing to a taunting far-off echo.

He dove down again, then he and Stu emerged with Rudy between them. We managed to lay him across the overturned boat and tow him to the opposite shore.

"Holy Christ!" Arnie said.

As we slid up on the beach an Indian's painted face stared out at us. My flashlight ran down his body, it was tin and rusted.

We stretched Rudy out on the sand and took turns pumping the water out of him. He quickly came to, gagging and retching. Arnie gave him the flask, and he made a good dent in the brandy.

"Why the hell didn't you ever learn to swim?" Star said.

"I got the carpenter's merit badge instead of swimming," Rudy solemnly replied.

And that big guy meant it!

The water was ice cold and the tunnel like a refrigerator. When the three of them started to shiver in their wet clothes, we divided our sweatshirts and heavy jackets, ripped up a blanket for towels and moved on. We had to portage across a short stretch of sand and rock before we reached the tunnel. The walls were dripping, it smelled cold and dank, like a tomb, I thought.

Bensonhurst—where are you?

We got into the boats and started to paddle. There didn't seem to be any movement of the water, it was motionless like a river of black glass. I tried to reach bottom with my paddle but couldn't, a rock just sank out of sight.

We had made a turn when Arnie silently played his flashlight on a rearing horse of tin. Its rusted rider in Confederate gray, arms raised, was flung back in the saddle as though he had been shot. Beneath the hoofs was what appeared to be a soldier pointing a rifle. Other rusted figures had toppled over.

Most of the niches we passed were empty but some held remnants of a scene. We seemed to be going deeper and deeper into the hill, twisting and turning endlessly. Suddenly, when Star and Rudy were in the lead, I caught the glimpse of something on both sides of the tunnel's walls.

"Don't move," I shouted but it was too late. We should never have underestimated Morenci; he was too smart to let someone walk right into the tunnel after he had garrisoned the outside like a fortress.

"What's the matter, Sam?" Stu asked as he came up.

I pointed to the electric eyes on either side of the tunnel.

"I don't know what it does, maybe touches off an alarm inside the house."

Star, who always had the ears of a fox, held up his hand.

"Listen!"

For a moment I didn't hear anything, then I caught it, the faint sound of rushing water.

"Jesus! It's rising!" Rudy shouted.

His voice boomed off the walls.

"It's rising . . . rising . . rising . . ."

"The dam!" Trev called out. "Remember the series of locks?"

"Locks . . . locks . . . locks . . ."

That was it, of course! In some fashion Morenci had electrically controlled the series of old iron locks that crazy colonel had installed nearly a hundred years ago to hold back the waters of this subterranean stream. Breaking the electric eye beam released the water. Curiously, while I was terrified, I was also unconsciously admiring Morenci's thoroughly professional security measures. He had made Grand Vista tighter than the Pentagon.

We paddled like wild men. The splashing, curses, and grunting echoed and echoed. We made one turn, then another. A tin guy dressed in what appeared to be a Pilgrim's hat, leading some rusty figures, stared out at us. Then someone in a uniform standing on the tailboard of a wagon with a rope around his neck. Major André.

By the time we passed André I could touch the top of the tunnel with my fingertips. The water was rising very fast.

At one point a whole display had fallen over and we had to maneuver around it carefully to prevent the ragged tin edges from cutting the canvas.

Then Stu who was in the lead boat waved his flashlight.

"There're the stairs."

We paddled like college crews down that last stretch. Stu swung out of the boat onto the old iron stairs. The water was up to his waist. He played his light on the ceiling. Directly above him was an iron plate like an extra large sewer cover. We automatically made way for Rudy who joined Stu on the stairway.

"See if you can lift it, Rudy."

Rudy put his shoulders under the cover and pushed upward. The plate didn't budge. Now we were all stretched out on the boats, watching him. I refused to consider what would happen if that plate didn't swing up. Then Arnie joined Rudy and Stu.

"One . . . two . . . three . . . heave."

This time Star got in the head of the sledgehammer. When I reached up, the palm of my hand was flat on the roof of the tunnel.

"Come on, Fatso," Star said, "you can do it."

280

Trev, Tom, and I trained our flashlights on Rudy. He gripped the iron railings on both sides and put his shoulder under the plate at the point where Star held the crowbar and Stu and Arnie the sledge. The water was now shoulder-high.

Rudy began moving upward. The cords in his neck grew taut, like strands of rope under the skin. His face turned dark red, his eyes bulged as if they were about to pop from their sockets, but the plate lifted with agonizing slowness while Stu, Arnie, and Star frantically used the crowbar and sledge as wedges. Inch by inch, step by step, Rudy lifted the cover high enough so the others could help him to force it to one side. When I climbed out the water touched my chin.

"What the hell took you so long?" Star grunted as he lit a cigarette and handed it to Rudy.

Our flashlights showed we were in a large, almost empty room. A slab of concrete was bolted onto the heavy iron cover. In the center was a ring. A hoisting chain hung from the ceiling; off to one side was a small generator.

"I guess they brought the other loads in this way," Arnie said.

"How do you feel, Rudy?" Stu asked.

"Fine, Major," he said.

"When we get out of here I'm gonna give him swimmin' lessons," Star said.

"Ya know somethin', Injun?" Rudy said solemnly, "I'd like that."

I love those two crazy *klutzim*, I really do.

We were in a large room. Trev, who had brought along the architect's plans for the house, spread them out on the floor. The room we were in was in the rear of the north wing, adjacent to the kitchen. We found the door; it wasn't a fire door but old and formidable.

"Jeez! Look at this, Injun!" Rudy said as he examined it. "They don't make 'em like this anymore. Remember that plywood crap they tried to sell us out in the desert? Hey, looka the lock!"

It was a big old-fashioned iron lock, and while they began to remove it I walked across the room to a dark corner where I had noticed a tiny red light. It was in a new-looking gray panel box. There were two lights, white and red, each with a button. There were no directions or any indication of what it was. After I traced some of the wires I knew it had to be the control for the dams in the tunnel. When I pushed in one of the buttons, the red light was replaced by the white.

There was a faint whine under my feet. Morenci had a reactor control system which could flood the tunnel in minutes but also empty it in the same time.

"What's up, Sam?" Stu asked.

After I explained we went over to the tunnel's exit and studied the receding water; in minutes it was halfway down the ladder.

"Do you want me to flood it again?"

"No. Let's keep it clear. We may have to get out of here fast. Let's leave a couple of flashlights back here—just in case."

Detail. You couldn't beat him . . .

By now Rudy had the lock off. He fumbled with a long screwdriver, there was a click, and the door inched open.

"Can you put it back together again, Rudy?" Stu asked him.

"Sure, Major."

"What's the difference?" Tom asked.

Stu pointed to the tunnel exit. "If we have to move out, the locked door could give us a few minutes."

Tom examined the heavy lock Rudy was putting back on the door.

"How could we lock it, Stu?"

Rudy inserted the screwdriver into the lock. "I have the tumblers set—all you have to do is turn it."

From this room we stepped into the kitchen; ancient and new were mixed. Shining copper-bottom pots lined one side of a wall. There were huge, nineteenth-century iron stoves, stainless steel sinks, and a hand pump for well water.

Again we consulted the plans. The kitchen led into a long hall which ended in an enormous entry hall with dark oak paneling. Riding across the domed ceiling I could make out figures in gray and blue on horseback with cannon firing all around them. Then tearing through the battle smoke was a guy even a no-talent *putz* like me could see was General Grant. This guy Abbott, I told myself, certainly knew how to butter up the right people . . .

In the center of the hall was a sweeping staircase with red carpet thick as sod which Trev said led up to the rooms of the north wing. Hanging above the top of the stairs was a stunning chandelier.

Off to the left of the entry hall was the formal dining room, to the right the library with more books than the Bensonhurst Library and a fireplace big enough to drive a horse and wagon through, a rec room with a fantastic amount of stereo, tape, and movie equipment, another room stocked with wine racks and liquor of all kinds, which Trev said was listed on the plans as "The Spirits Room," and a ballroom that reminded me of a movie called *The Great Waltz* I had seen when I was a kid.

It had several chandeliers, smaller than the one that hung at the top of the stairs in the main entry hall, the windows were covered with heavy drapes and the walls mirrored. When we turned on the lights the chandeliers began to turn slowly. We moved in cautiously, walking across the waxed parquet floor like kids testing a frozen pond. We checked the smaller adjoining dressing and powder rooms, then the rest of the main house which ended in another entry hall and a staircase leading to the floors of the south wing.

It was eerie. There wasn't a speck of dust, everything was in place, ashtrays were clean, the fire in the library was a bed of coals, blinds were drawn, bearded ancestors glared down at us—the place seemed to be deserted.

We decided to make our command post in the formal dining room. To someone like me who had been spent most of his formative years in a railroad flat, the room was tremendous.

The table looked like something out of King Henry VIII's court. There wasn't a thing on it but the top glowed as if it had been polished only minutes before.

Stu had just spread the plans out on the table when suddenly a guy with a dog walked out of the library and into the entry hall. The dog caught our scent, froze, then made a wild, snarling lunge into the dining room. As the surprised guard fumbled for his gun, Star hit him. He went down like a steer in a slaughterhouse. The dog leaped at Tom but Rudy caught him in midair. The animal weighed at least a hundred pounds; Rudy backed to the table, the mutt fighting him every inch, that big furry head twisting and turning in a fury, the snapping teeth trying for Rudy's jugular.

Then Arnie slid a blade into the dog's side. It gave a short yelp and Rudy swung it to the floor.

"You don't like water, I don't like dogs," Arnie told Rudy and wiped his knife on a pants leg.

We should have known that one snake means a family.

He was a big guy who passed the dining room door like a sprinter going for the tape. Star caught him on the stairs with the sledge in the knees and he came tumbling back down. We stood there as if we had been nailed to the floor, but the house remained quiet—the only sound was the moaning and cursing of the guard as he pulled himself up.

We pushed him into a dining room chair. Stu put the silencer to his head.

"We want some answers to some questions. Start talking or I'll shoot you through the arm. You have three seconds. Where's Morenci?"

"Who's Morenci?"

Stu stepped back. The silenced automatic jumped in his hand. Pain and disbelief replaced the arrogance in the man's face as the bullet tore into his upper arm.

"You have two seconds," Stu said stolidly, "then it's the other arm."

"Upstairs."

"Where upstairs?"

"The north wing."

"Where in the north wing?"

"Midway down the upper hall."

"How many cutters?"

"Nine."

"How many guards?"

He held his arm and moaned.

"There's two teams, one for the house, the other for the grounds."

"How many in all?"

"Twelve. Jeez, this hurts!"

Star said, "So you're lucky. You only got it in one arm. How many of you bums are in the factory?"

"Two."

"Why the guards? Can't you trust your own cutters?"

"Nobody leaves without a guard, that's the boss's orders."

"Where's Morenci?"

He licked his lips.

Stu stepped back.

"Wait a minute! He's in the factory."

"Where's the girl?" Trev demanded.

"The chink? She's with the boss."

"The other one—where is she?"

He looked surprised.

"I don't know of any more women . . ."

"She came in with the load."

"I wasn't here. I was in the south wing."

"Who's in the south wing?"

"Nobody now. The cutters sleep there."

"Is the junk upstairs?" Stu asked.

He nodded.

"You're not feds . . ."

Stu nodded to Rudy. The big fist came up in a short, vicious arch and the guard flew out of the chair. Arnie caught him before he crashed to the floor, both were tied, gagged, and dumped into a closet.

But we missed the third one. While we were working over his buddy, he tiptoed past the dining room and started yelling as he ran upstairs. When he heard us rush out into the entry hall he turned and fired, the bullet smashing into a wall. Stu's automatic made a soft *plop* and the guard slumped over the banister, slid down and crumpled at our feet.

We hugged the wall and waited. I thought, they didn't hear him . . .

But they did.

Two guys ran out of the rooms above us, leaned over the rail and began firing.

Then, as they say, the ball opened.

"The front door," Stu yelled.

It's funny, how in some crucial moments small details stick in your mind. I will always remember one of my first patrols; a guy in front of me was hit. He had a comic book stuck in his back pocket. It said "Horror Tales" and had a monster's face on the cover. For weeks I had nightmares about that face.

Now I could see the front doors had panes of thick, old-fashioned engraved glass. One side had a leaping stag, the other a woodland scene. Through them I could see guards and dogs running across the lawn.

"Let's go!" Stu shouted and started up the stairs, followed by Star

284

with the M-30, Arnie with the M-16, Trev and me with handguns, and Rudy and Tom in the rear. Rudy, who had the other M-30, shattered the beautiful glass panes and outside the guards dove for cover.

Going up that stairway was like taking a hill under frontal and rear fire. The guards outside sent in a ragged volley through the doors, while we also took fire from guards on the second floor. I will never know how we got to the top, the hallway was starting to look like a body-count area. Two guards were sprawled behind the banister, a portrait of some ancestor had more holes than a target in boot camp and the pockmarked yellow walls could have been slabs of Swiss cheese.

But we had casualties. Rudy had been hit in the leg and shoulder; Tom's kneecap was shattered and he was bleeding badly.

We overturned two heavy tables at the top of the stairs and re-formed.

"Any casualties?" Stu shouted.

"Tom's hit, so's Rudy," I shouted back.

"Hell, it's nothin', Major," Rudy roared indignantly, "these gooks are pigeons!"

"How about you, Tom?" I asked.

The pain was evident in his face. He drew deeply on a cigarette and pushed home another clip.

"I'm okay."

Now from the top of the stairway I could see the physical layout of the north wing's second floor. Midway down the hall on the right side were the heavy fire doors, the sheets of iron, as the contractor had told Stu, carefully paneled to blend in with the decor.

Across the stairway along the hall on the left were other rooms. One had a partially opened door. At the far end was a large foyer and a third staircase with a suit of armor at the bottom.

This crazy *meshugeneh* began to wonder if it would fit him.

Stu pointed to the partially opened door. This was our next target.

Star hit it like a fullback charging center to cross the goal line. It flew open. Luckily he was crouched over, for the blast of handgun fire whistled over his head and tore apart the beautiful crystal chandelier; it came down with a crash, prisms flying like bits of ice.

There was a guard behind a desk. Star's M-30 turned it into kindling wood. Objective secured.

Now the upper hallway was cleared but below us the other guards, under cover of heavy fire, had forced their way through the front doors and into the library.

I left Tom and Rudy behind their table barricade and joined Arnie, Star, Trev, and Stu.

"Are they hurt bad, Sam?" Stu asked.

"Tom's kneecap is shattered and Rudy's bleeding all over the place."

"We better wrap this up fast," Stu said, "Let's get the factory—"

"Toni may be in one of those rooms," Trev pointed out.

"If we don't stick together they'll pick us off one by one," Stu said.

Arnie opened the burlap bag and carefully took out what appeared to be two cigar stubs taped together and attached to a blasting cap. He tore some pieces of tape with his teeth. "Cover me."

He took off down the hall in a crouching run, taped the dynamite to the fire doors and came back. Star handed Stu the rifle with the scope. He waved us down, then sprawled out on the floor, took careful aim and fired.

There was a deep, thumping noise, the house shook violently and the doors blew in with a shatter of plaster, wallpaper, and wood.

We ran down the hall and into the factory through a billowing cloud of smoke. I could make out the cutters, their faces half-hidden behind surgical masks—to avoid inhaling the dust of the drugs—standing behind a long table. A guard fired at Star but missed. A vicious upward swing of the butt of the M-30 sent him reeling against the table and he crumpled to the floor. Another guard cried out and clutched his arm.

It was over within minutes. The cutters were mechanics in the drug traffic, not gunmen, they wanted no part of violence. They backed to the wall, hands raised and shouting in English and Spanish, they were unarmed and wanted to surrender.

Two attack dogs went for Star but Arnie got both before they could leap off the ground.

Trev straddled the wounded guard shouting, "Where's the girl . . . where's the girl . . . where's the white girl . . . ?"

Arnie jammed his M-16 into the stomach of one of the cutters.

"The boss? Morenci? The boss?"

The man, so frightened he couldn't speak, pointed to a door at the end of the room.

Arnie blew off the lock and he and Stu disappeared while Star lined up the cutters and ripped off their masks.

"Toni's upstairs!" Trev shouted wildly as he ran past me.

I followed him down the hall to the far end staircase. Behind us Rudy's M-30 crashed as he and Tom held off the guards below in the entry hall.

On the third floor Trev kicked in two doors and, while I covered him, rushed in but both rooms were empty.

He didn't wait for me on the third one and that was a mistake. He had kicked in the door and moved in as I ran up. I heard a shot and Trev staggered back against me; the slug had shattered the butt of his rifle. I couldn't see if he was hit.

Inside the room a stocky dark-haired man frantically tried to work his jammed automatic. On the bed was Toni. She didn't move. Then the guy tossed aside the pistol and threw up his hands.

"I'll take the pinch," he shouted, "okay . . . I'll take the pinch."

Trev didn't say a word. Carefully, accurately, he shot Cardillo through the heart twice and was bending over Toni before the body crashed to the floor.

286

Toni's face was battered and bruised but she was breathing.

"There's a funny smell," Trev said, looking up.

I bent over and sniffed; there was a faint sweetish odor about her mouth.

"They drugged her," he said. "The bastards drugged her!"

Downstairs there was an outburst of gunfire.

"I'll take care of her, Sam," he said. "You get back to the others."

Then I noticed the large bloodstain under his armpit.

"You're hit, Trev."

He didn't even look at it.

"Toni," he said softly, "Toni . . ."

I ran back to the second floor to find the guards moving up from the entry hall. Behind the splintered table Tom was firing his rifle but Rudy's M-30 had jammed. With a triumphant yell the guards started up the stairs. Rudy, bloody as a butcher, flung a heavy chair that sent one guy flying and I let go with a round; the rest couldn't get back down fast enough.

"Trev found Toni," I told them. "We think they drugged her. Where's Stu and the others?"

"Stu and Arnie have Morenci trapped on the roof," Tom said. "Star's looking for you. He needs help with the cutters."

"How's it with you, Rudy?" I asked.

The big guy shook his head and slammed the M-30 on the edge of the table.

"Goddam those grease guns!" He aimed downstairs and it suddenly coughed into life.

"Whaddaya know—it works!" I heard him call out delightedly as I ran down the hallway to the mill.

Arnie's bomb had gouged a deep hole in the wall, leaving splintered slates and twisted wire mesh. Plaster covered the floor and a part of the banister was missing. Inside the cutting mill the shattered windows had helped clear away the dust. The cutters, hands raised, torn masks hanging from their necks, had their backs to the wall. Stretched out on the floor were the two guards, one slightly wounded, the other dazed.

Star was standing in the middle of the room, his rifle aimed at one, then another. His face was set, emotionless.

"I ought to kill every one of you bastards," he said in a hard, bitter voice.

I said quickly, "Take it easy, Star."

He gestured with his rifle. "Look at the stuff they've been workin' on—"

The wooden boxes we had seen the deliverymen remove from Mary's house were piled along one wall. Scattered about were scales, bowls, spoons, spilled boxes of quinine, powdered milk, and several of the hollow bells. In every corner were stacks of cardboard boxes. Star kicked one, and it came down in a shower of glassine envelopes filled with junk.

"You're garbage!" he told the cutters. He ripped open an envelope and flung the powder into their faces. They raised their hands still higher and kept pressing against the wall. I'm glad they remained quiet; I am quite sure Star would have killed the first one who opened his mouth.

"Trev found Toni," I told him.

"How is she?"

"I don't know. It looks like they drugged her."

The M-30 swung to the cutters.

I said quickly, "Tom said they got Morenci."

"He's on the roof with one of his hoods and that Chinese dame. You can see 'em from the window."

"On the roof?"

"We caught 'em headin' for the ladders we put up. How do you like that? Our ladders!"

"Where are they now?"

"Pinned down behind one of the chimneys."

"Where's Arnie?"

"He's over in the south wing. We have to come up behind them. Stu will cover us. How's Rudy and Tom?"

"They've been hit but they say—"

There was a burst of fire from the hallway.

Star said calmly, "They'll never get past Fatso." He waved his rifle at the guards. "Watch these bums, Sam. I have to help Arnie. The major wants to take him alive. I say the hell with him, why waste time?"

"It's too late to run, Star."

"I personally don't care," he said stolidly. "I'm ready to fight the whole goddam country right here." He pointed his M-30 at the cutters and said loudly, "They're shit, Sam. If they move, kill 'em."

Then he was gone.

I made the cutters turn the table upright and herded them and the guards behind it.

"You heard him?"

A row of heads bobbed up and down.

"Well, keep your hands up and your mouths shut!" From the shattered window I had an excellent view of the roof. The north wing we were in looked down on the main house and its sheer gray cliffs of slate roof, gutters edged with rusty grillwork about eighteen inches high. The south wing, like the north, had turrets at either end. They were clapboard, bleached to a light gray by the weather, with small wooden roofs like cone-shaped hats.

Two huge fieldstone chimneys, each with a narrow platform, poked up through the roof near each wing. Each had an iron ladder installed by Star that led to the courtyard below.

The wind was blowing in sharp, sudden gusts, and I can remember how it moaned, like grieving women, around the corners and eaves of that crazy place.

Just then, from another room in the north wing, Stu began a rapid fire; simultaneously I could see two windows open in the south wing and ropes thrown out. Star came down like a cat, Arnie descended more cautiously. As they straddled the spine of the roof to move toward the shelter of the south chimney, someone shouted a warning and I could see bullets smashing the slates about them and ricocheting off the stone walls.

Finally they reached the chimney and its platform. They huddled there for a moment, then Arnie jumped up, his M-16 crashed, and the guard threw up his hands and slid down the roof with agonizing slowness, to stop finally at the iron fence.

In a brief lull, Stu shouted, "You have five seconds to surrender, Morenci!"

The reply drifted up to me.

"Who are you?"

"Throw your guns down the side of the roof," Stu ordered.

Silence.

Stu yelled, "One . . . two . . . three . . ."

Two guns made a rattling sound as they bounced down the slate, cleared the small fence and crashed below in the courtyard.

"Now stand up."

The guy I had seen in the country club dining room slowly rose from behind the chimney. He was wearing a sport jacket and a turtleneck sweater to match. Then a woman, it was Mary Chang Winslow, the wind molding the green suit to her body, long black hair flying about her face.

Arnie came from around the south chimney, gave his rifle to Star, and straddled the roof. He was halfway toward them when suddenly Morenci dropped down, fumbled with his pants leg and came up with a small handgun. His first shot caught Arnie in the side. He swayed, slumped over but held onto the peak of the roof.

It had happened so fast everyone, including myself, was caught off balance. Mary grabbed his hand and they started swaying back and forth on the narrow platform like partners in a weird ballet. Mary tried to twist the gun from Morenci's hand but he contemptuously pushed her to one side. For a heart-stopping moment she teetered on the edge, clawing at the air, then fell backward screaming, sliding down, nails and heels helplessly trying to dig into the polished slate. Several feet from the ladder she slammed into the iron grillwork. Part snapped off; I thought she was gone, but a piece remained to hold her and the dead or unconscious guard at the very edge of the roof. A sneeze could have sent them hurtling to the courtyard.

Star rose from behind the chimney, the M-16 looked down

Morenci's throat. The hood fired frantically. I could see chips of stone fly up around Star; I swear there was a thin smile on his dark brown face as he took careful aim.

I smashed what was left of the glass in the window.

"Fire! Fire, Star!"

But then I heard Stu's even, shouted command.

"Don't kill him, Star! Don't kill him! We must take him alive!"

The M-16 wavered. One shot rang out.

Morenci screamed and grabbed what remained of his right hand.

Then Star flung the rifle over his shoulder and scrambled to where Arnie was hugging the roof. The Mohawk tied him with ropes then carefully brought him back to the rear chimney and down the iron ladder to the rear courtyard.

He came back up the ladder, coils of rope around his shoulders to stand there for a moment, silently studying the roof. Below him Mary was stretched out along the gutter against the tiny iron grill fence. I could see her agonized face as she looked up and cried out something that was shredded by the wind.

Star first fashioned a line around the south chimney then disappeared behind it for a moment. When he reappeared I couldn't believe what I was seeing; he was barefoot and walking along the sharp peak of the roof in the gusty wind with the grace and ease of a circus tightrope performer.

When he reached the middle, he straddled the peak and made a lasso. He whirled it around his head and tossed it at the north chimney where Morenci was crouched at its base clutching his bleeding hand. When the rope fell to one side he nonchalantly pulled it back, whirled it around his head again and made a second toss. This time it slid over the chimney. He had roped it as easily as any cowboy I had ever seen rope a steer in the Garden.

Now I could see Stu slowly making his way along the peak. Star shouted a warning and waved him back but Stu kept on; he was leaving a streak of blood along the slates. He reached the chimney, said something to Morenci, and moved past to join Star.

Stu pointed to Mary and appeared to be telling Star something. Finally the Mohawk nodded and tied together both ends of the ropes leading to the chimneys. Then he looped three more around the single line. One he wound around his waist and between his legs to fashion a bosun seat, he did the same thing for Stu with the second, the third he snaked down the side of the roof until it came to rest in the gutter near where Mary lay.

He spoke to Stu, tested the ropes, then both left the peak, inching their way down the sheer cliff to the gutter. Star quickly tied the third rope around Mary's waist. When Stu knelt beside her, she put her arms around his neck and he carefully raised her while Star pulled on the ropes to keep them taut.

For a moment they seemed frozen against the darkening sky; the slender girl in the dark green suit, her hair blowing and twisting in the wind as she held Stu around the neck in a death grip; and Star pulling on the lines like a ghostly fisherman hauling in his catch.

I could see Stu talking intensely to Mary and she kept shaking her head. Suddenly a piece of cornice fell along with a shower of slates. Mary screamed and Star worked desperately to keep the ropes taut. Stu remained on the edge with Mary clinging to him.

Then she began screaming hysterically. I thought she was saying "Yes . . . Yes . . . ." over and over.

Stu motioned to Star and they started to lift Mary over the wavering rail. More slates fell to the courtyard and for a long heart-stopping moment they clung together, swaying, before Star grabbed Mary and went over the edge. Stu peered down; then, like a mountain climber making his descent, he followed. After a while the ropes became slack and I knew they had reached the courtyard.

It wasn't long before Star reappeared climbing the ladder of the south chimney. He repeated his spine-chilling walk along the roof's peak and this time slid down to where the guard was caught in the gutter behind what remained of the iron fence.

The third time he climbed the ladder of the north chimney to get Morenci, Star yanked him to his feet and slammed him against the chimney. Then he quickly tied a rope around his waist and gestured to the ladder. They went down, rung by rung.

I felt weak and drained. The cutters and guards, their hands still raised, looked at me curiously as I turned away from the window.

"Who are you guys?" one of the guards asked.

"If you don't keep your mouth shut I'll kill you," I told him and I meant every word of it.

I heard footsteps in the hall and jumped behind a door. It was Rudy, pale as death, his shirt and pants soaked with blood.

"The guards left," he said. "They ran away."

I kicked a chair toward him.

"Sit down, Rudy, you don't look good."

He slumped in the chair but his M-30 swung up to cover the guards and cutters; they raised their hands still higher.

"You miserable creeps," he said.

He motioned with his rifle to the overturned card boxes and glassine envelopes.

"That the junk?"

"It's all over the place."

"Sons of bitches!" He wiped his face with his sleeve. "Trev's in the hall with Toni. He said she's drugged. He can't bring her around."

"How's Tom?"

"Not good, he's bleedin' a lot."

"Can you watch these bums, Rudy?"

"Sure." He told them, "In Nam you guys would be a body count." He kicked a pile of envelopes and one broke, the powder spilling out on the floor.

"We ought to make 'em eat it—bag by bag. How would you bastards like that, huh? You don't eat it fast enough, we'll stuff it. Right?"

The cutters were exchanging uneasy glances when I left.

Outside in the hallway, Trev had Toni propped up against the wall. She was still unconscious.

"I can't bring her around, Sam," he said.

I bent down and took her pulse. It was slow, very slow.

He gently touched her bruised mouth.

"We've got to find Cardillo," he said savagely.

"Trev," I said, "You shot him—he's dead!"

He looked at me bewilderedly.

"I shot him?"

"It's not important now." I pointed to his arm. "You've been hit."

He studied his bloodstained shirt in a surprised sort of way.

"Yeah. Maybe I have," he said. He gestured to where Tom lay behind the table at the top of the stairs. "Tom's bad. I did the best I could but he needs a doctor. Where's Stu?"

"They're coming in. They got Morenci. Arnie's hit."

"Bad?"

"I don't know. I'm going to see what I can do for Tom."

"I'll help you . ."

We did what we could for Tom but that wasn't much. It seemed like a long time passed before we finally heard doors open and close below us.

Star appeared in the entry hall prodding Morenci before him. They were followed by Mary, then Stu who was limping and carrying a paper bag with one hand and helping Arnie with the other. They came upstairs and I helped Stu lower Arnie to the top step. His sweatshirt was soaked with blood. Morenci, clutching his hand wrapped in towels, slumped to the floor. Mary sat on the step near Arnie. She looked dazed and different.

I knelt down and offered her a cigarette. She accepted it gratefully.

"I saw it all from the window," I told her.

She rested her head on the banister and closed her eyes.

"Every time I took a breath," she said, shuddering, "I could hear that little iron rail make a sound as if it was going to break off."

Arnie held out his hand and she gave him the cigarette. He inhaled deeply and gave it back to her.

"She stopped that bastard from killing me," he told me.

She turned to look at him.

"Clint Fontaine?" she asked bitterly. "What really is your name?"

"What difference does it make now?"

I told her, "Arnie Harper."

She repeated, half to herself, "Arnie Harper." She laughed wildly, "And I believed him!"

Arnie said slowly, "Mary met a guy who was ready to pull the trigger, Sam."

"He acted as if he was crazy," Mary said trembling. "He said he would throw me off the roof if I didn't answer his questions." She put her face in her hands. "It was horrible . . . only the little fence and the guard with blood all over him."

"It's too late to play Mary's little lamb," Arnie told her harshly. He went on to me, "She told Stu everything. Now we have the answers."

She pleaded, "Please tell me, who are you? What do you want?"

"I told you that doesn't matter now," Arnie told her, "not now." He lit another cigarette and gave it to her. "Now it matters for you to remember what you promised. I'm telling you this because the next time he won't hesitate, he'll fling you off that goddam roof like you were a sack of rags. He means it, Mary, and I mean it!"

She stared at him unbelievingly.

Then Stu, a bundle of sheets over one arm and still carrying the paper bag, walked out of a room.

"Did Arnie tell you, Sam, Mary has promised to cooperate with us? She cleared up everything." He bent over and said solicitously, "I'm sorry it had to be that way, Mary, I really am."

"Who are you?" she demanded. "What do you want? Are you the police? If you are not the police, who are you? People don't do such things!"

"And people don't smuggle in five hundred pounds of junk to sell to kids!" Arnie said roughly.

She didn't answer and turned away to rest her face on the banister railing.

I asked, "Any surprises in what she told you?"

"A few," Stu replied.

Arnie looked at him. "A few!"

"I'm going to put all my notes together and then we'll go over them . . ."

"What's in the bag, Major?" I asked.

"Morenci's guns. They're slightly battered."

"Why carry them around?"

"His fingerprints will prove he isn't Mr. Pascal Nicolai."

"We're giving them everything in a package," Arnie said fiercely. "Let's see them blow this one!"

His face had a greenish tint and he sat bent over as if to favor his wound.

"How's that dressing, Arnie?" Stu asked anxiously.

"It's fine," Arnie said, closing his eyes and biting his lower lip, "just fine."

Stu held up the sheets. "I found these in a closet. We can use them for bandages. Sam, give me a hand with Tom."

Tom was very pale and there was a large pool of blood under his knee.

"How do you feel, Tom?" Stu asked him.

"Not good, Stu. I feel sick."

"He needs a doctor," Trev said as he joined us.

"We'll get one," Stu said, almost mildly.

"Goddam it, Stu, we need one now!" Trev shouted. "For Tom and for Toni!"

"What's wrong with Toni?"

Trev pointed to Morenci.

"Either Cardillo or this bastard drugged her." He walked over to where Morenci sat on the floor, holding his wounded hand. "Why didn't you kill this son of a bitch!"

"Because I want him alive," Stu replied calmly.

"What did you do to her?" Trev asked Morenci.

Morenci looked up at him.

"I don't talk to crazy people," he said.

I was surprised, his voice, instead of being harsh or guttural, was cultured, with a slight accent.

I reached Trev before he could get to Morenci and with Star fought him back to the wall.

I pleaded with him, "Easy, Trev, for crissakes, take it easy."

Stu said loudly, "I want him kept alive. He's important to us."

Tom said in a weak voice, "Will someone get me a drink of water? Please."

That broke the tension. Trev went back to Toni, and I got Tom the glass of water. Then Stu tore up the sheets and we cut away the torn and bloody pants leg and bandaged the gaping wound.

"We'll get a doctor," Stu said. As he rose he asked me, "What about Cardillo?"

"Trev killed him. He was in the room with Toni."

He nodded as if satisfied. "I'm going to have a look at Toni and Rudy."

Star, his M-16 swung over his shoulder, knelt down beside Tom. "How's it going, Tom?"

Tom tried to smile. "I feel like I was kicked by a horse."

"I know what you mean," Star said. "When I was a kid I was kicked by a bronc. I walked on my heels for a week. How about a cigarette, Sam?"

I gave him one and he let the smoke seep from between his lips.

"I saw what happened on the roof," I told him.

"You should have rigging hawsers for a job like that," he said with the air of an annoyed professional. "For a few minutes I didn't think we were going to make it. I wonder what that hick contractor would have done if he'd seen us?"

"Had a heart attack," I suggested, "like I almost did."

Star gestured to Mary. "You owe her one, Arnie."

Arnie nodded.

"You okay, Arnie?"

"Good enough to climb trees," Arnie solemnly assured him.

Star looked over at Morenci. "What does the major have in mind for that creep?"

"Turn him over to the feds," I said to Arnie. "Right?"

Arnie didn't reply.

I repeated, aggressively, "You listening, Arnie? I said we're going to turn Morenci over to the feds—"

"We talked about it outside," he said at last.

"And?"

"Let Stu tell you . . ."

Oh no, I told myself, not something new at this point . . .

Star stood up. "I say we shoot him and then pull out of here. Leave him and his junk as a present for the government."

"I'm no executioner, Star," I told him. "You can pass me on that one."

"It will save the taxpayers a hell of a lot of time and money, Sam," he said with mock seriousness.

"Let's wait until we have a talk with Stu," Arnie said.

Star walked over to where Morenci was sitting on the floor.

"I just hope you make a break for it, creep," he said softly.

For a moment Morenci didn't reply. His face was emotionless, but murder glared out of his cold black eyes.

"I'll remember you, my friend," he said, and patted his wounded hand.

"Next time I'll make sure it's your head," Star told him and hurried down the hall to the cutting factory.

Something about Morenci's hand puzzled me. The missing fingertip? No, it was something else and it eluded me, teasing me as it hovered on the edge of my subconscious . . .

I broke off trying to remember what it was and watched Star march the guards and cutters out of the factory; one of the guards had his arm in a sling and Rudy had bandages around his shoulder and thigh.

"We oughta have a Snakepit for 'em, Major," he called out as Stu limped into the hall.

The big *meshugeneh* is really enjoying this, I told myself.

Then Star gestured with his rifle and the guards and cutters, face down, stretched out on the carpet.

"How's Toni?" Arnie asked Stu.

"They used some kind of anesthesia, I would say chloroform. Cardillo gave her a terrible beating . . ."

Arnie said to Mary, "Toni's one of the reasons why we came here."

"I never knew that girl was here," she said. "What does she mean to you? Why is she here?" She begged him, "Why don't you answer my questions?"

"It's a long story, Mary," Stu told her, "and we haven't got the time."

"What's the next move, Major?" Star asked.

I pointed to Morenci.

"Make arrangements to turn him over to the feds. What else?"

"We're not going to turn Morenci over to anyone," Stu said abruptly. "At least not yet."

"Then what the hell are we going to do with him?" I asked.

"Shoot him, I hope," Star said.

"We're going to put Morenci on trial," Stu said loud enough for all of us to hear, "and on national television."

Morenci slowly lowered his cigarette and stared at him. So did I. All of us. Even Mary.

Trev jumped to his feet.

"That's insane! You wanted Morenci and you got him. Now let's turn him over to the feds. To the cops. To any one, but for God's sake, let's get out of here." He pointed to the bodies of the two guards off to one side of the hall. "Isn't that enough?"

"What do you think will happen if we turn him over to the law?" Stu said savagely. "A thousand hearings? Finally bail? Then a trial? With witnesses either killed or so frightened they won't testify? And if he is convicted, what will he get? Five years with probation at two? A presidential pardon because he knows the right people?" He added, "I'll let Star kill him before I do that."

"But what will we prove by putting him on trial on television?" I asked.

"Let's face it, Sam," he said. "Today if it's not a headline event on television it just didn't happen! It's not history, it's only a foul ball forgotten with the crack of the bat. But we're going to make sure it's not forgotten! Morenci's going to help us to wake up this country. If something isn't done soon we'll all go down the drain—"

Suddenly a bullhorn began blaring outside.

"You people inside the house! Throw down your weapons and come out one at a time! With your hands up! This is the State Police!"

Star ran to one of the front windows.

"Holy Christ!" he shouted over his shoulder. "There must be a million cops on the road! And there's guys with cameras on the tops of trucks . . ." He read off, "Columbia Broadcasting System . . . NBC . . ."

"That's what I mean," Stu said. "We're going to put Morenci on trial—and on prime time!"

BOOK THREE:

TRIAL BY TELEVISION

Chapter **11**

Trevor David- Prime Time

I find it difficult now to remember much of that afternoon. At the time hours lost themselves in each other, like a series of nightmares blended into one horrible dream. But I can recall there was for me only one question in the world—Toni's condition. She had all the appearance of being drugged or anesthetized. When I bent over to kiss her I could smell a faint, sweetish odor about her lips. I agreed with Stu, it could be chloroform. Her pulse was slow, terrifyingly slow, and there was no reflex reaction. Bruises on her face and arms confirmed her sister's story of how Cardillo had beaten her.

I must have carried Toni downstairs to the second floor like a sleepwalker; Tom's voice seemed far off, muffled as if coming through a thick mist. I suddenly found myself staring down at him. He lay on the floor behind a splintered table, his face pale, deadly pale, and a pool of blood under his knee.

"Trev! Trev! For God's sake answer me. How is Toni?"

"I think she's drugged. I can't bring her around." I knelt down. "How do you feel, Tom?"

"Not good." He bit his lower lip. "It hurts like hell. Can you get me a drink of water?"

I found a bathroom and gave him a drink, then I took off my jacket and made a pillow for him.

"Where are the others, Tom?"

"Rudy and Sam are in with the cutters . . . there's been a lot of firing outside."

"What about the guards?"

"They ran away. We have to make up our minds damn fast of what we're going to do now, Trev."

"You and Toni need a doctor," I told him, "that's number one as far as I'm concerned."

I didn't know I had been hit myself until Tom pointed to my bloody shirt. Apparently the slug had shattered my rifle butt, then freakishly torn through the skin and muscle inside my upper arm near the shoulder.

Then the others arrived. We had the battered appearance of a combat company back from a bad patrol. We sat on the stairs, sprawled out on the carpet, or leaned against the wall. Our sweatshirts, jackets, and pants were torn and blood-smeared. Our pockets bulged with shells and we held onto our weapons like lost children or laid them close to us.

Suddenly Stu sprung it on us, how he planned to put Morenci on trial on television. I lost my head but that didn't ruffle him—he promised we would soon have a doctor. Curiously, I believed him and so did the others. It has always been that way.

For the first time I really appreciated Tom's insight that night in the Automat when he said Stu had never left Vietnam. Now I knew he had been planning something like this from the very hour of our reunion when he had talked about the awesome power of television to focus an entire country on a single event, unifying millions as they have rarely been before. I could still hear him say:

"To bring home a message to the American people, Trev, all you need is blood and pageantry . . . television can't resist this combination."

Blood?

The bodies of the two guards we had killed in the rush up the stairway were covered with prisms and glass from the big chandelier.

Dead men were no strangers to me but my insides crawled at the sight. I guess I wasn't the only one; Star abruptly got up and dragged the bodies into the room where he had killed the other guard; I could see his hand sticking out from behind the shattered desk.

There was another one below in the dining room; Sam said still another was outside in the courtyard.

And Cardillo.

Among us only Sam and Star had not been wounded. There was also a wounded guard in the cutting factory and, downstairs, the one Stu had shot in the shoulder.

Was that enough blood for television?

A sudden feeling of weariness swept over me, this one afternoon had been longer than any week I had known. It seemed to me that I was dreaming, and it had to be a dream that I had taken part in the raid on Grand Vista and the capture of the man who sat on the floor glaring defiantly at all of us.

Then the bullhorn blared outside. . . .

The agent we met in the library came in under a white flag. He was a prissy young man with a petulant mouth and a thin, precise moustache.

As he hurriedly took notes, Stu identified us and quickly sketched what we had uncovered in our investigation of Morenci and had found in the house. Then he opened one of the cardboard boxes and gave the agent a glassine envelope.

"Heroin. There's a large amount upstairs in the cutting factory. We found Morenci directing operations—"

The agent snapped, "The local police identify him as a man named Nicolai, an international contractor, and a very respectable citizen."

Stu gave him the paper bag.

"These are his guns. You'll find his fingerprints on them. A Colonel Bouquet in Paris at the Brigade Criminelle of the Police Judiciaire will give you his file. They also have a sketch done by a police artist and a sketch of his right hand showing a missing fingertip of the right hand. Police headquarters in New York has his yellow sheet listing charges for shylocking, policy, assault, and drugs. Don't bother to look for a picture—there are none. Something the cops over there had better look into."

"I would like to speak to Mr. Nicolai—or Morenci."

"Not yet!"

"Is he wounded?"

"Let's say he'll have trouble firing a gun again."

The agent picked up the glassine envelope and held it to the light. "How do you know it's heroin?"

Arnie gave a short, contemptuous laugh.

"Taste it, for crissakes! It's pure heroin and cocaine."

The agent shut his notebook with a determined snap.

"Well, what do you intend to do? Turn this man over to us and—" he hesitated, "surrender yourselves? And your weapons?"

"Before we do anything," Stu said. "we want to talk to a pool television crew."

"May I ask the reason, Mr. Harlow?"

"We wish to make a public statement."

"I will have to consult with my superiors."

"Consult with anyone you want, but we're not going to make a move until that television crew gets here."

The agent repeated as if for the record, "Then you do not intend to turn this man and his alleged illegal narcotics over to us for lawful prosecution, nor do you intend to surrender yourselves and your weapons."

Sam broke in, "This guy is wired for sound, Major."

"I couldn't care less," Stu replied. "Maybe it's just as well we get things straight. We are not going to surrender Morenci to you, nor do we intend to give ourselves up or our weapons. In fact, you should warn your—" he underscored the word with cold sarcasm, "superiors, that if any attempt is made to infiltrate or storm our position we will use all the firepower we have to repulse you. We are all combat veterans and can easily pick you off. However, we don't want any more bloodshed. But that's up to you. Now please follow me."

He led the agent to the entry hall and pointed upstairs to the big holes gouged in the walls by Arnie's bomb.

"We used explosives to blow in the fire doors of the cutting factory. We have more we will use if you try to bring in armor."

They returned to the library.

"We have an endless supply of explosives and ammunition," Stu went on. "If you move in it might be another Attica. Of course the dead and wounded could include Vietnam heroes. We have two or three silver stars plus some other stuff."

He studied the agent.

"And that wouldn't be very politic, don't you agree?"

The agent replied as if by rote, "I will have to consult with my superiors."

"You do that," Arnie said, "but come back with the TV crew."

In an hour the bull horn blared again, and a cameraman, technician, and a young TV reporter came up the driveway. We met them in the library where Stu made his statement, not written but off the cuff.

There was an aura of unreality as he sat behind the oak desk, the wall of books and burning logs for a background, while a rifle leaned against his chair and all around him were armed and wounded men.

He first said who we were, reviewed our service records and the time we had spent in Tong Le Mai, then went into the reason for the raid on Grand Vista:

"Our lives were severely altered by imprisonment in a war which many Americans believe was stupid in its conception, dishonest in its motives, and ruthless and corrupt in its execution. History will undoubtedly agree with them, but the conception, motives, and execution of that tragic war had nothing to do with us; we were not professional soldiers; as civilians we obeyed the laws of our country and took up arms in the jungles of Vietnam.

"We were captured and imprisoned for periods from four to eight irreplaceable years. During that period some of us lost homes, wives and children, dreams and hopes. We have never complained and we do not intend to do so now. If there is one thing you learn in a prison camp it's not to feel sorry for yourself.

"Our desire was to return home, each to live out his own life. However, we discovered we had come back to a world which God knows was not perfect when we left it, but now was in chaos, with crime, indifference, apathy, and corruption in both high and low places affecting the lives of our fellow citizens to a degree never before experienced in the brief life of our Republic.

"We felt like men who through some outrageous trick of time had been misplaced in another century in which our old ideals were viewed with contempt and even amusement.

"We found the elderly barricaded behind locks and iron gates afraid to venture outside, afraid to walk a few blocks to worship in their church or temple.

"We found that women played Russian roulette when they walked down a street after dark or even when they went to a store in midday because it was a question of whether or not they were to be stalked by a drug addict who was ready to kill for the few dollars in their purse.

"We found drugs ravaging young people to a fantastic degree, and while there are commendable programs to try and salvage their lives, we were amazed to discover that federal and local law enforcement authorities are seemingly unable to stop the flow of drugs at the source—namely, Turkey and the nations in Indochina who, despite world opinion, continue to harvest opium crops and allow their drug merchants to smuggle cargoes across their borders and into the United States.

"We have found an incredible amount of crime in our cities, a great deal connected with drug addiction, but we have also found a shocking lack of interest in, even disregard for, the rights of the victims of these crimes and the rights of potential victims.

"In contrast we found an overwhelming concern with the rights of criminals and those charged with crimes. The latter concern is legitimate, even necessary, but in the society to which we returned, the scales of justice never seemed to balance: we believe there has been a disproportion in concern for the rights of the criminal.

"We have examined our history and, although there have been periods when life in American cities was unsafe, there has never been a precedent for the violence sweeping our cities today; when night falls most urban citizens feel they are living under a state of siege.

"There is little doubt that drug addiction is the basis for a great deal of this crime. In the past, crime against property was attributed to poverty, but now, in those areas where poverty has been eliminated or diminished, drug addiction is rampant and so are the crimes not only against property but against people.

"Combined with this rise of drug addiction and violent crimes there has been an increase in official corruption, cynicism, and political opportunism at both ends of the social spectrum.

"We discovered corruption firsthand when we tried to help our community combat the sale of drugs. Purely by chance we were able to uncover an international drug syndicate operating not only in New York City but in many urban areas of the United States. We are not skilled in law enforcement procedures, and actually the information we received was through the efforts of a courageous young woman who was kidnapped from her Brooklyn home and taken to this place where we found her drugged. She is still unconscious.

"This syndicate had a terrifying objective: to make addicts of as many schoolchildren as possible, mostly of elementary school age. The motive for the leaders of this syndicate was simple: greed.

"We not only turned this information over to Mayor Dwight Kerr and his police commissioner, but cooperated fully, only to be betrayed by official corruption, apathy, and incompetence. It was then that we decided to continue the investigation as individuals.

"We have taken this action to dramatize what is happening to our country and to alert its citizens that there has not been enough sense of outrage against these evils: official corruption, in both high and low places; apathy, cynicism, terrorism in the name of some twisted cause, political opportunism; political lying and political double-talking—in all parties, minority and majority. Watergate, the judicial committee's hearings, the presidential resignation, are part of what we mean.

"What we find hard to believe is the lack of public outcry, of national revulsion. A year ago Congress reported after a worldwide survey that since 1968 two hundred and thirty public places have been bombed by terrorists and a hundred aircraft have been hijacked. Almost two hundred persons have been murdered, including twelve innocent kidnap victims, and three hundred injured, sometimes so critically they will spend their lives in a wheelchair or bed. Property losses have been in the billions.

"The head of the committee which made this survey warned that this reign of terror was threatening our country. Several months after he released his statement—I couldn't find it in our daily newspapers— there were two so-called political kidnappings, one of a young girl of a prominent family. And spokesmen for these terrorist groups predicted there will be many more.

"We are stunned at the lack of a nationwide cry of outrage against the senseless brutality of these crimes; politicians seemed occupied with projects for our convenience and comfort.

"It is evident to us we are so drugged with violence we have accepted the premise that nothing can be done about it so we must live with it."

His voice rose. "We believe that something can be done and must be done.

"We believe that Congress should take immediate steps to cut off all aid to those countries that insist on cultivating and selling opium. Street crime could be cut drastically if the flow of drugs to this country was stopped. This is the opinion of experienced law enforcement leaders.

"We call upon Congress to establish a supergovernment agency with powers to unify all law enforcement bodies, federal or municipal, in a national drive against crime, from street level to organized groups, with particular attention given to those who use official corruption to smuggle drugs into this country.

"We also believe this agency should have the power, with subpoena, to periodically survey not only municipal police agencies but also government law enforcement bureaus, should there be a legitimate complaint of apathy or corruption from responsible citizens. Since our return we have read of scandals in not only police departments in large cities but in dozens of smaller communities. This makes it plain that corruption has become a way of life for many of those charged with community protection against crime.

"Vietnam farmers say you can sleep just so long with a tiger before one morning he awakes and selects you as his breakfast. We believe that morning is dawning for all of us; we have too long been sleeping with the tigers of our indifference, cynicism, and lack of patriotism. We must restore love of country, love of neighbor, and love of community.

"We realize the action we have taken here at Grand Vista is criminal and perhaps repugnant to many, but in our opinion desperate times call for desperate measures.

"More than a decade ago we poured millions of man hours, fantastic talent, and billions of dollars into our space program.

"We believe the same national intensity is needed to wage a war against the crime and violence that are slowly eroding our lives . . ."

For a moment we stared back at the tiny red light above the lens eye of the camera.

"We don't care if you totally condemn our actions. We ask only that you listen as we present a case which we believe is a symbol of what is happening to our country."

The reporter broke in, "And what case will that be, sir?"

"This is the home of a man named Nicolai," Stu replied. "He has posed in this beautiful community as a wealthy and respectable international contractor. We will prove that actually his name is Del Morenci, a former New York gangster and head of an international drug syndicate backed by organized crime. It has smuggled an incredible amount of drugs into this country with the primary purpose of recruiting children as his customers.

"We will also prove that this syndicate is protected by official corruption . . ."

He paused.

"In fact we will name two high officials connected with the present mayoralty race who are linked to Morenci's syndicate."

The reporter looked startled.

"The New York mayoralty race?"

"That's right."

"And you have proof?"

"We believe excellent proof."

"What do you intend to do with this man Morenci?"

"Put him on trial on national television," Stu said. "On prime time."

"A trial? Will you have a jury?"

Stu pointed to the television camera.

"The American public through that camera will be the jury."

"If you have such evidence on Morenci, why didn't you turn it over to the proper authorities?" the reporter wanted to know.

"I explained that some weeks ago we had turned all the evidence we had uncovered over to what you call 'the proper authorities' and we were betrayed. The facts are these: on information we supplied a raid was made on a Water Street warehouse. Although the police had confirmed the place was a major cutting factory for drugs, those who operated it were not apprehended and a cargo of drugs was removed—despite a twenty-four-hour guard placed around the warehouse on orders of the New York City police commissioner who had been reporting directly to Mayor Dwight Kerr. The syndicate which operated that warehouse was also under the leadership of Morenci."

He went on, "I can now disclose to Mayor Kerr and his police commissioner that at least fifty million dollars' worth of drugs were removed on Morenci's orders from that warehouse on the eve of the contemplated raid by two men, one named Frank Cardillo, the other Michel Forelli, alias Mike Fortunato, both ex-convicts, by means of an old sewer pipe which goes from Water Street to a Sanitation Department garage a block away. The drugs were put into a truck and taken to another factory where it was subsequently diluted and sold on the streets not only of New York, but of many other American cities; the customers were principally schoolchildren.

"If the Mayor and his police commissioner are interested they can find this abandoned sewer pipe in the north, lefthand corner of the first floor of the warehouse. Apparently a wooden floor was put in some years ago but a hatch can be found under several boxes of old machine parts. I might say that when we received our initial information pinpointing the warehouse as the syndicate's main depot and cutting factory, we tried to obtain copies of the plans of this old building. Curiously, they were found to be missing.

"I would suggest that the mayor assign his commissioner of investigation to look into the reason why they were missing and also the reason why a sanitation truck left the department's garage without authorization at 3:30 A.M. although this same truck had been listed as inoperable and scheduled for extensive motor repairs.

"In closing I would like to make one final statement. Men have been wounded, killed, and taken prisoner by us in this affair. We do not believe them to be totally disinterested and innocent persons. We do not want hostages and those we took as prisoners will be released in a few hours. However, we would suggest that each man's criminal record be examined and that he be questioned as to his participation in cutting the drugs we captured or in guarding these premises. I believe you will find all have extensive records.

"I wish to state emphatically that the total responsibility for all the events which took place today rests with me. In fact I duped my companions into coming here under the guise of turning what information we had uncovered over to the federal authorities.

"I'm responsible for the killing here today—no one else.

"I am ready to stand trial and accept whatever punishment is given to me. I have no martyr complex nor do I have an ulterior motive. I simply love my country and I am afraid of what is happening to it.

"I believe our tigers are awakening and we should be prepared to face them. Thank you and good night . . ."

When the television crew was packing their gear, Stu asked the young reporter:

"Would you be interested in covering this?"

"By all means," the reporter replied. "I want to get this stuff back as soon as possible for a fast special . . ."

"If you intend to cover this trial," Stu told him, "you should remain here."

The reporter gave him an uneasy look.

"Why?"

"If you leave the authorities will never let you return."

Star said, "Don't forget the Department of Justice refused to allow reporters or TV crews inside Wounded Knee."

The reporter looked thoughtful and turned to his crew.

"Not me," the elderly technician said. "My old lady would hit the roof."

The cameraman in his early twenties nodded.

"Count me in."

"Can you work everything alone?"

"Sure. You can give me a hand with the lights if we need 'em."

The reporter said, "Can I use the phone?"

"By all means."

The reporter went into the next room and returned in a few minutes.

He tried to look casual.

"They said it's up to me. I'm staying."

"Me too," said the cameraman.

"Dave, you take back the rolls," the reporter told the technician.

"You got spare tapes?" Dave asked the cameraman.

"It just happens I do," the cameraman told him. "We were on our way to do two more jobs in Jersey when we got this call."

"I have only one request," Stu said. "Please remain on the first floor and nothing must be taped unless we approve. Is that satisfactory?"

"Fine with me," the reporter said.

"You're making a very grave mistake, Mr. Harlow," the agent said stiffly. "Any evidence you have should be turned over to us, along with Nicolai—er—Morenci. And yourselves."

"You said that before," Stu snapped.

"And I say it again, sir—"

Stu interrupted him. "All I want from you, sir, is a doctor."

The agent started to say, "I will have to consult with—" but Stu smashed his fist down on the desk with such force I thought surely the bones in his hand would be broken. His face twisted with rage and his green eyes became cold and bleak. I had never seen him like this before.

"Goddammit!" he shouted. "I told you we needed a doctor! We have a drugged girl and wounded men here! The men not only fought in Vietnam but were imprisoned for years—probably a hell of a long time before you even started to piss in your diaper! Now get that doctor—and get him fast!" The agent looked startled at this unexpected attack but remained silent. Then Stu and I escorted him and the technician carrying the box of video tape to the front door and they left.

"Before we go back in there, Stu, tell me something," I asked him.

"Anything."

"Where did you get that stuff about the sewer pipe and the sanitation garage?"

"Mary," he replied. "She told us just about everything we want to know. She's going to be our main witness."

"Stu, this is crazy!"

"Why is it crazy?" he replied coolly. "Somebody's got to wake up this goddamn country!"

"Do you realize what we did? Six people were killed!"

"This is a hell of a time to do a body count, Trev! You were all for it, remember? You couldn't get in fast enough! If we had turned it over to the police or the federal people, do you think Toni would be alive? They would be still out on the road making a deal with their bullhorn!"

"We got Morenci. We got millions of dollars in junk. You made your point—why this trial?"

306

"To show the country what's going on! Mary told us how we were sold out by Miles and Derby and the rest of those thieves. Wait until you hear her story. Maybe it's stuff you could never get out in a trial by jury, but by Christ, I'm going to make sure the American public hears it!" His voice became grim and taut. "I didn't give eight years of my life for this kind of society. After the first week back I was sick of it. Something's got to be done to change it."

"Like what?"

"Like waking up this country! If you have to give them a show on television to do it—fine. But I'm going to do it!"

"It's not going to change anything, Stu."

"That's exactly what I mean—we've come to a point where we accept anything. We can't fight them. Let's make a deal with them. No more, dammit, no more!"

"You said the public is to be the jury—"

"That's right. I want the whole rotten mess put out on the table. Let them get a sniff of it."

"How will you know what the jury came in with? Guilty or not guilty?"

"Let's see what the evidence says."

"Suppose *you* think Morenci's guilty?"

"That's something we'll talk about."

He stared at me for a moment, his face white and drawn, his hands, hanging at his sides, clenched and unclenched. Then abruptly he broke the silence with a harsh laugh.

"What the hell's the matter with us, Trev? Fighting like two idiots!"

"There's one thing I want you to know, Stu."

"Jesus. You don't have to say it like that!"

"If they don't send in a doctor, I'm taking Toni out of here and turning myself over to the cops."

"No one's keeping you here, Trev."

"Don't try to stop me, Stu."

"What would you do if I did try to stop you?" he asked. "Kill me?"

"If I thought you might be jeopardizing Toni's life? Yes."

He said slowly, almost meditatively, "I didn't know she meant that much to you, Trev."

"She means everything."

He put his arm around my shoulder and hugged me.

"Trev! Trev! For crissakes! You heard what I told that agent. They'll send in a doctor—"

"But if they don't you know what I intend to do."

Someone in the library turned on the color television set and we could hear the announcer describing Grand Vista from the air, then give some background history of the mansion and a recap of the events of the afternoon.

"... *the television technician who just emerged from the house said the group appeared to have plenty of weapons and ammunition and seemed determined, as he put it, 'to get their point across to the country'... the tape that was made by the leader of the raiders will be shown on this network as soon as it is processed ... police received the first news of this—"*

"Let's go in and see ourselves on TV, Trev," Stu said quietly.

I suddenly realized that it was twilight and the purplish veil was closing in over the grounds changing shapes. Trees lining the driveway were menacing, stiff-limbed giants, the fountain a dull patch of color and its splashing sound held a sullen note as if it feared the coming of the mute darkness. Out on the road a radio car had turned on its dome light; the flashing amber and the brief explosive bursts of the photographer's bulbs made it appear like a standard scene in a TV crime drama.

I thought of Riverview and my aunt staring unbelievingly at the big color set we had in the living room and I wished I were dead.

As we entered the library the cameras had zoomed to the road at the front gate where a crowd surrounded police cars with revolving lights.

"That's early stuff," the television reporter smugly told his cameraman. "Wait until they get my tapes." He looked up as we entered. "By the way, Mr. Harlow, when will that trial begin?"

"You'll be advised," Stu told him.

A reporter on the road was interviewing an elderly man in uniform who described how a local delivery man had found the gates of Grand Vista open, heard the volleys of gunfire and notified the police.

Then the excited delivery man told his story:

"After I called the cops I came back here. I seen some of the guards get in their cars and leave, some of 'em came out of here on two wheels. It's just lucky they didn't hit my truck. This one guy I know slightly, because he's always been at the gate, came running down to the gatehouse. I guess to get his car keys. When I asked him what the hell was goin' on he just shouted, 'Some crazy guys raided the house ... they got Mr. Nicolai ... !' Then he got into his car and left, so I just waited here until the chief arrived."

Suddenly the bullhorn blared again.

"We're sending in a physician, Grand Vista. If you have a flashlight blink it twice so we know you understand ..."

"Well, there's your doctor, Trev," Stu said with a smile.

Star found a flashlight and we walked out to the front steps. Star blinked his flash and floodlights suddenly turned the lawn and gardens into cold white daylight. A slender, solitary man with a deliberate gait and carrying a black bag walked up the long driveway and finally paused at the steps.

"I'm Dr. Wallace from St. Anthony's Hospital," he explained. "I was asked by the police to come here and treat some wounded—"

"C'mon in, Doc," Rudy told him. "We all have Blue Cross."

Wallace, frail-looking, white-haired, and wearing steel-rimmed

308

glasses, could have walked out of a Norman Rockwell New England village.

"We have some wounded, doctor," I told him, "but there's a girl upstairs who needs immediate attention."

He was unflappable. "Lead the way, please."

Going upstairs he asked, "Was this young woman shot?"

"No, we believe she was drugged," I told him.

"Is she on drugs?"

"Of course not," I snapped at him. "She was kidnapped and brought over here."

He followed me across the hall, doubting every word; frankly, I didn't blame him.

Wallace tested Toni's eye reflexes with a light, studied her respiration, took her blood pressure, then bent down, parted her lips, and sniffed.

"There's no doubt about it," he said with a puzzled air. "They used chloroform with something else."

"I don't care what they used—is she in any danger?"

"How long has she been unconscious?"

"Two, three, maybe four hours."

He took what looked to be a plastic siphon from his bag.

"What's that, doctor?"

"Ambubag. She's getting into respiratory distress. I have to ventilate her."

He adjusted the mask on Toni's face and began squeezing the bulb attached to the mask.

"Her breathing is weak," he explained, "we have to help her respiration."

"Doctor, is she in any danger?"

"She'll be all right now," he said and after a few minutes removed the mask. I noticed Toni was breathing more deeply and color was coming back to her cheeks. He added, "They first gave her a shot, then a massive dose. She's a lucky young woman. Only an anesthetist should use chloroform combined with another drug ... it can attack the respiratory system and cause cardiac arrest."

He listened to her heartbeat and timed her pulse with his wristwatch.

"May I ask who this woman is?"

"I don't want to give you a short answer, Doctor, and there's no time to go into details. There are wounded downstairs. What should I do when she comes around?"

"Nothing," he said, again the professional. "Don't give her a thing, especially liquids. If her respiratory system isn't active, she could choke. At first she'll appear dazed but gradually she'll come out of it. When she's perfectly clear give her some tea and toast. She'll probably have a terrible headache for a while. Let her rest." He added with irony, "No excitement."

Outside in the hall Stu asked, "How's Toni?"

"It was chloroform. She'll be out for a while, but the doctor said she'll be all right."

"Now if you show me the way to the other patients," Wallace said.

In the library he slipped on rubber gloves and carefully laid out his instruments on a towel.

He looked at Arnie.

"Is this gentleman first?"

"Take your pick, Doc," Rudy said.

When he removed the rough bandages from around Arnie's chest I could see along his ribs the double purplish bruises of a bullet hole.

"How is it, Doctor?" Stu asked.

"Well, let me say this, if you have to be shot, this is the best way" was Wallace's wry comment. He dressed the wound, gave Arnie a shot, and moved on to Rudy.

"There's a slug in your shoulder that must come out," he said.

"Sure, go ahead," Rudy said.

"Do you have any whiskey?" he asked Stu.

"There's a whole room full of it," Star said.

"Give him a bottle. I'll get back to him . . ."

Star went to the spirits room and returned with a quart bottle.

"Drink yourself silly, Fatso, this guy isn't foolin'," he said.

Rudy lifted the bottle and toasted Star.

"Here's to Custer," he said with a grin.

When Wallace removed the bandages from Tom's knee, he studied the wound for a moment then stood up.

"This man needs immediate hospitalization."

"I'm not going to leave here," Tom said flatly.

Wallace gave him a puzzled look.

"Why not, sir?"

"You wouldn't understand, Doctor," Tom said.

"But you could lose a leg, young man!"

"I'll take my chances."

"You should go to a hospital, Tom," Stu said.

"You'll have to kick me out first, Stu."

Stu looked at Wallace.

"Can you do something temporary, Doctor?"

"There's nothing temporary for a wound like this," he replied. "The bone is shattered and the cartilage torn. Undoubtedly there are fragments of the bullet which must be removed." He shrugged. "I can put on a dressing but if infection sets in . . ."

"Put on the dressing, Doctor," Tom said woodenly.

After he had cared for Tom's knee, Wallace removed Stu's blood-soaked shoe and sock; a slug had gone through the fleshy part of his leg.

Stu asked Wallace as he treated the wound, "What's going on outside, Doctor?"

310

"Well, you certainly put the town on the map," the physician informed us. "The television and newspaper people have taken all the rooms at the motel. I heard a bulletin on the car radio as I was coming over here."

"What did it say?"

"Well, at first they thought it was a robbery—"

"We're not thieves, Doctor!" Tom broke in. "Who the hell said that?"

"No, they corrected that. Now they say you were all former POWs. Is that right?"

"That's right."

"May I ask what you hope to gain by all this?"

"Justice," Stu said.

"For whom?"

"Perhaps for you, Doctor." He nodded to me. "Trev, you're next."

"You're lucky," Wallace said after he examined the hole in my upper arm.

"Why?"

"The slug just missed the axilla brachial plexus nerve."

"And if it hadn't?"

"Your arm would have been paralyzed" was his blunt reply.

"What about the police?" I asked him.

"There are more police outside than in ten St. Patrick's Day parades. There are also some government men. They have the roads blocked off and our chief asked New York for their police helicopter."

"What the hell for?" Star asked.

"Somebody said they're going to take pictures of the grounds," Wallace said.

"I hope they don't do anything foolish," Stu said.

"I'm a doctor, not a policeman," Wallace said. "Are there any more wounded?"

He followed us into the dining room where Sam had untied the two guards.

Wallace looked startled when he saw the body of the one who had been killed on the stairs.

"There are four more upstairs and another outside in the courtyard," Stu told him. "Perhaps you can suggest they send in a mortuary wagon."

Stu now spoke in an emotionless monotone. Curiously I felt the same way, dull and listless. The blazing battle in the house seemed as dim and faded as the bloodstains on the stair carpet.

Wallace silently examined the two guards. One pointed to Stu.

"Hey, Doc, this guy shot me in the shoulder for nothin'!"

Sam said roughly, "When was the last time you were busted for drugs?"

The guard glowered at him but remained silent. Wallace dressed his

311

wound and examined the other one, who had been knocked out by Rudy. He was not seriously hurt, only indignant.

Upstairs Wallace found Morenci had lost two fingers of his right hand and a great deal of blood.

"He needs hospitalization," Wallace told Stu.

"A temporary dressing will have to do," Stu said firmly.

"This man and the one downstairs are seriously wounded, sir," Wallace protested.

Star nodded to Morenci. "This bastard's lucky I didn't put a bullet in his head."

Wallace began, "You will have to assume the responsibility—"

Stu interrupted him impatiently, "It is my responsibility, Doctor. Please dress his wounds."

Wallace reluctantly treated Morenci's hand. Although he gritted his teeth and closed his eyes, Morenci didn't utter a sound.

Wallace abruptly asked him, "Are you Mr. Morenci?"

"Yes, I am," Morenci told him.

The old man looked up at Stu.

"The police chief told me this man is a respectable international contractor."

"Respectable he isn't—international contractor he is," Stu said. He kicked a glassine envelope toward Wallace—"Of this."

"What is it?"

"Don't you recognize it, Doctor? Heroin. There's enough on this floor to satisfy the habit of every junkie on the east coast. And most of his customers are school kids."

"Isn't there a law to take care of things like this?"

"We happen to believe the law isn't working too well these days, Doctor."

"Maybe it would be better to take the law that isn't working too well rather than the law"—he nodded to Stu's rifle—"that comes out of that."

"Eight years ago I would have believed that, Doctor," Stu told him, "but when I came back, I found a great many people had let this -" he patted the barrel of his rifle, "be their spokesman. The rest haven't done much about it . . . so I guess this is the way to make people listen."

After he had treated the guard in the factory for a slight flesh wound, Wallace bent over Mary who was still sitting on the top step of the stairway.

"Are you all right, Miss?"

"Yes, thank you, Doctor," she said with a wan smile.

We found Rudy and Star in the big ballroom. The lights were on, the drapes were closed, and Rudy was in the middle of the floor, swaying and dipping in a grotesque charade of a lone dancer. His eyes were half-closed, he was humming to himself, one hand held high, the other clutching the quart bottle of whiskey. Star leaned against the piano, cigarette smoke curling up about his impassive dark face.

"He said he had to have the last dance," he explained disgustedly.

By some trick of the light Rudy seemed lost in the vast emptiness of the mirrors while the shimmering crystal pears of the revolving chandeliers glowed green from the velvet paneled walls; the waxed parquet floor was a sheet of ice for this surprisingly graceful elephant of a man who swayed, dipped, and wheeled to the sweet flow of music from invisible violins.

Stu said quietly, "Come on, Rudy, the doctor's here."

"I was just having the last dance, Major," he said apologetically and took a long swig of the bottle. "Let's go, Doc."

"Just a big crazy bastard," Star said. But this time there was a note of affection in his voice.

In the library Wallace again spread out his instruments on a towel and slipped on the rubber gloves.

"I'm going to give you a local anesthetic just like you get when you have a tooth extracted," he said, picking up his forceps, "but I advise you to also suck on that bottle, young fellow . . ."

Rudy took a deep slug.

"This is the kind of prescription I like, Injun," he called out to Star.

But despite the liquor and the local, probing for the bullet was still excruciatingly painful. Rudy stopped talking. Sweat dripped off his pudgy pale face and the knuckles of both hands, which gripped the edge of the table and a chair, turned white.

Finally the doctor dropped the bloody slug on the table.

"Give me that bottle, Injun," Rudy said hoarsely. He toasted Wallace.

"Thanks, Doc."

After the doctor had bandaged Rudy, Stu and I escorted Wallace to the front door.

"Well, good luck," he said. "I don't know what you're after but I think you're going about it in the wrong way."

He walked down the driveway, a puzzled, disturbed old man.

A few hours later the bullhorn again shattered the stillness that lay over Grand Vista. The floodlights were still on and this time they told us the county coroner was coming in.

The gates opened and two ugly vans slowly drove up the driveway.

A thin man in black with long strands of hair carefully brushed to one side of his head, accompanied by two young and obviously curious assistants, walked into the entry hall.

Star, chewing on a cigar he had found and cradling the M-16, waved them against the wall where they were frisked by Sam. Then they quickly wrapped up the bodies in rubber sheets and slid them into the vans.

After they left Stu ordered the second floor shut off although Toni still remained in one of the bedrooms. The cutters and Morenci were put into the ballroom with Star on guard, and Mary joined us in the library where we watched Stu read his statement on TV. This was followed by brief bios of us and an interview with the night manager of the Eldorado who kept saying, "I don't believe it. I don't believe it."

It was weird staring back at a much younger picture of myself taken from the AP file stock and hearing my former city editor in Atlanta describe me as "an excellent writer and a fine fellow . . . but changed since he came back from Vietnam."

"Christ, they make it sound like your obituary," Arnie said when he saw himself in a college football jersey.

Then the scene shifted back to Grand Vista and a group of reporters hurrying down the road, thrusting mikes at Dr. Wallace and shouting questions at the old man who seemed happy to let the police push him into a radio car. But the coroner preened before the cameras as he gave a grisly account of the bodies he had carted off while to his constant irritation his two assistants kept interrupting to tell the reporters about the shattered interior and the "prisoners" who lay on the floor.

"Cornball stuff" was the comment of our television reporter in residence.

There was more then enough food so we put together a respectable supper; the guards and cutters cleaned their plates but Sam reported Morenci didn't touch anything.

"I tried to talk to him but he just stared at me," Sam said, "like he was cooking up something."

"If he makes any kind of move," Stu said shortly, "tell Star to kill him."

We locked the front doors and hung thick spreads over the shattered glass but the autumn chill still edged through the big house. Using the night glasses from the third floor, Star reported there were now twice as many newsmen, television crews, and cops gathered in the road at the front gates. I piled blankets on Toni and someone gave Mary a guard's coat. She put it on and huddled in a large leather chair before the fireplace in the library. At first she ignored her food, but after Arnie talked to her for a long time in a low voice she ate a sandwich and had tea.

When she finally fell asleep Arnie walked lopsidedly across the room to join me.

"You shouldn't be walking around with that hole in you, Arnie."

"As that old guy said, if you're going to be shot, this hole is better than most."

"How's Mary?"

"She's coming out of it. Stu gave her a rough time on the roof . . ."

"Do you think he meant it?"

"About throwing her off if she didn't talk? Definitely. And she knew it. How's Toni?"

"Still under. The doctor said it would be a couple of hours more."

He leaned his head back on the chair. In the glow of the dying fire his face looked greenish gray.

"About Cardillo, Trev," he said abruptly, "don't give him a second thought. This was not what we elected to do when we came back; it was done to us."

"We're not going to solve anything here, Arnie."

"You wanted to get in for Toni."

"And I'd do it again for the same reason but it was still a mistake, Arnie."

"It was a mistake," he conceded, "but it's done. It was a mistake that we waited too long. Coming back from Nam to what I found taught me one thing—it's a mistake to just endure because you think you can't escape or you don't understand. I'm not going to endure anymore nor am I going to accept. From now on it's got to be on my terms . . ."

"Maybe a time of making a choice is over, Arnie. We can't stand them off much longer."

"The Indians held out for seventy-one days at Wounded Knee. But we won't be here that long—"

"Why?"

"I told Stu that as soon as this trial is over, we should all pull out through the tunnel. They still don't know about it."

"How can you be sure?"

"Remember the switch Sam found? The water in the tunnel's back to normal. Our car is still over on the other hill. We could slip out at night and be miles away before they discovered we were gone."

"To keep running? To where? For how long?"

"Do you know how many fugitives there are in this world, Trev? South America's loaded with them. All you need is money and Stu has plenty overseas. We can come back when the dust settles—they'll never convict us."

"There were six dead men here, Arnie."

"But who were they? Innocent gardeners? Hell no!" He added disgustedly, "They all have records or Morenci wouldn't have allowed them past the gate. All we would need on a jury is one housewife who had trouble with drugs in her family. A good lawyer will throw these eight years in the Pit right in their faces. Hell, they'll give us a medal on the steps of City Hall."

"What about Morenci?"

"Well, what about him?"

"I asked Stu what happens if he believes Morenci is guilty."

"And what did he say?"

"We'll talk about it."

He lit a cigarette and in the tiny light of the match his face was

315

drained, weary. I was startled to see patches of white in the stubble along his jaw. But his eyes were cold and unwavering as he turned to me.

"I guess that's what we'll do, Trev—talk about it."

In the early hours of the morning, Stu arranged to deliver our "prisoners," as the reporters now called them, to the federal agents. It was eerie, watching him and Star on television escort the cutters and guards as they walked single file down the driveway.

At the gate a man in a topcoat holding up a wallet with a shield approached Stu.

"Are you Mr. Harlow?" he called out.

"Yes, I am," Stu replied.

"I'm Fredericks of the Department of Justice. Can we arrange a meeting, sir?"

"I don't think that is necessary, Mr. Fredericks."

"What about this trial you spoke of? Will we know when it's going to be held?"

"Sometime this evening in the dining room. The pool crew will make a televised record and the tapes will be sent down to you at intervals. Of course we insist they be put on the air immediately."

"I don't know if that's possible, Mr. Harlow."

"Well, you make it possible, Mr. Fredericks—or we'll stretch this thing out all month. Is that understood?"

In the brief silence the camera went from Fredericks to Stu; it was Fredericks who gave in.

"Very well, sir, we'll make sure the networks get the tapes. How they use them will be their decision. There is another thing—"

"That is?"

"The drugs. You told our representative you found a large amount of narcotics in the house."

"Did you test the sample?"

"We did, sir."

"And what did it show?"

"The powder in the envelope you gave our agent is heroin."

Stu pressed him. "Pure?"

"Yes sir. Can you give us an estimate of approximately how much you found?"

"One subject at a time, Mr. Fredericks. What would you say the potency of street heroin is today? A five-dollar bag?"

"Three to five milligrams of heroin."

"How much would you estimate was in the bag we gave you?"

Fredericks hesitated. Then he said, "Twenty to twenty-five."

"Would you call such bags 'catch-em' bags?"

"Well, in street language—"

316

Stu snapped, "Let's not deal in semantics, Mr. Fredericks. Would you call the bag we gave you a 'catch-'em bag,' which is used by pushers to recruit young addicts?"

Fredericks silently nodded.

"Would the dose in that sample bag be powerful enough to kill an inexperienced youngster?"

Again Fredericks nodded silently.

This time Stu shouted: "Dammit, Mr. Fredericks, don't nod, say it, man! Say it loud enough for the country to hear! Bags that we found in Morenci's cutting factory contain pure heroin, strong enough to kill a child who is inexperienced in handling drugs! Is that right or is that wrong?"

"That is true, sir," Fredericks said in a loud clear voice.

"Now you asked me to give you an estimate of approximately how much narcotics we found in Grand Vista," Stu said in a calmer voice. "The answer is slightly over five hundred pounds."

Fredericks looked startled. "Will you turn it over to us, Mr. Harlow?"

"Certainly," Stu said, "after we introduce it as evidence in Morenci's trial. At today's costs, Mr. Fredericks, how much do you think this cargo of drugs is worth?"

"Well, it is difficult to estimate—"

"Oh, come on," Stu said disgustedly. "If the drugs in the French Connection case were officially valued at seventy-five million would it be fair to say another twenty-five pounds would bring it up to near a hundred million?"

"I would say that would be a fair estimate."

"I told Dr. Wallace that there were enough drugs in this mansion to satisfy the habits of almost every junkie on the east coast. Do I exaggerate?"

"It's difficult to know exactly how many addicts there are, sir," Fredericks said uneasily.

Stu's strategy was plain—he was making the government representative act as an expert witness, not only for the millions of viewers but also for any future trials—if we were the defendants.

He finally let Fredericks change the subject.

"Are you turning these people over to us, Mr. Harlow?"

"Yes. As I told your representative we don't want hostages. But we would suggest you look into their police records. I assume you checked out the fingerprints on the guns we gave you."

"Yes sir. We have a report."

"Would you care to disclose what it shows?"

"Mr. Nicolai is Del Morenci as you claimed." He paused. "However, there are no criminal charges pending against him nor are there any warrants listed for his arrest, either here or in Europe."

"We are aware of that, Mr. Fredericks," Stu said smoothly, "that's one reason why we have decided to put him on trial. We suggest you view the evidence we introduce against him. There will be one very important witness—"

"We intend to monitor your proceedings, sir," Fredericks replied. He moved closer and said almost pleadingly, "Don't you think we should discuss this, Mr. Harlow."

"What is there to talk about?"

"We believe your evidence—"

Stu broke in with a flash of impatience, "We don't care what you believe."

"You could accomplish your purpose by turning Morenci over to us along with what evidence you have against him for due process."

"When we have finished presenting our case to the American public you can have him and all our evidence," Stu said.

Fredericks stood stock-still looking at Stu.

"I hope you realize a television spectacle will make it impossible to select a jury—"

Stu reminded him, "They tried Jack Ruby, didn't they?"

He motioned to the cutters and guards. Fredericks stepped aside as they passed him, hands on their heads. Beyond the gate men in plainclothes moved in. Then Stu and Star started to walk back up the driveway.

The camera followed them until they faded into the shadows, then returned to the announcer in the road:

"You have just witnessed the latest incident in this rather bizarre happening which some are already calling 'The Siege of Grand Vista.' A group of men, allegedly cutters and guards in a drug factory operating in this historic old mansion, have just been turned over to police and Department of Justice representatives by the leader of a group of vigilantes who earlier today raided and captured Grand Vista, which they claim is the headquarters for an international drug syndicate.

"To recap for those who have just tuned in, this story first broke late this afternoon when a man making a delivery to the house alerted police that a party of raiders, operating in an efficient military manner, had infiltrated the mansion and taken captive those inside, including the owner, who local police had initially said was a contractor who has done a great deal of work in Europe.

"The raiders, all former Vietnam POWs, were led by Stuart Fitzroy Harlow III, a prominent and wealthy New York hotel owner and realtor. The group has now been identified as seven former POWs who gained national attention some years ago as 'The Hounds of Tong Le Mai,' after their photograph, taken in a South Vietnam prison camp, was released by Hanoi and published throughout the United States.

"In a statement read to a pool television crew now inside Grand Vista, which was seen on national television a short time ago, Harlow said he and his companions hope to arouse the country by putting on television trial Pascal Nicolai, millionaire owner of Grand Vista, who Harlow insists is really Del Morenci, ex-convict and leader of the drug syndicate which has connections in Indochina, Marseilles, Corsica, Mexico, and Canada.

"This claim by Harlow appears to be correct. Just a few moments ago Norman Fredericks, special assistant attorney general in charge of federal strike force investigating narcotics in the metropolitan area, confirmed in a dramatic meeting with Harlow that Nicolai had been identified through fingerprints, supplied by the raiders, as Morenci, an ex-convict with a long criminal record for drug trafficking in the United States and Europe.

"However, Fredericks also pointed out to Harlow there are no known warrants or criminal charges pending against Morenci.

"Harlow answered Fredericks in this dramatic parley by suggesting he watch the proceedings of the televised so-called 'trial' and by the evidence they will produce against Morenci. The 'trial' will be held later this evening in the mansion's formal dining room. If this is true it will be a perfect setting for the drama now being played in this Gothic mansion built by a flamboyant Civil War hero who rode with Custer, dined with presidents, and became a power in nineteenth-century national politics.

"A pool television crew who taped Harlow's statement earlier this evening decided to remain behind and will televise Morenci's trial. Harlow has promised that the tapes of the proceedings will be forwarded to the front gates at intervals. They will be seen on this network as soon as they are processed."

The announcer then recapped Stu's charges that we had been "betrayed" by "elements" within the New York City Police Department and how the cargo of drugs had been moved from the Water Street warehouse by way of the abandoned sewer pipe. Mayor Kerr, he said, had rushed to City Hall where he was now conferring with the district attorney, Police Commissioner Fitzgerald, and his top aides. Suddenly he broke off to read a bulletin:

"This has just been handed to me. One of the six bodies removed earlier from Grand Vista has been identified through fingerprints as that of Frank Cardillo, a New York racketeer with a long police record for shylocking and narcotics arrests. Police who went to his last known address in Canarsie are now questioning his wife. It was unofficially reported that her sister is missing. As you recall, Dr. Wallace told police he had treated a young woman inside Grand Vista. Police say her description matches that of the girl treated by Dr. Wallace. This is a late bulletin and we will keep you in touch with developments as they come to us in the 'Siege of Grand Vista.' Now with us we have—"

The camera returned to the delivery man who had given the first alarm. By now he was a professional and repeated his story with a bored air as he turned without cue to the right camera.

The long night passed slowly. The house was still except for the wind moaning about the eaves; in the entry hall spreads covering the

319

shattered doors billowed with each gust. Morenci was asleep, his head on the dining room table. Sam, a rifle between his legs, sat in a corner. There was the sound of a typewriter in one of the rooms off the library where Stu was working on the statement Mary had given him. In the library Rudy's snores rose and fell, Tom was asleep on the couch and Star, a motionless shadow, stood guard by the window. Arnie was in a reclining chair near Mary, the tip of his cigarette a glowing arc as he flipped it into the fire.

After a while I went up to the second floor bedroom, switched on a night light and lay down beside Toni. I must have fallen asleep because I suddenly awoke with a start. It was still dark outside and Toni was regaining consciousness.

She moaned, moved her head, then opened her eyes. For a moment they widened and a scream caught in her throat.

"Toni! It's me—Trev."

She slowly relaxed and the terror went out of her face.

"Trevor! How did you get here?"

"We came in and got you. Don't worry, everything's all right. How do you feel?"

She closed her eyes and took a deep breath.

"My head feels light. They used chloroform. Someone held my arms but I could smell it . . ."

"Forget it, Toni. No one will ever hurt you again . . . never."

I slipped my arm under her shoulders and held her close.

"Oh, Trev, I kept thinking of you all the time when he was hitting me. I kept wishing you would come—"

"It's all over, Toni . . . don't think about it."

I touched her cheeks, they were wet.

"I love you, Toni . . . very, very much."

She lay still in my arms and I remembered that first day with the dull afternoon's slanting sun lighting up the tints on her hair and the tentative, shy smile.

After a while I said, "The doctor said when your breathing is all right you could have tea and toast."

"A doctor?" She looked up at me. "How did he get here?"

"We called him as soon as we found you, Toni. We were very worried about you."

She slowly lifted her head and I helped her sit up.

"God, I'm starting to have an awful headache," she whispered. "My throat is so dry. Could I have a glass of water, Trevor?"

"How about that tea?"

"Yes, maybe tea. I'm still woozy." She reached over to hold onto my arm and I winced.

"Trevor, you're hurt!" She felt the bandage. "What happened?"

"It's nothing. We'll talk about it later. I'll get the tea. How about toast?"

"You're not answering my question. Did the doctor come with the police?" Her eyes were clearing. She held on to me. "Frank caught me on the phone, Trevor."

"I know. We spoke to Teresa. We knew you were in here, that's why we came."

"You saw Teresa? Is she all right? The kids? He was a wild man when he caught me. He hit Teresa. He kept hitting me."

"Toni! Please!"

She went on in a low monotone. "He had been drinking all night, and when the phone rang I picked it up and heard a woman's voice say, 'The girl will pick up the bells this morning,' then hang up.

"I was so excited I never noticed that one of the kids, the four-year-old, had gotten out of bed and was standing near me by the bed. She's a sleepwalker and when I turned and saw her standing almost at my elbow like a tiny ghost in her nightgown, I dropped my hand that was covering the phone and let out a gasp. He heard it and I guess things clicked into place for him then. He came upstairs like a raging bull. The baby, yanked out of her sleep, began screaming. That woke Teresa who ran in just as he began beating me. Teresa tried to stop him but he was like a wild man. Did she call you?"

"Thank God she did or we wouldn't have known what happened."

"He dragged me downstairs, then he tore up some sheets and tied, gagged, and blindfolded me. After he made a phone call he pushed me into the trunk of the car. I was terrified. Once I heard a boat whistle and thought we were going on a ferryboat. That had to be Staten Island. After we stopped some men took me out of the trunk and put me into what I think was a small truck. Then we started riding again. I heard the gates and the water and knew we were back on the ferryboat. When we stopped they loaded the truck with boxes. I could feel them being piled around me.

"There was more driving before the truck stopped again. Something like a heavy door opened and closed. They unloaded the boxes and Frank got into the truck. He said I was going on a little trip and if I gave them any trouble they had orders to kill me. When he left I worked the blindfold so I could see out of a tiny slit. When the other men came, they loaded the boxes back onto the truck but in such a way I was completely hidden. Once I thought I heard a woman's voice.

"When we left this place we drove for a long time, I believe on a highway. We finally entered a garage where the truck was unloaded. After the others left Frank came and untied me. I was so cramped I could barely stand. He seemed very agitated and kept cursing me for a fool who had made trouble for him.

"When we reached the entry hall something told me I was in Grand Vista. There were drapes over the windows but I could see through the front door that it was still dark outside."

"Did you see anyone else besides Cardillo, Toni?"

"I'm coming to that. I recall we went up two flights of stairs, where a man met us and took us to a room at the end of a long hall. He knocked and went in, then came out in a few minutes and nodded to Frank who pushed me ahead of him.

"In this room there was a fireplace and a man sitting behind a desk. He was a good-looking man, I would say in his fifties. He was wearing a dark purplish brocaded smoking jacket.

"In the beginning he was polite, almost apologetic. He said something about how it was too bad we had to meet like this, but he had no alternative."

She squeezed my hand very hard.

"Then I noticed when he offered me a glass of wine that the fingertip of the middle finger of his right hand was missing."

"Morenci."

"I told him I didn't want any wine but I did want to go home and he just smiled and shook his head.

" 'Frank tells me you've been listening in on his phone calls, young lady,' he said.

"Of course I denied it but Frank told Morenci how he had found me." She added disgustedly, "How stupid that was!"

I kissed her and begged her not to go on but she refused.

"Morenci was still very polite. He asked me if I had given the police any information on the warehouse and of course I denied that. I kept telling him all I had wanted to do was make a personal phone call.

"Then he offered me money if I would tell them what I was doing with the information I learned on the phone. When I kept telling him I didn't know what he was talking about, he became angry and shouted to Frank that I must be the one who gave the cops the information about the warehouse. Then he said that if he had the time he would make me talk. He went out but returned in a few minutes to sit behind the desk. This time he didn't say anything, just kept staring at me.

"I thought I heard the door behind me open. When I saw Frank look over my shoulder I started to turn around. That's when someone jabbed me with a hypodermic needle and I smelled chloroform. I guess I became hysterical because I know what both can do. I was screaming but Frank held my arms and from behind someone put a towel over my face. I tried to hold my breath but it wasn't any use. As I went under I heart Morenci tell Frank to take me down the hall . . ."

Her voice was low and muffled.

"He said first came the business, then the pleasure. He said before they got rid of me he was going to have a party—just me and him. Frank laughed and said now he wouldn't be first."

I found myself wishing I had not killed Cardillo so easily.

She put her face in the pillow and wept. In between sobs she told me she was ashamed of herself for crying—in the last second of consciousness she wondered how I would ever know how much she loved me. . . .

Chapter **12**

Sam Hoffman- Judgment

We couldn't have been happier when Trev came down and told us Toni had regained consciousness, and with the exception of a horrible headache she apparently had not suffered any reaction from the drugging.

"If we had moved in on that truck they would have killed her," Arnie pointed out after Trev told us Toni's story of how she had been taken to Grand Vista.

It was one good piece of news after a long night. I had been relieved of guarding Morenci by Star and although I grabbed a few hours I was wound up, apprehensive, fearful of what this morning would bring, and still trying to figure out how this *nebech* from Bensonhurst was sitting in the library with a million books, six unshaven guys who looked as beat as I felt, and a chink dame who had been a beauty yesterday but now looked like the exhausted wife of a West Side laundryman.

After a quick breakfast we waited to hear Stu go over with Mary the statement she had given him and Arnie in the courtyard. He had just opened a thick folder when the bullhorn sounded and Star came in and said Fredericks of the Department of Justice wanted to parley with Stu.

They met in the middle of the driveway. Out in the road we could see the television cameramen clambering to the tops of their trucks while the newspaper photographers poked their lenses through the spaces in the fence. Flashbulbs went off, one with a loud bang that made a TV technician duck, to the laughter and jeers of the photographers below.

Stu and Fredericks spoke briefly, then shook hands. Stu came back up the driveway briskly as if he had made a sudden decision.

"What did Uncle Sam want?" Arnie asked.

"He promised that if we would turn Morenci over to them along with the drugs and surrender ourselves and our weapons they would immediately present all the evidence we have to a federal grand jury."

"And what did you tell him?"

"I told him that any one of you was free to leave at any time." He looked around at us, then went on. "I also told him that after all this time a few days more wouldn't make much difference. They will get Morenci and all the evidence we have against him—but only after we put him on trial." He picked up his folder. "I don't think we should wait until this evening. Let's start now."

"Did anything that Fredericks said change your mind about holding it tonight, Major?" I asked.

"He said he's under pressure to get this thing over with and he can't hold out much longer. I think those TV comments about how we have beaten them on their own investigation is starting to get under Washington's skin."

"Do you think they'll really move in?"

"That would be stupid on their part," Arnie said. "Don't they realize a couple of dead POW heroes as against some narcotics racketeers won't sit well with the public?"

"And the public doesn't exactly love Washington these days," Stu pointed out. "I brought that to his attention, but he said he was worried the county cops might try to come in alone. I told Fredericks that would be unfortunate."

"Very unfortunate," Star pointed out.

"How's Morenci?" Stu asked him.

"He sits there and we glare at each other," Star said.

"Who's with him now?"

"Rudy. He insists he's okay."

"And what did Morenci say?"

Star nodded to Mary. "There's a lady present."

"Mary, we're going to start the trial now," Stu told her. "Are you willing to repeat exactly what you told us?"

"Yes," she said in a low voice.

"I'll base my questions on your statement," he said, holding up the folder. "We don't have time to go over it but"— he gave us a grim smile—"it answers a lot of our questions. Where's Trev?"

"He took something up to Toni."

"Sam, tell him we're going to start in a few minutes. If Toni feels strong enough she might want to come down."

"Will she be a witness, Stu?" Arnie asked.

"No. Neither will you. There's no reason to bring out the Agency stuff. I'll describe the Indochina background, then lead into the warehouse business."

"Do you have the film, tapes, photostats, and the other stuff?"

He patted the folder. "Everything's here." He broke off and asked Star, "Are you sure Rudy's okay?"

"Fatso insists he's fine, Major," Star said. "Do you want me to take over again?"

"No, you take the third floor front window, Star," Stu ordered, "and keep an eye on those gung ho cops. Sam, you keep an eye on Rudy."

"What about Tom, Stu?" Arnie wanted to know.

"He's not too good," Stu said shortly. "He's in one of the rooms down the hall. I tried to get him to leave, but he insists on staying. He's one of the reasons I want to get this thing finished. Where's our demon television team?"

"Setting themselves up in the dining room," Star said.

"They're not taking anything of Morenci, are they?" Stu asked quickly.

Star took an electrical plug from his pocket.

"They're not in business unless they have this."

"Would Morenci talk to them?" I asked.

"Sure. In four letter words."

"Well, are we set?" Stu asked briskly.

"Let's go," Arnie said.

"Star, you're upstairs—"

"Right Major, I'm on my way."

"And, Sam, you talk to Trev and Toni . . ."

Toni was finishing a piece of toast when I entered the upstairs bedroom. She looked pale and drawn, and the bruises on her face and arms were starting to turn an ugly purple. When I gave them Stu's message Trev shook his head.

"Toni had better stay here for a while, Sam, she's still woozy."

"I'll be all right in a few hours," she protested. She added, a puzzled look on her face, "What's going on downstairs, Sam?"

"Stu is making a statement on television," Trev said with a glance at me.

"What kind of statement? I don't understand."

"It's about what drugs have done to this country," I put in.

"Sam, what's wrong?" she pleaded. "Something's wrong! I asked Trevor and he won't tell me."

"Nothing's wrong, Toni," Trev said gently. "Everything is—"

"But everything is not all right," she protested. "Don't treat me like a child. I want to know. Thy police are outside—why don't they come in? Where's Frank? And Morenci?"

"Morenci is downstairs, Toni. He's going to be turned over to the federal people."

"And Frank?"

I looked at Trev—he would have to take care of that department. He took a deep breath. "I killed him, Toni."

She closed her eyes and shuddered.

"Oh, God," she said. "I didn't want this."

"None of us did," Trev said wearily.

"Is there an answer to all this, Sam?" she asked, trying to hold back the tears. "If there is, do you happen to have it handy? Trevor doesn't."

I said, "Don't count on me, Toni. It's been a bad time but it won't last much longer . . ."

"It's my fault," she said.

"It's nobody's fault," Trev told her, "something went wrong."

What went wrong? rattled around in my head, as I went back downstairs. What had twisted and mutilated our high purposes and made us do the things we never wanted to do? Are we fighting another stupid, separate war with no future? I felt as if we were all on the sloping deck of the *Titanic* with "Nearer My God to Thee" loud in our ears. . . .

The ad hoc trial of Del Morenci took place at 10:00 A.M. in the dining room of Grand Vista with Lord Muttonchops glaring down from the wall as if he was impatiently waiting for the butler to come and sweep this human garbage from his sacred precincts.

The heavy drapes had been pulled aside with devastating results. The fall sunshine revealed hairline cracks in the plaster, the debris of battle, and faded carpet. Even Muttonchop's face was seamed and flaking. When I had first seen Grand Vista, the mansion had appeared romantic, mysterious, but now the crisp, cruel light made the place look like a grande dame caught by surprise without her corset—sagging, pathetic, violated.

Stu insisted the room have the sparse, stern, judicial look of a courtroom, so we pushed the big table to the rear and brought in a smaller one for him and two heavy captain's chairs for Mary and Morenci.

Morenci spoke only once and that was to call us "a bunch of crazy bastards."

Stu had one touch I thought was good; we lined twelve empty chairs along one side of the room; as he explained, every viewer was a juror.

I also set up a very expensive portable movie outfit and tape recorder from the rec room; we would show the films Tom and Trevor had taken of kids buying narcotics at the Lunch Box wagons. The recorder would play the tapes we had made—the statement of Adolph's girl friend, Stash's confession, Mary's taped telephone calls to Lennis.

Stash. I wondered how Stu would get around that part of the story . . . ?

The television cameraman and reporter sat off to the left with a clear view. Rudy, armed with the M-16, was stationed alongside Morenci's chair, just outside camera view. Arnie and I remained in the back of the room. I wanted to bring in one of the big reclining chairs from the library, but Arnie refused and insisted on leaning against the table. It was evident he was in a great deal of pain.

"When I sit down," he explained, "I find it almost impossible to get up."

"Dammit, you should be in a hospital and so should Rudy and Tom," I told him.

"Let's finish what we started, Sam," he said quietly.

We found a Bible in the library and put it on Stu's desk along with a yellow legal pad and a pitcher of water. It looked as solemn as the Supreme Court.

Adults playing a deadly game of make-believe? No, at the time it seems to me we were serious at what we were doing. Yet I think that no one who saw it ever forgot our play-acting courtroom. Stu was right, it helped millions of viewers believe they were actually sitting in the jury box.

Stu opened with an explanation of the proceedings:

"What we are holding here this morning can be called either a commission of inquiry or a 'shadow trial,' " he said. "I prefer the latter description. It is not new here or in Europe. In fact the 'shadow trial' is an especially American institution which has been frequently invoked in cases where a miscarriage of justice is alleged to have taken place or to be intended; in Europe it was widely used by groups in the years before World War II. A celebrated one was organized in London following Berlin's Reichstag Fire trial.

"Another one was held in New York in 1946 when a group of American airmen and officers who had been rescued by General Drazha Mihailovich of Yygoslavia, but who had been refused permission to testify during the general's puppet trial in Belgrade, decided to hold their own 'trial' in New York City. Not only the flyers testified but also several prominent individuals and Washington statesmen.

"However, this is not a political 'shadow trial' but an attempt to dramatize what is happening inside our own country. We hope we can persuade you something is very wrong with our society and what is wrong should be corrected.

"Perhaps the very fact that we are here is one of the wrongs. Why are we here? What brought us to this room? You, the American public, who will tonight sit as jurors in these empty seats, must supply that answer . . ."

He held up the Bible.

"This is not a court of law, the proceedings that take place here have no legal standing nor are any oaths binding. However, if they wish, witnesses may swear on this Bible to confirm their goodwill and integrity."

With the aid of a map we had removed from an atlas, he sketched the political situation in Burma, how the Burmese Communist Party had taken over the government garrisons at Mongyank and were fighting on the outside of the large city of Kentung, the irregulars equipped with AK-47 rifles, howitzers, and machine guns brought from China's Yunan Province, just across the border. Then he briefly went into the opium-crop area of Burma, Laos, and Thailand, the historic "Golden Triangle" of the Far East, which supplied much of the drugs smuggled into the United States, and how the United States was putting pressure on Burma's president, General U Ne Win, to do something about the opium crop or face the loss of aid.

He explained how the two Nationalist generals, with remnants of the Kuomintang army which fled China at the time of the takeover, controlled the region's enormously rich opium crop and were smuggling cargoes under protection of the BCP into Thailand, Laos, and South Vietnam. From there the drug was refined in Marseilles, then brought into the United States by way of Mexico, South America, or Canada. Combined with Turkey's renewed opium-growing program, these cargoes of heroin could create a whole new generation of American drug addicts.

After Indochina, he told the story of how the organized crime Families had outwitted the intelligence agencies of both the United States and Canada to hold their meeting and vote to return to the smuggling and sale of illegal drugs in this country. It was at this meeting, Stu said, that an international drug dealer from Corsica named Del Morenci was selected to head the world's largest drug syndicate.

The customers?

He nodded to me and I closed the drapes, put up the screen, and started the movie films with Stu acting as narrator. There was one harrowing shot: two kids running from the Lunch Box Wagon stopped alongside the car where Trev and Tom were sitting and unwrapped the "sandwich." The glassine envelope dropped out, the camera zoomed in on the kid's hand picking it up. At that moment I froze the frame and Stu said simply:

"The customers of this ring were schoolchildren."

After I had pulled back the drapes he showed photostats we had obtained at the medical examiner's office of the death certificates of

328

the kids who had died of OD, then we ran off the tape-recorded statement of Adolph's blonde girl friend.

There was no table pounding, shouting, or purple prose on Stu's part, he simply recited the facts in a brisk simple manner. It didn't take a genius to realize what he was doing: carefully laying the groundwork for the introduction of Morenci, Miles, Derby, and the rest of our cast. Morenci? He still didn't blink an eye. In fact once he yawned. I was glad to see the young cameraman was alert enough to catch it.

After a brief recess, Stu came to Morenci. He introduced his criminal record in New York, pointing out that his mug picture was mysteriously missing and followed up with the stuff we had obtained in Paris. Then he held up Morenci's ugly portrait and the sketch of the missing fingertip.

While the camera swung to Morenci Stu told the audience to look for the tiny lines, evidence of his face-lifting operation, and the missing fingertip.

Morenci continued to look bored. In a way I agreed with him; if it was a crime to have a face job done, half of Park Avenue would be in jail . . .

Police pictures of Cardillo and Stash along with their police records followed.

The Five Boro Anti-Narcotics League, its origin and goals, came next. In his folder Stu even had a notorized accounting of the monies spent for the league.

He told, without mentioning Toni's name, how we had received the inside information about the warehouse and how it was turned over to Mayor Kerr and Police Commissioner Fitzgerald. Stu introduced letters and reports sent to him by Kerr or Fitzgerald acknowledging the work of the league and its accomplishments—over one hundred thousand dollars spent and one pusher sent to jail for six months for parole violation despite the state's supposedly "tough" drug laws.

The films I had copied from the cops' teams watching the warehouse were rolled, showing the cutters arriving and leaving along with the panel truck delivering the cargo of narcotics.

The scorecard after the raid: Cardillo was arrested on a vague conspiracy charge and released on low bail. Not one ounce of drugs was confiscated.

There was a brief silence, then Stash's voice filled the darkened room. It was the first time Morenci showed any emotion. I thought he would leap from the chair, but he quickly gained control of himself.

But in that brief moment I shivered as I had done the first time I saw his portrait in Colonel Bouquet's office. Maybe it's melodramatic to say but I had never seen such evil on any man's face and that's including a lot of Charlies in Nam who stepped on my toes and generally clobbered me to keep their hands in.

The gravelly voice detailed how the syndicate worked and how he brought the money from the sale of drugs to schoolchildren to the Forty-fourth Street office of Bernie Lennis—Lennis, who he once saw enter a neighboring office—the Indochina Importing Company.

"Bernie is going to have plenty on his mind tonight," Arnie said softly.

Now it was time for Mary.

She insisted on being sworn in and Stu gave her the Bible.

"Do you solemnly swear that what you will testify here today will be the truth, the whole truth, and nothing but the truth?"

"I do."

I now quote from the stenographic record made by the Department of Justice which they later released to the press.

Q. Your name?

A. Mary Chang Winslow.

Q. Obviously there is no need for addresses, Mary, but can you tell us something about your background?

A. I was born on the South China coast. My mother's family was in importing, my father was an officer in the Kuomintang Army. When the Communists took over the mainland we didn't hear from him and presumed he was dead. My mother took me to Hong Kong, where she started an importing business. Later she married Captain Richard J. Winslow, an American naval officer, and we came to San Francisco.

Q. And your stepfather, Captain Winslow, died?

A. Yes, while I was in my junior year at U.C.L.A. My mother then opened a small importing company in San Francisco's Chinatown.

Q. Did you ever again hear what had happened to your natural father after the fall of China?

A. My mother received a letter from him. He is in Indochina.

Q. After your stepfather died did you continue college?

A. Yes, I received a B.A. degree from U.C.L.A. and later a masters in social sciences from Columbia University. I have more than half my credits for a Ph.D."

Q. When did you come to New York?

A. About four years ago.

Q. During that time did you meet anyone you knew from San Francisco?

A. Frank Miles. His family also owned an importing company in Chinatown and our families knew each other very well. In fact we went to high school together.

Q. What was your relationship?

A. He was my lover.

Q. Did you ever discuss marriage?

A. Yes, many times. But he always said he wanted to get his foot in the right door in the PD before he thought of raising a family.

Q. What did he mean by the PD?

A. The New York City Police Department.

330

Q. What job did he have at that time you met him in New York?

A. Captain in the bureau of intelligence.

Q. Did he ever mention a police officer named Brigadier?

A. Yes. He was a former police commissioner. Sonny—that's Frank's nickname—called Brigadier his rabbi.

Q. Was Miles subsequently promoted?

A. Yes. To inspector in charge of the new narcotics bureau.

Q. Did he ever talk of money?

A. Money was his favorite subject. Once he said he could never get enough of it. But he also said many times that cops who sold themselves for a few thousand dollars were fools. He said if he sold out it would only be to the highest bidder.

Q. Did he ever give his views about the police department?

A. He was always talking about when he would 'put in his papers,' as he called it. He said it was then that he would really start to live.

Q. Were you included in those plans, Mary?

A. Yes—in the beginning.

Q. Did he change his mind?

A. No—I did.

Q. Was there a reason?

A. I grew to hate him. He wasn't the same man I knew in San Francisco.

Q. In what way, Mary?

A. I really can't explain it. I was surprised when I first met him in New York. I hadn't seen him for some time. He even dressed differently and had different types of friends from those we knew back home. I would call them, well, rich swingers. He was always partying. In fact, when his father died on the coast, he didn't bother to attend the funeral.

Q. And did there come a time when you decided to break off your relationship?

A. Yes. He used to tell me stories about a fat bartender named Carlos whom he used as an informer. He considered it quite funny that he kept promising this man he would get him on the police department although the poor man was so fat it was impossible for him to pass any physical tests. Then one night someone called him at my apartment and told him Carlos had been recruited as an informer by a federal agent. He was furious and told whoever had called him that he was not to worry, he would take care of that fat slob. About three weeks later the same party called him, it was a man, and Sonny told him to meet him in a bar. When he returned it was evident that he had been drinking. He boasted that he had arranged for a drug pusher to be told that the bartender was a police informer. He said they had just found the body of Carlos in a car trunk. He kept laughing as he described how they had to saw away part of the trunk to remove his body.

Q. What was your reaction, Mary?

A. It sickened me to listen to him. That night I told him I was through with him.

Q. Did you break off your relationship?

A. No.

Q. Why did you keep seeing him?

A. He threatened me.

Q. Physically?

A. Physically—and in other ways.

Q. We will get to that phase in just a moment, Mary. Before the incident of the bartender, Carlos, did Miles take you to an East Side bar to meet a stranger?

A. Yes.

Q. How did that come about?

A. I hadn't seen Sonny for a few weeks when one night he came over. He looked very tired and said he and a special team of detectives had been working on a case of two young boys who had died of an overdose of extraordinarily pure heroin. During the investigation he had discovered a new drug syndicate was selling narcotics to schoolchildren throughout the city. Several days after that there were stories in the newspapers and on television about the case and how the city council had started an investigation of drugs in the schools. Then one night Sonny took me to a place called Barco's Lounge near Lexington Avenue and there we met a man named Pat Nicolai.

Q. Is that man in this room, Mary?

A. Yes.

Q. Can you point to him?

For a moment Mary hesitated then slowly turned to Morenci. It was a tensely dramatic moment in that quiet room and I never forgot it: Mary, pointing a trembling finger at Morenci who glared at her, the television reporter hurriedly making notes while his camerman swung from Mary to Morenci; Arnie, gripping the edge of the table as he leaned slightly forward; Stu, a grim look of triumph on his face as he handed Mary a glass of water.

Q. And he was introduced to you by Miles as Pat Nicolai?

A. That is correct.

Q. Did he subsequently tell you the man he introduced to you as Nicolai was actually Del Morenci?

A. Yes. Much later.

Q. At the time of your first meeting what did Miles tell you about this stranger?

A. Sonny said he was an importer who once had a firm in Hong Kong. During that first dinner we talked a lot about Hong Kong, and it was evident he knew the city, the importing business, and a great deal about Indochinese politics, especially in Burma.

Q. Did you see him again?

A. Yes. Several times.

Q. Each time you had dinner at Barco's Lounge?

A. Yes. With Sonny.

Q. Did you know the reason?

A. At first Sonny told me he was trying to work out a business deal with this man—something to do with importing and opening a New York office.

Q. Did you consider this strange—an inspector in the police department discussing an importing business deal?

A. No. Sonny's family was well known in San Francisco's Chinatown as importers. We both worked in our family's businesses when we were going to high school. He had told me many times that after he retired he would like to open an importing company and do most of the traveling himself.

Q. Did he finally tell you the truth?

A. Yes. One night he said he had finally sold out to the highest bidder and that bidder was Del Morenci. When I asked him who that was, he said, the man I knew as Pat Nicolai.

Q. Did he give you any details?

A. He said Morenci was operating what was probably the world's biggest drug syndicate and was ready to bring several big loads of drugs into the United States. I was shocked. At first I couldn't believe what he was telling me. Then he said I was going to work with them.

Q. What was your reaction to that, Mary?

A. I was horrifed. I told him I would never have anything to do with drugs and I insisted he leave. A few weeks later he pushed his way into my apartment and said he had to wait for a phone call. After he received the call he told me the story of that man Carlos, who was murdered. He said he could easily arrange for that to happen to me but he had something better.

Q. Did you learn what he meant by that threat?

A. Yes. A few nights later my mother called. She was almost hysterical. I managed to get out of her that she had come home a short time before after seeing a relative off to Hawaii. As she opened the door and switched on the light she was grabbed by two men and pushed into a chair. One was middle-aged, the other she recognized as a young hoodlum who had a bad reputation in Chinatown and was known to be in drugs. This man held a knife to my mother's throat while the older man, speaking in our dialect, told her that unless she got me on the telephone immediately, she would be killed. She told me this and then turned the phone over to the man who was doing the talking. Still speaking in our dialect he asked me if I loved my mother and if I wanted to see her again. By this time I was frantic. Of course, I said, I would do anything or pay all the money I had to make sure she wasn't harmed. The man said he wasn't interested in my mother but he was in something else—my word of honor that I would work with Sonny Miles. Of course, I said yes and he told me to go at once to Sonny's apartment, that very minute, tell him the same thing, and then to have Sonny call him at my mother's apartment.

Q. Did he warn you about going to the police?

A. He told me my mother would be cut up into little pieces if I called the police.

Q. When you reached Miles's apartment did you promise to work for him?

A. Yes. And then he called my mother's apartment and spoke to the man. After that they let me talk to my mother. The next night I had dinner with Sonny and Morenci at Barco's Lounge, and they told me they were opening an importing company on Fifth Avenue and Forty-fourth Street and I was to be the manager. This company was to deal in oriental curios and expensive museum artifacts from Indochina.

Q. What part did the company play in his drug operations?

A. We were in direct communication with an importing company in Hong Kong. They in turn transmitted and received messages from the Burma interior.

Q. What were the messages?

A. As to when a cargo of drugs was ready to be shipped out and when a courier was to proceed to Mandalay, then on to Shan State with the money.

Q. Who was that courier, Mary?

A. I was.

Q. In other words you picked up an amount of money in New York, then flew to—

A. No. I first flew to Las Vegas where I received the money.

Q. Where in Las Vegas?

A. At the offices of the International Vending and Amusement Machines Company. They occupy a suite in a hotel there.

Q. After you picked up the money at the vending company did you then fly to Hong Kong?

A. From the west coast.

Q. And from there you went into Burma?

A. Yes. From Mandalay to Mongyang, which had been taken by the Burmese Communist Party. When the government troops regained the city last winter, I met my contact in Mandalay.

Q. What made them select you, Mary?

A. The person I was dealing with spoke only the Chiu Chow dialect, which I speak.

Q. Was there another reason, more important than speaking a dialect, Mary?

Tears slowly trickled down her cheeks as she closed her eyes.

A. Yes. The man I gave the money to was my father, the man they call General Chang Pi.

I looked at Arnie. He was staring at Mary, a stricken look on his pale, drawn face.

"Arnie! For crissakes, is this true?" I whispered.

He nodded.

"When the hell did you find that out?"

"Remember when I told you I was looking for a reason why she was in drugs?" he said bitterly. "Stu got it out of her on the roof."

During the brief pause as Mary wiped away the tears and sipped a glass of water, I was startled to see the shadows on the wall were lengthening; I looked at my watch, it was late afternoon. Then Stu continued his questioning:

Q. Why did you give your father the money?

A. He and another Kuomintang officer have controlled the opium crop of northeastern Burma since 1955. Three years ago the Burmese Communist Party launched an attack on he main garrison at Kunlong in northeastern Burma. President U Ne Win who heads the Rangoon government ordered my father and the other officer to join his army and fight the Communist forces. My father refused and instead moved his people into Shan State across the Salween River.

Q. Why did he do this?

A. He told me that once he joined the government he would lose the opium crop because the farmers don't care about politics, they only want to get paid.

Q. But isn't Shan State controlled by the Burmese Communist Party?

A. My father and the other officer made an agreement with the BCP leaders to give them a part of the profits. They also allowed their troops to join the raid last year on the big government garrison at Mongyang.

Q. Your father and the other Kuomintang officer have an army?

A. More than a thousand soldiers. They are armed with weapons supplied by the Chinese leaders of Yunnan Province just across the border or stolen from the munition dumps left behind by the American forces in South Vietnam.

Q. Is the drug traffic profitable?

A. The last time I saw my father he showed me boxes of gold bars and bags of rubies and emeralds which he said had come back with the last caravan to Thailand.

Q. What was your reaction when you heard your father was in the drug traffic?

A. The first time I heard it from my mother I cried all night.

Q. Did you ever talk to your father about it?

A. He seemed surprised that I was disturbed he was in drugs. One time before I left he took me to see the opium fields and he spoke to some of the farmers. They regard growing opium as our farmers do tobacco and cotton. They have been doing this for generations and my father said they will never quit.

Q. Did you have anything to do with the negotiations for the cargo of drugs?

A. No. I was the courier. Arrangements were always made before I left the country. A business letter in code was sent by the vending machine company in Las Vegas to a financial house somewhere in the Bahamas—I really don't know the name of this company—and from the Bahamas an order was sent to an importing company in Hong Kong. They in turn sent it on to their people in Mandalay who delivered the message to my father in northeastern Burma. I picked up the money and delivered it to my father. If I couldn't meet him I delivered the money to his representative who would meet me at my hotel in Mandalay. Lately it has been getting very dangerous. The frontier police have many spies. The last time I was there a friend of my father's in the Communist Party, who had been watching out for me, warned me to leave my hotel at once for the airport where they had booked a passage for me to Hong Kong. Later I learned the police had raided my hotel room a few hours after I left.

Q. Was there anything unusual about this last cargo?

A. It was the largest ever taken out of Burma, according to my contact in Hong Kong. He said it was leaving Burma in several caravans and would involve many people in smuggling it into Marseilles.

Q. How was it to come to the United States?

A. I don't know all the details, like names—Sonny only told me so much—but I understood the entire cargo was five hundred pounds of heroin and cocaine and took several months getting to Mexico or South America in parcels brought in by airline personnel, seamen, and a diplomat who was paid twenty thousand dollars to bring a package in his diplomatic pouch. Also some came in the diplomat's car, which had a double roof. Sonny told me they brought the drugs in by fast planes from Mexico flying under the Customs radar system, and from Canada.

Q. Where eventually was the cargo assembled?

A. In the Indochina Importing Company on West Forty-fourth Street.

Q. Was the attorney, Bernard Lennis, aware of all this?

A. Bernie knew everything that I did. Many times he delivered money from Morenci to the vending machine company in Las Vegas so it could be "laundered" as he called it, through the Bahamas financial connection.

Q. After a cargo of drugs arrives in the United States, how is it distributed around the country?

A. Several months ago at one of our dinners in Barco's, Morenci was very upset because a load of drugs had been found hidden under a tire by a state trooper in Arizona. He said that from now on he was going to move the drugs from point to point by more sophisticated means. Now in the west the drugs are transported by horse vans.

Q. By horse vans?

A. There are usually three horses in the van, along with a bin of oats. The drugs are hidden in the oats.

Q. How was this big cargo delivered to Grand Vista?

A. I must first explain that the Indochina Importing Company had a legitimate business selling Far Eastern antiques to museums and private collectors. One of our specialties was silver temple bells, some hundreds of years old. It was Morenci's idea to use bells as a method of transporting the drugs from New York to any eastern or midwestern city.

Q. Can you tell us how this was done?

A. The Hong Kong office employs a very old man who is an expert counterfeiter of Far Eastern antiques. As it was explained to me when I was there, he would cast a spurious bell in three stages; the core, the dummy, and what he terms the cope. The core is made of bricks wired together and then coated with clay. Over that goes a wax dummy of the real antique bell with symbols and lettering added to the wax. The cope, which is a canopylike covering, is then placed over the dummy to shape the bell. When this is done the dummy is carefully removed leaving a space between the cope and the core where molten alloy is poured to form the bell itself.

However, at Morenci's orders the old man molded the bell but left it hollow. This was the master bell. Duplicates were then taken to our importing offices and filled with drugs. They were delivered around the country in this fashion.

Q. Did they appear to be legitimate antiques?

A. It is very difficult to know the difference when they are in boxes. Only the weight.

Q. Now, Mary, we are coming to a very important part of your testimony. When you returned the last time from Burma, were you met by Inspector Miles?

A. That is correct.

Q. How did he appear?

A. He was very excited.

Q. Before we go on, I would like you to make clear why you had gone this last time to Burma.

A. To deliver the money to my father's representative in Mandalay.

Q. And this was for the big drug cargo—the one they said was the largest ever to come out of Burma?

A. That is correct. It was to come by stages in many ways.

Q. But eventually the entire cargo would be assembled at one central point—your office on Fifth Avenue and Forty-fourth Street—and then put into the hollow silver bells and brought here to Grand Vista. Is that correct?

A. That is correct. The cutting mill was upstairs on the second floor.

Q. And there the drugs were cut and distributed to many American cities?

A. Yes.

Q. Did you find out why Miles was so excited when he met you at the airport?

A. Yes. He said he had finally made the deal he had always dreamed of making. He said he had arranged for Morenci to finance the mayoralty campaign of George Horatio Derby. He was going to resign from the police department and join Derby as an advisor. He intended

337

to write a white paper on narcotics in the city and really raise hell, as he put it, over drugs in the schools and crime in the streets.

Q. How did he intend to do that?

A. He said he had copies of all the reports he had made to Fitzgerald, the police commissioner, and he could use them to accuse the mayor of keeping the lid on the drug situation in the schools. He said he had written many of them with just this idea in mind.

As Mary reached for the glass of water I suddenly remembered Trev quoting Miles at their first meeting; how he boasted he had put everything in writing to the PC.

Mary appeared exhausted but when Stu suggested a recess she insisted they continue.

Q. In making drug conditions in the schools a campaign issue, wasn't Miles endangering his own operation in the police department, Mary?

A. No. He said they had everything so well covered not even the federal strike force knew Morenci was the head of it. He also said the people who were behind Morenci had excellent connections and if anything started to go wrong they would hear about it.

Q. What did Miles hope to get out of persuading Morenci to finance Derby's campaign?

A. He said with a lot of money to spend, Derby could walk into City Hall. He said the people were fed up with Mayor Kerr and he wouldn't be hard to beat. After Derby got in, he would appoint Brigadier for one year, then he would resign and Sonny would be made police commissioner.

Q. And how would that benefit Morenci?

A. Sonny said they would then own the city.

Q. What did you say to Miles at this time?

A. I told him I couldn't go on. I was finished.

Q. What did he say to this?

A. He said he was the one who would decide when I could quit. He warned me that if I crossed him he would not only have my mother killed but I would join her. I was frantic. I didn't know what to do. I finally decided to tell my mother the whole story. She was horrifed and begged me not to have anything more to do with Miles or my father; she said she would rather be dead. We sat in her apartment all night, two frightened women, wondering what to do. Finally we agreed on a plan—she would join our relatives who lived in a remote section of Hawaii and I would leave the country.

Q. Where did you intend to go?

A. I planned to accompany the man I love on his overseas assignment to China.

Q. May I ask who that man is?

She bowed her head for a long moment and when she raised it, her cheeks were wet with tears.

A. He is one of your friends, Mr. Harlow. I knew him as Clint Fontaine.

338

Q. Do you know his true identity now, Mary?

A. Yes. His name is Arnie Harper.

I was stunned and looked at Arnie. His face was stone and he was staring straight ahead.

Q. What was your relationship with Miles at this time?

A. He was very busy with the Derby campaign and I saw or spoke to him as little as possible. The few times I did speak to him, he never failed to boast that when his plans finally materialized he would be the most important man in the city . . . power seemed to be an obsession with him. . . .

Q. Did you ever see any cash passed between him and Morenci?

A. Yes.

Q. Please tell us the details.

A. One night during the campaign, Sonny called me. He said I would have to drive to Grand Vista and get some money for him from Morenci. The campaign was mapping out a high-powered television series and he needed a large sum of money immediately.

Q. And you came here to Grand Vista and got the money?

A. Yes. It was about ten o'clock at night. The guard let me in and I saw Morenci. He was with three men in the library. When I entered they got up and left. Then he went over to the second shelf of the bookcase, removed some books, and opened a safe. He took out several packages of money, put them in an attaché case and gave it to me. He then asked if I wanted a drink and when I refused he let me out. I returned to New York City and met Sonny in Barco's Lounge.

Q. Was anyone with him?

A. Yes. George Horatio Derby. He introduced me and Sonny wanted me to stay and have a drink but I refused and went home.

Q. Could you find that safe again in the library?

A. I think so.

Stu stood up. "Suppose we try, Mary."

I followed Stu, Mary, and the television cameraman and reporter into the library. Mary silently pointed to a shelf left of the fireplace. Stu quickly removed the books, then stepped aside. In the back of the shelf was a steel door covered with paneling. He opened it and there was the safe.

"Is this the safe you saw Morenci take the money from that night? The same money you later gave to Miles in the presence of Derby?"

"It's the same safe," she said.

"We will leave the safe to be inspected by government agents," Stu said and we trooped back into the dining room.

Hours passed. Stu kept up his relentless questioning of Mary. Every trip to Burma was described in detail; time, dates, names of airlines, hotels, rooms, landscapes from Mandalay to the small cities or villages in northeastern Burma where she had met her father; what her father had said, how he was dressed; of her meetings with Miles and

Morenci or Derby—detail piled upon detail until the authenticity of her story could not be doubted.

For some reason I turned to look at Morenci. He held his bandaged right hand close to his chest and nervously toyed with a cigarette in his left hand. For a moment I wondered again what it was about his hands I couldn't remember. Rudy was slumped in his chair, dull-eyed, slack.

I was about to turn to Arnie and ask him what he thought about Rudy when I saw Morenci casually take another cigarette from his pocket and slowly crumple it in his left hand. Like a bulb flashing on over my head, it came back to me; the old detective telling us that Morenci was not only a skilled gunsmith and underworld armorer but was also ambidextrous. I started to jump to my feet when Morenci acted.

He flung the handful of cigarette tobacco into Rudy's eyes, swooped down and grabbed the M-16, then like a graceful dancer, spun around. Rudy's outraged roar was drowned out by the crash of gunfire. He managed to get to his feet, then crumpled to the floor. Mary's scream broke off as the bullets pinned her to the chair. Stu's reflexes were perfect. He tipped over the table, Bible, glass, pad and pencil spilling over the floor but it wasn't much of a barricade; in seconds the M-16 reduced it to splinters. Then Morenci started for the door.

Arnie cried out, "Mary!" and lurched forward, staggered a few feet and fell. I tried to hurdle him but tripped. When I got to my feet Morenci was gone, there was a terrible silence in the room.

You didn't have to be a doctor to know Rudy and Mary were dead. Stu was still alive, the front of his shirt was covered with blood. His eyes were closed. There were shouts in the hall and footsteps on the stairs, then Trev rushed into the room.

"My God!" he shouted. "What happened?"

"Morenci shot them . . . he's got a gun," I told him. "Give me a hand with Stu . . ."

Trev lifted him up when Toni came in. I saw questions forming on her lips, but when she saw Stu they were never asked.

"Get him on the couch in the library—quick!" she snapped. She bent over Mary, then knelt beside Rudy. She didn't say a word as she ran out of the room, following Trev who carried Stu in his arms.

I heard a noise and turned. The young television reporter was throwing up but his cameraman was calmly recording the whole scene. The ridiculous thought came to me—now they'll see it all on television and on Stu's prime time.

As I came out into the entry hall, Star was racing downstairs.

"Morenci's got a gun—he killed Mary and Rudy and shot Stu . . ." I yelled at him.

Halfway down Star hurdled the banister and ran into the dining room. Seconds later he came out.

"Did he get out?"

"The doors are still locked."

340

"Then he's still in the house," Star said. "Let's go!"

I started to follow him into the library when suddenly I recalled the tunnel. The heavy old door that led from the kitchen to the tunnel exit was locked—Rudy had set the tumblers and Morenci had used the long screwdriver in the old lock. It was strong but I finally blew it to pieces.

The room was ink black. A match helped me to find one of the flashlights we had left behind, and I started down the ladder. I had just about reached the platform when I was caught by the beam of a flashlight; the roar of the heavy automatic weapon filled the tunnel with a solid sound. Bullets tore the rifle from my hand and ricocheted off the walls and I dropped the flashlight.

Sitting in a bobbing canvas boat and shooting with his left hand, Morenci was still an excellent marksman. I wasn't going to let him have seconds so I went back up that ladder with a rush.

I stood stock-still in the darkness listening to the splashing of the paddle. The cops and federal agents still didn't know about the tunnel, in a little while Morenci would make good his escape. I was swearing to myself, debating what I should do next when out of the corner of my eye I caught the tiny bead of white light across the room.

It drew me like a magnet. I lit a match and saw the two buttons on the panel board. I pressed one and the white light was replaced by the red; it glowed in the darkness like the fierce, unblinking eye of an owl.

I found I had run out of matches. I felt my way to the edge of the hole. Somewhere deep inside the tunnel I heard a faint shout. It rolled along the winding hole, bouncing off the granite walls.

I thought I heard another shout and the splashing noise that a frantic paddler makes but I wasn't sure. Then there was only silence, a deep, awful silence. I put my hand down, water, icy cold, touched my fingertips. When it reached my elbow, I got up and left. I felt sick.

Someone had torn away the spreads we had put over the front doors and through the shattered glass I could see cops and men in plain clothes crouched over, running across the lawn toward the house.

"Mary's dead and so is Rudy," Trev said in a dull monotone.

"I missed Morenci," Star said.

I forced myself to ask: "Stu?"

"Toni's with him . . . ." Trev replied in a choked voice. "I don't think he's going to make it."

Outside the bullhorn was giving us orders. Then something made me laugh in a crazy sort of way. We were doing what we had always done when Charlie marched us out of the stable in Tong Le Mai; form a single line, put your hands behind your neck and keep your eyes down. . . .

Although it wasn't Charlie we faced when we walked outside, the goddam guns were still pointing at our heads. . . .

THE NOTCH, FALL, 1974

341

EPILOGUE

Two years after the "Siege of Grand Vista," a New York newspaper assigned a reporter to do an "anniversary" feature story on the event. During his research he sought out those who had played major and minor roles and determined what had happened to them in the interval. In brief here is a summary of his findings:

A few days after Dr. Gordon J. Wallace, the country general practitioner, announced at a tumultuous press conference in the lobby of St. Anthony's Hospital that despite all his efforts, Stuart Fitzroy Harlow III had died on the way to the operating room, spokesmen for senators, congressmen, and the White House revealed they were receiving a swelling tide of mail and telegrams commenting on Harlow's televised plea that his fellow citizens do something about their country's apathetic society, its violence, cynicism, and lack of compassion. The mail, spokesmen said, was three to one favoring many of Harlow's suggestions.

Large crowds attended a congressional committee hearing on the raid itself. The committee's findings condemned the raid but paradoxically recommended that a superagency be created to correlate the activities of other agencies fighting urban violence. The recommendation, however, continues to be met with a great deal of opposition from government law enforcement bureaus. Senators and congressmen representing the nation's urban areas plan another meeting on the proposed bill next month.

Harlow, leader of the group of former Vietnam POWs who raided Grand Vista, owned by Del Morenci, an international drug racketeer, was buried in the National Cemetery on Long Island. He has become somewhat of a folklore hero with at least one gold record based on his life, sung by Lincoln Dodd and the Coffeyville Raiders.

Harlow's thirty-million-dollar estate, which he willed to his six companions, has been tied up in Surrogate Court by a series of suits filed by distant relatives of Harlow.

A clerk for the justice presiding over the cases predicted it will be at least another year before they are settled. However, a $500,000 trust fund established by Harlow for needy medical students has not been contested. The Dr. Max Findeloon Fund was named for one of the group who committed suicide some years ago.

Trevor David, second in command of the so-called Hounds of Tong Le Mai, along with Arnold Harper, Sam Hoffman, Thomas Bruckner, and Kenneth Iron Star, were indicted by a federal grand jury and tried twice on the charges. The first trial ended in a mistrial, the second in a hung jury. The Department of Justice finally agreed to accept their plea to a lesser charge. They received sentences from eight months to a year in the Danbury, Connecticut, federal prison.

The trial of Bruckner, a former navy pilot, was severed from the others because of a hospital stay. His left leg, badly shattered by gunfire during the siege, was amputated. Like the others, Bruckner pleaded guilty and was given a six month sentence, also in Danbury. He had served three months when he committed suicide by hanging himself in his cell.

Harlow had dictated a deathbed confession in the emergency room of St. Anthony's Hospital to Norman Fredericks, assistant attorney general, in which he claimed sole responsibility for the siege and for the killing of six ex-convicts guarding the enormous load of narcotics discovered in the mansion and for the murder of a drug racketeer, Stash Fortunato. Harlow's statement, witnessed by Dr. Wallace, was effectively used by defense counsel in the trials. Fortunato's body was never recovered and Suffolk County murder one indictments against Hoffman, Harper, and Iron Star were dropped because a *corpus delecti* could not be established.

After their release from Danbury, the group dropped out of sight.

The reporter found Trevor David living at Riverview, his family's pre-Civil War homestead, near Jonesboro, Georgia. Shortly after his release from Danbury federal prison, he married Antonia Angeli, a pretty medical student, who, it was later revealed by federal agents, had played a major role in the bizarre episode. She is now in the last year of her residency in an Atlanta hospital. She is a pediatrician.

David, a former newspaperman, was named executor of Harlow's estate, which includes New York's famous Eldorado Hotel. Harlow's relatives had fought to cancel his appointment, but the court upheld it. At present he has an office in Atlanta. The reporter joined David and his physician wife for lunch in Atlanta but both refused to discuss either Harlow or the siege of Grand Vista.

Sam Hoffman was discovered living in Los Angeles where he owns a small but thriving electrical supply company. Before the seige he operated a properous private detective and security agency in New York but lost his state license. Following his release from Danbury, Hoffman married a Washington government secretary. Hoffman was reluctant to talk to the reporter, but did say he still hears from the others in the group. Last Christmas he and his wife spent a week at Riverview with the Davids. Arnie Harper and Kenny Iron Star, he explained, were out of the country.

In Langley, Virginia, a spokesman for the CIA refused to comment on Harper. However, sources close to the agency said Harper had returned to Indochina.

Iron Star, a full-blooded Mohawk from Brooklyn, was reportedly working for a steel company in South Vietnam.

Mary Chang Winslow, whose murder by Morenci was witnessed by millions of viewers on television as she testified in the now celebrated "trial" of Grand Vista, was buried on the West Coast.

Morenci's body was recovered from the historic tunnel used by the raiders to gain entrance to the mansion. Police theorized Morenci accidentally touched off the electrically controlled dams inside the tunnel and was drowned. He was trying to escape after fatally wounding Harlow and killing Miss Winslow and Rudy Webb, a member of Harlow's group.

After his body remained unclaimed in the county morgue for the legal thirty days, he was buried in a section of the local cemetery set aside for the indigent and homeless.

Webb was buried near Harlow in the National Cemetery.

George Horatio Derby, the New York mayoralty candidate, whose campaign was blown apart by Harlow's televised charges, which were supported by Miss Winslow's testimony, was indicted for bribery and conspiracy to violate the state election campaign laws. The former state senator and U.S. attorney pleaded guilty and was sentenced to a year on Riker's Island. While in prison he was indicted for tax fraud; he also pleaded guilty to those charges and served a year, ironically, in the federal prison at Danbury, where the "Hounds" had been confined.

Mayor Kerr, the incumbent who was defeated by Robinson Brown, candidate for the Independent Democrats for Integrity Party formed after Derby resigned from the race, has spent the last two years writing his memoirs: *Memoirs of City Hall: The Kerr Administration.* The book will be published next month.

A spokesman for his publisher said that the former mayor will tell the "real inside" story of what happened when he met Harlow and the others in the Five Boro Anti-Narcotics League, the ill-fated civic organization Harlow charged in his broadcast had been betrayed by crooked police and the apathy and incompetence of Mayor Kerr and his administration.

Frank "Sonny" Miles, the former inspector and head of the New York City Police Department's Bureau of Dangerous and Controlled Drugs, who was named as the "bag man" for Morenci and Derby, was indicted on bribery and sixteen counts of perjury before a federal grand jury.

He was tried, convicted, and sentenced to serve ten to twenty years, but his conviction was overturned by the Federal Court of Appeals due to a legal technicality in the judge's charge to the jury.

Miles was then indicted on a lesser charge but refused all plea bargaining efforts by the government. Another trial resulted in a hung jury. Last month the U.S. attorney appeared in court and requested that the indictment be dismissed on the grounds the government did not have sufficient evidence to convict Miles.

Miles's attorneys also brought a successful action in Supreme Court against the New York City Police Department which had attempted to discontinue Miles's pension.

Miles is now president of The Miles National Security Agency with elaborate offices on Madison Avenue. Last summer a Washington newspaper revealed his agency had received an eighty-thousand-dollar fee for installing an electronic security system in the palace of an Arabian ruler of an oil-rich country. Miles explained the Shah was "an old friend."

Several members of the New York City Sanitation Department were also tried and convicted of conspiracy and bribery, after the New York County district attorney's office investigated disclosures made by Harlow in his broadcast. A night supervisor of a sanitation department garage confessed he accepted a twenty-five-thousand-dollar bribe to help remove a cargo of drugs, estimated to have been worth millions, from a Water Street warehouse under the eyes of police who had the place under surveillance. Three drivers were also convicted.

An assistant superviser in the Building Department was convicted and sentenced to two and a half to five years on charges of bribery and two clerks received terms of fifteen months, after one confessed he and the others had accepted bribes to remove plans of the Water Street warehouse from the department's files.

A New York County grand jury presentment charged Mayor Kerr and his administration with incompetence, inefficiency, and "permitting acts to be committed which verge on criminality." The explosive presentment undoubtedly helped to oust Kerr from office.

Betsy Van Lyden Derby, the New York socialite who worked

closely with her husband during his campaign, divorced Derby several months ago. She had been employed until recently by a Hollywood public relations firm when she was confined to the Couch Sanitarium. Her physician said she was suffering from "exhaustion" and could not be interviewed.

Former Police Commissioner Theodore Fitzgerald, also charged with incompetence by Harlow in his televised statement, joined a large computer organization after his resignation from the police department. Cornelius Brigadier, another former police commissioner and close friend of Miles, testified before the federal grand jury that indicted Miles. Brigadier was named as a co-conspirator but not a defendant. He pleaded guilty and was given a suspended sentence after testifying for the government against Miles.

Bernard Lennis, Morenci's attorney, pleaded guilty to perjury charges in federal court and was sentenced to from two to four years. However, the sentence was suspended and he was put on probation. He did not contest the New York Bar Association's disbarment proceedings and was disbarred last year.

Books and records of the International Vending and Amusement Machines Company were subpoenaed by Internal Revenue agents, and officers of the firm were called before a federal grand jury. Four were convicted of income tax evasion and received two to five year sentences. The company later filed for bankruptcy and its assets were confiscated by the IRS.

Grand Vista, the grim, medieval castlelike mansion that sits on the peak of a hill overlooking a small valley several miles from the village of Cidertown, New Jersey, was taken over by the county for nonpayment of taxes. It was subsequently given to the state and is presently a home for disturbed children.

Shortly before his account was published, the reporter learned that the Davids had become the parents of a boy, their first child. David told his former newspaper colleagues in the Atlanta Associated Press Bureau that the infant was named Stuart Fitzroy David.

The five hundred and ten pounds of pure heroin and cocaine, valued at $100,000,000, which was "captured" by Harlow's raiders in the cutting mill of Grand Vista, was removed under maximum security measures by federal agents and local police. Last year some of the bags were found to contain talcum powder.

The incident recalls the theft of the famous "French Connection" drugs from the property clerk's office in the New York City Police department.

Both police and federal authorities conducted what was called at the time "an intensive investigation" but the reporter was told, "There is nothing new."